AF345965

The Hand We Are Dealt

The Hand
We Are Dealt

Robert Bordas

Copyright © 2022 Robert Bordas

Cover design by Dominika Mars (background photo: Todd Trapani)

Translation of Taras Shevchenko's poem by Ethel Lilian Voynich

This is a work of fiction based on a true story. Characters may be based on real persons, but their names were changed, and their personalities and actions may differ from the real person. Historical personalities and their actions are based on available sources. Places and incidents are either preserved to maintain historical accuracy or are the product of the author's imagination and used fictitiously for the benefit of the story.

All rights reserved. No part of this book may be reproduced, or stored in a retrieval system, or transmitted in any form or by any means, electronic, mechanical, photocopying, recording, or otherwise, without express written permission of the publisher, except by a reviewer who may quote brief passages in a review.

ISBN-13: **978-8090867512** (paperback)

To the memory of Anna (1922-2016),
my mother

Content

Chapter 1

"Don't give me meat with all the sinew, Mr. Hanzel. Who would want to eat that?" Anna snapped at the beefy butcher, wrinkling her nose at the cut he presented her. "That will do," she said curtly, pointing at a brightly colored piece cleaned of fat. Customers would fight for that beautiful cut of meat—the tenderloin. In times like these, it was impossible to get such meat in all of Czechoslovakia, even Prague. In Uzhhorod, Anna's small city in Subcarpathian Rus, you had to look for quality meat with a magnifying glass.

Anna spoke to him in Slovak, his mother tongue. She enjoyed the way the soft, melodic syllables rolled off her tongue, but wished they would sound harder to show her determination to make a good deal.

The proprietor of the wholesale enterprise, Hanzel & Son, looked at the sixteen-year-old girl with small, mousy eyes. Anna spotted a mix of pique and awe in them as he tossed the meat with the tendon back into the box and picked up the impeccable cut she had demanded. She had to suppress a smile. *I got you!*

Other wholesalers would display the cheapest cuts, full of gristle and fat left after the butcher had served his better customers: elite hotels and restaurants, exclusive delis, kitchens of the city hall, and mansions of the rich. But Mr. Hanzel always had something worthwhile to offer; it was why Anna frequented his shop. His butchery was cleaner than a hospital and smelled of fresh meat, smoked sausages, and salamis made with his own hands. He claimed they were better than imported ones. Nevertheless, he wasn't above misbehavior; he held out a cut of meat with a proud smile, knowing full well that the bottom was covered in fat.

He must have connections or relatives in the countryside, or perhaps he offers bribes? Rumor had it that some butchers went to Poland for meat, where it was much cheaper.

"This will be expensive, Anna. But I have to admit you have sharp eyes," Mr. Hanzel said, composed.

He dropped the meat into the brass pan of the scale and, not waiting for the pointer to calm down, declared, "Two kilos. That'll be one hundred crowns. Anything else?"

Anna's muscles tensed and she hiccupped. "Can you just look at the scale once again, please? I see 1.95."

"If you wish, missy, let's make it 2.50 less," Mr. Hanzel retorted with a shake of his head.

Anna tried to swallow, but her mouth was dry. She cleared her throat instead and hoped it sounded aggrieved.

"Mr. Hanzel, do you mean to charge fifty crowns for a kilo of tenderloin? Need I remind you that I am a loyal customer? Not to mention I'm also buying the salami, sausages, *and* bacon." Anna brushed her honey-blonde wavy hair from her shoulders. "I'd expect a discount for such a nice tab. You know we need to sell this at our shop and make a living from it."

He picked up a rag from the counter and wiped his greasy, bloody hands with it. Anna attempted to hide her disgust as his black eyes wandered from her face, fixing themselves on her heaving chest.

"I am not running a charity here, young lady." Mr. Hanzel offered a bemused smile and shook his head once more.

Anna straightened up and smoothed down her simple but elegant floral print dress. She gave her best attempt at bringing a captivating smile to her lips and lowered her soprano voice to a lulling tone.

"But you wouldn't want a long-term customer to switch suppliers, would you?" Anna tipped her head to the right, steering clear of the scale and forcing those mousy eyes back to her face. "In fact, I've just heard that the new meat wholesaler at the Czech factory is giving out discounts to build his clientele. And their excellent Prague ham is not the only thing they offer..."

Mr. Hanzel's always-pink face blanched, and an ugly frown appeared between his bushy brows. His eyes jumped to the entryway as a small bell rang and a customer entered the shop. Then he picked up the cleaver, raised it high in the air, and let it wedge itself into the butcher block with a thump. He blinked twice and gave Anna a cold stare.

"No problem getting the best Prague ham for you, young lady. I can assure you I also have the best connections in Bohemia." His fleshy hands reached for the butcher paper to wrap the cut in. "And just for today, I will give you the meat for forty-five a kilo. With all the other items, it comes to 131 crowns. Do you have a one-crown coin?"

Closing the shop door behind her, Anna hopped down the steps to her bicycle. She felt a heat wave hit her ears and ducked when she noticed the curious stare of a woman who had just reached the shop. Towing her bike in a hurry, Anna disappeared onto a side street.

Her mind was abuzz like a beehive. She had not only found an excellent piece of meat to attract premium customers, but it would also sell at an excellent margin! Warmth flooded through her chest that made her smile as she recalled Mr. Hanzel's expression when she had caught him trying to cheat her. Her mouth watered as she added up all the ice cream cups her savings would buy. It was a pity the confectionery didn't open until much later in the morning, otherwise she would devour at least one scoop.

There was no time to stop, though; she had to hurry home. *Stepfather must be sitting on thorns waiting for me.*

The bicycle was heavy with two large sacks of flour, another sack of butter, lard, sugar, and yeast, and a smaller bag with meat and sausages. Anna made this trip every morning to get the daily non-essential items for her family store. She pedaled through the narrow streets—made narrower in the early morning hours by peasants from villages around Uzhhorod displaying their spread in the market.

She liked testing her haggling skills with the farmers, sweet-talking some, feigning indignation with others, and even cajoling a few into dropping their price by a few tens of hellers. Wholesalers also traded here, offering tools and household items for peasants: spades, shovels, plows, and even fabric, shoes, and soap...you name it. It looked like a jumble sale. Farmers did not require beautifully arranged displays. Anna avoided those stalls, as the prices were high compared to her contacts in the city. The wholesalers primarily focused on the peasants and their money, as they were ignorant of the cheaper sources.

That morning, Anna had been allowed to buy meat for

the first time. She had been pleading with Stepfather, himself a butcher, for weeks. She told him she wasn't a small girl anymore and that he could entrust her with such an important job. After all, she had been helping in the shop for six years. In the last two, since she had started attending high school, she had taken care of all the purchases from the grocery wholesaler and the market every morning. She knew enough about meat and bargaining.

Stepfather will be happy. I'll prove I can make all the purchases, and not just act a mule. After all, I'm not a porter but a clever girl who sees through the machinations of merchants and cannot be gulled.

The houses edging the road were smaller and less cared-for as she left the central area and neared the railway station. She turned a corner to take a shortcut and soon arrived at the old steel bridge above the railroad. It was quite steep, and she quickly got out of breath from pushing the heavy bicycle up to the top. She had to keep a tight grasp on the bike to prevent it from tumbling down, and that was even worse. As it was so early, there was nobody around to help. Anna prayed she could keep her balance and hold the bicycle straight. If it tipped and the sacks and parcels fell, she would not be able to get them back on the bicycle by herself. It took her forty minutes to reach her family shop, by which time it was already past seven.

As Anna pushed the bicycle into the yard, Stepfather darted out of the shop. His mustache trembled as he hurriedly approached her, brows meeting above his nose as he rolled his shirtsleeves above his elbows. She cringed with a sense of foreboding, a result of past encounters. Her stomach churned, and her vision blurred as she spotted him.

He held out his hand for the change, counted, and then pocketed it.

"Show me the meat!"

He started turning over the items in the sacks.

"How much did Mr. Hanzel charge you for this mock tender?"

"What mock tender, Dad?" Anna swallowed, dutifully addressing him as Mother wished. "I paid forty-five a kilo for this tenderloin. He gave me a ten percent discount. It's almost two kilos, he wanted to cheat me..."

"You let yourself be fooled, you worthless girl! He cheated *you*. He's a scoundrel alright!" His face was getting red, and he waved the meat in front of her face. "A mock tender from the chuck, good only for roasts because it's so tough! No steaks from it unless you marinate it for long. Has a value of no more than thirty-five from the wholesaler. I'll be lucky to get forty-five per kilo for it myself." Flecks of spittle assailed Anna's face, and she moved back a step, trembling. "You are a ne'er-do-well, a good-for-nothing!"

The slap on Anna's left cheek sounded like a gunshot and had a similar effect on her: she collapsed to the ground. Her mother ran out of the shop and looked at the scene, but did not intervene. Her stepfather turned and took the bag with the butcher's goods inside.

"Take the flour and grocery items in," Mother said, hurrying after Stepfather.

Anna started to cry. She clambered to her feet, hastily brushed the dirt off her dress, and carried the sacks into the shop one by one. No time to dwell on Stepfather's bile. She had to go; she could not be late on the first day of the new school year. She caught a glimpse of her face in the hall mirror—red as beetroot with an imprint of four fingers on her cheek. The handkerchief she squeezed to her left cheek would mask it. Pretending to have a toothache. The calendar next to the mirror featured a red-penciled circle around the date: September 5th, 1938.

The main road to school went through the city, but Anna chose the path next to the river instead. There were fewer chances of meeting her schoolmates there; she would die if they saw her blemished face. Her chest was still heaving irregularly, although the tears had dried up.

Anger took the place of self-pity. Anger at Stepfather for being such a bully, anger at Mother for not standing up for her, and anger at herself for being such a silly goose. She began to doubt her capabilities. Profound shame heated her face more than the slap, and she was close to forgiving Stepfather. After all, it was her mistake not to catch Mr. Hanzel's trick.

She passed the railway bridge, but the footbridge was still some distance away. On the right side of the river, dark gray clouds were gathering above the castle. The August rains had made the river swell, and September wasn't promising better weather either. Below the castle, a swimming pool with its functionalist building was the most recent luxury for the city. Anna could rarely afford the entry fee, and her friends would rather take a bath in the low waters of the River Uzh. Behind the swimming pool and the Greek Catholic Basilian monastery, the buildings of the historic center rose to a modest height. She could easily recognize the top of the cathedral above them.

As she left the orthodox church on the Palacky Embankment, traffic became dense. Horse-drawn carriages and wagons were increasingly being replaced by motor cars and buses that created a new type of morning noise with a distinctly different smell—engine whirs and honks instead of wagon squeaks and clatters and cracking whips and shouts of the carters; petrol fumes instead of the rancid stench of horse manure.

She had to cross the bridge full of pedestrians hurrying to their workplaces. People had also transformed in the past years. Men wore better suits and silk hats instead of felt ones and oozed self-confidence as they walked to work. Women looked as if they were going to a theater performance instead of their office or administration jobs. Anna noticed some of her classmates among the crowd and touched her face under the handkerchief. It was no longer warm or puffy, and the hanky could go.

The gleaming windows of the Bata shoe shop opposite the city theater had always lured her to make a brief stop to admire the new arrivals. But this morning, she did not even glance at them.

After a left turn at the synagogue toward the cathedral, she hiked up the cobblestoned street to the small castle hill and made a right turn at the Jewish rabbi's school. She would always titter at the sight of the students with their billowing black coats and long earlocks, but today, she barely noticed them. It was another hundred meters before she looked up at the school building that awaited her with its large windows, yawning wooden gate, strict nuns, and relatively friendly male teachers.

The "goose castle", as the locals called it. The still-tender trace of the slap on her face heated up again and her throat constricted. Her left fist closed tight around the handle of her briefcase, and she pressed her lips together. Her eyes met those of the janitor at the gate, and she gave him a respectful nod.

I will show them this nickname is wrong. To Stepfather, to Mother. To the teachers. To myself.

Chapter 2

Anna was furiously calculating and making notes to finish the math test on time. Miss Plishkova liked to give the class an assessment during the first few lessons of the year to see how much they had forgotten over the summer. It was already the second week of the new school year, and the test was due. Same as last September. This did not cause Anna much hardship, as she counted in the shop every day. During the summer, there were even more calculations to do. Instead of attending school, she needed to help all day. She could calculate in her head, writing on paper only for larger lists of items. Customers standing in the queue had little patience, so she had to be lightning fast. This practice honed her math skills and gave her an advantage in Miss Plishkova's flash assessment. It had to be finished on time, within fifteen minutes, and slow students had points deducted for every extra minute. Losing five points meant a fiver, no matter how good your calculations were—the mark of unsatisfactory performance.

Anna's friend, sitting next to her, was struggling. Marika was much better at literature and grammar than math or natural history. Anna had finished the sums and was thinking of raising her hand, but on seeing Marika's pleading expression, she looked over her sheet once again. Moving as slowly as a snail, Anna turned her work toward her friend while steadily gazing at their teacher. Miss Plishkova was watching over the students at the far end of the class, so Marika could look at Anna's results for at least ten seconds. That was enough for her to copy the answers. When Anna saw Miss Plishkova turn, she pivoted her sheet back to her desk. Their teacher began to scan the work of the students in the window row next, so Anna looked at Marika to see how she had fared. Anna saw her sighing with relief and finishing her sums. She put up her hand to signal that she was ready to submit her answers. Thirteen minutes, excellent result!

During the big break, the two friends took a walk in the yard and Marika thanked Anna, hugging her tight.

"I don't know what I'd have done without you. I cannot afford to lose points and it takes me so long to finish those sums."

"You can pay me back by helping me during the grammar lesson, especially in Russian."

"I've never understood why you have so much pain with Russian. You attended the Ukrainian higher elementary school, didn't you?"

"Aye, I did. But don't forget that for the first four years of elementary school, I went to the Slovak school closest to us. It was convenient because there were many Slovak families in the neighborhood and I grew up with that language." She wrinkled her forehead. "During the summer, I had to learn

Ukrainian from scratch as the Slovak school had no further grades. It was okay to learn how to speak and the basics of the Cyrillic alphabet, but not for grammar. Stepfather, being Ukrainian, helped me a lot, but he is also not very good at grammar. And you can imagine how it is when parents try to help you with your studies."

Anna finished with a giggle that turned into a sneer as she remembered the scathing hits of his leather belt. "He is but a butcher, you know."

Marika nodded, but her mind seemed to be elsewhere. "What about the Saturday ball? Are you coming?"

"Now? In September?"

"It's not a traditional ball. It's a party that's organized by the Rusyn Brotherhood in the ballroom of the Urania cinema. You know how beautiful it is, full of mirrors. It will be fun, you must come!"

"Saturday evening, you say? Who'll be there?"

"Oh, I know several guys coming from the teacher training school for boys and also from the upper grammar school. I'm sure there will also be students from the business academy. And don't forget the wonderful music! You could bring Laci, that dashing gendarme!" Marika's enthusiasm was contagious.

During the summer, Anna had gone to a couple of dancing parties. Having turned sixteen in July, she was finally allowed to go without an escort. Dancing parties represented her only opportunity to get acquainted with young men and have fun. She had met László Domeny, nickname Laci, a handsome gendarme, at such a party. She loved uniforms, and he was a gallant dance partner. Unfortunately, he was very busy, and he usually visited his old parents in the country most weekends. Marika's mention of him lit up the memory of a warm August evening when he had accompanied her home after a party. She blushed.

Anna longed to get away from the everyday drudgery of the shop, roam freely without Stepfather's ever-following look, and enjoy the attention of a decent boy. She wished for Laci, but she had no contact with him. Would her parents allow her to go this time?

"I'm not sure, Marika. I'll have to ask for permission at home. And I don't know about Laci..."

"Oh. It's a pity, he was really gorgeous. Do ask at home. You should tell your stepfather it's a Rusyn ball. If you have a yellow and blue dress, you'd fit in tremendously!" She laughed at her own joke, hinting at the Ukrainian national colors.

"What should a Hungarian girl do in yellow and blue?" Anna answered, puckering her lips, but then broke into laughter at the idea. The bell had just rung, signaling the start of the next lesson, so they directed their steps toward the classroom.

Mr. Savchenko, the teacher of civic education, was a middle-aged Ukrainian with a full goatee and circular glasses. He liked his own voice, a velvety baritone, and could recite several stanzas from the poems of Taras Shevchenko, his almost-namesake national Ukrainian hero. He loved "The Testament", especially the last verse:

> *Bury me, be done with me,*
> *Rise and break your chain,*
> *Water your new liberty*
> *With blood for rain.*
> *Then, in the mighty family*
> *Of all men that are free,*
> *May be sometimes, very softly*
> *You will speak of me?*

In the past year, it had become common to hear more about Ukrainian history from him than the political system of the Czechoslovak Republic.

"You should know, dear ladies, that the question of the autonomy of our region—that I prefer to call Carpathian Ukraine over the degrading, confusing, and unnatural Subcarpathian Rus, which has, unfortunately, become a common name in the current political system—has still not been fully solved despite the twenty-year-long promises of the government. Fortunately, with the national movements, demonstrations, and political pressure, we can hope for some changes. Not too far in the future, we may see our region receive its well-deserved autonomy."

Anna was confused. Her mother tongue was Hungarian, and until six, she had spoken no other language. When Mother had gone to enroll her in a school, the administrator had asked about her nationality and she had proclaimed in a low voice, "Well, Rusyn." Anna had stamped her foot then and raised her head in childish pride.

"I am a Hungarian girl!"

During the ten years that followed, she had learned not to emphasize her Hungarian origins. Her mother had explained—"Hungary is a matter of the past. After the Great War, we became a part of Czechoslovakia, and insisting on your heritage will only get you in trouble."

She learned Slovak, Ukrainian (they called it Russian, sometimes Little Russian), and Czech, and made friends with students from all nationalities—even Jews. Having people of every nationality was natural in Uzhhorod. Mr. Savchenko, however, accepted no nationalities other than Ukrainian. He strongly believed that whatever your heritage was, if you attended this school, you should accept being Ukrainian. The school belonged to the Greek Catholic Church, had a mixed staff of Rusyn, Slovak, and Hungarian origin, and the medium of instruction was Ukrainian. It had become much easier for Anna after her mother had started to live with her stepfather some eight years ago, who was a real Ukrainian from Galicia that had become part of Poland after the Great War. They spoke more and more Ukrainian at home, as his Hungarian was terrible, although with the local Rusyn dialect that Mother forced on him. Their neighbors to the right were Slovaks, and behind them lived several Rusyn families and some Jews. Others were Hungarians. Her schoolmates were also a mix of these nations, except for the Jews and Czechs. These two nationalities had their own schools. The Greek Catholics were locals.

When Anna was younger, her mother used to say, "Rusyns have lived here for more than a thousand years. My father and grandfather all considered themselves Rusyn, even when our region belonged to Hungary. And it had belonged to Hungary for almost a thousand years, too. Your birth father came from a mixed Hungarian-Rusyn family. I was born in Hungary; you were born in Czechoslovakia, and we were born both in Subcarpathia. States change, people remain."

But now Mr. Savchenko said they should call their region Carpathian Ukraine. Does this mean the state had changed? Or the people? Marika said the Rusyn Brotherhood had organized the dancing party. Should she go?

After school, Anna hurried home to help in the shop as always. She tried to do her best to be fast and polite to customers, but she could hardly wait for six o'clock, which was when they closed. It took her another half hour to clean the shop and prepare things for the morning. Her mother cooked dinner at seven o'clock.

"It was a good day today," Stepfather said while slurping down the broth.

"People still have some money to spend on food," Mother answered, and also looked satisfied.

All four of them were at the table. Anna's five-year-old brother was sitting to her right on his highchair. Anna let the adults talk while she tried to gauge their moods. Asking for permission just after dinner would be best. Stepfather would be in a relaxed mood after a good meal.

"Bondarenko will come over after dinner to have a chat," Stepfather said.

Holy cow! I will have to wait.

"What does he want?" Mother asked with a frown as she poured a hearty helping of the brown gravy onto the pork neck on Stepfather's plate. He helped himself to some boiled potatoes to accompany it.

"He wants to discuss the situation in Bohemia."

Bondarenko was Stepfather's old buddy from Galicia. "I heard the Czechs are mighty busy with the Germans in Sudetenland," Bondarenko said as he sat down at the kitchen table. He was a stocky man with large hands that handled the smith's hammer every day. They made a good pair.

"There's a rumor that Czech police stations were attacked after Hitler gave that fiery speech on Monday in Nürnberg demanding to end the oppression of the Sudeten Germans by Czechs."

"Yes, I heard. The government has declared martial law in some of those regions." Stepfather frowned and poured two small measures of vodka. He beckoned to Bondarenko, and they chugged down the shots at the same time.

"If the Czechs are so occupied with the Germans, they might be more lenient in Subcarpathia...this could be an opportunity for us."

"What are you thinking?"

"We're calling for quiet demonstrations for autonomy.

Some peaceful events are also being organized in the city—some balls for the young—just to test the waters."

"I am all for autonomy. What I don't like is the too-loud voice of the Muscovites insisting we should side with the Russians. They cannot mean to adopt their Bolshevik system, what nonsense!" Stepfather threw up his hands and then bent closer to Bondarenko, pointing his index finger at his face. "It's autonomy we need! And you may be right; as the government is in trouble, this may be the right time for action."

Anna was helping Mother clean the dishes, and she perked up at that. She was praying that Mother made less noise as she scoured the roasting tin. Fortunately, the two friends raised their voices while discussing the discreet events and their chances of success.

"Will you join us for the demonstration on Sunday?" Bondarenko asked, pushing his glass toward Stepfather. "To the other leg, too."

Stepfather poured another shot for both of them and shook his head.

"I'm not sure. I have a lot of different customers: Slovaks, Hungarians, and even some Czechs. It wouldn't look good if they saw me at a demonstration for the Ukrainian cause. I will support you financially, but don't ask me to take part in person."

"Hmm, I thought you had more pluck in you, Dimitri. But as you wish."

Stepfather saw Bondarenko to the door, came back, and plonked himself in his favorite wing chair. Anna saw her moment arrive. She bit her lips, jiggled her hands to shake off the excess water, and grabbed a kitchen towel to hide her trembling hands. Her croaking voice startled her.

"The Rusyn Brotherhood..."—she cleared her throat—"...is organizing a party this Saturday. It is like a ball. I'd like to go with Marika. May I?" She took a big gulp.

Mother opened her mouth to react, but Stepfather was faster.

"The Rusyn Brotherhood?" Stepfather seemed surprised. He screwed his eyes. "Bondarenko mentioned something about a ball." There was a brief silence. Mother did not want to interrupt Stepfather. "If you help in the shop on Saturday afternoon until closing time, you can go."

Both Mother's and Anna's brows shot up, and they looked at each other. Anna could not believe her luck.

"Of course, I'll help as always. The dancing party starts only at seven."

"Why, it's a good idea to be seen to be close to the Rusyn movement. They are, in fact, Ukrainians who have lived too long under Hungarian rule. I cannot make a bold demonstration for the Ukrainian cause with our multinational clientele, but I would wish my stepdaughter did." Stepfather had a sly smile on his lips. "Maybe you'll even find yourself some clever Rusyn boy."

Anna's little brother giggled. She glared at him, and he stopped. *Should have known. This is why he agreed. He wants me married off as early as possible. I still have two years of high school and this is the priority. But I can still have some fun, can't I? And I will not support Stepfather's Ukrainian cause, whatever it is. I'm just going dancing.*

Anna approached her mother after Stepfather retired to his bedroom.

"Do you think, Mummy, you could make my Sunday summer dress look new?" Mother did not answer right away, but continued to mend a skirt on her sewing machine. The kitchen also served as her workshop in the evenings. A long minute passed and Anna's heart was beating in her throat to the rhythm of her pedaling.

"I'll sew you a new dress. I have some delicate light blue satin fabric that would look good with yellow trimming around the neck and arms." She turned to Anna with a smile.

"Oh no, that's really unnecessary! The summer dress will do, just add some decorations to make it look different from what I wore the last time."

"Don't worry, I have some time in the evenings. I want you to look fabulous. And those colors will attract attention."

Anna loved the idea of having a new dress, and the satin would look elegant. She was sure that few girls could afford a dress shining with novelty nowadays. She was smiling in bed that night, imagining the skirt of her new dress forming a radiating, fluttering bell while she danced the Vienna waltz with a handsome boy.

What she was not sure of were the colors.

Chapter 3

Saturday saw increased traffic in the shop. Anna joined Stepfather after school at midday, and both worked hard to serve all the customers standing in queues to make their weekend grocery purchases. This satisfied Stepfather and he seemed to be in an outstanding mood, bantering with the most familiar patrons. Anna could hardly wait to see and try on the dress Mother had been working on late through the night and that morning as well.

When Anna locked the door behind the last customer after four o'clock in the afternoon, Stepfather presented her with a ten-crown note. "You should have some money for the ball," he said, and put the note in her palm.

He really wants me to represent him. Or he wants me to catch a suitable boy. I don't care. At least he paid for the entry and I can also have a lemonade. I don't need to spend my meager pocket money.

"Thank you, Dad!" she said, forcing herself to be all cool

politeness, and ran to the kitchen where Mother was still sewing.

"Here, try it now!" Mother said as she glimpsed Anna. "But be careful, some stitches still need to be strengthened."

The dress was a dream. Anna thought she had never seen such a beautiful garment in her whole life. It was turquoise and very fashionable, and from up close she could see its floral self-pattern. The plunging neckline with gathers at the shoulders and cap sleeves made it elegant. The gathers were top-stitched with yellow thread. Again, there were gathers below the bust that slimmed the waistline. The skirt was mid-calf length—just perfect.

"Mummy, this is beautiful! How did you make this skirt so wide? It will be grand for dancing!" Anna exclaimed as she put on the dress gingerly and did a pirouette.

"They call it a 7-gore wrap skirt pattern. You make it from 7 pieces, each wider down than up, and this creates a great bell." Mother looked at Anna with a smile, then she frowned and made some adjustments to the hem of the shoulders. "Take this belt, and I also have a clutch for you. I used to wear it as a young girl..."

The belt and the clutch were yellow, the same shade as the thread on the dress. The belt was made of fabric, but the clutch was smooth leather, if a bit worn.

"This is just wonderful!" Anna exclaimed. But then she had a worrying thought. "Don't you think the color combination is too obvious?"

"Ancika, you're going to a Rusyn ball after all."

"But Mummy, I don't care about the Ukrainian movement. I feel Hungarian and these colors show that I've forgotten that."

"You are who you are. It's not the colors of your garments that define your feelings. Displaying your innermost feelings may sound brave, but in most cases, it's just foolish. You can do this for Stepfather. It won't kill you, will it?"

Anna contorted her face like she had tasted pickled cucumber.

"I...I hate to lie."

"Not lying, just going with the times. You may not like Mr. Hanzel cheating you over the meat, but you'll go back to him because he has the best meat available. You must be clever. If you want to go dancing, you must sacrifice something for it."

Anna's mind was in a whirl while undressing. The dress was so beautiful, cooling her body. She would be so attractive in it. When was the last time she had a new dress? She handed back the garment with her final decision—she could not miss this opportunity. A longing to get out and have a great evening, meet interesting boys, and dance in their arms washed away bothersome feelings that she was cheating on her nationality, like a tumultuous spring flood overcoming flowering pastures.

There was another hour before the party began, good enough for a quick bath, and Mother could finish with the stitches. Anna put on the dress and was on her way. She met Marika on the bridge in the city center before half-past six.

"You look amazing!" Marika called to her from a distance. Anna noticed pedestrians turning their heads to look at her.

"Hush, you also look beautiful, Marika!" Anna said in a low voice and commented on her floral peach-colored cotton dress with puffy shoulders. "I'm sure we won't have problems finding dance partners!"

Anna hooked her arm into her friend's arm and they started toward the Urania cinema. It was beyond their school, further up the hill. They had to be careful on the cobblestoned streets in their delicate shoes. The warm Saturday evening had drawn out lots of pedestrians who were strolling.

The luxurious Purma cafe in the corner was full to bursting, and half of the sidewalk was occupied by guests enjoying the weather along with the confectioner's delicious cakes. The sweet smell of vanilla and coffee followed the girls as they tried to carve their way uphill through the idle crowd. Opposite Hotel Tatra, they ascended the stairs leading to the state's real grammar school on Druget Square that boasted a new roof. Between the school and the spa, they glimpsed the new modernist building of the People's House of Enlightenment on the square at the end of the street. This building housed the Urania cinema on its second floor and a big assembly hall on the third floor.

The young people gathered at the square had already started entering the building, and the two girls hurried to join them. They exchanged greetings with some school friends. It was difficult to ignore the loud remarks from the boys, who could not take their eyes off the girls' slender figures enhanced by their attractive dresses. Several steps led to the double doors of the building. They found themselves in a spacious hall with gilded stucco ornaments. On the left side, a large door led them to the staircase hall. There was a queue at the cashier's window, but they got their tickets after ten minutes, and after the usher checked them, they ascended the stairs.

A handsome young man greeted them in Rusyn at the head of the stairs. He gazed into Anna's eyes and gave her a ravishing smile.

"You dressed up for the occasion, young lady. I am Volodymyr Paliychuk. Welcome to the ball of the Brotherhood."

The girls giggled, introduced themselves, and stepped around Volodymyr, who seemed to be unwilling to let them go.

"I hope to see you later on the dance floor!" he shouted

after them and then turned to welcome the other guests.

As they went up the stairs, they admired the decorated walls. The marble on the columns displayed marquetry of geometric shapes that gave a modern look to the interiors. The assembly hall on the third floor was indeed a wonder. It had mirrors around the entire perimeter with cushioned, elegant benches every three meters, some of them occupied by young people. Most of them were talking and laughing with animated gestures.

On the left side of the room, there was a stage for a folk ensemble. The musicians were still rehearsing—one could not hear the tunes because of the loud conversations.

The two girls went to the buffet to pick up some lemonade, and when they returned to the room, they glimpsed Volodymyr on the stage just about to speak. Anna admired his ability to address so many people with ease, his words filled with pathos and excitement. He spoke Rusyn but borrowed Ukrainian phrases where he could not find the high-flown expressions in his local dialect.

"We have arrived at a unique stage in our history, to a long-awaited moment when we are close to achieving our right for self-determination as a nation. We have suffered under foreign rule without rights for centuries. Governments have promised us autonomy but never delivered on their promises. It is time we raise our words for our freedom and rights that governments should have granted us a long time ago. Our organization, the Rusyn Brotherhood, welcomes the new generation that will lead this victorious fight!"

The folk band started to play the official anthem of the Subcarpathian Rus. The melody, without the Czechoslovak anthem that should have preceded it, rose above their heads. "Subcarpathian Rusyns, leave your deep sleep, the voice of the people is calling you..." The young people in the ballroom sang along, and they continued to sing when the second national song followed. "I was, am, and will remain Rusyn, I was born a Rusyn..."

When the song was over, it took several minutes for the hum of conversations to begin. A cheerful folk song thawed the lofty atmosphere.

Volodymyr approached Anna and asked her for a dance. His attention flattered her. Marika was alone only for a few seconds longer. The ballroom was soon full of pairs of dancers moving around the perimeter to the rhythm of the polkas and mazurkas.

"I wanted more Rusyn dances, but they advised me it would be too much for this audience," shouted Volodymyr into Anna's ears while shuffling around, trying not to bump into other couples. "I know these dances are much more popular. After all, polka made its way into our culture too." He grinned and did not take his eyes away from Anna as he turned and hopped. "We'll need to work a lot to raise Rusyn music to the level where it will be accepted on social occasions. And, last but not least, I could not have hugged you while dancing a circle khorovod or karichka, could I?" He winked and turned even faster.

Anna politely smiled but did not comment. She admired Volodymyr and enjoyed the dance with him, but felt uneasy to commit too much to the case he represented. The colors of her dress were more than enough for her already.

After a couple of dances, Volodymyr had to leave to fulfill his responsibilities as the chief organizer of the evening, and Anna could escape to sit on a bench. She was enjoying the short break alone, but that did not last long.

"I didn't know you were such a fan of the Rusyn movement." She heard the familiar voice on her left as a young man sat down next to her. "How're you doing, Ancika?"

Anna's eyes popped out when she looked at the boy. "What are you doing here, Michal? This is a surprise indeed." She greeted her cousin with a fleeting kiss on his face.

"This is one of the rare occasions in town when a young man can get acquainted with beautiful young women. I wouldn't have missed it for the world." He looked at the dancing couples and his smile was full of mischief. "Who are you here with? It's not Volodymyr, is it?"

"What do you have against him?" Anna pursed her mouth and her eyes began to search for the organizer.

"He is too much of a nationalist. Did you hear his speech? He wants to pull all the youth into his movement and give them guns to go against the Czechs, Magyars, or whoever stands in the way of his independence."

"You're exaggerating. I think he's a jolly boy. But I am here with Marika from school and we've just met him. I'm also here to get acquainted with nice young men. It was a suitable occasion to get my parents to agree to let me attend."

"Just be careful," Michal said, his face turning grave. "I know your stepfather would like to get you married as soon as there's an appropriate match on the horizon, especially one with Ukrainian or at least Rusyn origins."

"He's not the only one." Anna looked into Michal's eyes. "I'd give years of my life to be out of the house."

"Ancika, you cannot mean that." Michal took her hand in his. "You have a brilliant future in front of you. What would other girls give for the opportunity to learn a regarded profession as a teacher? There are not many choices for a lady yet. When you receive your diploma, the world will be open to you and you can finally stand on your own feet."

"I know, Michal, and I'm not ungrateful. I'd love to teach. It's just..." Anna fell silent. How could she explain her oppression at home? "Sometimes it becomes so unbearable that I wish I could escape from home with somebody I love."

"You know, Ancika," Michal said, his eyes holding hers hostage, "marriage is not a contract of equals, whatever you may have read or heard. We are in modern Czechoslovakia but also in Subcarpathia—the husband rules. Therefore, it is important that you finish school and not seek an escape from home through marriage. Working and financial self-reliance are the only ways to gain independence."

"Shall we dance, miss?" A boy offered his extended arm to her. Anna heard the waltz start. She could not miss it. She was wearing the part, after all.

The boy seemed familiar, but she could not place him. He was tall, in his late teen years, and wore a black formal suit, somewhat old-fashioned. His classic oval face would have been attractive if not for the large reddish pockmarks covering both his cheeks. She nodded to him and gave an apologetic look to Michal. He gestured for her to go, regret overshadowed by the smile on his face as he watched her graceful movements on the dance floor.

"My name is András Egri. We met at the city pool during summer but were not introduced," the boy said, looking into Anna's brown-green eyes. His brows were asking for her name.

"Anna Onisko," she answered and nodded. The boy held her like she was a delicate porcelain figure, and she felt herself flying. Anna enjoyed how her dress formed a bell shape as they rotated to the melody of the Vienna waltz—as she had imagined it would. A smile appeared on her face and the boy's face answered alike. She forced herself not to look at the pockmarks, but they drew her like a magnet. *Beauty and the Beast—this is how Belle must have felt. Can András also have a secret? Could I learn to love such pockmarks? And kiss them?*

They spoke little. He told her—surprising her with her

mother tongue at a Rusyn ball—that he was a senior in the teacher training school and his family came from Beregovo. She liked that he said Beregszász, the Hungarian name of the town. She closed her eyes and lost herself in the soaring sensation that rose above the crowd. Her toes left the dance floor, and she felt free. He had strong arms that held her safely and tenderly.

A polka followed the waltz, and he moved with the same effortless expertise. But as she opened her eyes to mind her own steps, the spell broke.

"Shall we continue our dance, Anna?" Volodymyr said, showing up out of the blue and not even waiting for András to release her. He pulled her off from him and hopped away with her to the rhythm of the polka. Anna was so surprised that she could not utter a word. She just sent an apologetic smile toward András.

"Such a beautiful girl should choose better dance partners," Volodymyr said, grinning. "You deserve a more handsome boy than this Magyar."

"Do you mean yourself?" Anna said with a crinkle of her nose.

"Why not?" Volodymyr's harsh laugh made the neighboring pairs turn to look. "Why not?" he repeated, and grabbed her even more fiercely. His steps became faster, bolder, and longer—demanding a larger free circle in the surrounding space. Anna felt her stomach jump into her throat. The safety and tenderness she had felt in András' arms had turned into a fight against a whirlwind. Volodymyr's smile was devious. She longed for the dance to end.

Volodymyr invited Anna for a drink and she accepted, her throat parched from the speed of their hopping polka and her mixed feelings about him. The sheer force with which he handled her had confused her. She could not put it together with the disarming smile that Volodymyr had greeted them with at the stairs and his gracious manner at their first dance. They stood at the buffet table while Volodymyr exchanged words with the other organizers. There was a break in the dance. A short-haired man stepped onto the stage and asked for silence.

"Who is he?" asked Anna, as they followed the crowd back to the ballroom with their glasses of refreshment—lemonade for Anna and wine for Volodymyr.

"Vasyl Ivanovchyk, the leader of the Ukrainian National Defense, a new organization. They'll be our future army," said Volodymyr proudly and pointed to the middle-aged man now standing on the stage with his glass raised for a toast.

Anna froze. *What's happening here?* She listened to Ivanovchyk's fiery sentences about self-defense and the need to arm his organization.

"We need to ensure we are capable of defending our cause with arms in hand if needed. We will not let the Czechs, Slovaks, and Magyars rule our country. If they don't give us power peacefully, we'll take it by force!"

Anna felt her face getting hot by the end of the speech. It was difficult to breathe. *Why am I here at all?*

There were shouts from the crowd, and to Anna's surprise, they were not of protest but agreement. More and more young men shouted phrases like "Freedom to Carpatho-Ukraine", "We are with you, Vasyl", and "Get into arms". Anna's worry transformed to fear and then dread. At that moment, she heard a shrill whistle.

There was a commotion at the staircase with the typical drumming of tens of heavy boots getting closer and closer. The gendarmes flooded the ballroom in seconds. Young men stepped into their way and tried to push them back. Some of them were beaten with rifle butts, but there were many people in the room and only fifteen gendarmes. Anna looked at the havoc and stepped back against the wall. She saw a familiar face among the gendarmes, but only for a second. The chaotic movement of the crowd hid them from view. She was in doubt. *It cannot be Laci! Or was it him?* Suddenly, a strong hand seized her arm and pulled her with great force out of the room. She crashed into several people across the staircase before she saw Marika at the buffet table and grabbed her arm. Only then did she realize that it was András who had pulled her. She said, "Marika comes with us!"

András nodded, but did not wait. They raced down the stairs and out into the street in a matter of seconds. The gendarmery had not left anyone posted in front of the house, and they could turn unnoticed into the very first left street leading down the hill. Anna heard the screeching tires of the police cars around the corner, but did not turn to look at them. The trio did not stop running until they reached the Roshkovich Embankment. Turning to the bridge, they began to walk slowly to catch their breath. They remained quiet while they made their way to the far end of the bridge.

Anna wanted to turn left to take the shortcut to home along the Palacky Embankment, but András stopped her by grabbing her hand.

"I cannot let you walk home alone. Marika, where's your place?"

"On the Munkácsy Street, just straight on and then to the left." Marika showed the path ahead.

"We'll accompany you and then I will walk Anna home."

"I don't think this is necessary," Anna said, hesitating, not wanting to use the kindness of the boy any longer.

"It is. It's getting dark and the situation in the city may not be safe." András was unwavering.

They continued straight and reached the Masaryk Square

where a throng of people was standing and shouting slogans similar to that in the ballroom. András pulled them close to the left side of the square and turned to the Munkácsy Street not long after. They could get away without attracting much notice.

Marika separated from them in the middle of the long Munkácsy Street. It was another five-minute walk to reach the end of the street, where the Carpatia Hotel stood opposite the main railway station. Gendarmes were picketing on the square, stopping anybody who approached the railway station, and asking for their identification. Anna guided András toward the railway crossing to Bolotina and they continued to walk along Antalov depot with its narrow gauge rails for wood transport. When the narrow rails turned to the right, they continued straight and got to the first houses of Anna's part of the city. It was more of a suburb, developed to make an affordable dwelling for craft workers and small shop owners. Everything was quiet here, as if they had arrived at a sleeping village. It was almost dark.

"You can return home now. Thank you." Anna said in a low voice.

"Can I see you soon?" András tried to take her hand, but she retracted it.

"I'll ask my parents."

"Which is your house?"

Anna pointed to the corner house and turned to go.

"I will remember," András said to her back. "You take care."

Anna slowed down, hesitated, then turned halfway and looked him in the eye. "Thank you, András. For everything."

The boy nodded, sighed, and disappeared into the darkness of the streets. Barking dogs dotted his way back home.

Anna found a willow basket full of beautiful hydrangea roses in front of their gate the next morning. She quickly hid the basket in the shed. *Can't let Mummy find it. How she had thrown away that bouquet of roses last time!* She wet a rag and tied it around the lower part of the stems. The bouquet would be waiting for her in the afternoon. She did not answer the note András had placed in the basket asking for a date next Sunday. András seemed to be a great boy, but she did not feel up to the role of Beauty. Instead, she went to Mass in the cathedral. *Our Father which art in heaven, Hallowed be thy name...and forgive us our debts...Forgive me, Father, that I forgot where I belong. I succumbed to sinful behavior, and you rightly corrected my ways by sending forces to destroy the ball. Give me faith and strength to keep my beliefs so that I am not following temptations. Give me the strength to bear my cross and succeed in my studies. Help me to get to what I want—independence. Amen.*

Chapter 4

On Monday, the students wrote a paper in natural history and Anna excelled in it. The subject was not her favorite, but she had made an effort during the weekend, poring over her books for hours, and it showed. Miss Plishkova praised her, too, and she was in a great mood. Nothing could spoil her world.

Wednesday evening was long. Stepfather sat in front of the radio the entire night, listening to the news with Mother.

"The government has accepted the requirements of France and Great Britain...Czechoslovakia will be responsible if there is a war over its refusal of the German demand for Sudetenland...Demonstrations against the government's decision..." It was confusing, but Anna did not dare bother her parents for an explanation. They were having a heated discussion about the consequences for their business, and she could not risk him throwing a tantrum. She concluded that her country had to agree to terms it did not like and complicated politics was involved.

Thursday started quietly, but Anna noticed the agitation on the streets during the morning rush hours. Everybody seemed to be hurrying somewhere. People were nervous and confused. In the afternoon, on the way back home from school, she heard the news before she read it. "The Hodzha government has fallen!" the newsboy shouted. "General Syrovy is the new Prime Minister." People were reading the newspapers on the street and talking about the general strike in Prague and other large cities. Anna had never heard of changes in the government. She had not thought about the stability of political institutions: only the safety and prosperity of her city that reflected the strength of the system. But the future of her country had now become an all-pervasive question. A shiver ran through her spine. *Could something happen to the school? It's my only way to escape from Stepfather. What if I can't finish it? No, the school must go on even if there is a war; teachers will be needed.*

She wanted someone to tell her that her worries were groundless, and everything would be fine. Marika always had an optimistic view of life. Her father worked in the city administration and had a lot of information. *Maybe she will know more about what the future holds for us.*

Marika wrapped an arm around Anna's shoulder and squeezed it as they sat on the bench in the schoolyard during the big break.

"Don't fret, silly! People will always need teachers."

"It's just that I don't have any other way to escape the slavery at home," Anna said, gratefully propping her head on Marika's shoulder.

"I know. But the Greek Catholic Church is strong, and with the Ukrainian movement, they are proud to maintain their school. At least this is what Dad always says. You also heard Savchenko—maybe autonomy is the solution."

"I hate politics! It just throws a wrench in the works for everybody."

"You are right. How that nice ball was destroyed by the gendarme last Saturday! I was enjoying myself until you grabbed my hand. I thought you liked Volodymyr, but then András saved us after all..."

"András is a nice boy, but not my type. And Volodymyr is gorgeous, but a brute..."

Marika giggled and said, "Aren't you a bit picky, missy? Take a bite." She shared her apple with Anna. The ripe red fruit had a bitter taste and she could hardly swallow it.

"I am not lucky with boys. I should focus on my studies instead."

"Balderdash!" Marika puckered her lips and pulled Anna up as she heard the bell. "You must always be on the lookout. You never know when your future husband pops up. And you can still study like a topper! Look at me!" She snickered and dragged Anna. They ran into the building so as not to miss the next lesson. Anna sighed and held onto Marika's hand like a lifeline.

Late evening, Stepfather and Mother talked in front of the radio and repeated the word "mobilization". Again, Anna was afraid to ask questions. She thought of Laci, and her throat constricted. If there is mobilization, a gendarme would be in more danger than most. Why did she feel so attached to the man she had met only a couple of times? She craved to see him now, feel his strong hands in hers, and listen to his Hungarian dialect from the countryside. She craved for even more...

She had gone to bed early but had difficulty falling asleep. She tossed and turned a hundred times before falling into sweet oblivion.

Next day, the queue in front of the shop reached the corner over thirty meters away. Customers pushed and elbowed their way in, cussing in the process. The shop saw an enormous turnover for a Saturday—over three times the normal. People bought everything from matches to food, and there was no flour, meat, or canned food in the shop by the time they closed much later than usual. Despite the profits, the family was exhausted from the mobs attacking the store. Even little Jancsi had to help move the smaller goods from the stock. Anna had planned to go to the movie theater with her friend, Bözske, to see the Burian comedy of the summer, "Duchacek will fix it". Until now, tickets had always been hopelessly sold out. As she reached the center to meet Bözske, an upside-down city awaited her. Army trucks occupied most of Masaryk Square, loading supplies from different shops. Masses of soldiers were marching across the bridge from the army barracks in the north of the city toward the railway station. In the center, on the other side of the bridge, she saw people gathered around the Morris column, discussing animatedly. Anna tried to get closer to the large placard on the column and read it through the gap between the two men in front of her, slightly bending at the waist to see better. "For fear of Germany's potential attack, the government has declared a general mobilization". All the soldiers in reserve had to report immediately to their regional centers.

"I am not in reserve due to age, but my son-in-law went to report in the morning," an old man said in Slovak to his neighbor.

"I heard that we would have more than a million soldiers—along with me, that is," the neighbor said, producing a sour smile. "I will report in the afternoon. I need to arrange some things for my family first." He waved goodbye and disappeared toward the bridge.

Anna felt a hand on her arm and turned to see Bözske. Her voice was impatient as she tugged on her arm. "Hi Ancika, come, we should get to the theater on time!"

The city movie theater was on the opposite side of the block, uphill. From the corner, they noticed the crowd in front of the building.

"Why don't they play, damn it?" a harsh female voice shouted in Rusyn, and the girls looked at each other. Shouts of "why" echoed through the throng. Placards at the entry doors featuring Burian, Czech's best comic, and his unmistakable lanky figure, were crossed by a long paper tape with the notice "Canceled".

A man sporting a pencil mustache and clad in an elegant double-breasted striped waistcoat and pants stepped out of the doors and held his arms high to catch everyone's attention. He could have stepped out of a film canvas, but was probably the movie manager. The throng calmed down.

"Dear audience, I regret to inform you that tonight's performance had to be canceled. All of our technical staff had to report to the army due to the mobilization." Because of the uproar from the crowd, he had to raise his voice. "As it is, we'll have to close our theater until they come back. Your tickets will be valid for the next performance after the theater opens or you can reimburse them at the cashiers now or tomorrow."

The racket of the crowd took time to diminish as people filed into the foyer toward the cashier boxes. When they finally got their money back, Bözske said, "Duchacek won't fix that. Let's have ice cream at least. I am not willing to let our afternoon be spoiled!"

Fortunately, the Korona hotel's ice cream window was

open. The girls walked home amid the Saturday crowd that resembled a disturbed anthill, leisurely licking at their creamy vanilla ice cream that had begun to trickle down the sides of the cone. But Anna did not feel relaxed at all. They had to stop at the Masaryk Square to let a troop of soldiers from the bridge on the north. Anna noticed a familiar face among the marching gendarmes. She ran to the column of uniformed men and tried to keep up with them. The ice cream fell on the sidewalk, totally forgotten.

"Laci! It's you! Where are you going?" She tried hard not to sound worried, but was not sure if she'd succeeded.

The chiseled profile turned toward her in surprise, and she glimpsed a trace of a wistful smile. It reminded her of those August party evenings when he had danced with her. But his smile disappeared in a second, and she saw the determined face she thought she had seen at the raid of the ball.

"Ancika! I can't speak now. We're moving to Bohemia to protect the borders." László Domeny looked straight ahead and pulled on the belt of his gun as it slipped when he looked at Anna.

"When will you come back?"

"Soon. I'll call on you as soon as I can, I promise." His eyes turned to her as she jogged along with the troops and stayed on her for a few moments. His glance made Anna blush, and she stopped moving. Then he looked ahead and marched toward the train station, holding himself erect and clutching onto his gun in an effort to draw courage.

Anna was now sure that it had been László among the gendarmes disciplining the crowd at the ball.

Bözske took Anna's hand, and they turned toward their city quarters. Anna was grateful that her friend did not ask any questions and let her get immersed in her own thoughts.

She waded through the weekend in a daze. She helped

Mother with all the chores like a machine and avoided answering her questions as to what was wrong with her. She saw Laci's handsome face everywhere. However much it seemed irrational, she could not help feeling that if she had been more persistent in seeking his attention over the summer, she could have prevented him from going away. She ended up in the shed late in the afternoon, weeping her fill until she became exhausted.

The next week was very busy in the shop, forcing Anna's attention away from her sorrow. She had to place large orders at the wholesalers, but they did not confirm half of them. They were out of several items, and Stepfather had to make additional purchasing tours during the day, leaving Mother to serve the customers. He could not resist picking on Anna.

"If the young lady is incapable of procuring basic things, I have to take care of it myself!" he said as he grabbed his coat from the peg in the hall. "If only she learned something useful and not how to teach stuff and nonsense to poor kids!"

The door banged behind him and the copper rod holding the little curtain on it hopped down from its peg. Anna ran to the outhouse to seek relief in a good cry.

They were closed on St. Venceslav's day on 28th September. Anna went to the celebration Mass in the cathedral and prayed for László. In the afternoon, radio broadcasts spoke of the shootings at the border with German Freikorps and even some SS units who had crossed the Czechoslovak borders. It frightened her to death. From then on, several casualties were reported every day, and on some days, several tens of them. Anna listened and trembled, but to her relief, she did not hear László's name.

"What's happening, Mummy?" she asked, washing the dishes with her mother on a Thursday evening.

"Nothing you should worry about, Ancika. The Czechs are fighting the Germans who want part of the country, but we have a very strong army. Fortunately, we are too far away to feel any effects," Mother said and squeezed her foamy, wet hands for a second. Then she resumed drying the dishes.

"We'll kill the Germans!" Jancsi shouted from his playing corner and banged two lead soldiers against each other, letting one of them fall. "Bang!"

"Are we at war?" Anna asked.

"This is just a trial of weapons. The politicians are still working on a diplomatic solution. Let's hope they will come up with one," Stepfather said, looking up from his paper. But the way he chewed on his pipestem warranted that he was more nervous than he was showing.

The politicians did come up with a solution alright.

They were in the shop on Friday afternoon when they heard that the Prime Minister would talk to the nation at five o'clock. They moved the radio to the shop so that the customers could also hear what was happening. General Syrovy spoke in a grave voice:

"After comprehensive consideration and examination of all the urgent recommendations, the Czechoslovak government has adopted the Munich resolutions of the four great powers. She has done so knowing that the nation must be protected and that no other decision is possible. The Government of the Czechoslovak Republic announces this acceptance, and at the same time, declares to the entire world its protest against the unilateral decision taken without its participation."

What does this mean? Is everything all right now? Anna scrutinized the solemn faces of the women and also noticed the fiery glance of the only male customer in the shop. Her insecurity led her to make a bold move.

"So, there will be no war, Dad. Is that right?" Anna asked when they were closing for the day, not long after the radio announcement. No customer wanted to remain; all of them rushed home. She was praying for the right answer but hid her hands under her apron to stop the tremor that always overcame them when she had to address Stepfather.

Stepfather furrowed his brow, but he was too thoughtful to be grumpy this time. "No, there'll be no war, but Czechoslovakia has already been defeated," he said and sighed. "They will truncate the country starting tomorrow, and I'm sure the Poles and Hungarians will follow. We won't be safe."

"Why do you say that?" Mother asked, pausing her task of setting the table for dinner.

"Poland wants the Teshin region and Hungary wants south Slovakia and Subcarpathia. The Munich agreement, due to which Czechoslovakia is handing over the Sudetenland to Hitler, without a fight, will encourage them."

"People will always need to eat, so what can happen to us?" Mother strongly believed the grocery business would survive even a war.

"The Ukrainian nationalists won't let this happen without a fight. They wanted autonomy, now they will want independence. I'll need to talk to some people to see what are the chances of that."

The Saturday papers confirmed Stepfather's notions. Anna picked them up from the kitchen table late in the afternoon after Stepfather was done with them. She read, with bulging eyes, how the four powers—Germany, Italy, UK, and France—had agreed that her country would be handing over Sudetenland to Hitler's Germany. It was more than one-third of Bohemia and inhabited by 3.5 million people, albeit with a dominant German nationality. Anna also understood that the agreement had further consequences: in three months, there had to be a solution agreed for the Polish and Hungarian nationalities of Czechoslovakia. Both nations had announced their territorial demands in line with what Stepfather had claimed the day before. The papers also reported that terrorist groups from Hungary had crossed the borders and were attacking police stations in villages all over south Slovakia and Subcarpathia.

Her country would be cut to pieces, but she had strange feelings of hope. *Could we belong to Hungary? Could I use my mother tongue everywhere I like? What would be like living in a kingdom without a king?* The thought was like a scene from a fairy tale. Only the terrorist attacks drew a frown on her forehead.

She could not imagine it at all. Uzhhorod (or Ungvár in Hungarian, as she liked to call it) was her home city with its mixture of inhabitants and languages—where it was no problem to call somebody in Slovak, Hungarian, or Rusyn. Even the Jews were part of the business and everyday life of the city, just like any other nationality. *What will happen to them now? How will the Hungarians handle this?*

She remembered the Jewish family, the Rosenfelds, who used to live in the neighborhood when Anna's family was living on Kralicki Street several years ago. Their religion did not allow them to make a fire on the Sabbath. They had persuaded Anna to prepare the wood for the fire on the tile stove. It needed to be lit on Saturday morning. Before going to school, she would stop at the Rosenfelds' and light the fire on the stove. When she returned from school in the afternoon, she stopped at their place again and made up the fire so the family could be warm the whole day. The Rosenfelds were grateful to Anna and offered her many delicacies, most of which she had never seen or tasted. Quince cheese, watermelon and honeydew melon preserves, matzo at Passover...She loved matzo, the crunchy Jewish flatbread. They even gave her some coins for her trouble. After a couple of months, Mother found the money and drew the information about where it came from her. Mother then told her that the Jews cooked Christian blood into the matzo before Easter. Anna never again visited the Rosenfelds.

A large and growing Czech elite, especially those in the administration, had moved to Subcarpathia when it had become a part of Czechoslovakia after the Great War. They brought their modern Western culture and architects and built numerous government buildings, the swimming pool, lots of schools, and luscious parks and alleys that Anna loved. They also brought business opportunities. The Czechs held their nose high, put their children in new Czech schools, and frequented expensive cafes. Anna met them only when she worked as a ball girl for a crown an hour at the tennis courts on Sundays.

Anna remembered well the poor Uzhhorod in the late twenties, during her childhood, full of horse-driven carts from the countryside on market days, the ragged clothing of the peasants, the not-much-better dress of the town people, and the Eastern and ancient provincialism of the city with lots of unpaved roads, dirt, and poverty. The change started in the thirties, but life did not get better until the middle of the decade when the consequences of the Great Depression disappeared. Uzhhorod prospered, thanks to the industrial, commercial, and even administrative moves of the Czechs toward the new province. Anna's parents had been profiting from this for the past several years. This made it possible for her to go to high school and get closer to realizing her dream of becoming a teacher.

What will happen to my school if the Hungarians come? When I finish, will I be able to teach Hungarian? I barely know anything about history and I don't write well in Hungarian. She shivered and locked her trembling hands together. Anna spoke Hungarian like a native speaker, but the written word was different. She was not used to reading in Hungarian. Stepfather had always bought Rusyn newspapers. At school, they spoke and read Ukrainian and Slovak. Writing in Hungarian was foreign territory. She had never learned the language at school, so grammar did not tell her anything.

Anna felt alone with her misgivings. Mother would not assuage her worries as she was pragmatic: we need to play the hand we are dealt. Stepfather seemed to be occupied with talking to his friends and business partners and always had too many wrinkles on his forehead that discouraged Anna from bothering him.

"Would they really be interested in having butchers?" Stepfather whispered as he bent closer to Bondarenko one evening when he had come over for a chat. Anna was standing close enough to hear them, so she dried the plates with care to avoid any clink.

"You bet. I'm also offering my services as a blacksmith. The army needs every hand. Today the Czechs, tomorrow may be our own," Bondarenko said.

"Dad is excited that the Hungarians could come. Finally, we'll be together again after twenty years, he says," Marika said, reacting to Anna's worries while ambling toward her home after school the following day. "We still have almost two years at school, don't worry. You'll have enough time to practice your Hungarian."

Of course, her father was a Hungarian national from Slovakia. Anna's stomach was still in knots.

"It's just a mess. I love this city as it is, with all its nationalities."

"I would love to use my mother tongue every day, everywhere, without being frowned upon."

"You can. We are speaking Hungarian, aren't we?"

"Go to the city council! Dad has to speak Slovak all day."

"We have no problem speaking our customers' language at the shop unless it's Hebrew," Anna said, giggling. "But we really haven't mastered that language!"

"You see? You are anti-Semitic!" Marika japed and cracked up as she grimaced.

They sauntered along in silence for a while as Anna thought of the Rosenbergs.

"Do you know how handsome Hungarian soldiers are?" Marika said, winking at her.

"Oh, come on, I am serious. My only chance to get away from Stepfather is to be a teacher. How can I teach in a Hungarian school if I have learned everything in Ukrainian?"

Marika hooked her arm along with Anna's and whispered, "We are best friends, aren't we? My Hungarian is good enough for two." She giggled. "I can teach you all that is necessary for grammar or history. I know some Hungarian songs for children, listen." She started to sing in a low voice, but Anna shushed her as a passing man glared at them.

"You see?" Marika growled, her cheerfulness evaporating.

Chapter 5

The funeral cortege progressed from the police head-quarters along the Roshkovich Embankment with its linden alley toward the new Masaryk Bridge that connected the governmental administrative complex of Small Galago with the southern bank of the river. The coffin was in a four-horse black landau with several huge wreaths on top. On both sides of the carriage, six police officers marched in parade uniforms with glistening rows of metallic buttons, spiked helmets, and the indispensable sabers. The family followed the landau, and behind them, a vast crowd walked in the middle of the cobblestoned embankment. Onlookers stood on both sides of the street, some with enormous banners raised above their heads. The Ukrainian slogans on the banners called for action: punishment for the terrorists and autonomy for the region. A row of policemen and gendarmes separated the onlookers from the funeral procession along the whole road.

During the entire week, Anna felt the city trembling with anticipation. She went to join her mother and stepfather in the shop on Monday afternoon after school. She made her way around the curtain that separated the living quarters from the shop but stopped short, as she wanted to hear her stepfather conversing with the customers unseen. It was safer not to let them know she was present if she was to gather information on how the war would affect their lives. Stepfather rarely offered Anna answers when directly asked.

"What about you, Dimitri? As a good Ukrainian, will you join the demonstration tonight?" A man with graying temples picked up his goods from the counter and put them in his bag. He looked at Stepfather.

Stepfather leaned on the counter with both hands as if he needed support.

"I am not sure. You see how much work there is in the shop—everybody needs goods today. I am busy till late evening looking for new sources in this beehive nowadays."

"Autonomy is important," the man announced in a loud voice, turning his head to see other customers nodding. "If our country is now declared a federal republic of the Czechs, Slovaks, and Carpatho-Ukrainians, as the radio announced yesterday, the autonomy of our region is a natural consequence. But we need to remind them!"

"You do that, Vasyl, and I will make sure you have food to buy," Stepfather said with a smile and waved the man goodbye. On Tuesday, all the papers were full of news about the new autonomous government led by Andrej Bródy.

"Bródy was born in the same village as your father, in Beregkövesd," Mother said in a low voice when Stepfather had gone to the bathroom. "I remember seeing Bródy at some of the village fairs in Kövesd. He was a rich Rusyn boy.

Later, he became a teacher and politician in Ungvár. Isn't he still a dashing man?" She gestured to the picture in the paper.

"Bródy will just side with the Magyars," said Stepfather, stepping into the kitchen. He had noticed Mother pointing at Bródy's picture. "He wants Subcarpathia to join Hungary. Everybody suspects that, and he wants it based on a people's vote. What a dreamer!"

They never spoke about Anna's father, not when Stepfather was around. Anna had seen him twice or thrice. The last time she remembered seeing him was when she spent the summer in his village with his sister's family after finishing higher elementary two years ago. She remembered the six children, her half-sisters and half-brothers, from a toddler to an almost teenager around the house—some playing, some doing chores. They looked at her with curious but hostile glances topped by the gaze of the woman of the house. Her father had invited her into the main bedroom.

She sat on the bed, feeling out of place. The picture of her father and the woman, hanging next to a picture of Christ above the rustic bed, bothered her. He asked about her mother and she gave laconic answers, mostly looking at her hands. When he asked about her studies, she gathered some courage and looked him in the eye.

"I am applying to the teacher's school," she said and glimpsed a spark of interest in his face. He raised his bushy brows that were still auburn like his wavy hair, without a trace of gray.

"Commendable!" he said. "I have a clever daughter. What subjects do you like the most?"

"I need support for the tuition fee."

She exhaled as though a large boulder had rolled off her chest. She had said it. Shame heated her cheeks, and she slid down the bed a bit.

He fiddled with his shirt sleeves and talked about the crops, the family, and the weather. She listened but wanted to be off. At last, he said, "After the harvest, I will send you money. You deserve a chance."

No money came from him that summer or later. It was pure finesse that Mother convinced Stepfather to send her to higher education because it would be easier to find a bridegroom for her if she was educated.

They heard a lot about the political changes at school. Most of the teaching board, loyal Rusyns and Ukrainians, rejoiced. Mr. Savchenko took extreme pleasure in explaining the changes and did not forget to emphasize their significance for Carpatho-Ukraine, proud to call it "the right way". He was radiating joy and making jokes until Thursday when he came into the class with a somber, even tragic expression. He announced that the school was attending a funeral on Saturday.

"We cannot remain behind in paying tribute to the brave protectors of our country who share our blood. Vasyl Kuzmik, a police officer, gave his life in a fight with the terrorists who are attacking our country and wishing to oppress our budding autonomy. It is no surprise to hear that our nation is calling for armed action. I celebrate the army and police's efforts to stop these Hungarian terrorists of the so-called Ragged Guard." He stopped and looked at the girls, turning his head to look into each pair of eyes for a second. "We will be there at the funeral procession as faithful children of our country and show them that we are not afraid of any enemy who imperils our freedom."

Hungarian terrorists?

They wore black, of course. Anna was among the onlookers, along with her schoolmates. The cold weather had persisted in the last few days, so their black winter uniform coats were coming in handy. The school canceled classes on Saturday because of the funeral, even though it was due to start in the afternoon.

The onlookers followed the procession, which grew with every meter as they turned onto Masaryk Bridge. Many people were waiting on the southern bank in the Market Square to join the procession. The congregation must have numbered several thousand by the time they reached the old city cemetery.

Anna caught sight of the handsome face of László Domeny in the throng. *He has returned!* She almost could not believe her eyes. But as fast as her excitement appeared, it subsided. *But he has not stopped by to let me know. The rogue.* She surprised herself by feeling a jealous bitterness. He was in his gray-green uniform but without the gun. He was standing not among the gendarmes who protected and accompanied the procession, but among the onlookers. How smart he looked! *He must be off duty today. Why is he here at all? Did he know the policeman who died?*

The Greek Catholic bishop himself led the service. Several speeches, including those by a police general and some politicians, followed. Anna was not surprised to see Volodymyr Paliychuk among the speakers. Her head was buzzing from the nationalist slogans she heard in every sentence.

Her questions about László found their answers only after the funeral ended a good two hours later. As the crowd dispersed, she spotted László again, and this time he also took notice of her. His solemn face brightened up, and he started toward her with his customary brisk steps.

"Anna! Ancika! Great to see you, even on such an occasion," he said, greeting her in Hungarian with a warmth in his voice despite his still-solemn mood.

"I thought I would need to visit a funeral to see you again," she said petulantly. "I just feared it would be yours."

"You don't mean that," he replied, and took her hand in his. "As soon as I returned from Bohemia, they stationed me at Mukachevo. I couldn't go to see you."

"Are you alright?" Her mood changed. It was not due to neglect that he had let her suffer—he had been stationed away.

"I am. But Vasyl did not come back with us."

"You knew him?"

"We were both ordered to Mukachevo early in October, but I've known him before from Uzhhorod."

Anna felt dizzy. László looked around and pointed to a bench at the cemetery gate.

"Why don't we sit down for a minute?"

As they sat, he took out a cigarette from a packet, tapped it on his knee, and lit it. He drew on it a couple of times before he spoke. "We thought it just being prudent of the Command that they were mobilizing us again, now closer to the Hungarian border. It turned out to be much more than that. We were not there a mere week when we heard about the terrorist groups coming over the border. The clash south of Mukachevo happened on Tuesday." He stopped speaking for a minute and just stared at the smoldering cigarette end. "We were helping the army units against a couple of hundred Ragged Guards. I cannot tell you more. It's enough that Vasyl got shot in the guts. No chance of survival. He died the next day. We have lost some others, too—Czech and Slovak boys. He was the only one of Rusyn origin and from Uzhhorod."

"You fought against Hungarian soldiers?" Anna searched his eyes. Her hands grabbed the edge of the bench.

"You could call them terrorists. They didn't even have a uniform. The name Ragged Guard fits them well. They had bad-quality and old weapons. After we crushed their main body, the army took a lot of hostages. Some of them succeeded in escaping, but almost a hundred remained. I heard them speak, and they were crazy."

"What do you mean?"

"They were deifying Horthy, Hungary's Governor, and were talking about reclaiming Subcarpathia. They didn't care at all about the losses they had suffered. Only hate and contempt radiated from their words. I didn't dare to show that I understood them."

"But they are Hungarian like you and me after all..." Anna said, looking at him, wanting to hear a solution.

"I was born in the last year of the Great War when we still belonged to Hungary. I am Hungarian, but this country brought me up. Czechoslovakia gave me a purpose, opportunity, and a decent life. I don't know what to do with my being Hungarian."

Anna was silent. *He is a grown man, and he doesn't know. How am I supposed to understand where I belong? What do I believe? Who is right and who is wrong?*

László finished his cigarette, threw it on the ground, and extinguished the stub with the heel of his boot.

"I need to go. I have an afternoon shift. I cannot walk you home now. Can I meet you next Sunday? We could have a stroll around the Uzh if the weather is pleasant."

Anna looked at his finely wrought face and could not say no. "Meet me on the bridge next Sunday at two," she said and walked away toward the center of the city. She wanted to cut a caper, but she was at the cemetery gate and had to control herself.

Dusk approached fast as it neared six o'clock. She needed to go through the Masaryk Square in the center. There she noticed a gathering crowd flooding the square. More banners swayed above the heads of the people. She dove into the smaller side streets and zigzagged in the direction of the railway station. She could still hear the shouting and the rhythmic chanting of the crowd in Ukrainian demanding independence for the region. "We won't give away Carpatho-Ukraine or our freedom! Give our homeland to the Poles or the Hungarians? Never!" She increased her speed. Several large printed pieces of paper lay on the ground. Looking around and making sure that nobody saw her, she picked one up. She did not dare to inspect it then and there, so she hid it in her pocket. It was dark when she reached home and slipped into the anteroom. She told her parents that she was not feeling well and was not hungry, so they left her alone. Her brother was with their parents at the dinner table. She rushed to her empty room to have a look at the pamphlet. The text was in Ukrainian.

Brothers and sisters! Liberation has come. The fate of Czechoslovakia has been decided in Munich. A country based on lies, on the suffering of its peoples, is divided. Rusyns! Get ready for this day! Your freedom is imminent. Do not believe the Czechs who want to spring new promises on you! You will be prisoners again in New Czechoslovakia! It is enough! Shake down the Czech yoke. The Hungarian borders are getting closer and closer to you. You should welcome them with joy. After the Czech misery and oppression, Hungary will give you grain, wine, and peace. Under the crown of St. Stephen, you will live in prosperity with religious, economic, and political freedom.

She fell back against the bed and looked at the ceiling. It was her childhood friend, helping her imagine things. Against its pure white canvas, she could project any scene she imagined—be it a fairy tale or a boy's handsome face. A movie appeared in front of her eyes: horse-driven carts full of wheat and wine barrels, decorated with wind-blown ribbons in the Hungarian national colors, were driving through the city's streets. The gypsy band accompanying them played bittersweet Hungarian songs. Young boys were dancing to the rhythm of the czardas. The unbelievable image then transitioned into the new buildings of Ungvár that had transformed her old and poor country town into a bustling modern city in merely eighteen years. Her city, with its theaters, cinemas, hotels, ballrooms, tennis courts, and its swimming pool, linden alley embankment, and the sakura trees in Galago. The factories built to give work to thousands. The city center with the smell of coffee, vanilla ice cream, and creamy cakes made fresh in its famous confectioneries.

She was tucked in bed by the time Jancsi came to the room. Anna was in no mood to read the customary tale to her brother. He complained, but to no avail, and eventually fell asleep. Anna looked at the ceiling for hours, thinking, until it all became blurry and she could not keep her eyelids from closing.

Chapter 6

The weather got colder by the following weekend. It was freezing in the morning and improved only a little by midday. A strong wind blew from the Carpathians, and sleet started falling when Anna walked through the garden gate for her meeting with László. *We aren't very lucky, are we?* She opened the umbrella she had brought with her in anticipation of rain. Anna had dressed for warmth, wearing her long reefer herringbone coat with wide lapels, a double row of buttons, and a wide belt. She took the shortest route to the center and reached the bridge in less than twenty minutes.

She spotted László in his uniform under the awning of the city theater, just opposite the bridge. As soon as he noticed her, he took big steps and met her in the middle of the bridge. László kissed her gloved hand and offered his arm while taking her umbrella and placing it above her head.

It made no sense to get soaked, so László suggested visiting the popular place in the Legio-house, Purma cafe, just a couple of streets ahead. Czech ex-legionnaires returning from Russia after the Great War had financed and constructed the building in which each of them had opened a different business and enriched the city with a Czech hallmark. The delicate and sweet smell of biscuits and coffee had lured them from two blocks away, and when they entered the huge parlor, they felt they had been transferred to Prague.

Anna and László looked around in search of a free table until they saw a couple emerging from the corner who were just leaving. Anna had been there only once on her birthday a couple of years ago after finishing higher elementary. Purma meant luxury, and she was full of anticipation about sampling their vanilla ice cream, the taste of which she still remembered. She might even ask for their signature cream cake and coffee.

After placing their orders, they began to observe the people around them. They were making fun of some overdressed ladies in hushed whispers. They stopped when the server appeared with a tray carrying coffee, cake, ice cream, and lemonade.

"Tell me about your school," László said, mixing sugar in his coffee, stirring slowly, and looking into her eyes all the time. Anna admired those large hands full of blisters and could not imagine them raising the miniature cup without breaking it.

He was an attentive listener. Anna stopped being shy and looked him directly in the eye as she talked. Those sparkling blue eyes had fascinated her during that first August evening. She rambled about her love for math, her success as a singer in the choir, her having to give up the choir last year because she had to help in the shop every day, her ambitions to be a teacher... He did not mind her jumping from school to friends and her love of dancing.

"I remember that you dance extremely well," he said when she stopped her monologue to dive into her cake and ice cream. "I regret that we could not meet at more dancing parties."

As she ate, he talked about his aging parents in the countryside and how he spent his off days and his holidays in the fields to help them bring in the crops. Now that the work was over, he had more time to spend with Anna.

When he took out a cigarette and asked for her permission to smoke, she realized she did not mind at all. She hated cigarette smoke and the smell of Stepfather's cheap pipe tobacco lingering on clothes. But she found László's smoking manly, his cigarettes fragrant.

"I am happy you sing," he said, and she felt a faint blush arise on her clean cheeks. "I have to admit, I love to sing, especially folk songs."

They were whispering melodies they enjoyed to each other, and both were surprised at how many songs they knew. When they stood, László helped Anna get into her coat and then offered his arm. She could not take her eyes off him and almost bumped into the swinging glass entry door.

"Whoops, careful, I didn't know they put alcohol in their ice cream!" László bantered as his strong arms stopped the closing door.

Anna giggled and hit his arm playfully. He had invited her into this shrine of peace, luxury, and glee, and now he had even prevented her from crashing her nose on the glass.

"We could come here every weekend if my duty schedule allows, don't you think?" László said with a content smile. Anna felt elated to have something to look forward to during the week. Life did not seem to be so dark and such a drudgery anymore.

The next weekend, however, László had to be on duty both days. Some weekdays, he waited for her in front of the school and accompanied her through the city after classes but did not go to her home. Anna always felt cheered to see him, and she reveled in the envious glances from her schoolmates. They tried to get her to talk about him and their relationship, but Anna gave curt answers. She was superstitious and thought that if she told them about László, it could somehow cause the end of their budding relationship.

László told her the city was going back on high alert from Thursday, October 27th, and that would mean they would not be able to meet on Friday, the twentieth birthday of the Czechoslovak Republic. Andrey Bródy had been arrested, and the Greek Catholic reverend Avgustyn Voloshyn had become the Prime Minister of autonomic Subcarpathia with a complete change of the government. The German-Italian negotiations in Vienna around Hungarian territorial claims against Czechoslovakia promised unfavorable decisions for the country.

Anna perceived the news through rose-colored glasses at first until she realized that those changes could be profound for her beloved city and even more for her beloved boy. Her city was in danger and her boy could be dragged away again. He had become a part of what she had embraced. She did not know what would happen, and it scared her. She wished for something to happen, anything so that she could take steps against her fate. She could fight for her future—her future with László.

By now, she knew she was in love.

They met on the bridge again and strolled toward Purma's cafe.

"There are some important things I need to tell you," László said, and his lips curved into a forced smile. "But let's have a seat first."

Anna just nodded; her mind was occupied with the news. She squeezed his arms closer to her body. Why couldn't she detect the sweet smell of delicious pastries in the air? As they turned the corner, they were shocked to see the cafe shutters down.

"What happened to Purma's, sir?" she asked a pedestrian who was walking past them in a hurry.

"You haven't heard? Purma closed his business and escaped to Slovakia two days ago. He's afraid of the Hungarians. I don't blame him." The man puckered his lips with a sigh and continued down the street toward the bridge.

"What's going on?" Anna turned to László with a puzzled expression.

He stopped and gestured downhill, leading with energetic steps behind the corner again. "You know what? I know the Korona isn't up to Purma's standard, but it's close and we don't want to walk in this rainy and cold weather. Let's go in and have a cup of coffee there so we can talk." Anna looked at him sideways and understood that he had something big on his mind that was not fit for the street. She let him lead her without a word, but her heart was in her throat. She bit her lip to stop herself from asking questions.

The cafe was almost full from taking in all the Sunday afternoon guests from Purma's. They were lucky to get a table, albeit next to the restroom. No one else wanted to sit there. They ordered coffee and Anna declined the server's offer of a cream cake. Her stomach could not have digested it, anyway.

"Ancika, they will station me far away," László said when the server disappeared after taking their orders.

"How come? And where to? What's happening?" Anna asked in a rush as if she thought that by asking so many questions the answers would become easier.

"The great powers have agreed to give the south of Slovakia and Subcarpathia to Hungary. The Czech forces have to move behind the new borders in a matter of days. I'll have to go tomorrow and my station will be in Nagyszőlős or Sevljus, as they now call it. This small town will remain in Czechoslovakia. All the government offices will move to Khust, twenty kilometers from there."

László's handsome face blurred, and she had to wipe the teardrops away from her cheeks. He reached for her hand and gave it a tender caress. Anna choked, but tried to fight it off.

"I can't lose you, Laci..."

"It breaks my heart, Ancika. I just cannot stay. I have my place at the gendarmes and..." László's eyes pierced into hers with indefinite sorrow.

Anna tried to think. There must be a solution. She took her handkerchief and blew her nose.

"You mean... Ungvár will be Hungary, and Sevljus and Khust will remain in Czechoslovakia? This is just crazy!" Anna grabbed the edge of the table with both hands, her thoughts in a jumble.

"We are to help in protecting the new borders of Czechoslovakia."

"Let me think... Beregkövesd, where my father lives, is ten kilometers north of Nagyszőlős so maybe it will also remain in Czechoslovakia. I can visit him. I am sure Stepfather and Mother will allow that. And then I could see you as well...maybe...if you want..."

"I would want that very much, Ancika. You can be sure of that!"

Their coffees had been hardly touched. László did not release her hands for even a minute. They were trying to console each other but could not find the words to do so. So, they remained silent and looked into each other's eyes, trying to hold a reflection of each other that would stay with them despite borders and changes. *We have to find a way.*

László walked her home. When the road turned away from the river near her place, she stopped and kissed him on the mouth, lingered for a few seconds, and then ran away.

She heard him say, "I will wait for you, Ancika!" But she could not respond due to the terrible dumpling in her throat that almost strangled her. She ran, hardly stopping to catch her breath, until she reached her house on the corner. Then she wiped the tears off her face and slammed the gate behind her.

The hussars, an elite cavalry brigade, came first—sitting erect in their saddles and letting their horses parade slowly. The late afternoon sun sparkled on the polished scabbards of their swords, the sabers themselves drawn and resting on the shoulders in salute. Their metal helmets reminded Anna of German soldiers she had seen in movie newsreels.

A military brass band followed, playing a familiar tune. Two infantry squadrons strode to the music proudly behind them and the soldiers sang the Hungarian words, "Rise, rise soldiers to the battle..." Anna felt fearful. It was an old song from the Hungarian revolution against the Habsburgs ninety years ago, but its fierce rhythm, fiery words, and enthusiasm with which the soldiers sang it radiated a determination that was above and beyond the peaceful overtaking of Ungvár. The soldiers seemed to come from a different world than

Anna's, and the more she observed them, the more dread she felt. They looked like they were ready to start a war.

On the Masaryk Square, the soldiers split and one group turned left toward the new Masaryk Bridge to Small Galago and the government buildings. Anna heard that the official celebrations would happen in front of the Governorate, a symbolic handover of the city keys. The other platoon continued right onto the solemnly decorated old bridge and the old city center on the other side of the river. Someone had wrapped the steel arches of the bridge in garlands that were also in Hungarian colors. Several enormous flags were flying on the bridge, and two huge ones on high masts adorned the bridgehead on the other side. Anna followed the soldiers to the bridge. Then she had to stop, not being able to penetrate the dense throng gathered there.

She could not imagine where all the small red-white-green paper flags, the Hungarian tricolor, mounted on thin wooden skewers, had come from. At least a hundred children were spread along the bridge, waving small flags toward the soldiers, and several women dressed in traditional Hungarian costumes offered bouquets to them. The soldiers accepted them with smiles and thanks. *Where did all the Ukrainians disappear?* Anna saw acquaintances who sympathized with the Rusyn movement among the bystanders. They were looking at the procession, did not have flags, and were clad in normal clothes. Their expressions deeply bothered Anna. She could not decide what was behind the sadness: mourning, resignation, contempt, or even resistance. She knew these people were conforming to the prevalent atmosphere and also knew that they would never voice their opinion in public. These were the people that had lived here for a thousand years, as her mother had told her. And they would continue living here always.

She had her own future to worry about. The school had suspended classes for the rest of the week. She felt all the pillars of her existence were falling down. The school, László, her city as she knew it, her friends who had fled to Slovakia... *Would she ever see them again?*

As much as she hated Stepfather's family business with all the drudgery he forced her to perform there, it seemed to be the only pillar of her life that still stood undisturbed and promised the livelihood her family needed. *How long can one pillar hold a building?*

"The new city council simply withdrew my license!" Stepfather roared, banging his fist on the table and making the plates jump and the cutlery clang. Mother stopped and held the glasses she wanted to place on the table close to her bust. "They won't let an honest Polish citizen run a grocery shop, the bastards!"

Mother winced at the word, but decided it was not the time to correct her husband. Instead, she put the glasses back on the sideboard and took out a bottle. She poured a generous shot of vodka and placed it in front of Stepfather. Anna was looking at them with wide eyes, and Jancsi was nestled in a corner next to her, embracing her right knee. His body was frozen and his blue eyes were jumping from one adult to the other.

"What's your plan?" Mother asked when he finished the shot. He exhaled and the veins in his temple stopped bulging. Then she returned to arranging the water glasses.

Stepfather shook his head. "Bondarenko was right. We can't stay here."

Jancsi raised his head and opened his mouth, but Anna

gave his shoulders a squeeze to stop him.

"I'll take the butcher's job in the army in Khust. You'll join me there after you find a good tenant for the house." He motioned to Mother to ladle the soup and beckoned to the children. "Come to eat."

Anna had no appetite. Leaving her home city filled her with dread. What would happen to her school? What would happen to her city? How would she pursue her dream of becoming a teacher? Would she find a teacher training school in Khust? She felt guilty, her thoughts consumed with Laci, but she knew she had to finish school to attain something in life. Jancsi must have felt the tension, too, even if he did not understand it. She noticed him listlessly stirring his soup, the spoon reaching his mouth only twice.

"I am not going anywhere," Anna blurted. Her voice choked as Stepfather's hand holding his spoon stopped in midair, his mouth open. Mother looked at her in horror.

"What are you babbling?" Stepfather put down his spoon and turned to Anna with squeezed eyes.

Anna straightened in her chair and raised her head. "I have my school here. I can't just escape. I want to be a teacher. Jancsi has to go to school soon. I could take care of him. Let us stay here."

Stepfather banged on the table, and the plates bounced again. Half of his soup spilled on the tablecloth.

"I am surrounded by idiots in my own household! We don't have a shop anymore, can't you see? We must rent the house to have some secure income. You must help us survive! Schools are everywhere, if that's your concern!" His face was red from the shouting.

Mother tried to put a hand on his arm, but he shook it off.

"I want to stay!" Despair replaced anger and determination, and tears flooded Anna's eyes.

Stepfather's hand swished through the air and smacked her head from the back with an enormous force. It was unexpected and her forehead hit the table next to her plate. As she raised it, she saw Stepfather jump and dart into the bedroom,

"So that you have reason to cry, you silly goose!" he said and banged the door.

Mother started collecting the dishes, shaking her head. Anna's head dropped on the table, and when she felt Jancsi's hand stroking her hair like a butterfly's wings, she let her tears flow.

The school announced that the next Monday, they would close their doors in Ungvár. The whole school gathered in the foyer, and the director told them that the school would move to Sevljus. To her schoolmates' amazement, Anna started to cry. One of the nuns stroked her back and tried to comfort her, but she shook her head and ran toward the bathrooms.

What a silly goose I am! I confronted Stepfather for nothing! The school will move to the city László is stationed! I can't believe my luck! She turned on the faucet and sprinkled cool water on her flaming cheeks. To stop her nervous hiccups, she drank water until she felt she would almost burst. Elation, shame, relief, and worry filled her head. She could not decide if she had cried from relief, self-pity, fear, or just shock. *Sevljus is only twenty-something kilometers from Khust. I should be jumping up and down because I can continue to study, I will be able to meet László, and I can go with the family to Khust! Everything is solved!*

Ungvár would be left behind. Her beloved city, now under Hungarian rule. Would she abandon the city, or would

Ungvár forsake her first? *I must follow most of my loved ones. The school, Laci, the family...whatever remains here that I cannot live without? The Uzh river? The castle? The cobblestoned streets of the old town? The sakura trees? The dancing parties? My friends? Friends will move with the school, I hope. And Laci will be with me...*

Stepfather thought his well-placed slap had made Anna change her mind. She told only Mother that the school would move.

"It's good you kept it between us," Mother said. "I will convince him that we could manage your commuting to Sevljus—if this is what you want."

"You know how much I want to finish school. It's only another two years and I can teach!"

"Who knows what can happen in two years in these insecure times... We should find you a suitable husband so that you can live your own life, don't you agree?"

Does she also want me to go, or it is just that she would wish me a better life without Stepfather? Why can she never take my side?

To Anna's relief, Stepfather left for Khust the next day. They remained behind to find tenants for the house and organize the move. It did not prove easy.

"You'll come with me tomorrow to the city authorities. They say they have lists of all the new clerks who are moving in from Hungary. We may need to stand in different queues," Mother said one evening. "It would also help if you prepared some advertisements for tenants. We could stick them on the lampposts in the city."

This started a daily routine: Anna accompanied her mother to the city council to find a tenant for the house.

Although there were a lot of newcomers from Hungary who found jobs in the government and city administration, they preferred to move into the center instead of the suburbs.

"No, we don't have anybody willing to live that far," was

the answer in most cases. "There are many empty apartments in the center after the Czechs escaped."

Nobody called based on the ads they placed in the city. Anna became nervous and noticed how Mother counted the remaining cash every evening after she had finished sewing. She accepted short-term repair work to get some income. They lived on the shop's stocks, and after three weeks, only wizened potatoes remained.

Anna missed school. She hoped she could catch up, but each day's delay made her more nervous. *What if I stay behind? I could lose a year!* She only found comfort in the idea of meeting Laci soon.

Jancsi had one more year before starting elementary, but he was doleful over the move because he was losing his friends from the neighborhood. Anna promised him that Khust had the jolliest Rusyn boys in the whole country. Jancsi smiled and believed her. He was only five. Eventually, they found a Hungarian family who needed a two-room apartment urgently. The Árpas moved in from Miskolc. The father worked as a lower civil servant at the city council, and they had three children. He could not afford the higher rent in the city center, and they were happy to have a house in the suburbs. Anna's mother set an acceptable price, and they agreed to lease part of the house.

The family left Ungvár two weeks before Christmas: Mother, Anna, and her little brother, two enormous trunks, and the sewing machine. A Rusyn peasant who delivered goods to the city was willing to take them on his back way north through the new borders. They were lucky, as the cost of transport had skyrocketed and they did not have the new currency the Hungarians had introduced. A truck journey cost as much as a small house–this they could not afford. Official money exchange did not function and the black market money-changers quoted outrageously low exchange rates, so they tried to use their money directly. The Rusyn peasant accepted the Czechoslovak crowns as he came from the areas where the crown still worked. He delivered them through the border to Perechyn, a small town twenty kilometers northeast of Ungvár. They spent the night in the stable of a farmhouse and waited for another cart going eastward. The one-hundred-and-twenty-kilometer-long route to Khust took them three days. They were exhausted, dirty, cold, hungry, and desperate to sleep in a bed when they reached the workshop Stepfather now rented.

"I have only one room. I did not expect you here so early," Stepfather said and sent them to his modest lodgings.

They had to squeeze themselves into his rented room and stand in a queue in front of the only bathroom for three rooms each morning. Eventually, they found an affordable apartment with two rooms just two days before Christmas.

"Now Khust is the capital of Subcarpathia with a hungry army I must help to feed," Stepfather said one evening after their move. "It gives us a chance to survive in this mess."

You could only hear Ukrainian, mostly with the Rusyn dialect in town, except around the Czechoslovak soldiers who filled the army barracks of the town. Blue and yellow flags were commonplace, although the Czechs frowned at them. They were not used to the region's autonomy showing not only by flags but also in how confidently locals behave. But it was still Czechoslovakia, their common country, that was under pressure from the Hungarians. The army here was also full of conscripted Rusyn boys. On the other hand, the Ukrainian nationalists were rumored to have organized their own home guard, the "Sich". Anna remembered Volodymyr from the ball and could imagine him participating in it.

Anna succeeded in getting information about her school

in Selvjus and visited the new school location before Christmas. She found her class decimated, as they had transferred only the Ukrainian and Rusyn students. The Slovaks and Hungarians remained in Ungvár. She looked for her friend Marika in vain.

The school allowed her to continue her studies from January only after a successful test because she had missed more than a month from school. She had received material that would help her catch up and succeed in the test: lecture notes from her teachers, and notes and papers her classmates had written during the five weeks she was missing. She spent most of her Christmas holidays hunched over the stacks of notes and books. Stepfather was busy slaughtering animals from morning to evening for the army and Mother was helping him make ends meet. Heavy snow covered the streets and the freezing temperature had forced people inside, except for Jancsi, who was throwing snowballs or riding on a sleigh with his new friends from the neighborhood. So, Anna found the ideal conditions to study without distractions. She was even able to block out Laci from her mind that week. Determined to prove she was capable, and that she craved to start attending school again, she even skipped meals to have more time to study. By New Year's Eve, she had become a shadow of her previous self, but she passed her test with distinction on the first working day of January.

So, what about that silly goose, hah?

Chapter 7

It was a bitter winter, and it took Anna an hour both ways daily to get to Sevljus and back by train from Khust. She wanted to look for László on her first day after school, but she could not find the time until Saturday when her lessons got over at noon. She inquired at the main gendarme station and left a message for him.

László waited for her on Monday morning at the railway station. He seemed to have changed—lost some weight, and gotten older over the couple of months they had not seen each other. But he was still the familiar Laci, she…she loved. A smile awakened on his handsome face as he glimpsed her descending the steps of the train carriage. He hastened toward her with his unfaltering military steps. Her hand became lost in his big ones, and he kissed it with a tenderness she was used to. *It's him, my old Laci!*

"Ancika," he said, his voice coming through as a whisper.

"Laci!" she cried. She wanted to hug him, but stopped herself. There were many people at the station.

"I couldn't believe you were here when I got your note!" He squeezed her arm and his murmured words heated her cheeks despite the freezing cold.

"We are lucky, aren't we?" she said with a smile and could not help but rub her cheek against his. His stubble tickled her sensitive skin and made her stomach jump.

"I haven't even had time to shave. I ran to meet you after my night shift," he said.

She shook her head, took off her gloves, and locked her fingers with his. She wanted to feel him as closely as possible.

"I missed you so much!"

"It was a nightmare to be here not knowing when I would see you again or if I would even see you."

The five-minute walk extended to ten minutes, then fifteen, as they looked at each other all the time. They could not walk too fast lest they stumble on the rugged sidewalk. The limited time allowed only a brief exchange that could not cover all that had happened in the past two months. Anna wanted to feel his closeness and hear his voice telling her how he had missed her. She listened half-heartedly to his stories about his life among his comrades.

"Can you wait for me after school?" Anna asked.

"I will, as much as my duty schedule allows it," László said in a raspy voice that had developed in the cold of the winter. "I'm free on Saturday afternoon. When does your school end?"

"That's good. Lectures finish at noon, and there is only a late afternoon train. We could have all Saturday afternoon to ourselves!" Anna was ecstatic and gave him a fleeting peck on the cheek before disappearing behind the gates of the school, along with her amazed classmates.

Since Anna passed the test with good results, teachers paid her less attention and she was grateful for it. She could not concentrate on her studies for several days due to László. She found herself daydreaming, looking at the blackboard but seeing his face and his smile instead of the lengthy citation on it.

"So where does the citation come from, Miss Onisko?" She heard her name and glimpsed Mr. Moroz looking at her from behind his thick round glasses, his bushy eyebrows in a frown and his hand slowly stroking his substantial salt-and-pepper beard.

"Ehm, yes, please?" she said as she stood, swallowing hard.

"The citation," the teacher said, pointing to the blackboard with an impatient wave of his arm.

Anna looked at the blackboard and read the first sentence with awe. "Aeneas was a lively fellow and quite a Cossack for a lad..." *We had Virgil last year, why now...wait, Cossack?* Then it clicked. She had read this on New Year's Eve and she had had a lot of fun.

"Kotlyarevsky's Aeneid," she blurted, then added with confidence, "of course."

"Of course it is, Miss Onisko!" Mr. Moroz accompanied his smile with a wave of his hand to bid her sit. "Kotlyarevsky, the father of Ukrainian literature."

Sometimes, however, she was unlucky, and teachers made comments about her absentmindedness. She had to make excuses about her home problems, that they had not settled yet in their new accommodation and she had to help her parents.

Several Saturday afternoons followed that first one. Anna explained to her parents that she was spending the afternoons until the evening train with a schoolmate who was helping her catch up with her studies. She felt strange about lying but could not tell the truth yet. Her parents were busy and exhausted by the weekend so she could get away with it. Mother had to take up more sewing jobs lately as Stepfather's earnings were low compared to what they used to earn from their shop in Uzhhorod. Without the occasional meat he came home with and Mother's sewing and knitting, they could not have made ends meet. Anna even learned to knit at Mother's prodding and spent her Sundays making shawls and sweaters. The hostile relations between the Hungarian and Czechoslovak part of Subcarpathia meant that they had still not received rent for January from Uzhhorod, and they had spent the first month's rent on the journey to Khust.

On their Saturday dates, Anna and László walked the little town's streets whenever the weather allowed. Sevljus was a little town with ten thousand people, predominantly Hungarians and Jews, and quite a lot of Rusyns. The life of the town concentrated on the main square with the large church and the modest but neatly ornated buildings around it, housing the best cafes and restaurants. It was like a piece of Ungvár but redesigned in country style. A large market occupied the square on Saturday afternoons that invited them to stroll around the stalls carrying goods of the local craft workers and from the neighborhood. When it was too cold or there was heavy snowfall, they visited some cafes and reminisced about Purma's and Ungvár. They especially took to a music cafe where a talented pianist played popular songs which they enjoyed humming together. The pianist even invited them to sing, but they shyly declined, laughing the offer away.

"Look at those carvings," László said, pointing to a stall full of woodwork. "I used to enjoy doing all the wooden work at home before I joined the gendarmes. My father taught me."

"And what did you carve—such ladles?" Anna asked, lifting one and hitting him with it tenderly.

"All our furniture in my parents' house. Even the window frames," László replied, fondling a delicate little box that was a masterpiece with tiny ornaments around the edges.

Anna looked at him with interest. *He has a profession. He could make a living as a carver or cabinetmaker.*

They liked to play word chain in different languages. László's Hungarian was much richer, but he was no match for Anna's Slovak. When she tried to play the game in Ukrainian, he used his vast knowledge of Rusyn agricultural words, which Anna was suspicious of.

"Friga? What is friga? No, that word has no meaning!" she cried and hit his chest with her small fist. "You are making that up! Cheater!"

"Oh, no! Of course, it exists! It is melted brynza, sheep's cheese. We will ask the Rusyn farmers on the market." László pulled her toward the stalls with potatoes, apples, cheese, and preserves.

The Rusyn peasants confirmed László's knowledge and bantered with them in Rusyn and laughed heartily. They did not let them go without taking an apple each.

Although Anna had passionately kissed him goodbye in Ungvár, she was shy to show her feelings here apart from giving him fleeting pecks on the cheek. The open spaces of the little town offered no privacy. They kissed the second time in early February on a sunny afternoon that emboldened them to undertake a walk up to the ruins of the Kankiv Castle. The experience surprised them both and they could not speak after, so they just walked back to the town arm in arm. When the time came to go to the railway station, László turned to Anna and looked into her eyes.

"I love you, Ancika." He swallowed hard. "I realize you are

not yet of legal age and there is school to finish, but I wanted to tell you I would be delighted if we got engaged."

"I love you too, Laci!" The gray station building lit up in color in front of her eyes and she thought she heard music. "I would like that very much!"

Their next kiss sealed their engagement. She lingered at his warm lips, her stomach in her throat. His brawny arms held her close, and she wondered how they would hold her in a dance. The smell of tobacco on his clothes was bitter but exciting. She thought it was a kind of perfume and it belonged to him.

If it was that easy with my parents' consent... Anna sighed but pushed the worries away. For now, she wanted to enjoy their intimate moments and put her parents out of her mind.

During the train journey home, she decided that instead of asking for their permission, she would announce her engagement to her parents. That would put pressure on them instead of allowing them a choice. They might even think she must...

"Who's this man?" Stepfather asked.

"He's an excellent officer at the Czechoslovak Gendarmes. A Hungarian boy. And we love each other." Anna blushed.

"Must you marry?" asked Mother with angst in her voice, squinting her eyes. "Are you with child?"

"No, Mummy, I don't. I'm not." Now Anna became red, indeed. "But he is my love, and he is an amiable person, always gentle."

"You say he is a Hungarian at the Czechoslovak Gendarmes? That's not a winning combination," Stepfather said with a sneer.

"Oh, Dad, he is Hungarian like any of us," Anna answered with haste. *Except for you.* "He was born in Czechoslovakia like me and speaks Czech and Slovak. Only his name is Hungarian."

"How do you want to live?"

"Dad, we will not marry yet. This is about an engagement. To declare that we intend to marry. To declare that we belong to each other. So that we can meet and he can court me."

"If you invite him next Sunday, we will meet him and then we can decide," Mother suggested and Stepfather nodded.

Anna's parents were not impressed by László at all when they found out that he was a poor cottar boy from Beregszász and had no property. His salary as a gendarme was modest enough for one but inadequate for two or more. Anna would have to work if they married. Mother had a different view about the future of her daughter.

Anna's brow creased into a frown as she noticed László stirring his coffee with the little spoon too many times. He was not looking at her like he used to do at Purma's. He was jittery and kept looking into his cup. He excused himself, saying he had to get back to Sevljus on the afternoon train due to his night shift.

"I want you to marry a well-off man who can take care of you," Mother said after László left. "You shouldn't repeat the mistakes your mother made." She was adamant that the engagement should not go through.

Curiously, Stepfather took Anna's side. Anna understood that his concern for her feelings was not the reason—it did not exist.

"The girl is grown up enough to stand on her feet soon. If she wants that boy, why not? I would have been happier to see her in a good Ukrainian or Rusyn family, but he's as good as she can get nowadays, it seems." For Stepfather, it was the end of the matter.

"Finish school. This is my condition. A lot of things can happen in a year and a half." Mother started collecting the dinner dishes, showing that she had closed the dispute.

"I'll finish school and then we'll marry." Anna stood and went to help with the washing up. She found consolation only in her little brother's smile.

"We'll see." It was all Mother said.

"Ancika, do you really love him?" Jancsi asked later when he had squeezed himself into her embrace under the quilt. One bed had to suffice for both of them in their small apartment in Khust.

"If only you knew how much, my little bedbug," Anna said, and ruffled his blond locks, wet from his bath.

"I want you to be happy," Jancsi said. "What's today's fairy tale?"

László came again the next Sunday, and they had an official engagement dinner without special formalities. He gave her a sparkling silver ring, created by stacking two thin bands that formed clasping hands on the top, in a delicately carved small wooden box that must have been his own work.

"I am happy to be with you," Anna said simply and kissed him. Mother was morose and László ill at ease. Her parents' rigid demeanor during dinner must have made it difficult for him. They did not ask after him more than politeness required and the atmosphere became heavy. He held her hand, crushing the ring on her middle finger between his forefinger and thumb. Anna did not feel the strength that had always radiated from him that she loved so much. He left soon after dinner with a hazy look in his eyes.

Their dates continued on Saturdays, but only in Sevljus,

as Anna's parents did not invite László again to their home.

"I was so happy to get to belong to your family," he said, while they listened to their favorite pianist play a melancholic melody. "Now that my parents remain on the Hungarian side of the new borders, I have no family in the country. I thought I could belong...not only to you, but to your family."

His admission wrenched her heart.

"They will come around, you'll see. What's important is that we love each other," Anna said, encouraging him, but he just nodded. He spoke less and seemed content to listen to her chatting, but she could not suppress the feeling he was somewhere else. Once they even had a row.

"Why couldn't you come tomorrow to Khust? You told me you weren't on duty. We could be together the whole day. Spring is almost here and we don't need to sit at home," Anna said, impatient.

"I have to visit some relatives."

"Your parents are in Beregszász, over the new borders. I thought you didn't have anybody in the remaining regions."

"There's a cousin who has moved over the new borders and he's got news from them."

"An important cousin, I see. More important than your fiancée."

László did not answer, but released her hand and lit a cigarette. Anna hid her hands in her coat pockets, straightened her posture, and quickened her pace. He had to hasten after her. Anna's abrupt stop at a hatmaker's shop window caused him to almost bump into her. When he regained his balance, he just stood there, waiting. Instead of the attractive creations on display, she was looking at his reflection in the glass: how he held his cigarette, how he drew on it and let the smoke encompass him like a shawl of mystery.

They ambled through the town side by side in the mild

early March breeze like strangers throwing in a word or two. Anna was still pouting when they arrived at the railway station.

"So, you haven't changed your mind, have you?" Anna asked, swinging her bag like she did not mind as she placed herself opposite him on the platform.

"I can't, it's important."

She stepped into her train compartment without a further word. She felt his eyes on her back, but steeled herself not to turn. It almost killed her to sit on the other side in the coupe from where she could not be seen. The tears did not bring relief.

The following Saturday, he was waiting for her in front of the school, smoking. Anna frowned at him.

"Ancika, I've something to tell you."

"Do we have time for a cup of coffee or you'll spit it out on the street?" Anna said, jerking on the strap of her bag. They started for a cafe on the other side of the street. Her anger rose again after a miserable week alone. She had no intention of letting herself be kissed after his smoking. László dropped the stub and strode behind her.

They sat at a window table in the empty cafe, Anna deciding to keep her coat on. The place lacked comfortable heating. She was eyeing László, but he did not start until the server had placed the cups in front of them.

"Your parents don't want me," László started.

"What's got into you?"

"I thought I found a new family, but..."

"Who do you want, me or my parents?"

"I'm sorry, Ancika. Something has happened."

Anna's hand, holding the cup, stopped midair. Her eyes were on him, her brows raised in a question mark. Ice-cold sweat trickled between her breasts.

"In December, when I was here alone for a month already with no message from you, I lost faith in getting to see you again. I thought I had lost you to another country. Why would you come through hostile borders, across a hundred kilometers, to meet me again?" László took a cigarette and lit it. Anna was looking at the smoke in horror, turning in the air, embracing him, and taking him away from her.

You knew that the post was not working when they set up the new borders. How could you think that I had forgotten you? How could you lose faith in a month? It was only me falling in love?

"I learned last Sunday that I'm going to be a father, and I'll marry the girl."

The cheap coffee cup fell to the saucer with a clang that echoed in the empty cafe. In another second, the ring flew at him and rolled down his coat. It fell to their feet, tinkling on the gray stone floor, and then rolled toward the other tables. It disappeared in seconds like their love.

Anna jumped and ran as if her life depended on it.

She could not speak to him again. He had cheated on her all this time. He must have been meeting the woman during their courtship. Or was it before their engagement? Before Christmas, when he was here alone, he said. He had promised her in Ungvár that he would wait for her in Sevljus. And she had come after him and found him just a couple of months later. Did he use that time to get under another woman's skirt? How could he?

I hate him! Oh, how I hate him! He was my love. I wanted so much to marry him! Everything is gone now, everything! He is a dirty son-of-a-bitch, that's what he is! You cannot believe a man. They are all the same. They want all the same.

She was sitting on the bench of the deserted railway station that she grew to hate in seconds. It was a witness to their sweet reunion in the first days of January. It saw them saying tearful but happy goodbyes on Saturday evenings, always believing in an even more joyful next week. It was a witness to their angry separation last week. And now, when her heart was broken, the ugly station was still here, indifferent and cold, forcing her to wait another two hours for her train. She wanted to disappear from this godforsaken town.

But he loved me! It could not be true that he was just pretending! He was so kind and always so polite. And he wanted to marry me. He told it to me, to my parents. Maybe he just had a weak moment, and the woman used it? And now she is in trouble and he is in trouble and he must do the right thing.

The idle train carriages on the station started to swim in a haze and hot drops of tears burned her hands as they fell.

But he had a... He was with another woman when he courted me and let me think he felt something for me. How could he? How could he kiss me when he kissed another woman also?

Anna bent her head to her knees and cried.

I hate him! I hate all men!

Mother's stare betrayed her knowledge that something had happened. The missing ring on Anna's finger could not escape her eyes. As was her custom, she did not leave it at that. She bugged her the entire evening and then some on Sunday until she got her to spill the beans. She sighed and said, "Don't you cry, Ancika. It's for the better. I told you he was not for you. We'll find you a much better man."

"I never want to marry! I hate all men!" Anna continued to weep with all her heart.

"Hush, you don't want Dad to hear us. Don't fret, you see I found my man, and I had a child, you, at the time. Be happy that it is the *other* woman who *must* marry and not you. We'll find you a well-off husband to save you from going through the hell I did."

Anna ran to her room and threw herself on the bed. Jancsi walked around on tiptoes until she sobbed herself into a dreamless sleep. She woke in the middle of the night with his hands on her shoulders as he had fallen asleep holding her. She placed a kiss on his cheek and looked long at the empty ceiling. It had no magic, like the ceiling in their home in Ungvár.

Going back to school on Monday was an ordeal. She had to concentrate on her studies and had to handle the inquiries from her schoolmates about the missing ring. She told them she had broken her engagement because he had proved to be a crook who had no future.

The following weeks justified her words. On March 15th, the radio announced that Slovakia had proclaimed its independence the previous day. Anna was afraid to go to school, as the entire town was full of military movements. The Czechoslovak army was pulling out and the local militia was taking their place. Blue and yellow flags were flying all over the town by midday and masses were marching with banners to celebrate the new independent Carpathian Ukraine. Czechoslovakia ceased to exist. The radio remained their only contact with the world. In the evening they heard the parliament in Khust proclaiming Carpathian Ukraine an independent state and the local militia its army. Voloshyn became president.

"What a farce!" Stepfather said. "They are playing at independence *now*, the fools! Now, when the Hungarians are on the borders ready to attack and we have lost the Czechoslovak army! What are our chances, as a small region, of staying independent for more than a couple of days? Zilch."

The parliament ordered a general mobilization, but it

was too late. In the morning, gunshots awoke them. Heavy trucks rumbled under their windows while they hid in the pantry. They remained there the entire day, sneaking out only to go to the bathroom once or twice. The shooting finally stopped at dusk. The neighbors ventured out and came back with the news: the Hungarian army had occupied the town. Anna's family remained closeted in their apartment till the weekend. They would rather nibble on week-old bread than venture out.

The radio—now announcing in Hungarian—informed everyone that, on Sunday, the Hungarian army completed the military occupation of the whole Carpatho-Ukraine. Miklós Horthy, governor of Hungary, had arrived at Khust. The newscaster also emphasized that the time had come to realize the autonomy of Carpathian Ukraine inside the Hungarian state.

This news did not beguile Stepfather. Instead, he was frantically trying to find a solution for their sustenance. As a Polish citizen, it would not be right to supply the Hungarian army with meat. His job had ceased to exist with Czechoslovakia. He might not even be welcome here under the Hungarian rule. Without his income, they could not afford the rented apartment in Khust. They survived on their meager savings for two weeks and Anna stayed at home as the school had shut. Classes were rumored to resume in Ungvár. At the end of March, after several consultations with colleagues and friends, Stepfather presented the family with the solution he had worked out.

"The Germans are desperately looking to increase their workforce. There are too many soldiers and nobody left to work. With my profession, I am promised a good salary in Germany that would enable me to send half of it home to you. You three are to go back to Uzhhorod."

"Dimitri, but we rented the house!"

"The shop is still free where you can furnish a room and you can free up some more space in the lean-to. Don't be afraid, I will send money as soon as I get my first salary. The Hungarians will not give me work here."

He departed the next day. As much as Anna was still mourning her lost love, she welcomed the opportunity to be without Stepfather again.

Moving back to Ungvár was easier. Trains were running on a regular schedule now through Beregszász and Csap to Ungvár. It took only one day with two changes. The sewing machine and the two trunks had to travel separately as Mother and the two children could not have carried them. They hired a cart at the station to take them home. Squeezing into the only free room that was supposed to be the corner shop was difficult. The family allowed them to go through the kitchen until Mother could have a separate door cut to the shop from the yard, which she arranged with the last bit of money she had. The exchange rate of the Czechoslovak crown was so low by now that they had almost nothing.

By the end of April, they were penniless. The next rent was due on the first day of May. It was not much, so Mother had to manage the money to last for the entire month for the three-member family. She hoped that by June she would get something from Stepfather. They learned, from a letter, that he had reached Germany safely and had started working at a slaughterhouse.

Mother was trying to find some sewing work, but she got only small repairs.

"Mummy, how will we manage?" Anna asked her after she had tucked her brother in bed. She had seen her mother brooding over the sewing machine, not working but looking at it with glassy eyes.

"We've gone through worse, Ancika. We'll manage again."

"You mean when you remained alone with me, pregnant? How did you survive?"

"I've told you the story at least ten times." Mother sounded tired.

"I want to hear it again." Anna put her hands together, pleading. Mother sighed and looked beyond the walls and years.

Chapter 8

"The Great War had already been raging for three years when I got the typhus. Supposedly, even if somebody recovers, they remain bald forever. This witch neighbor, Marie Onisko, convinced my widowed father he could not get me married if I remained bald. So, he accepted her offer to get me married to her son. I had never loved János Onisko. I only remembered him from school and considered him a scapegoat, but nobody asked for my opinion. János did not seem to mind the eventuality of me losing my hair. I think he liked me, but he liked my dowry much more. I came with six acres of land and a calf—my father was well-off. However, it did not take János too long to turn it into vodka, wine, or whatever he and his cronies drank.

Mother shifted on her seat, then stood up. She could never be idle for too long. She sprinkled flour on the baking board and made a small heap of it.

"As you see, I did not lose my hair," she said and smiled at Anna. "I recovered from the typhus, but not from our marriage. I became with child at once, but he was a weak one and was not even a year old when smallpox took him. We lived with my mother-in-law, as was the custom, in one room with her and János' three siblings. I worked like a horse to keep the house clean and managed the homestead to make a living. János sometimes found work as a farmhand, and when he did not drink away all the money, he gave me something. This was when I started sewing in the evenings, until János sold the sewing machine, too, and drank away the money.

"I bore it for three years. We were already part of Czechoslovakia when I went to Nagyszőlős, Sevljus, where you went to school this year. I carried eggs and milk to sell to a shopkeeper couple who I knew from earlier. I was in such despair that I complained to them about my life and they took pity on me. They offered to let me move into their household in exchange for helping out in the shop and with the housekeeping. So, I did. Soon they began to pay me a salary and I could save some money. János never looked for me. This was a God-blessed period.

The dough took the form of a ball under her hands as she began kneading it on the board. She put it into a keeler and continued kneading with fast, circular movements of her hand. Anna never understood how she could do that for half an hour—it was heavy work.

"I met István Csehil, your birth father, at a saint's day fair in Beregkövesd, where I was visiting my old girlfriend, Mariska Kuzma. You have met her. I am her son's godmother." Mother pointed at a picture on the window sill wherein she was holding a baby in her arms in front of an altar. "István and I liked each other and enjoyed the fair. He sat with me on the merry-go-round, even if he got sick later." Her wistful smile transformed her face. "He shot me a paper rose, at the stand with the air guns where youngsters shoot at sticks, holding small presents. I still have it in the attic somewhere. He was a good dancer with strong arms and we danced together maybe a thousand times. It was already summer in 1921. István then started courting me and came to visit at Nagyszőlős. He was two years younger than me. That year, he came of age to be drafted into the army. He came to visit three days before his joining date on October 20th to celebrate my birthday. We spent the night together.

Anna's eyes fell to her lap.

"When I realized I was pregnant with you, Christmas was closing in. I visited my brother. He lived in our house that he, as firstborn, had inherited from our father, who had died a couple of years before. I told him I was pregnant, and I loved the father who would be in the army for three years. I also told him I had written to the father that I was with child and he was thrilled. Mihal, my brother, became furious. You know, he had been elected village head after coming back from France, where he had worked for a couple of years, just after the war in a silver mine. They respected him and considered him a well-traveled man who could also read and write. He could not afford a scandal in the family. After all, I was still the wife of János Onisko, and now with child from another man. I understand it now.

"He did his best to get me as far as possible from our village. Sevljus was too close. He had an acquaintance who worked at a Jewish family's house, the Meinls, in Uzhhorod as a cook. Mihal wrote to her to find me work as a seamstress. The Meinl family was preparing to get their daughter married and was completing her trousseau, which needed a lot of sewing. They could not believe their luck to have their own seamstress to help. So, I got to Uzhhorod."

"Where I was born," Anna said.

"Not yet," Mother said. "I was working a lot at the Meinls, but I enjoyed it. Being respected, having good food, a separate bedroom—who wouldn't? I worked on the trousseau, all the linens, bedclothes, skirts, and dresses. Why, I was even asked to prepare the bridal gown. From the leftover fabrics, I could sew for myself—so I made the most necessary things for the layette for you. They couldn't see it, as I couldn't say I was with child. It showed soon, anyway. When they realized I would deliver my child in July, they asked me to leave the house a month earlier. As Jews, they couldn't afford to allow a Christian woman to have a baby in their house. I arranged with the hospital to move a month earlier in exchange for my work as a seamstress. I even got a room for myself where I could sew for all the hospital employees and mend hospital laundry."

Mother stopped kneading and put the keeler on the stove and covered it with a clean cloth. She sat down and drank her tea, which had already gone cold.

"I'll bake the bread later and we'll have it fresh in the morning. Where was I? A spinster, Aunt Rózsika, who worked in the hospital, learned that I had nowhere to go after you were born. The hospital could allow me to stay for only a week. Aunt Rózsika rented a one-bedroom apartment in a house where the family also needed a seamstress. It was a Hungarian family, the Szabós (isn't it funny when your name is Taylor but you need a seamstress?), and they wanted to move to Hungary as they did not want to get Czechoslovak citizenship and give up their Hungarian one. They wanted to get a lot of bedclothes sewn that would have been expensive in Hungary and I came in handy.

"We lived with Rózsika and the Szabó family for six years,

almost as family members. It was a great period in our life. You speak such good Hungarian because you lived with them throughout your childhood. The Szabós delayed their plans of moving several times as the situation was so bad in Hungary, with prices going sky-high. Hungary introduced the new, stable currency only in 1927. Even then, it took them a year to sell the house and organize the move.

"When you were six, I rented a one-room apartment (mind you, it was really only one room and only nine square meters) and we moved there. It was a difficult five years until Dimitri came along. I worked three shifts at the printing house. There was no work for a seamstress. The new factories established by the Czechs hired for cheap, and people didn't have money to sew new things. Dimitri saved us. He rented a room next door and after a year of eyeing me, he asked me out. Only with him we could then start the shop and build a house of our own. And that would feed us through now.

"Do you understand now why I want you to marry well?" Mother looked into Anna's eyes and she saw warmth in her greenish-brown eyes that were identical to hers.

"There must be other ways to succeed," Anna said. "I want to be a teacher; this is what I study for."

"I'm not saying you shouldn't study, well, when the school starts again, now that they are moving back to Ungvár. But for a woman, a husband is the best solution. I didn't have the chance of a good husband until Dimitri proposed to me. Your father was weak and let his mother command him. We went to Beregkövesd when they discharged him from the army after three years. His mother, your granny, declared that his son would marry only a virgin. Well, I was one for him. When she said that, I left and never looked back. He could not stand up to his mother. But he wanted to keep you. I had to call the gendarmes to force him to let you go. But did he help you when you asked him?"

"No, he didn't."

"We've had everything with Dimitri because he's a good man. He will send money for sure."

"Why do you allow him to abuse me and let him run you around?" Anna asked and felt a boulder on her chest.

"He has a short fuse, you know, but he is mostly right. I have never let him use his belt on you after that first occasion when you were so stubborn and did not want to study in the Ukrainian school. It was too much, I admit. But a slap here or there is just to put you in place."

"It's so humiliating! I hate him!"

"Was he right about Mr. Hanzel? He was. Did your school move after all? It did. You should have listened."

Anna let it drop. *I need to find my way to independence by myself.*

"In the meantime, until he sends money, we have to find some way to survive. I have always done so. I'll tend the garden."

"Mum?" Anna could not believe her ears and snickered. "You've never done any gardening work! You despise it!"

"You'll help me. A person in need will always find a way."

Although it was May, they had started a kitchen garden. After a rainy April and warm early May, the mushrooms had started their first season in mid-May in the neighboring forests. Inquiries resulted in some good hints about where to find parasols and boletes, especially birch bolete and porcini. Mother had some earlier experience, and they did not need to risk their lives over an occasional toadstool: they were picking only mushrooms they knew well. They were lucky with picking. They could even go to the market and sell some of them. Lots of Hungarians who had moved into the city did not know about mushroom picking, the Czechs' national sport they had brought to Subcarpathia. The Hungarians were good customers of mushrooms and Anna became a better and better seller. She enjoyed offering her wares and found a special joy in setting the right price for each customer. Should she see an older woman with a lot of supposed experience, she set her price reasonably. The male customers proved to be the source of extra profit as they had no clue of the market value of the mushrooms and they all fell for her sweet talk and appearance.

They had scrambled eggs and mushrooms for breakfast, mushroom and potato soup for lunch, and mushroom schnitzels for dinner until July. By then, their kitchen garden was ready to spice up their menu with carrots, cabbage, beans, onions, and potatoes. School finished in mid-June and Anna could spend all her time helping in the garden and foraging for mushrooms. They did not see meat until August. And even then, it was not for eating but for selling.

Chapter 9

"1.80 for a kilo of sausage, 2.00 for a kilo of paprika lard, and 1.60 for the kilo of pork cracklings—the 6 pengő should be enough," Mother said, putting the coins in Anna's palm. "Ask for the change in small coins so that we have them when we need to give back to customers. They will each buy for less than a pengő's worth, for sure, so we must be ready with change. By the time you return, I'll make you some scrambled eggs and mushrooms for breakfast."

Anna took her bag and set out for her first tour to the meat wholesaler after a long time. She was still sleepy; it was only five o'clock on the first day of August. They wanted to open at six, so she had to hurry.

Mother spent every other day in July at different offices to get her trade license. A lot of time was spent in long queues, but it was worth it. It was easy to prove that she had several years of experience based on running the shop with her husband, and she was Hungarian enough for them to qualify. Mother spoke the language without an accent, and she did not have any political records or attachments. Her coming from a Rusyn-Hungarian family helped her cause. She asked for a grocery license but wanted to build on their meat wholesaler contacts first. Although Mr. Hanzel had escaped to Slovakia, there were still acquaintances in his former enterprise. This was now owned by a Mr. Csontos, who had moved from around Debrecen. Anna did not feel sorry for Mr. Hanzel, remembering how he cheated her with the mock tender not even a year ago—it seemed now like ages...

She wore a light summer dress that had seen better days. It floated around her slim waist, which had become even slimmer during the summer. However, the dress was taut on her prominent bust, luring men's eyes away from the threadbare details of the fabric. Mr. Csontos' assistant, who remained in the enterprise after Mr. Hanzel escaped, served her and remembered her well. She made sure to examine the cut of the sausage first to see how much fat it contained and how fine the grinding was. She also looked for the color to see if there was enough paprika in the filling and had to admit that Hungarian sausages were unbeatable. It was like the Czechs with beer—you do not cheat on the quality of items of national pride.

Saliva filled her mouth as she looked at the pork cracklings and she risked asking nonchalantly.

"May I sample it?"

"Of course, Ancika, go ahead," the young assistant answered with a buoyant smile on his round face. He could not take his eyes off her. Anna did not believe her luck. Mr. Hanzel had never allowed customers to sample his wares.

The crackling piece she had picked up was almost half

meat, crisp, and smelling gorgeous. It burned her fingers, coming just out of the grease. It filled her mouth with a long-forgotten taste and melted like butter.

"A kilo, please, and also a kilo of the paprika-boiled belly, but mind your choice," she said in her best commanding voice.

The lard showed over a kilo on the weight, but there was no extra fee, so she thanked him with a radiating smile, paid, and collected her change.

She was back home just before six, after which she wolfed down her scrambled eggs with mushrooms in minutes, and they opened the shop just on time. It was an event in the neighborhood—they had announced opening beforehand—and soon several customers were asking for fifty grams of this and hundred grams of that. Before noon, their stock was empty. They had double the money Anna had paid for the merchandise in the small cashier. She made a second tour before the wholesaler closed at two o'clock. By the end of the week, with two tours a day, they could save enough money for some meat that tasted like manna from heaven after several months on a vegetarian diet.

In order to widen the types of goods on offer, Mother went early to the market and convinced a man from Szabolcs, the county over the Tisza River, to give her a cart of potatoes on credit. He came back after two weeks, and having received his payment, left another cart of potatoes with them. There was a good, cool basement below the shop where they could stack the potatoes, which would remain fresh even in the biggest heat wave of the summer.

The new school year started on September 4th, Monday. Anna met Marika in front of the school building after half a year. They just hugged for a long minute, not minding the tears.

"I attended the Hungarian grammar school in the city, Papa wanted it," Marika chattered as they started up the stairs. "No fun without you! I succeeded in convincing him to let me come back this year. After all, the teacher's diploma is important." She winked.

"How come our school accepted your half year there?" Anna asked.

Marika shrugged and allowed herself a mysterious smile. "I suppose it is good that Dad works at the city council. They must have put pressure on the church. I did not even need to write an aptitude test. I could continue with the next school year."

They had run into each other a couple of times during the summer, but Anna was ashamed of how they had to eke out a living. Now that they had their shop, she felt confident again.

"Silly, silly! I would have loved to join you for mushroom picking!" Marika said when Anna admitted to evading her. "You cannot imagine how we struggled until Papa got established in the new administration. He was without a job for six months! I could afford my first ice cream of the summer only in August."

Anna told her about Laci during the long break. She couldn't help crying, so she turned to the wall beside their bench. She could finally share her heartbreak with somebody who would understand.

"But I am free from Stepfather," she smiled through her tears. "He went to work in Germany."

"I wonder how long it will last," Marika said.

The previous Friday evening, they had learned from the radio that Germany had run over Poland. By Sunday evening, it became known that Britain and France had declared war on Germany. Mother became deathly pale when she realized what this could mean for Stepfather, a Polish citizen, work-ing in Germany. She was almost immobilized in the first few weeks of September as her thoughts circled only around him. A letter from him on September 15th informed them that he had succeeded in keeping his job because he had declared that his residence was in Ungvár, in the Hungarian Kingdom, so they considered him a Hungarian, the allied nation of Germany. He and his job were safe, and he promised to send money home soon.

Nobody talked about anything else in the school other than war. Especially when, two weeks later, everybody learned that the Soviet Union had also attacked Poland, and the country had collapsed between the two great powers.

On a late September afternoon, Anna and Marika were walking home after school, turning on Munkácsy Street.

"We are lucky, you know," said Marika, "that our street name did not need to change. Munkácsy was a great Hungar-ian painter." Several other streets had changed names from the Czech or Slovak heroes and state leaders to Hungarian ones.

"Yes, I noticed it. It's crazy to get used to all the new street names," Anna said.

They stopped at a commotion on the street. Blocking the sidewalk, workers were removing an enormous banner from above the door of a prominent fashion shop. The banner said: "Paris fashion by Schönberger and Son".

"I didn't know that Mr. Schönberger had sold his shop. It seems somebody else is taking over," Anna said. Other work-ers, standing on ladders, were preparing to put up a new ban-ner to replace the old one. It said, "Kovács fashion, straight from Budapest".

"Anna, this is a strawman," Marika said in a low voice so that she wouldn't be overheard. She pulled Anna away from the workers and other helpers.

Anna was puzzled and looked at Marika with a question in her eyes.

"A strawman—Sándor Kovács is taking over the shop from Mr. Schönberger for appearances' sake. Mr. Kovács is a good friend of the Schönberger family, so they agreed to let them stay and work in the salon," Marika said, pulling Anna to the edge of the sidewalk.

"I've never heard of such a thing! Why should Mr. Schönberger hand over his shop, even to his friend?"

Marika's information came from a secure source, her father, a Hungarian from Slovakia, who had gained a good job in the city administration. "Where have you lived in the past six months, Anna? Jews cannot run their businesses like before, according to the new laws, so they are giving them to acquaintances and remaining as employed persons. They call the new owner a strawman. At least they have a solution. It's worse that they cannot remain employed at the government or city offices or schools anymore. Papa says hundreds of Jews have lost their jobs in the city since spring."

Anna was appalled.

"The world has turned upside down. You remember László?" A wave of old anger heated Anna's cheeks, but she forced herself to be calm. He was in the past. "He remained with the Czech Gendarmery and they moved him back to Bohemia when Hungary occupied Subcarpathia. The Slovaks and Czechs escaped the city. Hungarians too. Here we are forbidding Jews to work and Hungarians are moving over to Ungvár from the mother country to replace them. Why can't they just let people stay where they are and let them go ahead with their life? What is with the people, for God's sake?"

"There's more to come," Marika said. "Haven't you heard about the Polish refugees?"

"Oh, no! What?"

"After the Soviet attack, Hungary opened the common border to them and they are now coming by the tens of thousands, Papa said. Fortunately, they are evading Ungvár and going either to Romania or Budapest and West Hungary. They are even getting a cost-of-living allowance."

"Are they running from the war?"

"They say both the Germans and the Soviets kill the Poles or enslave them. Their country has just disappeared."

Anna was speechless. She had to admit she had not noticed the changes. Her family had been too preoccupied with making a living. Now, as Marika mentioned, she remembered there had been, in fact, a lot of name changes above shops. She had first thought that this was also a consequence of Hungarians moving to the city. Now she understood they were all strawmen who were helping their Jewish friends.

By November, Anna was in the prime of her vigor. She was set in the routine of early morning procurement, then school till two, the entire afternoon spent serving customers in the shop, and cleaning after. She did not have enough time to do her homework and study and definitely did not have time for entertainment. Young men addressed her on the street when coming home from school, especially when she parted with Marika in the middle of her route and was alone. But the wound László had left in her heart was too fresh and she did not want to see any men. She would fall into bed after dinner for at least some hours of sleep before the next morning's early start. Her last thought would be that at least Stepfather was not there to pester her. *I must endure this! For me, for Mother, for Jancsi.*

The Christmas holidays gave them a small break. Christmas Eve was on a Sunday that year and they did not plan to open until December 27th. They placed a small decorated pine tree in the kitchen corner with painted glass and figures and a couple of Christmas candies for Jancsi's delight.

"Can you go into the shop and cut a decent piece from the peasant sausage?" Mother asked Anna.

"Oh, aren't we supposed to be on a fast until Christmas Eve dinner?" Anna said with a twinkle in her eyes.

"We haven't had a decent meal since morning. I am sure God will not fume over a slight bending of the rules. We have missed meat so long," Mother said and continued to cut the sour cabbage into small pieces and tossed them into the roux with a few bay leaves. "Look after the *bobájka* in the oven so that it's not too brown."

Anna received a red woolen scarf from Mother that she had knitted under wraps during the evenings. Mother's eyes popped out when she opened her small package. Anna had bought her a replacement for her broken reading glasses that she had sat on by mistake some weeks ago. She had since been struggling with sewing, not able to see the threads properly. Jancsi was euphoric when he tore apart the wrapping on his present and saw the shining, small red firefighter truck.

Christmas day awakened them with a freeze that made the walkways slippery after the abundant snowfall. Mother left the children to sleep in and went out into the shed to fetch a basket of firewood to fire up the tile stove. The full basket blocked her vision, and she lost her balance on the steps. The sawhorse toppled over, and the heavy saw fell under it. Her cry awakened Anna, who ran out to the yard in her nightgown but had the sense to avoid the walkway. She waded in the snow to get to her mother and helped her up to the wooden bench at the wall. She removed the saw from her left leg amid grievous cries. Mother's dress was soaked with blood and she could not stand up. Anna ran to ask Mr. Árpa, their tenant, to go to the closest neighbors who had a telephone and call for the ambulance. She picked up a warm blanket to cover Mother until help arrived.

Mother had an ugly bloody wound, but worse, she had a broken leg. She spent the Christmas holidays at the hospital and came back home only for New Year's Eve. Anna had to handle the shop alone for several days and also take care of Jancsi. It did not get better in the new year.

As school resumed, they had to shorten the shop's opening hours so that Anna could manage both together. They opened in the afternoon. Anna covered the purchasing tours in the morning and Mother could only take a few steps with her plastered leg. Jancsi was also going to school, so he could not help. Losing the morning traffic of working men who came to buy their breakfast severely reduced their revenue. It was a godsend when they received some money from Stepfather in February. The German Reichsmark had a stable rate to the Hungarian currency, and it more than compensated for the fall in the shop's profits.

In April, the Árpa family announced that they would be moving away next month. They had found an apartment closer to the center for the same low price. The dwindling rent money made them more dependent on the shop's profitable existence.

Mother could not use her leg properly after the accident and had to rest a lot. She could not cut back on meals, so she got heavier, and that did not help her physical recovery. She sat in the shop every afternoon, and either Jancsi or Anna had to help with moving the wares. She listened to the radio every evening while Anna did all the chores. Mother pointed out the escalating circumstances in the countries amidst war: Germany running over Norway, Denmark, the Netherlands, Belgium, and France during the spring and early summer. It was more about Stepfather's well-being in warmongering Germany than the fate of those Western countries that Mother was interested in.

The end of school came as salvation. Or at least, Anna thought.

"Mum, I am a teacher!" Anna said, running into the yard with her certificate on a late June afternoon after her graduation. It saddened her that nobody from her family could attend the ceremony. It had been a simple affair, though: a Mass in the cathedral followed by a procession from the church back to the school and a ceremonial handover of the diplomas. She couldn't help but stop at the confectionery on Kossuth Square, the old Masaryk Square, for a large cone of ice cream with Marika on their way home. It was the best moment of the entire day.

"This is a relief!" Mother said, smiling, and looked at the diploma. "I'm happy it's over."

"Now real life can start!" Anna said and did not understand why Mother looked so strangely at her.

"Now you'll handle the shop full time, won't you?" Mother asked.

"Mummy, I've received a job offer in Szolyva! I am to teach the first grade from September there. I was attending school for this!"

"You cannot be serious! Szolyva is sixty kilometers away! You want to leave us here? Me and Jancsi and the shop? How are we to make a living? And you'll live in a rented room at some peasant's hut when you have a house here?"

Anna was dumbfounded. She did not say more and went into the house to change and handle the shop like any other day.

What am I to do? Stepfather is still in Germany. The money he sends is not enough for Mother to survive with Jancsi. I need to start my career. I cannot let this job go. There are few jobs around, and there are none in Ungvár for teachers.

The next week, Anna went back to the school to inquire about a job in Ungvár, or at least in the neighboring villages. There was nothing. All the novice teachers had gotten jobs in remote locations. Marika would need to go to Csap, but she was thinking about it. However, she had a Papa who would probably get her a job in the city administration.

Mother could not stand the quietness at home for long. Anna did not speak to her. One day, Mother started to cry after dinner. Anna just looked at her until she spoke.

"How can you leave us here?"

Anna poured water into the kettle for tea and turned to face Mother.

"I've been working hard for this for the past four years. I want to teach. I want to have my own life. I'll come home every weekend and support you and Jancsi."

"I can't even go to the market. It's very tiresome for me. I'll have to close the shop. No news about Dimitri. We'll starve here."

Anna was quiet and went into her room, forgetting all about the tea.

She sat down in front of the mirror on her small desk and looked into it. A young, attractive woman was looking back at her with a confused expression, pursed mouth, and red eyes. *No, I won't give it up. I may stay for some time if Stepfather is not here. It's not so bad. I can manage the shop by myself. Teaching will have to wait. I won't forget what I've learned. With the shop, I can save some money for myself, and at the same time, I'll be here to support Mother.*

The large boulder sitting on her shoulders made her body slump. Breathing became a job. She always wanted to grow up and be as an adult. Now she understood how painful it could be. *I am not staying because I love her. I am staying because it is my duty.*

But she said nothing to her. Anna was still preoccupied with her thoughts, and her mother continued to sob each time Anna gave her the cold shoulder. One night in July, Anna could stand it no longer.

"I'm not going anywhere, Mum, don't be afraid. I'll stay with you and Jancsi."

"Truly, Ancika? Come here to me, and hug me tight!"

Mother had become big, the hug was awkward, and Anna's heart was elsewhere. She was still frantically thinking about alternatives, but got nothing. *If I had Laci...no, never...but then somebody else...*

Chapter 10

"Girl, could I get that corner of white bread, ten paper-thin slices of winter salami, and if you have sourdough cucumber, two proper pieces, please," said the dapper policeman. He winked at Anna, and at the same time, raised an eyebrow. His funny expression made her smile despite herself. She drew off the salami skin with the noble mold, cut the hard wide sausage into paper-thin slices, put it on the scale, then packed it with the bread and the pickled cucumbers.

"Here you are, officer! It is 1.20."

"Oh, this will be an expensive lunch, I say!" The policeman beckoned to his comrade, who was laughing, and stepped into the shop. "Pista, give me 20 fillérs. Pay some of your share at least!"

Anna had not seen the cheerful policemen before. They

had to be new at the station near the small Antalov depot. They guarded the wood terminal, a strategic industrial point.

"I also have fresh milk, officers, just 20 fillérs a liter. You can wash down the lunch and feel refreshed in this warm weather."

"Let us have it then, Pista, you pay!"

They sat down on a bench in front of the shop that Anna had placed for such customers who stopped by from work to get lunch—and there were quite a lot. Construction workers, employees of the Antalov depot, workers from the vicinity, and policemen...the shop was never lacking customers.

The two policemen could still see Anna from their bench. They made comments, sometimes accompanied by a buoyant laugh. Anna could only hear fragments of their conversation, but she definitely heard the dapper officer say, "she is a dish". She blushed and returned the wrong change to the customer she was serving. The customer complained, and Anna became even more embarrassed. It was good that Mother was preparing lunch and there were no other witnesses.

When the police officers had finished their meal, the cheerful one came back into the shop.

"Thank you so much for the lunch, miss." He flashed a smile. "I hope we'll be back in the following days. There are so many nice things here to taste!"

Anna blushed again, but tried to maintain decorum.

"You're welcome, officers. We always have fresh goods."

They came several times during the next week, always for lunch. Anna was surprised when the cheerful officer appeared one day in the evening, just before six, when she was closing the doors.

"Miss, I hoped to see you today, but I couldn't get away for lunch."

Anna did not reply, just nodded, and continued to pull down the iron blinds.

"May I help you?" The policeman was not intimidated by her silence.

"I've already finished. We are closed for the day."

"I supposed so. That's why I came at six."

Anna looked at him with a frown.

"I wanted to introduce myself: Lajos Zádori, at your service. I wanted to ask if you would be so inclined to take a walk with me at the Uzh. This promises to be a charming Indian summer evening."

"I'm sorry, I have my family to take care of," Anna replied quickly.

"Oh, I didn't suppose..."

"My mother and my little brother."

"You must be a generous young lady," the policeman said. "Maybe another time?"

"Thank you, but no, thank you." Anna turned, went into the yard, and closed the gate behind her.

She spied on him from the kitchen window and saw him standing there for a bit before walking around for some minutes. He looked at the ground with a frown on his high forehead, and eventually went his way. Anna felt a surprising jolt in her chest, and she had to admit that it was like disappointment. Was it?

She saw him only once next week, and he did not approach her. His comrade ordered and paid for their lunch. He waited outside the shop, not laughing but seeming more thoughtful. She had more time to observe him. He had a strong profile with a classic nose and a chiseled jaw; however, there was always a little curve around his lips as if he could not look at life without enjoying it. She liked his deep brown eyes and wavy chestnut hair. He was slim and tall and the uniform looked like his second skin. *Dashing!*

Mother and Anna were sitting in the kitchen on a Saturday evening. Mother was at her sewing machine pressing the pedals and discussing shop traffic, revenues, and future prospects.

"We now have enough money to hire a contractor to have water pipes laid in the house. It would make the bathroom fully usable," Anna said as she checked the figures in her little notebook where she was totting up the accounts.

"I'll ask around for a craftsman—there are many around here."

The clear voice of a fiddle and an accordion from the street startled them. The tune started slow in the low registers and gradually elevated into higher and higher ones with sweet accords and a familiar melody.

"What's that, so late in the evening?" Mother stopped sewing, could not hide her curiosity, and stepped closer to the window. She moved the blackout curtains a bit and looked out. "My God!"

Anna jumped to the other side of the window. The scene outside fascinated her.

She could only make out the contours of five male figures under the large sycamore tree in front of the kitchen window. Four of them were holding musical instruments: two fiddles, an accordion, and a contrabass, while another figure stood apart and started to sing. It was a melancholic tune, finding its way to the heart, seizing it, and not letting go. A pressure lifted from Anna's chest and she could not suppress a smile. She stood there, unable to get away, flying with the tunes like Aladdin on his carpet and letting herself soar in the warm October night toward the sparkling stars like the djin's treasure over the quiet suburb. The half-moon rose over the houses on the opposite side and Anna could imagine the scene in a romantic painting. It was so appealing.

"Who can it be?" Mother asked impatiently, not wanting to be left out of something important.

"It looks like that police officer, Lajos Zádori, who stops for lunch in the shop several times a week."

"So, you know his name? And why have I not heard of this man before?"

"Oh, Mum, he's just a frequent customer who tried to take me out for a walk last week. I don't know more about him."

"And still, he is serenading you in front of our kitchen window! What will the neighbors say?"

"I think they will enjoy the music," Anna said, grinning, and peeped through the gap between the curtains again.

"Well, they might enjoy the music tonight, but what will they say tomorrow? This is a serious appeal for a relationship!"

"Come on, Mother, we don't live in the 19th century!"

"People know what a serenade means. And you have to answer accordingly."

"What should I answer?" Anna asked, amazed. Her fingers were fiddling with the curtains.

"If you accept the serenade, light a candle. If you don't, stay hidden. But if you don't, it's a disgrace to you. You must have encouraged the man and now you're not accepting his advances."

"But this is not true! I have not encouraged him, just the opposite!"

"The neighbors don't know this, nobody knows. You better find a candle if you don't want to destroy our reputation."

Anna got enraged. *The rascal! He must have set this up deliberately!*

She listened to the music. A strain spread through her entire body and her anger disappeared. *But he is a lovable musical rascal, after all!*

She found a candle in the pantry. It appeared in the window with a tremulous flame, giving a sign to the band that they could end their performance.

Anna forced herself to go to the garden gate where a male figure was waiting. The other members of the band stayed away to give them privacy. She could not see well in the dark night and hoped it was Lajos. She was thankful when she heard his melodic voice.

"Thank you for accepting," he said over the closed gate. Anna noticed that his lips had become a note more curved in the dim light of the moon.

"*I* thank you for the performance. You have an excellent baritone," Anna replied in what she hoped was a not-too-enthusiastic tone.

"When it's worth singing, I'm all in for it. Will you still reject an invitation for a walk?"

"I will, if you mean now. I may not if you find a suitable time," Anna said with a smile.

The left bank of the River Ung became their place. They met frequently there and enjoyed the mild late October weather with the myriad colors of fall playing with the trees of the City Park on the opposite bank. The water was so shallow that even an origami paper boat would have difficulty navigating the large boulders of the riverbed.

He was a jolly fellow making jokes that made Anna smile all the time, but he was also kind and attentive. Anna felt secure holding his hand and looked forward to each of their dates. He belonged to a small village around Munkács and visited his parents at least once a month. He spoke about them a lot, and she envied his attachment to them.

Anna invited Lajos on a Sunday afternoon for coffee into their home with the secret plan of introducing him to

Mother. She must have liked him because she asked a lot of questions and not all of them were about how much land his parents had. When she learned he was a single child, her interest became even more pronounced.

"And what are your plans for the future, young man?" Mother had the ability to ask the most unsuitable questions of potential suitors.

"I want to pursue my career as a police officer in Subcarpathia, if duty requirements allow. They recently proposed my promotion to sergeant—a significant improvement in my financial situation. Further promotion to master sergeant in a couple of years will put me in a comfortable position that would allow me to raise and support a family."

Mother was nodding with great satisfaction.

From that afternoon, she always invited Lajos to stay instead of going with Anna for walks. It was for the better, too, as the weather became rough by December. They spent almost all their subsequent dates in the children's room with the doors open, Mother sewing in the kitchen, and Jancsi playing. Sometimes he took his guitar, and they sang popular duets together. Anna enjoyed these afternoons but missed the excitement of meeting something new, something unexpected. She missed meeting new people or children and creating something that survived: the changing of young minds, the forming of new characters.

Lajos was lucky with his duty schedule and could spend Christmas Eve with Anna and her family.

"An excellent dinner, Mrs. Movchan!" Lajos said when he swallowed the last piece of *bobájka*. Anna wondered why there was not much poppy seed on it and then remembered Jancsi's smile before dinner. He always took several spoonsful from the tempting sweet ground seeds mixed with powdered sugar on the sly well before the meal. He did not realize that the small black remnants on his teeth betrayed him. "My mother doesn't do better!"

Mother beamed and let them have a quiet evening to themselves, taking care of Jancsi and not bothering them in the children's room until nine, when she started pestering the boy to have his bath before bed. It was a sign to Lajos that it was time to leave.

The young couple spent New Year's Eve in the city where the Bercsényi hotel organized an evening with dancing and entertainment. The tickets were Lajos' present for Christmas. The Korona also advertised their own evening, but Anna let him know in time that she did not wish to go there. Lajos raised his brow but did not pry, although he claimed the Korona was more elegant.

Anna received a new dress from Mother for Christmas and she remembered the last time she had gone dancing at the Rusyn Brotherhood's evening two years before. The two events could not have been more different. Now it was a gypsy band playing in Hungarian folk costumes. The hotel restaurant was full of uniformed Hungarian officers and there was no sign of blue or yellow. Instead of grand robes, Anna saw all black and silver cocktail dresses around her. Her simple black chiffon dress fit perfectly, her only adornment a strand of white pearls.

On a Sunday afternoon in January, Lajos came with exciting news. He was enthusiastic and could not wait to tell Anna. "I've received the promotion: I'm to be a sergeant from February!"

"Congratulations, darling!"

"This is not all! I'll get an apartment from the Force!"

"Oh no! Now, that's wonderful! Where will it be? Close to the station?" Anna was fascinated.

Lajos became soberer suddenly. "It's in Kőrösmező where

I'll be the commanding officer of the station from February."

Anna opened her mouth, but no words came out. Her eyes fluttered, and she felt sick. Dizziness took over her.

"You'll abandon me," she said.

"No, Ancika, quite the opposite!" Lajos smiled, grabbing both her hands and kissing her right palm. "This is our chance! I made inquiries and they are looking for a teacher for small children in the school in Kőrösmező."

"Where is it?" Anna's voice was weak, a low whisper at most.

"It's a beautiful place. I saw pictures. It's below the Maramures Alps, full of green forests in the summer and snow in the winter. Rich people go skiing there. Kőrösmező is a little town, but an important station close to the border."

"Maramures Alps? Border?" Anna tried to find the meaning of the words. "It's close to Romania?"

"It's almost on the border with the Soviets, and the Romanian border is thirty kilometers away. But there's a contingent of soldiers to protect the borders, don't worry about it. They need an outstanding police officer to keep things in order and they chose me."

"Lajcsi, I can't leave my mother and brother here. We must wait till my stepfather comes back."

"Ancika, it's your life! We could support her and come visit every month if you wish."

"I tried it before when I received a job offer in Szolyva and it was only sixty kilometers from here. Mother had a nervous breakdown."

Lajos looked at her and bit his lip. "I could make a home until you'd come."

"I've done that before, Lajcsi. Love doesn't work over a distance."

"I'll write you, Ancika, every day! Write to your stepfather that you need him at home. Write to him about how well the shop is doing and he can come and run a well-established business. Then you'll be free. I'll wait for you."

"Don't promise." It was all Anna could say.

They held hands for an hour. Anna then sent Lajos away, saying she needed time with her mother.

"Kőrösmező? It's in the alps, below the mountains!" Mother's eyebrows ran up. "It's twice as far as Khust!"

"It is, and therefore, they are looking for not only a police commander, but also for a teacher. This is a great opportunity!"

"You want to leave me here again?" Mother was already sobbing.

"We'll write to Dad and ask him to come back from Germany. Now you have had an established business for almost a year and a half. He can work under your license. The shop can feed him, too. Why stay in Germany any longer? Also, with all the German wars going on, he would be much safer here. You said so."

Mother was trembling, and her sobbing did not stop. "I don't want you to go! We need your help! You are so deft in the business..."

"I'll wait till Dad comes home," Anna said between her teeth, then sighed. "Let's write to him together tonight."

Anna told Lajos about the agreement with her mother the following week. They had an enjoyable afternoon together in the city. It was cold and sunny, and Anna was in a better mood. Lajos promised to write as frequently as his duty schedule would allow. He also said that as soon as her stepfather returned, he would come, propose, and then take her away. In the meantime, he would secure the teacher's job for her.

Their goodbye kiss was long and passionate. Anna took a

deep breath and gulped down her tears. *I want to follow him.*

There was no answer from Stepfather for two months. Then he wrote that they couldn't release him before June. They had to find a substitute. In June, he would come home.

Anna lived on Lajos' letters during the whole spring. He wrote about the snow-covered mountain peaks, the fresh air, the pretty houses, and the kind people living there. His letters were enthusiastic and full of promises. It sometimes took letters two weeks to arrive and neither of them waited for an answer before writing another letter. At least in the beginning.

Early June, after having written four letters in a row and having read none, Anna realized she had not received a letter from Lajos in more than a month. She continued writing her letters in despair, one after the other, like she wanted to force them to answer themselves. In late June, she decided it had to be the fault of the war. After Germany attacked the Soviet Union, Hungary also declared war against them. When Stepfather arrived from Germany in early July, she lost her patience. As an excuse that she needed to do some miscellaneous purchasing, she started after lunch for the police station close to the Antalov depot where Lajos used to serve.

"Miss Onisko, nice to meet you! How are you doing?" She recognized the police officer Pista, Lajos' comrade, with whom he used to visit her shop. He was standing guard in front of the station.

"Good afternoon, Pista. Thanks for asking. Just on my way to the city. I was wondering what became of Lajos Zádori, your colleague," she said as effortlessly as she could.

"Oh, they stationed him in Kőrösmező from February, I thought you knew."

"I know that, but we have lost contact lately. I was just curious how he was faring as the commander there." Anna's attempt at a laugh sounded so hollow that she scared herself.

Pista seemed not to notice.

"As I am hearing, very well. A further promotion seems to come his way soon and best of all, he's getting married after the harvest, he wrote."

The physical pain in her guts took her breath away. It could have been a knife stab.

"Great news!" Anna inhaled and could hardly emit the words. She forced a smile on her face with utter effort.

"He's a lucky fellow. He's marrying a young local widow, quite rich as I hear," chatted Pista merrily, not noticing Anna's frozen smile at all that could have stopped a more attentive police officer. "The lucky bastard, forgive my language, Miss. I'll write to him that you wish him well!"

The turn of the knife took Anna's breath away.

"You do that, Pista!" She turned toward the city and it took her all her willpower not to run.

She arrived at the Kossuth Square, not knowing how she got there. She bought some small things at the wholesaler and escaped to the quay on her way home. It was early afternoon, so there was nobody, thank God. She wanted to cry, but no tears would come. She wanted to shout, but her vocal cords had stopped functioning. She wanted to kill, but the quay was empty.

Stepfather did not yet have the complete picture as to what replenishments the shop needed so he made no comments on her merchandise. Anna took her place at the counter and went through the afternoon with the same frozen smile she had had on her face after the meeting with Pista. Some customers were quite bewildered looking at her, and they spent no more time in the shop that afternoon than was necessary.

"Mum," Anna said after dinner with an even voice. "Lajos Zádori won't come back. I just wanted to say I'll marry my next suitor, whoever it is."

Chapter 11

Miklós Móri hated the police barracks. Sleeping with eight other policemen in one room was nobody's favorite, but he was used to better things. He spent as little time as possible in the barracks, taking long walks instead in the city that was still new to him. The cold weather did not bother him. The police uniform included a long woolen coat and comfortable long boots that he padded with thick flannel footwraps.

Ungvár had a spell of its own. It was so different from Tokaj, the small town where he used to serve at the beginning of his police career, close to his home village. The Subcarpathian capital boasted of the atmosphere of the Austro-Hungarian monarchy. It may have officially disappeared after the Great War, but it survived in the buildings, streets, and people of several small cities and towns in the realm. Even the

Czechs could not destroy it in the last twenty years. True, they had raised many modern cubic buildings, but they meant nothing to Miklós. He preferred the classic style of the Korona hotel, the cathedral, the theater, the old castle, and even the synagogue. They showed the inherency of something majestic, the dream of an empire, the strength of an omnipotent ruler. This brought him to the police. The job came with a pleasing uniform, accommodation, and a decent salary but chiefly it bestowed power and emphasized one's importance. And let's not forget, it protected him from being drafted and ending up somewhere on the front in Russia.

The barracks also lacked palatable food. In one of the small streets of the city center, after several weeks of searching, he finally stumbled upon what he was looking for: an inexpensive diner at the edge of the center that was open from noon till late in the evening. The patrons were workmen from the surrounding factories and workshops and high school students of different institutions. Despite the simple furnishings, the food was delicious and akin to home cooking.

"Don't spare the gravy, madame. I like the beef paprika stew when it's juicy," he told the cook, who also served the meals.

"Eat with gusto, dear officer," said the plump woman in the white apron with pinkish cheeks. She gave him a coquettish grin with a wink and poured another ladleful of steamy, deep reddish gravy on the *galushka* noodles on Miklós' plate. He couldn't miss the additional several pieces of meat in it.

Miklós found an empty table, which was a rare blessing in the packed eatery at dinner time. The far side opposite the kitchen window allowed him to follow the cook as she served the other customers. She was plump but well-proportioned and her curvaceous figure was attractive to most male customers. *She is a double win for this place.*

He stopped by one evening after his day shift. He had to take a long walk in the city to arrive at the diner just before closing time.

"Out for the chilly night again?" she asked with sympathy and placed a bunch of pickled cucumbers on the edge of the plate with the fried chicken and potato meal.

"Not tonight, I am free. Just in for a late dinner after my day shift," he replied, and risked a wink. His reward was an uncommon glance from the corner of her eyes under thick lashes that was worthy of a cancan dancer at a cabaret.

Miklós sat down close to the kitchen window and attacked the breaded chicken legs. He noted with gloom that the meal was lukewarm.

"Oh, so you can help me with closing the diner after your meal? My help has already left, you see." Her pink face became even more heated and it could not be due to the steam from the hot meals.

He could not wait to swallow the piece to answer. "With pleasure, madame!"

"Actually, it's mademoiselle. Mária is the name." Her grin kindled her emerald eyes as she adjusted the cleavage of her blouse. A hot wave flooded Miklós' guts. He did not mind the tepid meal anymore.

After pulling down the heavy shutters, Miklós waited a couple of minutes for the cook to close the service door.

"Why, if you're not in a hurry, you could escort me home, couldn't you? A woman would feel secure at such an hour with a policeman." Her voice became husky.

Miklós swallowed and cleared his throat.

"A distinction for me, mademoiselle!"

Her room was cozy and warm, like her embrace. He visited her as many times as he could during the winter, but as soon as the nights lost their freezing edge, he began to come up with excuses. Mária was eight years his senior, which was an advantage in bed as she proved to be extremely skillful, but it was not favorable for a more serious relationship. She was also too coquettish for his taste and he could imagine that she behaved similarly to others. He wanted a young woman only for himself. A young, beautiful woman on his arm the entire city would admire. A young lady who had her own standing, who came from a good family. A girl who could become his wife.

His inspection routes varied, but he recognized certain people with similar routes at similar times—workers, craftsmen, and clerks—depending on the hour. He saluted some, nodded to the others, and received recognition in return. It was good to be familiar with the people of this city. He noticed a young woman on his early morning routes, either before he finished his night shift or at the start of his day shifts. Sometimes she rode a bicycle to the wholesaler on the Kossuth Square or pushed the heavily loaded cycle along the River Ung on the Roshkovich Embankment and through the bridge, after which she turned left to the south. She had a proud posture and wore an elegant coat that did not fit the menial job she performed. A fashionable dark blue beret confined her wavy light brown locks.

The girl piqued his interest, and he directed his routes more frequently toward the wholesaler in the mornings. He was lucky one day in March when he glimpsed her stopping with the bicycle in front of the Csontos wholesale store, propping up the vehicle against the wall next to the entrance, and going in. He drew himself up and strutted into the store after her.

She seemed to be familiar with the assistant in the store because she asked for several items with an air of confidence. Miklós asked the assistant some banal questions about the traffic and if he had seen a certain man in such-and-such clothes. Hardly waiting for the answer, he rushed out of the store as she had already left. He could follow her with his eyes as she was pushing the bicycle down the small street, turning toward the river.

He went back in and learned from the wholesaler's assistant that her name was Anna Onisko, the daughter of a shop-holder in the city's southeast part. Miklós made a mental note of the address, but it was too far from his zone to include in his routes and make an incidental meeting possible.

She was a remarkable girl. She could not be more than twenty, three years his junior. The freezing late winter mornings filled her cheeks with pink, that became even more pronounced as she struggled with the heavily loaded bicycle. But she went and pushed with a determination and strength he could not miss.

He had to come up with a way to meet her.

Immediately after his return, Stepfather took over the management of the shop and restricted Anna to purchasing. It became more and more difficult to find certain merchandise. The country was officially at war and it had driven up prices and created a lack of goods. In two and a half years since the opening of the shop, the prices had more than doubled and Anna had to use all her charms and contacts to get basic food like meat, flour, and sugar. Her old bicycle was again instrumental in the delivery of goods. They had to be bought in small quantities, rather frequently, sometimes several times a day. Markets were expensive. All purchasing happened through contacts, agreements, and personal meetings.

He has not changed a bit. If possible, he has become even worse. Now he is just giving orders. He must have learned it from the Germans—they are very good at commanding. I must get away.

It was most difficult to deliver goods on the bike in winter. Pushing the vehicle packed with wares through the snow or city slush could consume the strength of a much stronger person. They could not afford the occasional cart deliveries anymore. Fewer and fewer customers could pay for expensive goods, so their palette of wares had crumbled to a very modest level, and this change evaporated most of the profits.

Anna was panting from the effort of pushing the loaded bicycle on her way home that Monday morning. It was her second round of the day. The streets were crammed with trucks and horse-drawn carts, and when some overtook her, she choked from the dirt and petrol fumes and got sloshed, too. She saw the familiar figure of a policeman on the other side of the street. He was looking in her direction and she could have asked for help, but he was too far away. She gave a hard push to the vehicle to lift it from the roadbed to the sidewalk, but the curbstone was high and she lost her balance. *Jesus, no!* The bicycle began to fall down with its load on a heavily polished black oxford. A pair of gray slacks above them caught the sack of flour—or were they black before? The contents of two satchels spread on the sidewalk.

"I am terribly sorry, sir!" She hurried to gather the merchandise one by one.

"I should apologize for not helping you get that bicycle to the sidewalk. It is dangerous to push it on the roadbed with such a heavy load," the man said. His shoulder nudged her arm as he helped put the goods back into the satchel. A whiff of cedarwood and bergamot teased her nose. "Let me set up the bicycle."

"You will smudge your clothes and hand." She straightened and looked into the deepest violet eyes she had ever seen. Light brown brows and a straight nose that held round glasses framed the eyes. His mahogany hair fell onto his forehead as he bent to raise the bike and he threw his head back to get them out of his vision. The cedarwood scent overwhelmed her and the winter scene dissolved into an awakening of spring. *The curve of his smile is like a gondola in Venice in that movie, what's it called?*

She must have gaped and stopped gathering the merchandise. She did not notice it until his eyes twinkled. A smile showed glowing white teeth, and she heard him laughing.

"You look like you have spotted a ghost!"

Anna felt the blood flooding her cheeks and put the satchels in the baskets of the bike.

"Thank you, sir. It's really kind of you to help. I hope I haven't destroyed your clothes."

"I better help you with this purchase so that you get home in one piece."

Despite her protests, he insisted on accompanying her and held onto one side of the bicycle. It was only a ten-minute walk. Either he was good at making conversation or she was still under his magic spell. She told him a lot about herself, including the shop and her family. He introduced himself as István Fedor, a teacher at the local lyceum.

The morning encounter diminished into an improbable fantasy as she fell back into the daily drudgery of customers in the afternoon. Then he showed up in the shop on Friday. She quivered and seized the edge of the counter. He was exquisite in his light gray suit *(it was really gray, and not from the flour!)* and had come to ask her out during the weekend. A thrill ran through her.

Stepfather grumbled something unintelligible to Mother but Anna took no notice. She stammered her agreement to meet István in the city on Sunday after lunch.

The sharp wind chased them into a new cafe on the embankment. They ordered malted coffee and a Sacher that had little in common with the famous Vienna chocolate cake except for the color. István was not only good at asking the right questions, but he was also an excellent listener. Within half an hour, Anna felt like she was talking to Marika. Talking about her life, completed school, and dreams, she admitted her aspiration to become a teacher.

"So, it seems we are almost colleagues," he noted, and raised a toast with his coffee cup. "I teach Hungarian and history in the lyceum."

Subcarpathia did not have enough teachers who could teach Hungarian, so the authorities tried to import them from the hinterland. István came from Miskolc, an industrial city in the northeastern part of Hungary.

Anna did not need to pretend to listen attentively when he recounted his own story. She was immersed in his velvet voice that caressed her like a feathery eiderdown. She laughed at his stories about the students and their mistakes in Hungarian. *I would have made those mistakes myself!* His monologue did not last long, and he again asked about her plans. She admitted her teaching dreams were impossible to realize: she had to work at the family shop.

He offered limited sympathy.

"I trust everyone is the architect of their own future. You should not give up. It is commendable that you help your parents, but you will be legally mature, I understand, in a year. You can and should go after your dreams. I came from a poor family, but had a teacher who supported me. A scholarship enabled me to go to high school and then I worked during the evenings as a server to pay for my tuition at the University. You must follow your dedication."

She had no mood for dinner and went to bed early that night. She could not tear herself away from those violet smart eyes, delicate figure, and dignified appearance. István differed from everyone she had known. *Why couldn't we have such teachers at school? Oh, of course, we would have fallen in love with them, all of us. A girl's school deserves only nuns and ripe, middle-aged, bearded teachers with a potbelly and a dedication to nationalism.*

"Can I help you, mademoiselle?" Miklós stopped next to the girl who was pushing the bicycle. "It seems to be hefty."

"Oh, no, officer, I can manage it, really!" The girl's voice testified to the opposite.

"Look, I'm also going in this direction. It's no bother," said Miklós, and flashed his captivating smile to the girl.

The girl gave in and passed the handlebars to him. She did not reciprocate the smile, just sighed, straightened up, and adjusted her woolen coat and scarf. He noticed that she still reached only an inch above his shoulder. *The perfect height.*

"I've seen you carrying loads of merchandise a couple of times. Is this your job? Delivery service?"

"We've got a family grocery store in the direction of Radvánc and I'm helping my parents."

"Good, so I can go with you as far as the railway bridge. There my zone ends. Shouldn't you be at school?"

"I finished the teacher's school almost two years ago," the

girl said. She had sad, wistful light brown eyes with green points in them. Miklós looked into them a second longer than he should have and averted his glance to the road in front of them, embarrassed. *Slowly, don't startle her.*

"And why don't you teach? A husband is taking care of you?"

"You're a curious police officer!" The girl's face now shimmered from the smile she finally allowed to sneak onto her face. "No, I'm unmarried."

"So am I," said Miklós and stopped talking for a while, giving his statement an emphasis. The girl had a singing voice with a soft local accent that was amiable to his ears.

They parted at the embankment below the bridge.

"I'm sure we'll see each other some other time in the city," he said. *I'll make sure that it happens.*

The girl just nodded, thanked him, and disappeared behind the bridge pillars.

Miklós stood under the bridge and looked at the receding figure until the girl disappeared behind the bushes after a turn of the path on the riverside. He sighed to becalm the drumming of his heart.

He saw her in his arms. He imagined her revolving around the stove, cooking his dinner in a pretty kitchen. With her strength and determination, she could be an asset in his vineyard at home. A teacher must be clever enough to learn anything. And if she sees how prosperous a wine-maker's wife can be, she will forget about teaching.

She is the one, he decided.

Anna looked forward to the weekends with István. They had developed a habit of meeting on a certain bench on the embankment at two on Sundays. Mother asked about him, but she was not in the mood to let her into their budding relationship. *Whenever she has mixed with my affairs, it has ended in disaster.*

He took her to the movies to see Hungarian films. He borrowed Hungarian books from the city library for her because she did not have time to go there on weekdays. As the weather became milder in April, they ventured out for more walks. They talked for hours about Hungarian history, and how Anna was grateful for the opportunity to fill the gaps in her education! It amazed her how little she knew about the country and its language with which she felt an unbreakable bond. *But where does it come from?*

"What makes you Hungarian?" she asked him on one of their dates that was sweetened with a cream cake from Hotel Korona. The puff pastry was as light as a feather, and there was real whipped cream on top of the vanilla custard. She had to admit that the new Hungarian chef was better. *Hmmm...much better!*

"I guess it starts with childhood. This is the language you grow up with, in which you talk to your parents and buddies. Then school forms you. They tell you stories and what you must believe in and what you must be proud of. Then life comes, and it creates and forms your opinions and political views. I suppose I cannot be anything other than Hungarian, as I do not know any other culture except for the fact that I learned Latin and German. And what about you?"

"It's difficult. My mother tongue is Hungarian, but soon I had to learn two other languages in my schools. Our neighbors were mostly Slovaks and Rusyns. Also, living in Czechoslovakia does not foster your Hungarian feelings. We learned almost nothing about Hungary. What I know is from my mother. I would even say that what we heard about Hungary and Hungarians were ugly things—and the Ukrainian movement made us believe that since we lived in Subcarpathia, we were all Ukrainians or Rusyns. Sometimes I think my feeling Hungarian is just girlish stubbornness."

"Stubbornness is a substantial force. But you surely know Hungarian tales and songs—you like to sing, you said."

"I also know a lot of Rusyn songs and some tales I heard in other languages, too. Little Red Riding Hood seems to be internationally known."

His laugh was more refreshing than their already-tepid coffee. They were sitting on the terrace of the Korona and enjoying the early June air.

"So, you think you are lost between cultures."

"And current events don't help. The rulers don't care about people, they just want to rule. For Czechoslovakia, we were cheap labor, and our exotic, wild, and romantic land was an added tail to their country. Ukrainians also wanted to forget history and demanded the land for themselves. And with Hungary..."

"You do not mean you feel oppressed, Anna?"

"How else should we feel? My stepfather lost his license. He was not trustworthy enough for the new rulers. People are losing their jobs not having the right nationality or being considered not dependable enough. We were not encouraged to speak Hungarian before, and now languages other than Hungarian and maybe Rusyn are banned."

"Rusyn is the second official language in Subcarpathia."

"Try to go to the city council and speak Rusyn. In the best case, there will be nobody who understands you. In the worst, they will treat you like a foreigner. Unless you speak Hungarian, you cannot make arrangements."

"This will change, Anna. These are hard times with the

war around us, and Subcarpathia is still in turmoil due to Ukrainian nationalists. You should find the motivation through this, though, to develop your Hungarian knowledge so that you can be an excellent teacher."

"I could teach the mixed children well. Everybody in the villages speaks both languages and needs them."

"You should consider that you may be a teacher in Hungary in the future. I mean in the mother country."

"My mother didn't allow me to take a job at Szolyva or Kőrösmező. She doesn't want me to leave Ungvár."

His violet eyes scrutinized her, and he gulped the cold coffee.

"I thought you wanted to get away from your stepfather."

"I do, I still do. It's just tough...I've never been outside of Subcarpathia."

"Miskolc is three times bigger than Ungvár, with growing opportunities. A teacher would find a job in no time."

"Why are you telling me this?" She frowned and resisted his spellbinding glance.

He straightened in his rattan chair and adjusted his glasses.

"You are a captivating young lady with a lot of talents, Anna. We have been enjoying each other's company for the past three months. I'm at the age where I do not relish remaining a bachelor anymore. I'd love to share more than a couple of Sunday afternoons with you." István smiled and his eyes continued hypnotizing her through the round lenses.

The hidden proposal flabbergasted her. *But he did not say it, did he? What does he expect?*

"I...you're confusing me." She looked down at her fingers fiddling with the hem of her dress.

"You should think about it. I'm planning to go to Miskolc for the school vacation. You could join me for a weekend. To see the city, the surroundings. Of course, I will find you reputable accommodation."

"You should meet my parents."

"I'm interested in you, not your parents."

Anna was still trembling when she arrived home. She could not talk to Mother about the proposal—it would have to wait. She must sleep on it and look at things without the cloud of cedarwood scent blurring her mind. *But how to burst those balloons so that they do not raise my tummy to my throat when I meet him?*

Miklós dropped his forehead into his palms, looked at the shot glass, and then dashed down the slivovitz.

I made a mistake. I should have talked to her sooner. How did she meet this showy fellow? Is it because he is a teacher? Or at least his landlady said he was. And he is from Miskolc—is he here for long?

They're meeting every weekend, it seems. But only in the city— he never accompanies her home. They always part in the city. She goes home alone. So, he doesn't know the parents. It cannot be a serious matter if he doesn't even meet them. But they're together every weekend.

Maybe he is only a spring flirt.

The pub was full of cigarette smoke that he detested. He beckoned to the innkeeper for another shot, went to drink it at the bar, paid, and left the dirty joint.

The early summer evening air was mild and fragrant, a relief after the choking bitter fumes in the pub. His mind cleared as the alcohol evaporated with the smoke. He staggered at first, but soon walked steadily with a purpose as his plan became clearer.

He worked on his plan for the whole of next week. He

talked to colleagues in other departments, pulled some strings, asked for some favors, and wrote reports. By Friday, he had even received an official commendation for revealing the suspicious individual.

He woke up early the next Monday morning. Fortunately, he was not on duty, so he could finish his plan. As he crossed the city, he made sure he went around the wholesaler on the Kossuth Square and saw Anna's worn bicycle propped up against the wall next to the entrance. He sped up, and in ten minutes, he was in front of the grocery shop. The door on the corner was already open, and he marched in.

"Good morning, may I speak to Mrs. Onisko? I mean, Mrs. Movchan?" He saluted the small but brawny man on the other side of the counter.

"My wife is in the kitchen. Just a second—Teréz, come here!" He looked at Miklós and produced a smile. "What crime did she commit now?"

"Mr. Movchan, I suppose," Miklós looked at him with a raised brow and he nodded. "It's just a routine check we're running on store proprietors."

Teréz Movchan shuffled into the store. She was heavy and moved with difficulty.

"Officer, what can I do for you?"

"Good morning, Mrs. Movchan. We need to ask some routine questions to store owners concerning an inquiry. Can we find a quiet place for a few minutes?"

Teréz invited Miklós into the hall and offered him a seat in the kitchen.

"I can't imagine what this is about," she said. "Can I offer you some tea?"

"Thank you, no, I will be brief. It's a personal matter I need to inquire about. Do you know a person named István Fedor?"

"Doesn't ring a bell, no. Who's that?"

"I'm afraid your daughter has a close relationship with this individual."

"Anna? No, I should know about that. True, she has been going out Sunday afternoons, but I assumed she was meeting with her girlfriends... Who's that man?" Teréz sat down on a chair that painfully creaked.

"I can't divulge the details as it's part of an investigation, but this person is under police surveillance because of supposed communist activities."

"Oh, no! You're sure he's meeting my daughter? Anna is not interested in politics."

"They were observed several times in the city having intimate conversations."

Teréz's face crumbled, and she emitted a sigh.

"What should I do, officer?"

"I don't know how far the investigation will go. It would certainly be inconvenient if your daughter was summoned for interrogation. Maybe you could speak to her about the person and convince her he is dangerous."

"I most definitely will, officer. You can't imagine how grateful I am that you let me know of this. I'm sure she's just...probably it's just a harmless...you know how it is with silly young ladies. A dashing gentleman like yourself can turn a girl's brain so easily, wouldn't you say?"

Miklós allowed himself a self-indulging but also forgiving smile.

"I'm sure you'll handle the situation properly, Mrs. Movchan. I would also advise you not to share the matter with your husband. You know, this is a delicate matter and I shouldn't be giving you any information. The fewer people know about it the better. You could tell him that we discussed your customers, and I was interested to know if you had heard subversive statements from anybody."

"Yes, I certainly won't share this with Dimitri. Trust me, he could get furious. It makes little sense. I'll talk to Anna and fix it. You can rely on me. And I'm grateful to you, officer..."

"Móri, madame, Miklós Móri. But we should keep my name a secret, please. I'll stop by some time later just to make sure everything is in the best possible order."

"Please do, you'll be welcome!"

Anna was preparing to go out after Sunday lunch. Stepfather went to have his nap in his bedroom and Anna remained alone in the kitchen with Mother.

"Where are you going today?" Mother was thumbing through newspapers that she did not have time to read during the week.

"I'm meeting with Marika and may end up in the movie theater or just stroll in the city and eat ice cream."

"Interesting...I thought she had gone to her relatives in Kassa."

"No, you must be mistaken." Anna's voice broke. She tittered and took the brush from a drawer with slightly trembling hands and started to re-brush her hair.

"I talked to her mother yesterday. She has gone on Friday and won't be back till next Sunday."

"The little devil! She must have forgotten we agreed to go out again today."

"Who is István Fedor?"

Anna's hand stopped brushing for a second, then continued with vigor. "I don't know anybody by that name."

"Don't lie to me, Ancika! You've been going out with that man for several months."

Anna's heart missed a beat. "And what if I have? I am twenty, I can go out with whoever I want."

"That man is under police investigation."

Anna pivoted to look at her mother. She did not seem to be joking. "What are you talking about?"

"A policeman was here the other day and made inquiries about your relationship. He must be in some unlawful political conspiracy."

Anna forced out a cackle. "This is nonsense. István is an esteemed teacher at a lyceum."

"He wouldn't be the first teacher to get involved in a political conspiracy. We have always remained away from politics. You must stop seeing him."

"This is insane! István is a very intelligent teacher from whom I'm learning a lot about Hungary and its culture. He is interesting, has seen so much of the world, and is willing to spend time with me. He has even...he invited me to Miskolc."

"What has gotten into you, Ancika? Have you gone crazy?" Mother stood up and put both her hands on the table, leaning closer to Anna. She could not shout because of Stepfather, so she hissed. "With an unknown man, a criminal?"

Anna's breath became heavy, her chest contracted, and her eyes started to burn. Her voice came out in hiccups.

"He proposed to me...you want to take him away from me...like Lajos before..."

"Lajos was a careerist. It would have ended badly, anyway. Now, you must think with your head and not with your heart in a serious relationship. Your life will depend on your choice." Mother dropped back in her seat and sighed. "If he's such an esteemed person, why didn't he come to your home to propose? He must have something to hide and this proves what the policeman said."

Anna staggered to the water can, poured herself some water, and took some sips. She blew her nose, nodded, smoothed her dress, and said in an even voice. "I'm going, Mum. I'll get proof that he is an honest man."

"Don't force me to speak to Stepfather about this. He would go mad if he knew. Just end it with this Fedor. There are so many trustworthy men available in this city. Why would you pick up some doubtful individual?"

Anna grabbed her purse, dashed through the door and into the garden, then the street, and did not stop until she reached the riverbank. The sad willows created a refreshing shadow in the June heat above the footpath. There was a slight breeze petting her burning cheek. It helped her to quiet down by the time she reached the paved embankment that soon became full of well-dressed people on a Sunday afternoon ramble. Seeing the couples arm in arm, she developed a cramp in her stomach and sped up.

She had already been waiting for an hour on their bench, but István was nowhere. She went to buy ice cream at the cafe close by so as not to look suspicious sitting alone. She ate the ice cream quickly, again finding her sitting there, alone.

Something must have happened to him. He has never been late. Is it connected to that alleged police investigation? Could it be that he is involved in something unlawful?

She did not notice the policeman approaching the bench, so she jumped when he addressed her.

"What a surprise! Good afternoon, Miss. It's refreshing to see you without a loaded bicycle!"

Anna sighed and forced a smile on her closed lips.

"Good afternoon to you, too, officer."

"Are you waiting for somebody?"

"Yes, it seems my girlfriend has forgotten we agreed to meet today."

"It's a pity. May I offer you my company? I was just think-ing about some refreshments in the Korona. I am not on duty today. Would you mind joining me?"

"Well, I...," Anna started, but then she changed her mind. "Thank you, officer, it will be just right."

Anna accepted the offered arm, and they strolled toward the square.

It could have been a pleasant afternoon on the terrace of the Korona, but Anna was constantly looking at the pedes-trian traffic on the bridge and their specific bench all the time. No sign of István. The policeman's mellow voice did not always reach her mind, and she gave distracted answers. *Could this policeman—what's his name, Miklós—know about the investigation?* She looked at him with interest.

"In what department are you engaged you said?" she said and took a sip of the malted coffee.

"At the public police, but I'm also helping with investiga-tions. Taking tours around the town gives me a lot of oppor-tunities to monitor people."

"Are there a lot of crimes? I've always found Ungvár a safe city."

"It might have been before the war, Miss Onisko. Now, more and more subversive elements are popping up. Ukrainian nationalists, anarchists, communists—you name them."

"I wouldn't have thought that. It must be dangerous." Anna shivered, as if the words frightened her.

"There are some elements who may well be. Even among the intellectuals, we can find sinister people who are... But this is not really a topic on which I can divulge details or something a young lady would be interested in. Tell me more about yourself."

It was difficult to concentrate on talking about her life

and showing enthusiasm when, at the bottom of her mind, all her thoughts swirled around another person. But Miklós was talkative and when he did not receive more information from her, he talked about his life back in Hungary. Something about a vineyard, his house, land, and his plans to go back to a quiet life after the war. When he shifted closer to her to repeat a question that got lost in the noise from the party at the next table, she smelled a mild scent of clean soap, maybe Flora. How different it was from classy cedarwood! She did not understand why she liked the simple soap.

He offered to accompany her home, but she declined. She wanted to be alone, to think and ponder her next steps. He nodded, said goodbye, saluted, and went on his way. *He did not ask for a date...why?*

She stopped at the lyceum on her second purchasing tour the next morning.

"Mr. Fedor has gone for the vacation period," the janitor said.

"Are you sure? I had some private hours agreed with him on history for my studies..."

"I am, Miss. There's only the schoolmaster in. Do you want to see him?"

"No, it's unnecessary. There must have been a misunderstanding." Anna turned and left the empty lyceum.

István knew her address. They had agreed he would send her a note if something came up and they could not meet. She would contact him through the lyceum if she had any difficulties. Now she was stuck waiting for his letter.

She saw the policeman frequently in the city. Sometimes he came to talk to her, and on a Friday, he asked her for a date to see a new movie starring the best Hungarian comic. She wanted to forget that she had received no letter, no news about István for almost two weeks.

She said yes.

Chapter 12

Miklós could have been the ideal partner to go out with. He looked fetching as he strode toward her in his uniform with unfaltering steps. He looked taller than he really was because he held himself erect and had a thick mane of wavy black hair rising two inches above his forehead. Even with her Cuban-heeled sandals on, she barely reached the thin lips that granted him a manly, serious expression. Not that she wished to reach them. She greeted him with a nod and a modest smile and let him offer his arm.

"Zombor, my village is on the plains, but blue-green hills surround it from two sides like the Tokaj hill. Everything is green—apple and apricot orchards, maize fields, and most importantly, vineyards," Miklós said as she inquired about his home. Anna looked at him with awe as his eyes glazed over and he seemed to be looking far away.

"Oh, and the fragrance of the blooming trees: you have a lot of acacia, linden, and bountiful ragweed. Some of the neighbors make good honey with bees. By now, the wheat should have been harvested, the fields are full of large straw stacks that some use as secret huts," he said, squinting at her. Anna blushed as she understood it was meant as a wink.

"Do you also have a vineyard?" She wanted to get back to neutral topics.

"And what a vineyard, you should see! Several acres, some old, some newly planted. We let the grapes ripen to get more sugar during the long, warm Indian summers, harvesting only in late October or even November. There is always a cheerful harvesting crowd composed of family and neighbors who help each other on different days to manage the whole hillside in a couple of weeks. Everybody gets a shot of the pomace *pálinka* that breaks the morning chill. It's a grape brandy that smells strong but helps digestion and definitely increases the performance of the harvest teams," Miklós chuckled.

"I'd like to see it," Anna said. The romantic harvest scene came to life in front of her eyes. She wanted to be among those buoyant people. Suddenly, the shop seemed like a prison.

"And when the women start to sing! There is always laughter, especially at places where the words become, hmm, a bit indecent." He made an embarrassed grimace that was so funny that Anna almost laughed out loud. "The men carry the heavy wooden baskets with the harvested grapes and work their way down to the carriages. When full, the horse-drawn carriages go downhill to our homes to get the team pressing the grapes started." Miklós stopped as they got into the queue in front of the movie box office.

Anna was happy to escape. She let Miklós held her hand

during the movie.

The cream cake at the Korona topped their afternoon. Miklós told her about his life as a policeman, the long walks on duty around the city, the crummy accommodation, and the even more dreadful canteen. She noticed how lively his black eyes were when he told a story. His eyes became round, the thick brows danced above them, and he liked to accompany his narrative with hand gestures that made the story vivid.

Weekends became occupied with work again. Anna quelled Mother's worries by telling her that she had broken up with István. She could not tell her he had disappeared. Mother took the news suspiciously and wanted more details, but Anna snubbed her by announcing that she was going out with a policeman. Mother blinked with sudden amazement and Anna almost broke into laughter.

"What policeman? Some colleague of Lajos?"

"He's not from the station here, but from the city. We've met a couple of times during the day when I was on my tours. He'd even helped once with the bicycle."

"Does he have a name?"

"Oh, Mum, is it important? He's some Miklós, Miklós... Móri, that's it."

Mother blinked again, and her eyes narrowed. "Why don't you invite him for lunch next time so that we know who is courting our daughter?"

"It's nothing like that, Mum. He's just friendly...it's nice going out with him. He's entertaining, pleasant company..."

"No friendship exists between men and women. Just invite him for your birthday. We'll have a small celebration next Sunday. I'm sure he'd appreciate some home cooking. Police canteens have a bad reputation."

Miklós's eyes radiated with warmth when she passed the

invitation to him. He kissed her hand and looked into her eyes as if she had just proposed to him.

"Just a simple Sunday lunch. It's pure chance that it happens to be my birthday. My mother's a curious being and she can't stand things happening without her being involved." She grinned and threw back her hair with an embarrassed shake of her head.

"You're most beautiful today, Annoushka, if I may call you so."

"They call me Ancika at home, but it's your choice."

"Annoushka, Noushika, I like how it sounds."

Anna chuckled, took his arm, and they strolled on the embankment among the parading couples like they were one of them.

"You are an excellent cook, if I may say, Mrs. Movchan! I haven't had such a fabulous broth since the time I left home. And the schnitzel! It could have come directly from Vienna!" The boisterous praise from the policeman made Mother blush and drop her fork and a knife with a clatter on the kitchen floor. Miklós jumped to collect them.

Stepfather's creased brow showed that he was thinking about how to trump that. He had to collect all his Hungarian vocabulary to come up with something.

"She cooks with good meat—and that's my area." He beamed with pride.

"I'm sure it is, Mr. Movchan. It's difficult to find good meat at all nowadays. The army takes the cream, the rich people follow, then those who have contacts. The police canteen is at the end of the queue, I can assure you." Miklós grimaced, then grinned and toasted to the couple.

Anna noticed Mother was following Miklós closely. Mother had accepted the posy when Miklós had arrived, but she could not take her eyes off the policeman. It was most curious. *Does she like him or what?* Anna received the other bouquet along with a Pelikan fountain pen and lengthy birthday wishes. She was amazed and embarrassed and looked at the expensive pen for so long that she almost forgot to thank him.

When Mother placed the coffee cup in front of Miklós, she noted, "You must be a busy man, Mr. Móri. These times are confusing for many people. They can easily get mixed up with the wrong elements."

The smile melted away from Miklós's face, and he looked Mother in the eye.

"Very true. We must be vigilant. We find criminal elements in all classes today. But good police work means we can remove untrustworthy or suspicious individuals before they can cause harm to honest people."

"That's most commendable," Mother said. She had a faint smile on her face and Anna heard her emitting an inaudible sigh as she was sitting down. *She must be nervous because of him.*

"What do you think of the war, officer?" Stepfather wanted to be part of the conversation. "The German forces are closing in at Stalingrad with the help of the Hungarian army. Will Stalin let them take his city?"

"My profession requires no mixing with politics, Mr. Movchan. I believe the police need to keep the order in our own country and I am happy to do that. The war is not my business."

"Clever stance, and very safe," said Stepfather. "So being a police officer is your vocation."

"It's difficult to say. I am too young to commit to a life in the force. It has its advantages during these troubled times, though." Miklós's eyes sparkled as he looked at Anna. "I have land to return to when the war ends. Vineyards around Tokaj make an excellent base for a living."

Stepfather looked at Mother and stood up to go to the kitchen cabinet where he kept his vodka. Mother prepared four small glasses.

"To life after the war!" Stepfather said.

Tears flooded Anna's eyes from the breath-stopping liquor and the kitchen became blurred and painted in rainbow colors. Miklós's chiseled features softened. The waves in his hair doubled and moved like the water in the Ung in spring. Both Mother and Stepfather smiled with a lightness she had never seen before, and Jancsi grinned at her as he slurped his raspberry lemonade. She wiped her eyes, and the world was restored to its gravity. Only Jancsi was still slurping his lemonade, his smile real.

Anna took Jancsi's hand, and they hastened through the streets to reach school on time. They had to be there before eight o'clock for the ceremonial opening of the school year. Anna had become accustomed to the fact that Hungarians loved to celebrate and grabbed all opportunities to show their national flag, decorate buildings with flower and paper garlands, and let the band play music that suited the occasion. Jancsi was excited to meet his friends and chitchatted the entire way about what they would do after the celebration ended. It was supposed to be brief.

"Jancsi, I'll return for you in an hour, agreed?"

"It's fine if you come back by ten. We'll be in the playground!"

Jancsi's school was in the suburbs, close to their home,

and the city center was half an hour away. She had enough time.

She left her brother with the teachers after a quick peck on the cheek and dashed toward the center. When she reached the lyceum, the students had gone inside to celebrate the new school year, and she could knock at the small glass window of the janitor's office, unnoticed.

"Do you know by chance if Mr. Fedor is in today?"

"He's not."

"I thought all teachers are in on the first day…"

"He's not teaching here anymore."

Anna's mouth fell open, so the janitor continued.

"He's moved back to Miskolc permanently. We have a new teacher taking over his job from today."

"I suppose… I'll need to find another personal lecturer for my history exam preparation."

Anna turned and stumbled out of the building. She stopped on the street and tried to collect herself with little success. *They moved him back permanently. He didn't bother to let me know. He may be in prison for all I know. Or he's just forgotten me.*

She kicked at the curb that made a young lady with a pram wince and glare at her but she could not care less. Wandering aimlessly in the small streets, she could not remember how she ended up on the embankment at the bench. Their bench.

She could not sit down. It was not their bench anymore. It was just a few wooden planks and prisms nailed together, and now she noticed how worn it was. A small piece of wood had broken away at the corner of the backrest, and the varnish had disappeared in places. It was an ordinary, corny bench—cold and ugly.

She turned to march back to Jancsi's school. Her mind

was as empty as the ugly bench on the embankment.

Anna went on more dates with Miklós. They worked like medicine—they soothed the pain in her heart and helped her spirit rejoice. She invited him for Sunday lunches in September at her parents' encouragement. They would saunter into the city after lunch and end up in the movie theater or a cafe. Once, they even attended a Lehár operetta that they both enjoyed and sang the tunes on their way home. He would hold her hand and had once also attempted to hug and kiss her in front of Anna's gate, but she slipped from his arms and whisked away in a second.

The next Sunday, he came with two gigantic bouquets and a bottle of wine. He presented one bouquet to Mother and the other to Anna, but said nothing. Mother melted like one of her cream cakes in the warm October weather.

The lunch went well with the customary praise from Miklós. Only when the piteously melting cream cake arrived at the table and he had received his malt coffee, did he stand up and turn to Stepfather and Mother. Anna's heart skipped a beat. She tried to stop Miklós, but it was too late.

"Dear Mr. Movchan and Mrs. Movchan! I have been enjoying your hospitality for the last couple of months. I am not a man of big words, but I have become very fond of your daughter. Please, allow me to ask you for her hand in marriage."

Anna stomped out of the kitchen in a fit.

She stood under the vine arbor in the garden with hands crossed on her chest and turned when she heard the door opening behind her. Miklós took a couple of steps toward her and held out his hand. She took a nervous step away from him.

"Noushika, I just wanted to make it easier for you. Even if your parents accept my request, it's still for you to decide if you want me. I needed to ask them first. You're still not twenty-one."

"You could have told me about this before. I am not prepared for marriage."

"We have time! I wanted your parents to know that I have serious intentions. You did not let me express my feelings toward you. I want you to know that I love you."

His eyes were begging, and he still held out his hand, palm up. Anna clenched her teeth and hissed.

"I don't know if I want to be your wife."

"Think about it, Noushi. I can offer you a much better life than the one you have here as your stepfather's servant."

"To be your servant instead!"

"Don't you know me yet? I would pamper you all day if you allowed me. There are lands, vineyards, and a house in Zombor. We would have a beautiful life. We just need to wait for this war to end and I can quit the police force."

"I want to be a teacher, not a peasant!"

"You could teach *and* be the wife of a winemaker—no peasant!"

"You talked to my parents without even consulting me. How will you behave when you're my husband?"

"I explained to you that it was a formal request. You always ask the parents. I also thought that you felt something for me."

She started to play with the belt of her dress.

"I like you, Miklós, but I'm not sure it's enough for life."

"We need to spend more time together. Once we're engaged, we will. You'll come around to love me, I'm sure."

Anna looked at his begging eyes and put her palm into

his outstretched hand. He closed it around hers and gave it a squeeze. It was time to return to the kitchen.

He is my chance. What can I do without a man? Now that István has disappeared, what else is there for me? He can take me away eventually and I'll have my household in Zombor. My own! It must be a charming place, from what he has told me.

"I need to think this over. It's so sudden," she said to her parents. "Give me a week to answer Miklós."

Stepfather grimaced, and Mother sighed, but there were no objections. Miklós nodded and took her out for a walk to the Ung, but she was silent and ended it soon. She wanted to be alone.

"This is *wonderful!*" Marika jumped up from her seat to the amazement of the passersby on the embankment. They were sitting on a bench on the promenade in the cool evening. Anna made sure to pick a different bench than the one she had come to hate.

Marika worked at the city council where her father had found a job for her in the education department. She was monitoring teacher vacancies for Anna without success, and they were meeting from time to time during evenings when it was nice outside.

"This is what you wanted! A handsome policeman. I recognized him on the street the other day based on your description. Mind you, I think he looks much better than you depicted him. He's not that chunky type you don't like. A slim fellow who can wear his uniform to his advantage, a serious man who knows what he wants, and as I hear, even has a pot to piss in!"

Anna sneered.

"But I'm not in love with him, Marika! How can I get engaged if I'm not sure?"

"Listen, you don't want to miss this train, too, do you? Is he good-looking? He is. Does he have a decent income? Well, a policeman's salary is nothing to boast about, but if we consider his lands and vineyards, that's not to be sniffed at. Does he kiss well?"

"You...you are terrible! I don't know," said Anna. She could not look at Marika and turned toward the river.

"What? You haven't even kissed him?"

"I... I was in love with István until..."

"He. Is. Gone. End of story. Whether he is a villain and in prison or just a man who cannot keep his promises, it's all the same. He's not worth your attention."

"It's easy to say, but he was so perfect a partner to speak to. A beautiful person! An ideal partner who could have supported me in my ambitions."

"A high school teacher is a good party even if he doesn't have land, I have to give that to you. But is he around? No. He's been gone for four months without a word. You should have forgotten him by now."

"I tried, I really tried."

"You must try harder. Otherwise, we'll not be neighbors."

"What do you mean?"

"Didn't I tell you? My fiancé's job will move to Patak next year and I'll follow him there, of course, after we marry. I'm sure we can find me a job there, too. That's less than forty kilometers from Zombor. We could visit frequently!"

"Oh, Marika, that would be great! I'm horrified to move to Hungary alone, not knowing anybody. This is great news!"

"Now you must quiet down, think about Miklós, and decide. Grab your chance."

Mother welcomed Anna's decision. They appointed the

following Sunday as the official engagement, and Miklós kissed Anna for the first time when she told him. She forgot to protest. *I should have let him do that earlier.* She smiled. *He is skillful.* She frowned.

Chapter 13

The cruel November weather with the frosty sleet and biting wind chased Miklós into the eatery. It smelled of cabbage and damp woolen coats, but it was warm and promised a hot dinner. The cook noticed him only when he got in front of her in the queue. She was alone in the kitchen.

"Long time no see, officer!" She sneered and put a hearty portion of steaming cabbage stew on his plate. "Wintry days arrived?"

Miklós hummed something unintelligible and took two thick slices of bread and a glass of hot tea to give the cabbage stew company. He sat in a corner and deliberately did not look at the cook. Closing hour neared and before he could notice, he was alone in the diner. He was mopping up the last of the stew with a piece of bread when Mária came out of the kitchen, locked the door, staggered across the room to his corner, and stopped in front of him with her hands on her hips.

"You seem hungry," she said. "Still hungry."

"No, I've just..."

She got down to her knees and started to unbutton his fly. He could not see her face due to the white cap that covered the top of her head. It moved to and fro, slowly, together with her head. His cheek was in flames, but he was unable to stop her. Feeling hot, his eyes shifted from the white cap to the white ceiling as he slumped gradually on the seat. He heard only his own heavy breathing.

Ten minutes later, Miklós was out on the street, floundering behind Mária.

"I am on duty tonight," he said in a low voice.

"I thought so, but you can still accompany me home at this late hour."

They did not speak during the five-minute walk, but Mária kissed him on the lips before going through the gate of her tenement building.

"Stop by after your day shift."

The thoughts in his mind made his shift last longer. He wandered through the cobblestoned streets and tried to take shelter under the gateways when the sleet was strong. The cutting wind blew away the warmth of the meal, and in its aftermath, he saw only Anna's apprehending brown-green eyes. Her slim figure was so close to him that he could touch it. He reached with his hand but the hip became twice as big, the breasts swelled, and he heard a voice say, "Still hungry." The white cap on the bowing head. Moving slowly.

He was almost frozen when he stomped to the barracks early morning. No hot water waited for him, so he just fell onto his bunk and into dreamless oblivion.

He awakened to a sunny but cold afternoon with a painful

hunger. Lunch was already over in the canteen. He washed, had a change of clothes, and went to meet Anna at her home. He would pick a sausage at the butcher for now and he could have a better dinner at her place. Her mother cooked almost as well as Mária.

Miklós halted for a second, then shook his head and muttered something to himself, much to the amusement of his roommates. He snarled at them and darted out of the room, smelling of the horsehair covers, old uniforms, and too many male bodies. He looked forward to Anna's home with its mixed fragrance of lavender, malt coffee, and smoked paprika sausages that Mr. Movchan liked to prepare for the store.

One weekday, when Miklós was off duty, he and Anna were comparing their progress on getting their birth certificates. They were pretty sure that neither had any Jew ancestors, but they had to prove to the authorities that there had been no Jews in the family for three generations.

"It's such nonsense!" Anna cried. "I have to go after the relatives of János Onisko with whom I have nothing to do!"

"Shhh, Noushi, God forbid you mention such a thing at the city council! We would get into trouble over proving who your biological father and relatives are."

"I know, it's just such a pain! The whole ordinance is ridiculous."

"I couldn't agree more, my dear. I thought we could marry by Christmas and this endless correspondence will prolong our engagement until... I can hardly wait to make you mine!" Miklós hugged her close and kissed her on the mouth. Anna shifted away.

"You must be patient and... I need time..."

"I know, I know, it's so frustrating. We could..."

"No. We couldn't."

Anna stood up, went to her dressing table, and began to

comb her hair. Miklós was looking at her back. Actually, at her buttocks.

"Did you receive answers from Zombor?"

"Yes, but the information is not complete. There are some missing certificates from my mother's side. I guess I'll have to make a trip there. I hope they will let me take some days off."

"Same with me. I may need to go to my mother's village to get the Onisko certificates; they are unwilling to send them."

"Come to dinner, children," Mother called from the kitchen. "I prepared cabbage stew. It has real sour cream and good pork shoulder. I hope you like it, Miklós!"

He grimaced, and Anna raised her brow.

"They had it in the canteen yesterday," he whispered.

"Mother's is much better."

He had to tread to the kitchen carefully in his tight trousers.

"You're a stallion, you know?" Mária's voice came through his dizziness in the dark, musky room full of sighs.

He was lying on his back and letting her caress his body. With closed eyes, it was easy to imagine Anna petting him. The idea aroused him.

"I'm saying, a stallion!"

Her voluptuous plumpness excited him, but it was even better to imagine Anna when he lay with Mária. He loved Anna's cleanliness, the lavender soap she used, the waves in her honey-colored hair, the tremble of her bust when she laughed... Closing his eyes, he could have all this, and in addition, he could feel the hand moving around his chest, playing with the hair on it, then slowly making its way to his navel, playfully circling in the small cavity, then continuing down...

Miklós preferred to do it with Mária in the dark. He did not even need to close his eyes, although that made his senses much sharper and increased his concentration. Giving a last thrust, he fell on her in exhaustion. Then he turned over, gasping for air.

When he was back from oblivion, he saw Mária going to the kitchen for the wine he had brought. He turned his tongue in his dry mouth. He took the glass from her and the strong, gold-colored nectar from home delighted him. She lit a cigarette.

"I hate it when you smoke," he said.

"I hate it when you say that." She went back to the kitchen.

He was looking at her silhouette—the muscular arms, the mighty breasts rising and falling as she inhaled and exhaled, the vast buttocks that showed through the cheap dressing gown and lifted its light material. He turned to his back and looked at the ceiling.

"I must go. I have a day shift tomorrow," he said and started to put his uniform on.

She stubbed out the cigarette, turned toward him slightly, and opened her mouth, hesitating.

"I thought...you would stay. We could have an entire night together...drink wine and talk..."

"I need to go. Maybe next time."

He grabbed his coat and was out of the door before she could react.

He tramped on fresh snow on the sidewalk on his way to the barracks. Christmas decorations were hanging in most store windows, visibly more modest than a year ago. The war was hiding in all corners of life and jumped out on you un-expectedly. His friend, Mihály Kovács, was drafted a week af-ter Miklós had applied to the police force. He had to be somewhere east, at the Don, close to Stalingrad. The entire Hungarian army was told to be there to help the Germans in the siege of the city. If he still lived at all. The news about victory had been less boisterous lately, and it was a clear sign of trouble. God bless, he had chosen the police.

Christmas meant small presents and a modest meal at Anna's house. The small bottle of pomace brandy from his brother-in-law served Anna's stepfather well. A large package of ground paprika his sister had sent made Anna's mother exclaim in delight. The tiny bottle of perfume had cost him a fortune, but was worth every pengő. Anna beamed and kissed him in front of her parents. They graciously chose not to comment. She will come around soon, he encouraged himself. But their physical closeness remained at stolen kisses, no more. It caused him more and more distress.

Frustration impelled him to visit Mária more frequently before Christmas and also in the following weeks and months. She was moody, especially when he appeared with no Christmas present but a bottle of wine. But she remained welcoming in bed. That was what he was looking for, anyway.

The last birth certificates arrived from both sides by Feb-ruary and they could apply for permission to marry at the police headquarters. They decided to set the date of the wed-ding for the end of April. Anna's mother insisted there were a lot of things to be arranged and it couldn't be done earlier. Miklós was sulking, damning her in his mind, but he had to play the good groom. He directed his steps to the eatery after his next afternoon shift. He hoped for a satisfying evening, but did not know how to break the news of the wedding to Mária.

It surprised him that the diner was almost empty. Another cook stood behind the serving window.

"Where's Mária?" he asked nonchalantly and held his plate out for the lentil pottage.

"You'll have to settle for me, officer, this week. She had an accident, and will be in the hospital for some days." The middle-aged cook's smile uncovered her missing front teeth. The concrete-thick lentil pottage with two thin slices of horse sausage was even less inviting. At least the bread had not changed. He took two hunks.

He visited the city hospital the next morning and was directed to Mária's room. All the patients in the room turned to look at him as he entered and he had to clear his throat before he could utter a "good morning". One woman sneered, another nodded, and the others just grinned. He straightened his back and addressed the nurse who had just entered the room.

"I am here for the investigation into Ms. Polgár's accident. Can we have a retreat, maybe?"

The nurse nodded, took Mária's bed, and pushed her out of the room and into a small visitor's cabin. The other patients grimaced.

Her face was paler than the bed cloth. She had one hand in a plaster but otherwise did not seem to be seriously injured. He sat on a seat close to her bed and patted her hand.

"I slipped on the icy sidewalk and had a terrible fall."

"Unfortunate. When will they release you?"

"I lost the child."

"What child?" The chill froze his innards and his limbs went limp. He straightened.

"I was ten weeks with it."

"Come on..."

"Yes, it was yours."

Miklós got sick. The bile was burning his throat and his stomach heaved. *Hold on, she said she had lost it*, he thought. So, it's alright then. No reason to worry. He exhaled.

"Mária, I..."

"We can have another, they assured me."

"I'm going to marry in April."

Roses blossomed on her cheeks, her lips opened, and she inhaled fast a couple of times. Her eyes were burning two holes in his face. He felt it.

"What are you telling me, for fuck's sake?"

Miklós stood up, not feeling safe so close to her.

"I have a fiancée. We were engaged in October and we'll marry in April. She is a young teacher from a respectable family."

"You scumbag! You fucking crumb! And I'm what, your whore? You were crawling into my bed like a slug while you were courting the cheesy little cunt, weren't you? She didn't give it to you in a jiffy, did she? So, you figured I'm a khaki wacky and you can enjoy yourself while you wait for your fucking wedding, right?"

She was beetroot red and shaking. She held onto the iron frame of the bed and convulsed. Miklós was taking a step back, one by one, toward the door. When she grabbed a glass from the nearby table, he did not hesitate and ran. The glass crashed with a bang as the door slammed shut.

The afternoon traffic was at its highest. Stepfather was making chitterlings in the kitchen and Mother was preparing dinner, so Anna served the customers alone. The queue reached through the door to the street.

"Madam, can I help you?" Anna greeted the portly thirty-something with a reddish face and muscular arms that could have done credit to a butcher.

"Yes, you can. You can fuck yourself, you little cunt!" Spittle sprayed from her mouth. "I may have lost his child, but he'll be mine. I'll tell you one thing: I'll pour a bottle of vitriol on you in the church before you say 'yes' to Miklós. Enjoy your beauty until then."

She turned, pushed her way through the queue, and disappeared.

Anna stood as still as a salt column. She saw the astonished people in the queue looking at her and murmuring to each other, but she could not move. The noise brought Mother into the store.

"What's happening here?"

"Some crazy customer has just threatened your daughter!" A woman standing in the queue leaned on the counter and sneered. "You may reconsider the wedding, Mrs. Movchan."

Mother's eyes bounced between the woman and Anna for a second, then she pushed her daughter inside.

"Go into the kitchen and finish cooking dinner, Ancika! And what can we do for you, Mrs. Novák? I suppose you came for the liverwurst and not for gossiping. Don't hold up the queue! What will it be?"

Anna walked to the kitchen in a daze. *Who was that woman? How does she know we are going to marry? Why is she threatening me?*

She spoiled the dinner; her mind was elsewhere. Stepfather burbled but ate. Mother must have worked on him. In the evening, after Anna explained to her in detail what the woman had said, Mother started to work on Anna.

"Must be a madwoman. You should not take it seriously. I'm sure there is a good explanation."

"I must see Miklós immediately."

"Ho-ho, hold your horses! You should tread carefully."

"Carefully? I was called a... I can't even utter those words...she evidently knows Miklós, and she wants to frighten me away from the wedding. Miklós needs to explain this."

"Good, but wait for the weekend when he comes for lunch."

"No, I have to know what's happening. I will go see him in the morning."

Anna left very early with her bicycle so that she could complete her purchases after she talked to Miklós. At the barracks, she had to wait until they called Miklós to the gate. She propped the bicycle outside.

"Noushi, my dear, what's the matter?" His otherwise penetrating black eyes were now hazy. *Is he worried about me or of me?*

"A woman came to the store yesterday and threatened to pour vitriol on me at the wedding."

"Oh...that's curious!" Miklós raised his brows and directed Anna to the visitor's room.

"Do you know a tall woman, plump, strong, bosomy, reddish complexion, about thirty?"

"There are many such women in the city. I may have met some of them."

"And how does this woman know we are getting married in the church soon?"

Miklós kept quiet and looked at his boots.

"Who's that woman? And why does she call me names? How does she know me at all? Will you answer me?" Her voice became hoarse from shouting.

"I really don't know. Must be some misunderstanding."

"You should have a better excuse. She's your lover, isn't she?"

"She's just..." Miklós raised his eyes to look into hers, but they were blank. She saw nothing in them.

She pulled down the ring and placed it into his palm. She had to clench her teeth to touch his hand.

Pivoting and making the four steps to the door sucked out all her strength and she could hardly trudge onto the street. It was good to lean onto the bike and not fall down. Thank God she did not hear any steps behind her. She did not have enough strength to run. She looked at the passersby. Nobody noticed the tears rolling down her cheeks. Nobody cared when she stumbled. And it was nobody's relief when she prevented her fall by holding onto the handlebars. She straightened and pushed on the vehicle with vigor. *It's for the better. God did not want this to happen.*

Chapter 14

Mother's eyes stopped her from escaping into the children's room.

"He was cheating on me with her!" Her voice ended shrilly, like she was asking for help.

"Now, now..." Mother opened her arms and took her to her bosom. Her palms stroked her hair as Anna leaned on her broad shoulders.

"He didn't deny it. Had no excuses." Now the tears came freely. Her sobbing filled the kitchen.

Stepfather appeared at the door and took the purchased items into the store without a word. He left the two women in their mourning.

"Sit down for a second and drink this." Mother put a glass of water in front of Anna.

"I gave the ring back to him. I can't marry him."

"That was not a clever step. You are just thrusting him

into her arms."

"What do I care? He doesn't love me, he wants that...woman!"

"How do you know? Did he tell you that?"

"He couldn't even give me a petty excuse."

"We must invite him to explain himself."

"Mum, I don't want to see him ever again!"

"You'll see him in the city. He will not disappear, so you better meet him now. Men are different. They have needs they must satisfy."

"I don't love him, Mum." Her piteous voice was begging.

"That has nothing to do with this. You have to take care of your reputation. Thank goodness, people don't know about Domeny and that he left you in Sevljus. A second broken engagement would finish you once and for all."

"I won't go to the barracks again."

"Alright, I'll do it. I'll send him a note that we expect him next Sunday for an afternoon coffee to explain his behavior."

Mother was true to her word and saved Anna from the disgrace of going again to visit the barracks. She hired a boy to deliver the message she wrote on a decent sheet of paper. She made the boy swear to wait for an answer from the policeman and bring it back. In his note, Miklós promised to come "with pleasure".

Anna was distracted since morning. She did not sing at church, only looked in front of her, and left her lunch untouched at home. Her trembling became visible early in the afternoon and Mother sent her to fetch wood from the shed, made her clean the tile stoves, and prepare a fresh fire. Mother convinced Stepfather that it was better for him to go card-playing with his buddies that Sunday afternoon and he needed little urging. Jancsi was out playing with his friends, as always, so the two women remained alone in the house.

Miklós arrived at four o'clock sharp, as requested. Mother began the conversation by talking about the war, and the tide turning with the Hungarian army being defeated at the Don. When the coffee was poured into the cups, sweetened with crumbs from their secret stock of sugar, and the apple pie offered, Mother eventually changed the topic.

"You owe us an explanation, Miklós."

He straightened in his seat, as always, when he wanted to emphasize his words.

"Mária Polgár is an old acquaintance of mine, from the time I didn't even know Anna. She's a cook at an eatery I went to sometimes to escape the inedible canteen grub. She might have imagined that the two of us could have a future together. When she heard I was going to marry... She found out about you through other policemen, Noushika, and that is how she got here."

"She said she had lost your child. And she said it was now," Anna said, her voice hollow.

"I heard she was in the hospital. They say she miscarried, but that could be anybody's child."

"So, you had nothing to do with her?"

"I had, but it was long ago."

"If it was long ago, why did she come last week to threaten me?"

"I may have recently boasted somewhere that I'm going to be married..."

"Boasted to the cook in the eatery?" Anna spit the words like fire squad bullets. They found their target.

Mother drank her coffee and stood up. "I will leave you alone. I think it will be better."

When Mother closed the door, Miklós tried to take Anna's hand, but she moved away. He sighed deeply and looked at her, but she turned to face the window.

"Noushika, I don't want to lie to you. I was in physical need. When I'm with you and I kiss and caress you, I imagine things that never happen. I couldn't wait half a year till the wedding. I needed to let out steam. It's unbearable not to be able to have you. I needed a woman. I was thinking of you all the time..."

She turned her head, grabbed the corner of the table, and hissed. "You were fantasizing about me when... Do not mention me in one sentence with that trollop!"

"I love you! I just needed to..."

She put her hand on her cheek and slowly let it fall to her breast and then to her lap like they did not belong to her. "Your fantasies make *me* dirty."

Miklós stole a glance at her. "You're the most beautiful and cleanest angel. I ask for your forgiveness. I'll never cheat on you again. Please, take the ring back."

She was shaking her head like she wanted to clean it from begrimed thoughts. "I can't love you."

"Noushika, dear, I'll prove you can. I'll be the best husband. We'll be the nicest couple in Ungvár, and Zombor when we go there. I'll give you the world!"

"Love would have been enough." She looked at him, and her lips curved into a soulless smile, and she shook her head. "I don't believe you."

"Noushi, I'll give you time. I won't bother you for a week, two weeks if need be. Please think it over. I want you. I want to marry you."

She turned her head back to the window, her face rigid like marble. "You should go."

Miklós arose, and his hesitant hand touched her hair. She did not move away, but her sudden convulsion made him snatch his hand back.

Mother must have heard his steps fading and the door

closing. She stepped into the kitchen seconds after. Her eyes were two question marks.

"I don't want to discuss it today, Mum," Anna said and went to her room.

≈

The next morning, Anna slipped out of the house without breakfast, but her mother saw her through the kitchen window.

"I must be first at the wholesaler. There will surely be a queue due to the long weekend," she said and left before Mother could stop her.

Late in the afternoon, she announced she had to see Marika and went out as soon as the store had closed.

"I don't envy you," Marika said. They had ice cream in a new parlor that had become fashionable lately. This week they had launched ice creams in national colors for the upcoming festivities: strawberry, lemon, and pistachio. The two girls could not resist. "I would kill my fiancé if he did what Miklós…" She stabbed the colorful scoops several times with her spoon and made a gray mess of it in a matter of minutes. Anna stared at her and her heart warmed. Marika rarely showed extreme feelings.

"This is exactly what I wanted to do! But I will definitely cancel the wedding."

"…but I am not you," Marika stopped destroying her ice cream, reached out for the whipped cream in a cup, licked it from her spoon, and then clicked her tongue. "You're in a peculiar situation. You want to get away from your stepfather. He's just a despot and you'll never be master of yourself otherwise. Miklós is the way."

"Have you gone crazy? Should I trade the despot Stepfather for a cheater husband? You can't mean it!"

"Look at it this way: is he a good party? He is. You told me eventually that he kisses well," she giggled. "Hopefully, he does other things well, too."

"Marika, shh!" Anna looked around, blushing.

Marika showed no signs of distraction.

"He slipped once. It would be worth forgiving for your own sake. But you must show him who wears the pants in your future house."

"I'm not sure if I can do that."

"You must work on it. I told you, I don't want to lose my future neighbor in Hungary!"

She returned home at dusk, said that she did not want dinner, and immediately disappeared into the bathroom. When she heard her parents in a discussion in the kitchen, she slipped into the children's room.

She invented different excuses to escape the fated talk with Mother until Thursday evening. Stepfather said he would go for a beer with his cronies and Anna was late to come up with an escape plan. As soon as the head of the family closed the door behind himself, Mother took Anna's hand and pushed her down to one seat at the kitchen table. "You will go nowhere until we have spoken!" There was an edge in Mother's voice that could slice you into pieces if you did not watch out. Anna knew when to give in.

Mother sat down heavily, put her elbows on the table, and rested her chin on her hands with fingers locked together. She looked into Anna's eyes, waiting.

"What? He admitted he had cheated on me after our engagement, and not just once. I can't love a man who doesn't love me. And he doesn't. How could he lay with that trollop? How could he make her pregnant?"

"Pregnant?" A hand went to Mother's chest.

"She lost the child."

"Thank...hmm..." she coughed. "And he told her about the wedding."

"He must have. But I don't care. I don't want him. I'm lucky that all this came to light now. At least I'm not marrying the wrong man."

Mother looked at her and shook her head. "Ancika, you can't dump a man for a slip."

"What do you want from me?"

"Men are impatient and their needs must be attended to."

"If he loved me, he would have waited. For me."

Mother took Anna's hands and caressed them. "Clever women don't show the bill to their men as soon as something happens. They collect them and wait for an opportunity. Debt makes men manageable."

"I want to marry a man who is worth it."

"Miklós is not a wicked man. He is a man, though. If you want a sissy, henpecked husband, you should have picked somebody else. He has a strong will and this will advance him. You should stand behind him and let him go, but where *you* want him to go."

"What are you talking about? I need an honest man and a partner for life. I don't want to manipulate him."

"You can't be so silly, Ancika, you're not sixteen anymore. A man achieves what his woman wants if she's clever. I never go into direct conflict with Dimitri. I let him do what he thinks he wants to do. But I prepare his thinking before he knows."

"This is just disgusting. I can't live with such a man."

Mother opened her arms wide as if the entire world could fit in. "And what do you think, Ancika, will happen? You'll be alone again, left by your fiancé. People will wonder what happened. Is she stained? Is she a slut that cheated on her fiancé? Does she have a temper that's not possible to handle?"

"Mum, why do you torment me? You know I am neither!"

"You'll be so in the eyes of the neighbors. He's a policeman, a respectable person. You're a girl not too young anymore. You can't afford to miss another suitable party."

Anna straightened her back and her voice became stronger. "I am still a good-looking girl who can turn men's heads in the street. I can find an honest man to love."

"Don't mix desire with marital interest. The war is on us and there are fewer and fewer men. You should be happy to have Miklós asking for you."

Anna clenched her teeth and her hands. "I want to cancel the wedding!"

"Anci, we have told everybody. We have bought furniture and most of your trousseau. The fabrics for your wedding dress have been ordered and will be delivered any minute. We have invited tens of people. You'll become the laughingstock of Ungvár."

"I don't care! I hate him!"

Mother stood, leaned toward Anna, and her voice made the candelabra above the kitchen table vibrate. "I won't let you spoil your life, you silly girl! You'll marry Miklós and it's done."

Anna was already standing. "Don't tell me what I am to do!"

The slaps were unexpected. Her head bobbed right and left, and there was only a high-pitch ringing in the silence.

"Until you live in this house, I will tell you what you do!"

Anna dropped back in her seat in shock. She opened her mouth to protest, but it was to no avail. She had lost another battle in a war without weapons.

Only Jancsi heard her sobs during the night. He slipped into her bed, and Anna hugged her little brother close to her. He fondled her hair and her cheeks and whispered nonsense into her ear until she fell into dreamless oblivion.

Mother forced Anna to send a note to Miklós saying they awaited his presence at Sunday lunch, and she had to emphasize "as always".

Anna greeted Miklós with a face that could have been borrowed from an antique marble statue. Miklós chatted idly and appeared to notice nothing. Mother and Stepfather were handling the conversation and Anna let them enjoy it. She did not say a word during lunch.

At coffee, Mother suggested that Miklós put the ring on Anna's finger again. He wavered, but Anna gave him her hand. Miklós produced the ring and slipped it on her middle finger. He leaned close to kiss her cheek. Anna wanted to turn away, but Mother's piercing looks stopped her. Miklós planted the kiss and inhaled.

"I love you!" he said and squeezed her hand.

Anna remained silent and focused entirely on her coffee.

Mother chatted about the wedding preparations and tried to involve everyone in the conversation, but Anna was not willing to break her silence. Miklós nodded enthusiastically and added, with radiant eyes, that the police were highly interested in making the wedding ceremony a memorable event. The city police office had promised guards in festive uniforms, a police brass band, a red carpet, and lots of flowers. Stepfather began to worry about the costs, but Miklós assured him that it was free. They discussed the invitations. From Miklós' side, nobody would make the long journey from Zombor. The newlyweds would visit them on their honeymoon and Anna's family would invite only Michal, her favorite cousin, and Marika—if she was still around before they moved to Patak—and some of their closest neighbors. Anna was still silent and looked uninterested.

Mother sent the young couple into the children's room to have some private time. It was awkward. Anna did not speak and Miklós tried his best, but soon they were just sitting next to each other in silence. Anna moved away from any touch and when he wanted to hug her, she stood up. Eventually, Miklós said he had to go, as he had an early morning shift the following day. Anna saw him off to the garden gate but did not reciprocate his kiss on her cheek. She just nodded and made to close the gate.

"Wait, Noushika, next Sunday? Or earlier?"

"Next Sunday." Her voice was otiose like her life seemed to be.

Anna went into the house and then to the children's room. She could not lock the door as Jancsi was expected later from the playground. She prayed Mother left her alone.

Lying on the bed, she stared at the ceiling. It knew her glare so well. How many times did she lie there and scowl at the white walls, counting all three branches of the small unlit candelabra with the tiny crack on the left glass?

I can't get away from here unless I marry him. He'll return to Zombor eventually and take me with him. Maybe Mother's right: he can be my bridge to freedom. Isn't the price high? I don't love him. Can I ever learn to? I liked him once, but now I'm not sure anymore. He crushed my trust. How do I trust him again?

She hugged her pillow and pulled the eiderdown to cover her. She craved warmth, inside and outside.

I'll need to let him prove his love. Let him be tender, let him be a real man, for me, only. Let him step up for me with Stepfather and Mother—this could be useful.

Isn't it sad? I had loved twice, really loved. They left me. Now I have to settle. Lord, give me strength. Teach me how to love him, so that I don't spend my life in a devastating marriage.

Chapter 15

The Holy Cross Cathedral loomed above them, its triple crosses on the two high belfries scratching the clouds. The incessant clanging of bells awakened the city, heralding the commencement of the ceremony on a late Tuesday afternoon in April. A small crowd had gathered on the square in front of the church, hoping to see the ceremony. The onlookers had created a natural playground for the local children who were running around them playing tag, interrupting the chatter with shrieks that clashed with the jingling of bells. The adults tried to discipline them but they slipped away like small lizards to continue their game in the greenery of the nearby park, with many statues that offered an excellent place for hide-and-seek.

Anna and Miklós stood at the end of the red runner that ran straight to the marble steps below the classic portico with the four Corinthian columns. Twenty police guards lined the carpet, ten on each side, wearing festive uniforms and saluting by holding their sabers high at an acute angle. The young priest standing under the portico raised both arms, and the guards began their stride on the carpet, marching in time with the clangs of the bells. Anna grabbed Miklós' right arm to keep in step with him while holding up the train of her dress with her other hand so as not to trip. The floral lace dress was Mother's masterpiece and attracted envious glances from the onlookers. Periwinkle leaves were sewn into the white lace here and there to augur the crowning wreath they would receive later during the ceremony. A simple lace tiara with a veil adorned her wavy honey-colored hair. Miklós' black uniform was decorated with a single medal and a white carnation flower on his left breast, but the white gloves and the silver saber with a white tassel dangling from his hip made him look stately.

They both wore a solemn expression, absent of a smile—not that either of them could fathom it in their nervousness. Miklós was apprehensive, as he was new to Greek Catholic ceremonies. Anna had other reasons not to smile. Her eyes were scanning through the onlookers to locate the woman.

"I made sure she's gone, I told you. She's gone far away and she'll never come back," Miklós whispered into her ear when they stepped on the stairs leading to the portico and squeezed her arm. Anna did not react but kept her gaze steady on the clergyman in front of the church's huge large wooden doors that were left wide open.

When they reached the young priest who would lead the ceremony instead of the ailing bishop, he invited them into the vestibule. He raised the tray with the gold wedding bands, blessed the rings, and placed them on the ring fingers of the couple's right hands. With that, they proceeded to the church. The bells stopped their crackling, and the choir started to sing, "Blessed is everyone that feareth the Lord". The congregation sang along. Anna glanced at Mother and Stepfather and took in the few relatives, friends, and neighbors who were present for the occasion. She looked around expectantly for her father, whom she had invited, but he did not seem to have come. Her dejection at his absence quickly turned to elation when she spotted Marika and her new husband. *He has six other children to care about. Why would he attend his firstborn's wedding?*

Anna noticed Miklós' sorrow when he could recognize only a couple of his comrades. None of his family could come from such a distance. Miklós saw her look at him and their eyes met. His gloom softened, and she saw in his black eyes something that she had not seen before: gratitude. She inhaled deeply and felt a warm wave inundate her chest and belly. She squeezed his arm with her left palm and they stepped up to the tetrapod in unison. The Cross, the Gospel, a golden chalice with red wine in it, two wreaths woven from periwinkle branches, and two embroidered towels lay on the table. *There is no way to escape now.*

The priest lit the candles and gave one to each of them. They knew they would have to hold on to them through the whole ceremony, so they clasped them tightly. The priest placed one of the towels in front of them and Anna stepped on it, Miklós following suit. Miklós did not know that he had made a fateful mistake. According to superstition, whoever steps on the towel, the rushnyk, first, was supposed to be the actual head of the family. Anna's face betrayed a faint smile for the first time that day. Miklós relaxed in his innocuous ignorance.

The singing stopped as they placed their right hands on the Gospel and repeated the vows after the clergyman. He put their hands together, tied them with the other rushnyk, and placed the wreath on their heads while saying his blessings. The choir began another solemn psalm that celebrated the union. When the song ended, the priest opened the Gospel and read about the wedding at Cana. When he reached the part where Christ turned the water into wine, he raised the chalice high, waited three seconds, and then presented it to the couple to drink one by one. He took them by the embroidered hand and, on the rhythm of another hymn, walked with them around the tetrapod, circling it three times.

Anna's stomach fluttered, and she bit her lips. The words, sung in Ukrainian, spoke of the love that does not burn for itself but is ready to sacrifice for the other. Where is the love the song speaks about? She is sacrificing herself, but not for Miklós. She thought only about herself. This is the way to escape. It is too late now to turn. *Learn to love. Learn to love.*

What about him? Does he sacrifice himself for me? Or is he just pursuing his own bliss?

Anna could not stop her blinking as her eyes were stinging from the teardrops filling them. Her heart was in her throat. She swallowed to push it down.

We must make amends for this to work. Both of us. Lord, give me strength!

The priest blessed both the groom and the bride, and they listened to the last hymn from the choir. The congregation moved outside the church to offer their felicitations and the couple accepted the godspeed from the young priest first. It was after many handshakes, kisses, and smiles that they could step into the chariot that took them home. Anna's parents and the guests followed them through the town, much to the amusement of the mid-afternoon passersby returning from work. They continued to smile and wave to the crowd to acknowledge the cheerful shouts of best wishes and well-meant advice until Anna felt she couldn't move a muscle in her cheeks.

Vodka and Miklós's pomace brandy were offered to the guests at the garden gate. Miklós insisted on taking Anna in his arms when stepping over the threshold of their new room, which used to be the children's room. It had a full set of new furniture, including a new double bed, as Anna had wished. Jancsi had to settle for sharing his parents' room until they could make some changes. Anna hoped, and also explained to Jancsi in secret, that this was a temporary arrangement as Miklós would arrange their move to his home in Zombor as soon as possible.

When Anna returned to the kitchen after taking off the train and the veil to make herself more comfortable, the humor of the guests was already high given the free-flowing alcohol. Mother directed everyone to take their seats at the dinner table and the feast began. The meal was simple but contained enough meat to call it luxurious at war times. Cream cakes topped up dinner, followed by cookies and biscuits brought by the neighbors as wedding gifts. It was no time for expensive presents. Anna was happy that she had new furniture.

A gypsy band arrived after dinner and set up in a corner of the garden where the paved deck and walkways served as the dance floor. Soon, couples were whirling to the melody of czardas masterfully played by the gypsies. There was also an attempt at a bereznianka, the Ukrainian folk dance of Subcarpathia, but only the older neighbors took part.

Anna changed into a homely dress as custom dictated that the bride change into one after midnight. Because of the blackout regulations, she knew they would have to end much earlier. The white-on-red polka dot dress was a special present from Mother that she adored, and it was perfect for dancing with its narrow waist and wide skirt. The bride had to dance with all the men for the "bridal dance" and Michal, her cousin, volunteered to collect the price of the dance from the participants—a way of gifting the newlyweds. She was out of breath by the time Miklós came to grab her and whirl her around, finishing the bridal dance and offering her some rest at the table. She had time only for a few sips of lemonade before Miklós asked her again for a polka.

She fell onto a bench close to the shed, reclining against the wall, hardly breathing after the fast dance Miklós had dictated. She was amazed at how he continued to spin around with a neighbor. Then she felt somebody sit next to her with a thud.

"Cousin!" Anna said and leaned onto Michal's shoulder.

"A great wedding, Ancika! Are you happy?" Michal asked with genuine interest.

"What else would I be?" Anna said, her voice wavering.

Michal looked at the hopping couples for a few seconds.

"Looks like we meet only when there's dancing," he said, and gave her a lopsided smile.

"You mean the Rusyn Brotherhood event? How long has it been, almost five years now? Another century," Anna said. In another country, another age.

"I remember you used to have ambitions..." Michal turned his gaze to the arbor above the dancing pairs. The sky beneath was becoming violet. Somebody had lit kerosene lamps to disperse the dark.

"I couldn't leave Mother alone at the shop. Teaching jobs were available only in the countryside." *Why do I need to justify myself? I found a way to break out of this prison.*

"I'm happy for you, little cousin. But never forget your dreams. They might check in at the right moment and then you have to grab them."

Anna sneered at him.

"That's not the most suitable wedding wish, is it?"

"You need no wish—you've got what you wanted. I just hope you'll have more chances." Michal kissed her brow and stood up. "Must get home before the gendarme starts harassing people after the curfew starts. We have had no air raids yet, but they still arrest anybody breaking the curfew rules."

The blackout started strictly from ten o'clock, so the music stopped an hour earlier to let the guests return home on time. Saying goodbye to the guests took another half an hour. Anna held Marika in a long embrace and she promised to visit them soon. She would be leaving for Patak the following month. Anna hoped it would not take long for Miklós to move as he had promised.

When everyone had gone, Anna wanted to help Mother clean the kitchen, but she refused with a smile.

"You go off and prepare for your wedding night, Ancika!"

Anna's cheek blanched like she had not danced at all. She looked at Mother, but she had turned to the dishes. She hoped Miklós would be half-drunk and fall asleep soon, but he had only been sipping some wine during the evening, leaving the shots to the guests.

She spent half an hour in the bathroom, and then she had to let Miklós in. She lay on their new bed and tried to enjoy the touch of the cool damask bedsheet that nobody had used before, but it did not calm her. Her stomach was in knots and her breathing became ragged. The familiar ceiling did not offer any consolation. She switched off the lights in the room as she did her last thought.

Miklós slipped into the bedroom like a tomcat. She saw nothing in the dark, just felt his presence, and heard the click of the door tongue. Another metal scrunch made her almost jump—it must have been the turn of the key as Miklós locked the door. She froze. His freshly ironed pajamas swished as he probably took them off and let them fall on the floor. Her forehead was bathed in tiny drops of sweat. The other side of the bed creaked. She felt the air move. She had held her breath for so long that she had to inhale deeply now.

"Noushika!" His voice cracked. She twitched when his fingers found her cheek. His rough fingertips were softened by a bath and she caught a whiff of floral soap. Clean and honest. The fingers did not move away but wandered around on her face, caressing her forehead and eyes and came down to her nose to halt at her lips, circling around them and finding their way across her chin, and ending at her neck. She straightened her back and raised the nape of her neck as she was feeling hot. His fingers slipped behind her neck and his hot mouth found her cheek.

She shuddered. His voice came as waves, whispering and puffing, murmuring and cooing. She did not understand a word, but she did not mind. The susurrus of the waves lulled her and washed away all her worries like they had never existed. She slipped into his voice and let it encompass her. Her hot skin was rapt as his coolness embraced it and her muscles relaxed. Her mouth found his, sweet and hot, full of doubtful but tempting promises that could not be distrusted at the moment. Not knowing how her arms were moving and how her body was reacting, she let him take her away to the flowering, scented fields of his homeland that he had spun so many yarns about.

She woke in the middle of the night. Her gaze jumped from one black shadow to the other until it came to a halt on the face next to her as her eyes became used to the darkness of the room. A soft ray of moonlight sneaked in through an incidental gap between the blackout curtains. She felt, rather than heard, the even rhythm of a satisfied man's breathing. His handsome mouth twitched, his tongue came out to dampen his lips, and he exhaled in some dream. She wondered if she had a role to play in his dream now that she was his wife. *His wife...*

She felt sore in a certain place but her body was extremely mellow, as if she was floating in the water of the Ung in June when the water was still high. The damask bedsheet cooled her hot skin and surrounded her with its feathery touch. A lavender scent emanated from the little pillows full of seeds she had collected last August with Mother. She had just met Miklós then and learned that István had abandoned her. She had found consolation in going out with Miklós and then getting engaged to him, who then cheated on her...

A coldness ran through her veins. *I enjoyed being with him despite not loving him. I let him make me his, and I liked it. What does it make me then?*

Her heartbeat doubled and beads of sweat appeared on her forehead again. One tear trickled down her temple onto her cheek, making its path slick like that of a snail. She shuddered. *Oh, Lord, forgive me! Why did you allow this to happen? Or is this what you want? Is it alright to feel...to be...when I don't love him? I promised to love him, but I don't. Am I cheating on him, you, or myself?*

Chapter 16

Anna and Miklós had to be at the railway station at eight o'clock. There was no time to waste. Both had knapsacks on their backs and were pushing the borrowed bicycles for the long trip ahead. Miklós had simple garments on, probably his only slacks, shirt, and jacket apart from his uniform, but Anna could not help dressing up for her honeymoon. She had a light blue suit on with a matching hat and white blouse. Miklós joked about her attire, playfully teasing her about how she would ride the bike later, but she did not heed him. She wanted to look like the bride on her honeymoon. When he saw her scowl, he added in a conciliatory voice full of admiration:

"You are gorgeous, my love, don't listen to me!"

The locomotive was impatiently puffing white clouds when they reached the station. With the help of a railway worker, they got the bikes into the freight wagon and then found their second-class seats. The journey took about two hours to Újhely, and Miklós was secretive about their next destination.

"It's a surprise!" he said and would not budge despite several attempts by Anna to find out where they were going. As the train turned at Csap from south to west, Anna realized that she was leaving Subcarpathia for the first time in her life. She admired the green plains that stretched as far as she could see. Lots of brooks and small lakes expanded to large water surfaces at some spots. High reeds covered the fields in most places with intermittent floodplain forests. They had reached close to Újhely when the train clattered on a long bridge over a river that widened to several hundred meters, covering the surrounding plains. Trees rising from the water fringed the original riverbed.

In Újhely, they took the bicycles and drove along the rails to the town's south end. Miklós stopped at a railway guardhouse and knocked on the door. A young, plump woman, with a small boy holding on to her skirt, opened the door. She wore an apron with flour spots (and who knows what else!) above her several petticoats and skirts. She pinned her auburn hair that was falling into her eyes behind her ear with a hand that looked twice aged than she seemed to be.

"Miki, welcome! You've arrived finally!" She hugged and kissed him, to Anna's consternation.

"Bözske is my cousin," Miklós said, patting Anna's back gingerly. "She married a railwayman and moved here a couple of years ago. My brand-new wife, Anna."

Bözske laughed, hugged her, and invited them into the cottage that had a sizable kitchen and two tiny rooms. A large cook stove sat in one corner with some water buckets next to it. A long credenza covered most of the main wall and a large rustic wooden table with four chairs around it took up the middle of the kitchen. Opposite the sideboard, a small wooden chest occupied the wall between the two doors to the rooms with a home blessing embroidered in blue thread above it. "With faith, comes love; with love, peace; with peace, blessings; with blessings, God is present; with God present, there is no need." Anna was amazed. *A Hungarian country home.*

They probably hadn't seen each other for several years, as demonstrated by the million questions fired on Miklós. Where did they meet? How is a policeman's life? Is Ungvár beautiful? He tried to answer them but had no chance: he was still answering the first one while five others had been fired in the air, waiting to fall on him. Bözske did not seem to mind and was content with the scarce answers while she skipped around the kitchen. Her attention was split between the cookstove, where she was stirring something that had a spicy aroma with a long ladle, the sideboard from where she took a few glasses, and the table around which her guests sat. In addition, the little boy had not let go of her skirt for even a second, and Anna admired the fact that she did not trip. After a couple of answered questions, pomace brandy and glasses of water materialized on the table. They raised their shot glasses to her bidding. The brandy burned like hell and Anna was happy that she was sitting. Bözske drank it like water and continued firing her questions, fueled even more by the brandy now.

The faint ringing of the midday bell at a nearby church crept in through the open window, and the door was flung open as if by command. After planting a kiss on his wife's cheek, a man in a railway uniform introduced himself. He grabbed Miklós' hand in his shovel-sized palm, shook it heartily, and thumped his back a couple of times. They were soon discussing what the weather would bring for the crops that year. Anna asked if she could change and Bözske showed her into their bedroom.

Anna could not miss how Miklós enjoyed the hot, rich goulash soup along with fresh white bread that had a crisp brown crust.

"Give me some chili, let me make it even hotter!" Miklós said with a half-full mouth and winked at Bözske.

"It's a pity I must go back to work after lunch. I would have loved to show you around," the husband said.

"We still have a long way to cover. We'll need to go, too." Miklós put a finger on his lips to stop Bözske from commenting. "The destination is a surprise for Anna."

Bözske packed some apples for them and Anna said goodbye to the couple as if she had known them for years. She hugged and kissed Bözske warmly and even gave the husband a peck on his unshaven face, which scratched her tender lips that were already burning after having the hot goulash soup. It seemed so easy to warm up to these simple, welcoming people. *Would all Miklós' relatives be so welcoming?*

Emerald hills with vineyards sneaking among their midst were on their right, and light green floodplain meadows with lush grass and wildflowers fringed their route on the left. Anna noticed the foggy clouds above the hot springs at Patak, the castle with three towers behind it like a bride lurking under her delicate veil, unprepared to show herself to the world yet. She inhaled the scents of freedom and pushed harder on the pedal to catch up with Miklós, who was keeping an even tempo and was not enchanted by the view, since he must have seen it a hundred times before.

They stopped to take a rest after crossing the next village

at a place where the river was close by. They sat on the dyke to look at the yellow water whirling by just a couple of meters below them. The flood extended to the other side of the river where there was no dyke, and they could see only small islands of meadows.

"They let the river overrun those fields for several kilometers to make fertile pastures," Miklós said and hugged her closer as a gush of chilly wind swept over them. They shared a couple of apples and drank from Miklós's flask.

Anna shuddered, but not from the wind. The uncontrolled river frightened her. Large tree trunks floated in the water, torn from the bank somewhere up north—maybe close to Ungvár. Miklós told her that several smaller rivers supplied the Bodrog, the mighty yellow river in front of them, and the Ung was one of them.

"You could sit on a raft and float from Ungvár to Tokaj," he said, and smiled at the idea. "Lots of wood comes from the Carpathians this way to Hungary."

"I prefer the train, even a bicycle is better," Anna replied, still shuddering, and stood up. "How long do you want to torture me?"

"We have passed the midpoint of our trip. Another two hours and we'll be there."

They left behind several villages with small and untended houses hidden between meadows and fields of wheat and maize grown to full height and almost ready to be harvested. The men and women working on the fields wore old and ragged garments. Some of them stood and stared at the bikers on the road, whereas others continued to hoe the potato fields or scythe the meadows with bent backs. Anna was thankful that she had changed into simpler garments than the light blue suit. Else she would have stood out more than the occasional cornflowers among the wheat ears.

Her behind was totally numb when Miklós motioned her to stop. They were at a crossroads above which a quarry emerged to open the belly of the hill for everybody to see. Pushing the bicycle, Anna stumbled after Miklós on the lumpy path that became more and more elevated. Anna had been silently cursing throughout the trip because she was feeling sick and tired and wished she could have a bath somewhere at a boardinghouse. How beautiful it would be to take off her shoes, put her feet up, and let her sore body soak in warm water! Her bicycle bumped into Miklós as she did not notice him stop.

"Ho-ho, here we are!" Miklós cried, releasing his bike and letting it fall. He opened his arms like he wanted to hug the hillside.

There were rows of vines as far as one could see. Thick, brown-gray trunks emerged from the ground every two meters. As they reached a height of one meter at the "head", the trunks were forced to run horizontally to create the "cordons", Miklós explained. These cordons were bound to wires. The wires ran along the row of vines, fastened to pickets standing between the trunks. Tiny green shoots appeared on the upward-facing brown spurs that sat at about a hand's span on the cordons. The ground showed fresh hoeing in some of the rows—somebody must have tended to the vineyard recently, maybe earlier that day.

"The shoots will be soon growing long. It will need a lot of work to keep it under control: shoot selection, spraying, binding, hoeing, and hoeing again..." Miklós touched the green shoots and caressed the cordons as if he were patting the head of a child.

"Is this all...yours?" Anna looked around in awe. A sea of grapevines.

"Ours, Noushi...seven acres. It can make sixty small barrels of wine, four hundred liters of good Tokaj wine."

"Who is working on it now?"

"My brother-in-law. We will go to them now and stay there. They live close."

"I thought we'll go to your house?"

Miklós turned and took the knapsack to his back.

"We will, but my sister and brother-in-law will take care of us, and I want you to meet them, anyway."

After a few minutes of pushing their vehicles on the bumpy hillside path, they reached a straight road on which they could finally pedal. Zombor was a ten-minute ride after that. Anna saw a small Greek Catholic Church, which they left behind at a road crossing, and then turned to a small street where Miklós stopped at the second house. The old cottage had small windows with a thatched roof that was begging for repair. Miklós had to lift the wooden gate an inch to get it to open. Anna followed cautiously because of the barking mongrel chained to its kennel and reaching half the yard. A sturdy man with a frown stepped out of the cottage at the noise. His strict features shifted into a wide smile when he recognized Miklós.

"Miklós, brother, come on in! We thought you must have gotten lost on the way!"

As they embraced, the man spotted Anna over Miklós's shoulders, standing like an orphaned flower. He disengaged from the hug and extended his arms toward her.

"And this must be the beautiful brand-new bride! Welcome! I'm Imre, his favorite brother-in-law, and now yours, too!" He placed a good smack on her cheeks, causing them to bruise to an angry pink with his two-day stubble. Anna's fragile body felt crushed under his embrace.

"You must be famished. Dinner is ready. Kati will set the

table in a snap."

Kati was a quiet, slim young woman. Her embrace was shy but warm. However, she welcomed Miklós with a bump on his shoulder and offered her cheek for a kiss. Her two small children, a boy and a girl, were running wildly in the kitchen until the arrival of the guests stopped them. They disappeared into a room and peeped through the gap left by the open door. Kati put a large open casserole with reddish-brown crispy potatoes onto a wooden plate in the middle of the large rectangular table. She invited everyone to the table while placing plates and cutlery. She smiled at Anna and asked her to sit next to her.

The potato casserole was simple but fulfilling, with the paprika sausage, eggs, onion, and sour cream giving it a special taste. Imre poured wine from a demijohn enclosed in wickerwork that he brought from the cellar through a trapdoor in the far corner of the kitchen. Anna remembered their own trapdoor at home and how cool the cellar kept the vegetables and smoked sausages, and felt a stab of homesickness.

Miklós turned the drink in his mouth for a long time before swallowing and clicked his tongue.

"Maybe even better than last year," he said, raising his glass toward Imre, who was also drinking with gusto.

"I'd say so—now that you weren't here to spoil it, bro!" The men guffawed and started discussing acidity, sugar content, and Botrytis, which was all Greek to Anna. She did not enjoy the wine, as she found it too sour for her taste buds. Kati noticed her scrunching up her nose, and she turned to Imre.

"You should give us some aszú to taste, or at least the yellow muscat, not this sour furmint." She turned back to Anna. "He refused to put some sugar in it even when he knew how rainy the Indian summer was last year." Imre made a face at her but went to the cellar and came back with a small bottle containing a lemony yellow liquid.

"I don't have aszú here, it is yet to ripen. But this muscat should be more to your liking, girls. It's from before the war!" He opened the bottle and gave it to Kati.

It was different and Anna cast a grateful glance at Kati, tasting the fragrant drink that filled her nose with the scent of elderberry, apricots, and pears, as well as other sweet aromas she could not determine.

The honeymoon couple received a room with a tiny kitchen at the back of the house that had served Imre's late parents. Miklós was still discussing something outside with Imre when they retired, but Anna was dead to the world in minutes.

The sharp crowing of the roosters awakened Anna at dawn, but she was unwilling to hand herself over to the day so early. She crept under the eiderdown and put her head below the pillow. She awakened only when Miklós shook her shoulder tenderly. The sun was high by now and peeping in through the small windows.

"Could we see your house today?" she asked at breakfast.

Miklós chewed on his bread and cheese for some time before he answered.

"We'll go around the village later and stop by. It's on the other end."

He showed her Imre's garden with the field behind it where the maize crop reached her waist and the fresh wind covered the ground with petal snow from the apple trees. Anna tried to help Kati with some gardening, but she slowed her down instead.

"You'll learn fast," Kati said to encourage her. "You could help me with preparing lunch."

That work suited her much better. The two women chatted as they cleaned the vegetables and prepared the dough. Kati left Anna alone sometimes when she needed to discipline her wild children who were running around the yard.

After lunch, Miklós and Anna took a stroll to his house. They walked through the village and the two-kilometer journey took them an hour as Miklós stopped at every second house to greet neighbors, friends, and old schoolmates. Anna arranged her face into the obligatory bridal smile and shyly accepted compliments for her attire and beauty.

Miklós pointed to a middle-sized house with shingles, and a picket fence painted green. "Here we are."

The house was old but reasonably maintained, in much better shape than Imre's. Anna brightened up and wanted to compliment Miklós when she noticed two children playing in the yard around a large cherry tree and two other older ones working in the garden.

"Who are they?"

"My nephews and nieces. Children of my other sister, Margit."

"And they live here? In your house?"

"She takes care of it. My father is supporting them with money from America, and he wanted them to live here until I got married and needed the house."

Anna's cheeks became pink.

"And now you need it, no?"

Miklós shrugged. "How can I send away a widow with four kids?"

Anna bit her lip and nodded. But her gaze burned Miklós' cheeks red.

"You shouldn't worry, Noushi. We'll build a new house. Until I am stationed in Ungvár, we can live with your parents, can't we? The vineyard will support us. We'll save money and we can prosper! Just have a little patience…"

Miklós' words sat on her shoulders like boulders. Her heart was in her stomach. She struggled to stand erect and fought back a wave of nausea. He took her hands and led her to the house. The children stopped their play and work and came to welcome the guests. The house had only two rooms. Margit eyed Anna suspiciously and asked where they were staying. Learning that they would stay with Imre and Kati, she relaxed. She offered them some tea that Anna did not want to accept, but Miklós pushed her down on a seat. Anna listened to their conversation and her fingers created ugly creases in her nice skirt as she constantly kneaded the hem. She did not touch her tea at all.

"I'm still stationed in Ungvár. We are going back in a couple of days. You don't need to worry, Margit, we'll not need this house in the next couple of years. I'm sure we'll find a solution by then."

While Margit drank her tea and complained about how difficult it was to bring up four children as a widow, the children gave them sulky side glances. Only the biggest girl, who also served the tea around the table, showed openness and smiled at Anna as if she understood her.

Anna's blood was boiling, but she forced herself to stay civil and not start a quarrel in front of these foreign people. It was not until they were back at their lodging and alone in their room that Anna put her hands on her hips. She exhaled like a steam engine and spat venom at Miklós.

"So, this is how we'll live, right? Your sister's family lives in your house and your brother-in-law manages your vineyard. And we'll live in Ungvár with my parents. You promised me something else." She was shaking and had to grab something to steady herself. Luckily, there were no plates or dishes on the table, only his discarded shirt was lying on the back of a chair. She crumpled it and threw it into a corner. Miklós squinted at her.

"I believed you! You boasted about your house, your vineyard. You told me just yesterday that we would buy a car to go there so that we don't need to cycle. What baloney!" The sobs came naturally. "What's a car for, Jesus, when we don't even have a roof to our name?"

Miklós took a chair, set it close to her slowly, and sat down. His eyes focused on hers and they were full of promises. "We will manage this, Noushika. Why would we need the house now? Who would look after it? I'm still employed in Ungvár, so we can't move here yet." He tried to touch her shoulder, but Anna pulled away, still sobbing. "Imre takes good care of the vineyard, and if the summer goes well, we'll have a lot of money from the stum by selling it to large farmers; maybe even from the wine, if he can gather enough barrels and we can make it ourselves. I swear I will look for a plot to build a house and we can have it ready in a couple of years."

"I...want to have our...own life...and not sssslave for Stepfather."

"Shh...Noushi, dear..." He cleared his throat to gain some time. "Look at it from the other side: in these times, it's a blessing we can have food in the shop where you work. We can live on what you make at your parents' place, and we can save my salary and buy the plot."

The tears seemed to dry up, but she was still sniffing.

"Money's just losing value month after month. You should buy the ground now!"

"I don't have enough. We need the summer to save and the harvest to start building."

He held out his arms toward her, but she dismissed it. She went to the small kitchen and poured herself a glass of water.

"Noushi, this is our honeymoon. Let's not spoil it." He was

standing behind her, his hands on her shoulders. Even through the dress, she felt how hot his palms were. After a second of hesitation, she moved away.

"Can we spend some time in the next few days looking for a suitable site?"

"That's exactly what I wanted to do. We will, don't worry. Come on, now."

There was no sense in fuming. They could not move now, and Miklós was right. Her parents' store provided them with a means of living. They could move once they had a house to move into. Sharing a lodging with his relatives was nonsense. *I must wait, I must wait again. I am fed up with waiting. Lord, will there be an end to all this waiting? I don't want much, only to claim my own life, to have my house, my work, my family. I am prepared to change my homeland if that is the price. I can even learn to love Miklós if that is the deal. But he must start fulfilling his promises. Or you, Lord. I don't care.*

In the last three days of their honeymoon, she was only interested in finding a suitable plot. They went around the village several times inquiring after sites but found only soggy, poor fields at the borders. Miklós made the village head promise to inform Imre as soon as something worthwhile became available and left word with his childhood friends, too. On the last day, he took her for a quick visit to the neighboring Szerencs to see the castle, but Anna did not enjoy the trip. She wanted to go home.

Fortunately, the return journey was fully by train although they had to change in Újhely. Anna breathed in the earthy smell of freshly cut tree trunks at Ungvár station, waiting to be loaded onto wagons. A wisp of a smile appeared on her face for the first time in several days. She could not believe that she was looking forward to being back at the shop, working for Stepfather. It seemed the only viable alternative.

She clenched her teeth, grabbed the handlebar of the bike, and darted toward their house along the rails. Miklós could hardly keep up with her pace.

Chapter 17

"Everything is in absolute order, Mrs. Móri!" The doctor stood up and put his gloved hands on her arm. "May I be the first to offer my congratulations?"

First, Anna thought he had spoken to the nurse. She had still not gotten used to her new surname. Married life had brought a lot of challenges to her life. It was not only the daily work from dawn to late afternoon, but also listening to her stepfather's grumbling and keeping her mouth shut at his acerbic remarks whenever he did not like what she bought or the price. He did not acknowledge that it was more and more difficult to get anything at all. The ration card system was in full swing, prices were fixed, and profits were diminishing. In addition, the official provisioning of the city was faltering. Farmers, wholesalers, and even some factories were holding back supplies to get better prices on the black market. Ordering beforehand at the wholesalers lost its meaning. She would have to stand in queues in front of the distributors every day, sometimes from midnight but definitely from dawn, just to get a day's worth of supplies. More frequently than not, something was missing. Meat was a rarity, offered only on certain days and, that too, only pork. Butter was unheard of. She visited the market frequently and tried to get some of the missing items, but the prices were horrible. Few customers could afford to pay such sums.

She washed, ironed, prepared Miklós' uniform, cooked his breakfast, packed his lunch box, and listened to him talk about his days and nights on duty when she would rather retire early and sleep. Once or twice, they went to the movies, but money became scarce, and her stepfather's comments about wasting money in uncertain times quickly soured their mood to go. There remained the occasional walks on summer evenings, but they had to return early because of the curfew.

Why the congratulations? Or... Jesus, not now... Anna could not help stealing a glance at her flat belly.

They were being careful. At least Miklós claimed he was. Having a child now was not in their plans. How could they save money for the plot if they spent money on a baby? Caring for it would mean...

She looked at the doctor, whose warm brown eyes conveyed a doting, fatherly tenderness that she had missed all her life. She gathered herself.

"Thank you. How far am I, I wonder?"

"You are in the second month only; the baby is due to arrive in late April."

Exactly a year after their wedding. What ideal timing! She stopped herself from scowling just in time.

Miklós's reaction was more blissful. His face broke into a wide, beaming smile as he lifted her and twirled her several times.

"Stop it, I'll throw up!" Anna cried, but could not help smiling.

He placed her on the table like a porcelain figure and hugged her. Her stomach somersaulted as the rank odor of his uniform hit her nose.

"Wear your other uniform tomorrow. I need to clean this one."

While her mother looked at her with a mix of tenderness and worry, her stepfather took their announcement with clear grouchiness.

"How can I manage the shop alone?"

"Dimitri, now!" Mother said.

"Inflation has already washed away our profits. They are not giving us a fillér to manage the household and now she'll be with child. I'll have to hire hands to help me run the shop. We'll go bankrupt in no time!"

Anna looked at Miklós, but he was sulking.

"Dad, I am fit to work as long as the baby comes. I'll perform my job until next April. And then I will return as soon as I can. You won't need helpers for more than a couple of weeks."

Her stepfather remained grumpy throughout dinner. He poured venom on Hitler for not keeping the fronts and cursed the war. The recent retreat of the Germans had surprised him the most.

"The Magyars have a talent to always take the wrong side. It was the same in 1918, keeping with the Kaiser till the end. And now...the Soviets have crushed the Germans in Stalingrad thanks to the impotent Hungarian army. Now they are surrounding Kiev! The Americans are landing in Italy. Starting a war is crazy, but only an idiot is losing it."

"Stop this dangerous claptrap. You'll get us into trouble!"

Mother jumped from the table and started collecting the dishes.

The young couple went to their room upon Mother's bidding but couldn't avoid overhearing Stepfather's mumbling the whole evening.

Miklós talked about how proud he was and how he would be boasting about it the next day at the station, but Anna paid little attention. She was not happy about her pregnancy. It was not nausea or the occasional strange tiredness: her goals were slipping away again. She chewed her lips and nodded at some questions from Miklós without understanding them. *How can I get a teaching job if I am pregnant or must care for a baby? True, Mother could help. I can't give up. Will the arrival of a baby push Miklós to speed up our move?* She looked at him. He was beaming as he strode across the room and gushed about how he would build the cradle, and that their room was just big enough to include the three of them. *He does not want to move away. I am stuck.*

Anna was thankful that the police gave long hours to Miklós, so he was too tired in the evenings to talk or make love. She could not have found the energy for any of that. She liked that he was content to put his hand on her belly to experience the baby moving. They slept until the merciless alarm clock rang at three and she had to leave the warm bed for another food hunt. The weather became frosty in November, and her voluminous cloak hid her condition. But her face became rounded and beautified, and she started receiving more compliments than usual from male vendors even though she had stopped applying paint and the perfume was also gone.

"How you do it, Ancika, is beyond me! You are becoming more and more beautiful by the day. If I didn't know you were married, I would start making indecent proposals!" One rather cheeky grocery wholesaler liked to flirt with her.

She just smiled, maybe coquettishly, but with good measure, and accepted the attention because a better piece of meat, an unexpected bag of nuts, cheese, or a jar of honey could appear on the counter. She soon found out that some items were impossible to sell profitably in their small shop to their lower-middle class customer base. Once she asked a vendor in the market if he could pay for her jar of honey with eggs. She received almost double the value in eggs for the luxurious sweetener that nobody could pay for in their suburb. The singular idea became a systematic plan—she collected luxury items that she either sold but preferably exchanged for basic need items, creating additional profit. She had no scruples about pocketing the extra profit she made. It was, after all, her slyness and not Stepfather's money that created the value.

Christmas came knocking on their doors again, but it was a poor one relative to those that had come before. Paprika sausages were missing in the cabbage soup for the first time in Anna's life, which was plain yellow and without the smoky aroma and the merry, reddish fatty blobs. She could only find a small bag of poppy seeds during her market hunt. It was probably two years old and made the *bobájka* bitter, and they could not fully remedy it with their limited sugar. For the first time she remembered, there were no black seeds between Jancsi's teeth when he grinned at her before dinner. The poppy must have been too bitter, even for him. Presents were missing; only Jancsi got some beautifully painted wooden soldiers that Stepfather had himself carved and decorated. Although they had mutually agreed with Miklós not to spend money on gifts, it was a disappointment to have Christmas without them. Anna felt each of her twenty-one years with double weight.

Pushing the heavy bicycle through the snow and slush into the city center was more than Anna could handle now. By February, she asked Stepfather for a helping hand.

"Katushka, the Rusyn girl from the neighborhood, is a strong girl and she could help me for a pengő a day to carry the goods. I can still handle the vendors who would be more lenient with a pregnant woman alone..."

Stepfather could not let it go without protest but had no choice. Anna had to listen to him grumble about wasting good money for weeks to come.

"The Germans are losing," Miklós said one March evening when they were preparing for bed. He seemed to have developed deep wrinkles on his brow lately that looked even more pronounced in the scarce evening light. Anna held her breath and waited for him to continue. Miklós sat down on the bed frame and sighed.

"They are talking about tactical withdrawals, but nobody believes it. The front is only a couple of hundred kilometers from the Carpathians. Today, I heard that the Soviets have taken Tarnopol, which is only 150 kilometers from the Hungarian border."

"What will happen to us?" Anna put a hand on her protruding belly and went to him. Miklós put his arms around her waist.

"I thought of sending you to Zombor. They will not let me go."

Dizziness took over her, but she tried to suppress it.

"I won't go anywhere. I need you next to me."

Miklós nodded. They lay down and held each other as closely as they could.

≈

In the following weeks, Ungvár resembled a fervent swarm of bees just before a thunderstorm. People were moving faster in the city, trying to buy everything they could. Prices went up and supplies became scarcer than ever. It was a miracle that Anna could still get something for the shop. Stores were closing for good, and every day she noticed several cars piled high with trunks going west. Anna and Katushka were returning from their second tour of the day in the afternoon on March 22nd. Katushka was pushing the bike. They had just crossed the river on the old bridge and were window-shopping on Kossuth Square as a reward for the day's work when they heard a rumble from the direction of Minaj to the south. They turned the corner to look at Liberation Street, the long alley toward Minaj, and saw a column of large trucks and cars full of soldiers coming toward them. People swarmed out of their houses to have a look and became transfixed like pillars of salt.

"They are also coming from the northwest!" Somebody whispered close enough for them to hear.

"They took Budapest on Sunday. It surprises me they have not reached us earlier!" Another man said and hurried back to his house.

A slightly distorted voice speaking in Hungarian through a megaphone could be heard through the streets.

"Inhabitants of Ungvár! Based on the agreement between the Führer and Governor Horthy, the German army is taking over Hungary's defenses." It continued with instructions to stay at home until further information.

Seeing the armed German soldiers, most people disappeared from the streets. Anna rushed Katushka to turn onto

Munkácsy Street toward their home. Looking back, they spotted heavy vehicles, with pipes protruding from small roof towers, lumbering like caterpillars behind the army column onto Kossuth Square. They stopped and it was just like the movies. Tanks, Anna recognized them. Hearts in their throats, the two women made a beeline for the railway station. They had just taken a left turn at Hotel Kárpátia when they saw soldiers marching from the station, evidently newly arrived by trains. Holding her protruding belly with both hands, Anna tried to keep up with Katushka. They were at home in ten minutes. Anna dismissed her help, closed the gate, then stopped and bent over her bicycle to catch her breath. She was in a panic that she would give birth there and then.

Miklós arrived much later, just before the curfew at eight o'clock. His brow was full of sweat and his eyes were bleary as he looked at everyone sitting around the kitchen table with eyes focused on his lips. Maybe he knew something that could explain the unbelievable.

"The Germans have occupied Hungary," he said and fell down on a seat with a thud, his mantle still on him. "They dismissed us today and asked us to report early tomorrow morning for fresh instructions. Supposedly, they will disperse the Hungarian forces."

Stepfather was beside himself. "Now we are stuck with the Germans, alright! They will make Hungary a battlefield."

Anna was breathing heavily, hands on her belly, and arched back on the seat. Miklós tried to quieten her. "We must wait for tomorrow. Maybe they will let us manage public safety at least. They need the police and gendarme; they don't speak the language and they have military tasks to fulfill for sure. It would be best if you stayed put for some days and not go out."

"And what will we sell in the shop when our stock finishes in a couple of days?" Stepfather said and threw his arms in the air.

"Dimitri, we have enough flour and marmalade. I could fry donuts." It was Mother's idea.

"What about meat? People will want lard, sausage..."

Mother was a woman of action, not of dispute. She took out her kneading board and started working.

The next day it was official. The German army was "extending its operations in the territory of Hungary in order to defend the nation from the war". Miklós came home in the evening partly relieved, but with more wrinkles on his brow.

"The police and gendarme headquarters will report to the German authorities. We are getting special tasks each day. They need us, as I suspected, but I don't like it. We have received a list of names to put under arrest immediately. All are respectable families—and I know some of them. Most of them are Jews."

Anna remembered the pictures she had seen in the newsreels from around Europe. Jews were being collected and segregated in closed part of the cities called "ghettos". She could not imagine this happening in Ungvár, where people from so many nationalities had lived together peacefully for centuries.

The donuts became a hot-selling item, especially for breakfast. After a week of waiting, the store became empty of fresh supplies. Anna collected Katushka, filled a bag with freshly made donuts, and went to the city to explore. The market was deserted; only a few vendors offered their goods. People were unsure about life under the Germans. It seemed better to hide and not give any reason to be noticed. Anna found a vendor who bought almost all the donuts in exchange for vegetables. Anna and Katushka loaded the bicycle, and they strode homeward along the Kossuth Square.

When they turned onto Mitrák Street to shorten their route, Anna took out the remaining donuts, wanting to share them with her help. She was holding a donut when they spotted German soldiers packing a black car with different goods. The loud crying and harrowing begging of a woman in German sounded from a window. They saw two other uniformed Germans coming out of the house holding several items, among them a silver menorah. A tall SS officer stepped through the door and slammed it behind him, emitting a German curse. The boxes tinkled as the soldiers threw them into the trunk. It was difficult to feign disinterest and tread among the soldiers, but Anna straightened her posture, pushed out her belly for all to see, bit into the donut, and ambled between them without stopping while chewing slowly. She bid Katushka with her eyes to follow her.

The soldiers were more interested in their loot than a pregnant woman and her housemaid returning from the market. The officer, however, had a different opinion.

"Madame!" He snapped.

Anna stopped short and turned, swallowing a too-large bite. She struggled for air and started to cough.

"Can we give you a lift? In your condition..." Anna had to gather all her knowledge of German learned at school to figure out what he was saying.

When she could finally breathe, she shook her head with a smile and waved to signal a polite refusal. "Thank you, we are very close." She only hoped she had remembered the words properly.

The officer bowed a little and instructed his soldiers briskly to finish the packing. When the black Mercedes disappeared, Anna passed the donut to Katushka, leaned on the wall of the house, and retched.

Miklós confirmed her story in the evening. "We have reported to the headquarters that the SS is making raids on wealthy Jewish people and robbing them of their valuables. I am afraid there will soon be further restrictions against the Jews."

Anna knew about the anti-Semitic views of the Germans and their hard policy that had also seeped into Hungarian laws and propaganda. She had seen it in the newspapers. After the anti-Jewish laws of recent years, more and more articles appeared about how Jews were exploiting Christian workers and how they had grown rich from the suffering of honest Hungarians. She remembered similar articles in Czechoslovakia about Hungarians doing the same with Slovaks and Rusyns, or recently, after the Hungarians occupied Ungvár, how the Czechs had exploited the Hungarians during their rule. She was always appalled when one nation threw dirt on the other. Therefore, she did not attach too much importance to them. However, there was a difference between reading articles and seeing open robbery on the street in full daylight by the authorities. She remembered the Rosenbergs from her childhood. They were such fine people. She regretted that she had believed the stupid tales about them sacrificing Christian children.

A week later, in early April, Anna stopped behind a throng of people gathered around a Morris column in the center. The mob parted when they recognized her condition and let her closer to the freshly glued poster, still damp and glistening in the morning light. "Implementation of ordinances related to Jews", the header read. It had been issued by the mayor. Jews were being ordered to wear a 4x4 inch canary yellow David star on the upper left part of their clothing from the next day, April 5th.

Her hand flew to her mouth. She remembered the pictures in newspapers and the newsreels showing Jews from other countries as they wore their discriminatory signs—from Berlin, Paris, Prague, Warsaw—everywhere. She could not imagine that it had come here, too.

She conjured up the Rosenbergs. They were standing close to each other, wearing their yellow stars and looking at her in shame. She could not decide if they felt shame for themselves or her. She thought of the certificates she and Miklós had had to collect for up to three generations back to prove that there were no Jews among their ancestors. *Am I better?*

"At least we know who we are dealing with!" said a man next to her and spat on the sidewalk. "Until now they could hide, but no more, the swines!"

Her stomach churning, Anna moved away and elbowed her way back to Katushka through the throng.

In the following days, the streets were full of yellow stars. Anna had always considered only the orthodox Jews with their caftans, hats, and ear locks to be Jews. Now every fourth or fifth pedestrian wore a yellow star. Her eyes rounded when she spotted Julcsa Novák, her schoolmate from the Slovak elementary, coming toward them with her mother, the yellow stars glowing on their coats. They crossed the street before they got too close to her, eyes downcast. Their efforts to become invisible drew tears in Anna's eyes. *Is it all we can do, look away?*

She saw the yellow stars at the shop, too. These people appeared mostly before midday or early afternoon when the shop was mostly empty. Anna was now shopping only twice a week. There was no need for daily scavenging. In the last few weeks, the turnover had become dismal, with prices shooting up like weeds after a good rain. Stepfather had never made a distinction among customers, and he was indifferent even now. Customers had changed, however. The yellow star wearers were especially humble and unsure, ashamed of their sign of distinction, and strove to finish their shopping in the shortest time possible. The customers without the stars behaved in three ways: some looked at the yellow stars with venom and contempt, some with regret and shame, and then there were people who came in the shop arm in arm with their yellow star acquaintances, indifferent to the stare of others.

Anna did not know how to behave, so she chose to do what she thought best: nothing. Smiling as she had always done, she greeted everybody the same way and did not notice the scowl of the hardliners who looked at the yellow stars with contempt. She felt ashamed but hid it. She fancied that the yellow stars were thankful for it, too.

"They will collect them and put them into ghettos," said Miklós after the Easter Sunday dinner. "Maybe it's for the better—we had to intervene in several street fights where citizens were beating up the Jews. The newspapers do not help with their fiery anti-Semitic propaganda."

"I read in the paper," Stepfather said, "that the Jews are to report next week to the authorities. They will list them as they do during a census. We'll lose them as customers if they move them to another part of the city."

Anna looked at him with scorn. *How can he think of business now?*

"They'll have to live somehow. How will they buy their food?" Mother asked.

"I reckon the city has to organize the supply chain," Stepfather said and looked at the far wall as was his custom when he went deep into thought. "I'll have to make inquiries about how we could be part of it."

"Why should we get mixed up in this?" Mother had become wary of new enterprises lately, believing that keeping to one's own business was the best survival strategy.

"We have to replace the missing turnover somehow. They have created a Jewish Council. There must be a way to get to them." Stepfather was adamant.

The next Friday, Miklós announced that he would be on duty during Sunday as the collection of the Jews into the new ghettos had begun, and he was among the policemen to guard the Glück lumberyard between Munkácsy and Mitrák Streets. He returned very late on Sunday, was in no mood to speak, and went to bed at once. He was on duty the whole Monday, but returned in time to have dinner with the family. After having the soup, he started to speak.

"We've already delivered over six thousand Jews from around Ungvár. As the Glück lumberyard is now full, from tomorrow, a new, larger ghetto on Liberation Street will open for further transport vehicles. They're building barracks to give them a place to live. They are also setting up a large kitchen to cook soup at least. Father, I am afraid, there is no chance to get into the supply chain—they are doing it centrally and there's little food. A few Jews have some food with them, but it won't last long. I don't know what will happen then."

"I'll go around tomorrow and see for myself," Stepfather said.

"I'm planning a purchasing tour to the market with Katushka in the morning. We'll come back past the Glück yard and have a look at what we can do," Anna said. Stepfather nodded.

The two women went through streets with almost every second shop locked. Big letters identified them as "Jewish stores". In some shops, the windows and seals were broken and scraps of goods lay on the sidewalk as bands of robbers had escaped with their loot in haste. Anna found nothing worthwhile to buy until they reached the market, where some village vendors offered their wares for shameless prices. Anna exchanged most of her donuts for lard and eggs, and they also found a load of wrinkled but otherwise healthy apples. They had their bicycle loaded by midday and took a route through the city to approach the lumberyard.

Anna had saved several donuts for Miklós from the morning lot. They were not warm anymore but still emitted a fatty and cinnamon scent when she opened the bag. Miklós licked his lips as he inhaled the aroma. He was standing at the main gate of the ghetto, where large trucks full of people were coming in. These people had but a couple of bags or small trunks but were wearing large coats as if they were prepared for the winter. With wrinkles on their brow but sitting erect and calm, they followed the regulations. They were hoping that segregation would protect them from the pogroms that had reared their head in the last couple of weeks, ending with the serious beating of the Jews and robbing of their belongings.

"Here, your lunch," Anna said to Miklós. She became aware of a middle-aged police sergeant's eye when she approached her husband. She planted a kiss on his cheek and passed him two donuts and some apples in a paper bag.

"Móri, you go into the office to eat your lunch! Don't fraternize outside!" The sergeant's voice reminded her of a whip crack.

She sent the sergeant a thanking smile and stepped closer to him, to Miklós's consternation.

"If you don't mind, officer, there is one donut more. I'm sure you like homemade cookies."

The sergeant's brows rose high up first, then he grinned

and took the ball-shaped sweet and hid it in his pocket. The sugar powder left a snow-white trace on the edge of his trousers.

"Sergeant, madam, at your service. Now it's clear why Móri has gained weight in the past year," he said, and let loose a loud guffaw.

Anna acknowledged the compliment with a gracious smile and looked over the sergeant's shoulders as she turned to leave. She saw black-clad people sitting outside roughly hewn barracks that had little chance of withstanding the heavy spring rains that were bound to come any day now. She waved goodbye to Miklós and bid Katushka to return to Kossuth Square. The Rusyn girl was unsure about it as it was in the opposite direction of their home, but Anna glared at her until she gave a push to the bicycle.

Anna turned right at the sharp corner on the square to follow Mitrák Street, that led to the back of the lumberyard. A policeman guarded the perimeter of the ghetto. Anna recognized Miklós's colleague, Sanyi. He nodded to the women with a clouded expression and strode behind them, taking slow steps until the next corner. There he stopped, looked around, and turned back. By that time, the women had reached the end of the lumberyard, bordered by a plank fence with sizable gaps between the individual boards. Dirty faces peered through the holes. Anna stopped cold when her eyes met the familiar, kind expression from her childhood. "Mrs. Rosenberg!"

"Ancika! Look at you. You're a grown woman now. We haven't seen you for a decade."

Anna's eyes filled with tears. "We moved from Kralicki Street..." She was embarrassed as the heat reached her cheeks due to the white lie. They had indeed moved, but several years later. She had stopped visiting the Rosenbergs much earlier.

"Oh, we moved too, to Minaj, where my husband had a business venture. Until now…" Her voice broke. "But we're together, my husband and the three children, all."

Anna looked into her bags. She had one last donut that she had saved for the walk back home.

"Mrs. Rosenberg, perhaps you wouldn't mind," she said, pushing the donut into her hand and motioning Katushka to open the sack with the apples. "Some apples, too."

Sarah Rosenberg grasped the gifts, and they disappeared into her large coat pockets in a twinkle, as if they had never existed.

"Careful, if the policeman sees you, you'll be in trouble!"

"Oh, don't worry, I know him. He's a pleasant chap," Anna said and looked to her right. Sanyi had just appeared around the bend in the street and was running toward them, shouting.

"Leave that fence immediately!"

"Sanyi, we're just…"

He drew his pistol and raised his baton as he reached them.

"No speaking to the Jews!" he shouted at Anna. He turned to Sarah Rosenberg and banged on the planks with his baton. Sarah jumped back like a frightened animal, fear in her eyes. She looked at Anna.

"Get the fuck to your barrack, you dirty Jewish bitch!" Sanyi shouted with venom and banged on the planks several times.

"We're going." Anna was able to say, and looked at Sanyi in disgust.

Miklós shook his head when Anna told him about her experience. She didn't feel it necessary to talk about the gifts, but Miklós guessed it.

"Helping Jews in the ghetto is a serious offense. You could have been arrested and we would have been in big trouble."

"Can you do something for them?"

"Have you gone crazy?" Miklós jumped from his seat and threw his hands toward the sky as if he was asking for help from somebody up there. He was not a deep believer, so Anna could not imagine who he wanted to call for help. "I saw people who had helped the Jews with gifts in the first few days. They are in prison now, some of them have fared worse."

"We cannot leave them to perish without food."

"They're getting some food, just enough to survive. I'm sure as soon as the city gets its bearings around the situation, it will set up a better supply chain. The Jews are allowed to cook and most of them came with some food with them, so they will last."

"*You* told me their supply is meager. I'm to go to the hospital any day. My parents won't help them, so that leaves you."

"Noushi, this is no game. I can lose my job or worse, I could be arrested and imprisoned! Because of some... Jews..."

"They were always kind and generous to me and Mother. I used to think ugly things about them once upon a time, having heard stupid rumors as a child. But they were doing none of that. This city has been flourishing due to their businesses, just look around to see how many factories and shops they have built. They are human, like any of us. I owe the Rosenbergs. I let them down years ago as a silly child. I won't let them down now." Anna turned her back to him and shuddered.

She felt him hugging her from behind. His face hidden beneath her honey-blond locks, she heard him inhale and stay there for a second. He always liked the fragrance of her hair that reminded him to hay. Then his fingers wiped the tears from her cheek.

"I could help in another way. Let me think about it."

Anna turned and kissed him. He tried hard not to get carried away. After all, she was to give birth in a week, according to the doctors.

Chapter 18

The authorities did not leave the Jews in the ghettos during the day.

"We need to organize workgroups," the sergeant said, his lips puckered, as he instructed the policemen at their morning meeting. "The SS needs men to handle dirty work like pumping of petrol tanks and cleaning of drains. There's also loading of goods at the railway station. We must set up women's groups to sort through the property left in the abandoned Jewish apartments, and the Gestapo headquarters needs cleaning women."

The war may end soon, Miklós thought. *Being in the police may have kept me out of the front, but today's enemies can be tomorrow's rulers. It's better to start collecting some scores that may be useful if (or when) the tide turns. Anna will be happy if I help the Rosenbergs, and later I could prove that I supported the oppressed.*

Miklós volunteered in the selection process, intending to

find Sarah Rosenberg and her husband. His sergeant was delighted to pass the task to him since he could not read and write well. It was not something he advertised, so Miklós kept his involvement a secret. He put the husband on the railway station team and assigned Sarah to the property sorting group. He also volunteered to be a guard for Sarah's group. It was an unpopular job among the policemen and gendarme, as it involved being a whole day in a Jewish apartment instead of outside. Five years of anti-Jewish propaganda through laws, politicians' speeches, most newspapers, and even movies had had its effect. It was easy to find scapegoats for their economic troubles, especially with the backdrop of the mighty German race theory. Hungarians, fighting alongside Germany, had accepted that Jews were below their level and were the cause of most current problems in their world. Most of the officers hated being with the Jews and the mere thought that they had to watch over dirty Jewish women was degrading to them. Some, however, volunteered, with the hope of plundering some valuables during the sorting.

Miklós was in a good mood until Sanyi appeared in the yard as the other guard. Sanyi narrowed his eyes when he noticed Sarah Rosenberg in the group. "Do you know that bitch?" He pointed to Sarah with his baton that he liked to knock against his thigh whenever he approached a Jewish group.

"Who's she?" Miklós asked, adjusting his belt and checking his buttons.

"Your wife was talking to her a couple of days ago at the back fence."

"Bullshit. We don't know any Jews."

"I'm not stupid, Miki." Sanyi spat on the ground and raised his baton as a warning, pointing it at him. "I'm watching you."

Miklós just shook his head, feigning disinterest, and hollered to the group of six women waiting in the yard to get into a line and prepare for departure.

The large apartment they had to inventory was full of expensive furniture, silverware, beautiful Persian rugs, and exquisite clothes. The women organized themselves in groups to make the work systematic. One policeman guarded the door, and the other walked around the rooms.

Miklós did not speak to Sarah until noon. Sanyi was watching him every minute, but before the brief break for food, he got busy with one of the young women. He dragged her into the bathroom of the apartment. Muffled cries sounded from behind the locked door. The other women tried not to notice and continued their work, unperturbed. Miklós approached Sarah, who moved away from him in fear. He produced a friendly smile and pushed into her hands a piece of lard and some bread packed in wax paper.

"Anna Onisko sends it. I'm her husband."

The woman's eyes opened wide, but she did not speak, just nodded. She slid the small pack between her ample breasts.

"We'll go around the market in the evening. Some vendors stay late and offer their goods to the Jewish work parties. It's forbidden, but if you have some money, you could try to buy food. I'll try to cover for you."

Sarah nodded again with a mix of disbelief and awe in her hazel eyes and then continued to sort the expensive clothes from the heavy baroque wardrobe. They heard the key turn in the bathroom lock. Miklós leaned toward another woman who was taking out silverware and crystal glasses from a beverage cabinet.

"Careful with that, woman, you'll pay dearly if you break it," he said in a gruff voice and moved to the main door with his back to Sanyi, who was coming out of the bathroom.

Sanyi adjusted his clothes and shouted at the women. "You can have your lunch now if you have some." He chortled at his own joke, took out a large sandwich from his bag, and bit into it. Miklós had to settle for a donut, his lard and bread gone.

As Miklós had promised, they went around the empty market on their way back to the ghetto with the last vendors putting their tired wares into boxes. Sanyi stopped at a vendor offering bottles of schnapps and started to bargain with him. Miklós nodded to Sarah, who quietly stepped over to a vendor selling old potatoes. She gave him a banknote for three potatoes that she could grab in seconds. Sanyi's attention was elsewhere. Another woman did the same thing, and the vendor received a bundle of cash for his sprouted potatoes. They disappeared into the big pockets of the women's coats.

The sergeant was standing in the yard when the group arrived.

"Line up for body search!"

Sanyi and Miklós pawed the women one by one. Sanyi's prodding concentrated on the intimate areas. He squeezed a young woman's breast and then reached into her cleavage with a lustful grin. Miklós pulled out a potato from Sarah's pocket.

"What do we have here, hah?" he shouted, raising the small yellow tuber with inch-long white sprouts above his head for all to see. Sarah's eyes froze with shock.

"Leave it, Móri. Look for valuables," the sergeant said, and pushed Sanyi with a sneer. "Search below the coats, you moron!"

Miklós dropped the potato in front of Sarah, who grabbed it and hid it in her pocket. She looked at him with angst and confusion. Miklós gave her a covert wink after turning away from Sanyi.

❦

"They took her to the hospital today," Mother said, and put some plates on the table in preparation for dinner.

"How? Why?" Miklós said.

"It's time. Her water broke."

Miklós turned and ran out of the house. The hospital was on the other side of the city between the market and the cemetery. Life and death. Such morbid thoughts. His mother had lost two children during his childhood. He could not stop hearing her screams and sobs. Running proved good for his mind, and by the time he reached the hospital gates, his mood had turned. *She'll be alright. She must be.*

They did not let him see her. Childbirth had started. He marched back and forth in the corridor. He could not sit down. His hands, locked together behind his back, were grinding each finger in a perpetual whirl. At first, he was alone, but soon another father joined him, who was much older and quieter. He sat down and looked in front, almost disinterested. *Probably the fifth child or more*, Miklós thought as he stopped for a moment before strutting again.

She is such a fragile girl. Even during pregnancy, she only gained a belly, albeit enormous. One could not have guessed by looking at her from behind that she was with child. Her slender form did not change. Yes, her breast swelled for his pleasure, but she remained his slim Noushi.

Her pregnancy was easy. She had not complained at all except lately because of the extra weight she had to carry. She had trudged from the kitchen to their room the day before with her back in an arc to counterbalance the weight of the baby.

What is taking so long?

A nurse came out and announced to the middle-aged father that he had had a boy. He stood up with a grin and went inside with the nurse. *Why are they done when Noushi is still there? We were here first! It should be our turn.*

It was almost midnight. Miklós was sitting on the bench, holding his head in his palms. Another nurse appeared. "Mr. Móri?"

"Here!" He got up with a start.

"You have a healthy baby girl. Will you come and see her?"

"Yes, sure, and the mother?"

"She's exhausted and must rest, but she's alright."

The nurse smiled faintly as he let all the air out of his lungs and collapsed on the chair again. He did not even know he had held it back and for how long.

They had names ready for both cases, boy or girl. A boy would have been László on Anna's request. Miklós could choose the girl's name.

Veronika was one of three children in the room. He was allowed to look at her through a window. The nurse pointed her out to him. She could have pointed at any of those babes, they all looked similar. He wanted to see Noushi.

"It's not possible. Come back tomorrow." The nurse was adamant.

Anna's mother was elated at hearing the news about her granddaughter and went to visit Anna and the newborn the following morning. He could visit only after his shift late in the afternoon. In the morning, he asked Mother to pack three large sandwiches and several donuts and made a show of taking with him a bottle of wine to celebrate with his colleagues. The wine had to be enough for the celebration, and he gave two of the sandwiches and the donuts to Sarah when unseen. She tried to pay him with some banknotes, but he refused, feeling embarrassed.

Noushi had just finished nursing Veronika when he stepped into the room. She beamed when she saw him, and he presented her with a bough of lilac he had picked from the garden opposite the hospital. Her thin lips, still slightly pale, curved into a wide smile as she took a whiff of the purple clusters, and a speck of pink spread on her cheeks. She was as beautiful as a mother could be.

He took Veronika in his arms, first clumsily, then with pride, and walked with her to the window to inspect her better. She opened her eyes for a few seconds and he saw Anna's likeness in them—the same brown with green dots in it. He planted a careful peck on her blond hair and smelled her baby scent. He had never been so contented in his whole life.

Miklós left both his women to get some sleep. Anna was tired but burning to ask about the Rosenbergs. However, the room did not offer any privacy because of her three roommates.

The following day, she ventured out of bed for a walk so they could talk. Anna cringed when she heard about Sanyi's suspicions, and how Miklós had to play around to baffle him. She sucked in her breath when Miklós told her about the body search.

"I think Sarah understood why I made a show with the potato. I succeeded in putting her husband into the working group at the railway station so that he could get some food. I also give her half of my rich lunches every day. Your mother must think I have gained an enormous appetite now that I am a father," Miklós said. It was a relief to grin like two co-conspirators. Her kisses tasted of gratitude and warmth spread through Miklós' body. As she let her head rest between his chin and collarbone, he allowed himself a smug smile.

Miklós got a day off to collect Anna and their daughter from the hospital and indulged in a taxi for themselves. Looking at her, he noted how she seemed to be proud of the bundle in her arms as she stepped into the car like a lady. He had fixed up an old second-hand carved crib and painted it. Anna's mother had lined it with soft white linen, pink cushions, and a quilt. Anna's soft lips trembled when she entered their room and spotted it.

"We have our own family now," Miklós said. He knew what it meant for Anna.

"I don't know why. They simply stopped the work groups," the sergeant said to Miklós. They were in the office after assembly in the yard early one May morning.

"It will be hard to engage the people all day inside the yard. They'll become restless and they are already hungry. The thin soup the city supplies is not enough for them to survive. The water is not enough for drinking, there's almost none for washing, and the latrines are full," Miklós said.

"I know, I know. It's not our worry. They'll move them soon, I heard. I'll call the headquarters for instructions. The commander has already collected all the Jewish barbers and directed them to shave off the children's hair and cut the women's hair short. This can help against lice."

"Move?"

"There's not enough workforce in the factories and fields in the hinterland. I have heard that work camps are being built to accommodate the Jews there. We will be rid of them for sure—this cannot go on forever." The sergeant put on his cape and stood up to signal that the conversation was over.

Miklós saluted and left the room.

When Miklós broke the news to Anna, she began to wring her hands and pace the room. "We have to send them some food. Is it possible to send packages to the ghetto?"

"I saw some packages coming. The guards opened them, and maybe even stole the better stuff, but some families got the rest. We must find somebody to deliver it. I can't be involved," Miklós said.

Anna did not hesitate for even a minute. She collected flour, bread, lard, rendered fat, old apples, and potatoes. Stepfather protested so Anna put some banknotes on the table. She had some savings left from the good barters in the city. "Consider them bought, Dad."

Stepfather muttered something to Mother about irresponsible people but went back to the shop.

Anna contacted a neighbor who was a postman and asked him to deliver the package officially to the Rosenbergs in the ghetto. She wrote a Minaj address on it where the Rosenbergs used to live. Miklós promised to monitor the delivery and try to prevent any pilfering.

In the evening he told Anna how the postman himself delivered the package at the pre-agreed hour when Miklós knew he would be guarding the gate. It had all the stamps, as if it had come from Minaj. Miklós reported to the sergeant, and he commanded a search of the package. When the searching policemen saw it was but low-quality food, they let it go. Miklós only relaxed when he spotted Mr. Rosenberg pick up the package and carry it into their barrack.

They could send another package the following week. After the weekend, Miklós came home and hugged Anna.

"They will transport them tomorrow."

"Where?" Anna's voice was strangled with fear.

"We don't know. A special squad of German soldiers and

Hungarian gendarmes is organizing it."

They put a package together again. Anna sneaked into the pantry and the garden after dinner. If Mother noticed, she did not comment. This time they packed food that could be immediately consumed: zwieback, lard, radishes from the garden, and a big flask of water.

"They could travel for a day or two. They must have water." Anna paced the room, her brow in a net of wrinkles and gaze jumping from the food to the door to the kitchen, then to the window, and then to Miklós. "I'll go to the station and give them the package myself if there's a way. I'll wear some old clothes and a headscarf for cover."

Miklós shook his head, but did not try to divert her from the plan.

Anna waited at the corner of the railway station building at six o'clock in the morning. She spotted some women and men also waiting there. If they were travelers, they would be waiting inside the station. She suspected that information about the moving of the Jews must have leaked through several channels and reached others as well as her. The people did not seem to be waiting for relatives to arrive because they were all holding small and large packages.

Anna had borrowed Mother's old brown coat from before the war. She pulled her brown scarf low over her brow. Her throat constricted when she noticed a group of gendarmes stepping out of the building sometime around seven o'clock. They systematically checked the papers of the people waiting at the square and sent some of them off with harsh words and impatient gestures. Anna strode across the crossing to the corner of Hotel Kárpátia on Munkácsy Street and lined up in front of the newsstand. After purchasing a newspaper, she turned and went into the hotel cafe. The white malt coffee had turned cold as she drank it for an hour while sitting there. Eventually, the gendarmes disappeared and let some people wait in the square.

The din from the street was audible through the open windows, and it brought her outside. Looking to her right, in the direction of the city center, Anna spotted the black-clad throng accompanied by the gendarmes and the policemen. The hundreds of yellow stars made it look as if the world had turned upside down, creating a night sky on the street. They trudged along the road, dragging their meager belongings— two-three bags or trunks. Even that was too much for some of the older people. They had to stop occasionally to catch their breath. The gendarmes pushed them on with the butt of their guns. One old woman fell, and a gendarme kicked her belly. A few young men tried to help her up, but found themselves facing bayonets. The old woman remained at the curb, not moving at all.

As the front of the throng reached the station building, Anna spotted Miklós marching along with the woeful mob. His almost imperceptible nod directed her to look behind him where she saw Sarah, her husband, and their three children who had grown into lanky adolescents. She remembered them as toddlers in her childhood when she used to light the fire on their Sabbath. She strode to them with determination and thrust the package into Sarah's arms. Their glances locked. Sarah's lips cracked into a pallid smile, but her eyes glistened as a tear dropped onto the cobblestones, lost in the dirt, and marched upon.

Anna withdrew before she was noticed by any policeman or the gendarmes and sought refuge under the awning of the hotel entrance. She continued to look at the sad procession for a few minutes, then turned left to go home. As she stomped across the rails, she looked back. A long train of cattle cars was waiting at the station. The gendarmes were pushing black-clad figures into the open sides. Anna could not take her eyes away. She stopped counting the figures thrown or pushed into a wagon when she reached eighty.

Her blood boiled with frustration at how the people were being handled. She hoped they would still reach the hinterland camps in good health—the journey to any place in Hungary should not take longer than one, or in the worst case, two days. Then they could receive proper food and do work. But still...she imagined soldiers pushing her into the same cattle wagon with Veronika in her arms, Stepfather and Mother thrown into a corner without air where they trembled and hugged a crying Jancsi...just because they were considered Rusyn...or Ukrainian...if there were different rules...would a Hungarian husband save her? Save them all?

Anna gasped and the shivers running through her spine froze her. Her brow felt ice-cold and pearls of sweat slowly slipped down to her drumming temple and burning cheek.

And what am I? And what is Veronika? Are we more Hungarian because of Miklós than my mother is? Or Jancsi, whose father is Ukrainian but speaks Hungarian like me?

The road to home had never been so long. She took Veronika from the crib, held her to her breasts, and wept.

Chapter 19

“I t would be best for all. You could have your own household and not be in a small room with the baby,” Mother said.

“We could rent your room to a student or a worker. It could partly replace the lost profit in the shop. We don't even need you to work there nowadays,” Stepfather said and coughed a couple of times as he realized that his arguments held no attraction for the young couple.

Anna did not think that her dream of having her own home would come true in such a twisted way. This could be the first step to real independence. But at what price?

“You are incredible! You want me to take a stranger's apartment?” Anna's cheeks were hot and her voice stepped up an octave. Her stomach turned, and she dropped her spoon.

“Noushi, it's nobody's apartment. All the Jews have lost

their property. Now these apartments are in the hands of the city and they are offering them to us to resolve our situation. So why not use it?" Miklós said and sliced the lard to go with his bread. They had a thin soup of vegetables and only a cold meal afterward. There was no meat, and he refused the lentil dish Mother had prepared.

"You're also against me?"

"It really makes sense. We'd have our own home. I'd be closer to the station. You could even find a job in the city and we could pay a nanny to watch Veronika. I have seen those apartments. They're large, fully furnished, and have hot water and central heating."

"What will happen when those families return?"

Only Stepfather's spoon, clinking against the plate as he ladled his lentil dish, broke the silence.

"The city will find a solution," Miklós said. "They may not be back for several years. During that time, we'll live comfortably and save money for a house of our own."

"I am at home here and will go nowhere." Anna stood up, having lost the last speck of her appetite. She ran into their room to find comfort in her daughter. She would surely not be against her.

How can I intrude into another family's apartment? They lost their property by law, they say. By some laws the Germans dictated. And now we are jumping on the quarry like hungry wolves. Disgusting!

Life in Ungvár had altered beyond recognition. Anna still went out for her purchasing tours but mostly returned with a light bicycle that was easy to push back home. Supposedly, ten thousand Jews had been collected from the city and almost the same number from the vicinity. The transport vehicles had cleared the ghettos in two weeks. By June, with one-third of its inhabitants missing, the city had become a lifeless skeleton and was less than a shadow of its previous self. She could not find a decent craftsman: no plumbers, no electricians, not even a shoemaker to repair their old shoes. Most of the shops were closed. The Christians who had taken over the Jews' businesses were incapable of running them efficiently. More Rusyn and Slovak were spoken on the streets. Anna rarely heard her mother tongue: half the Hungarian-speaking inhabitants had been Jews. Factories had gone bankrupt without their competent owners and management. Stepfather deduced from the papers and through talking to his friends that the city was struggling with finances. Offering the apartments of the Jews for rent was one way how the city tried creating a stream of income. She wanted no part of it.

The front began to edge closer every day. The Red Army was on the other side of the Carpathians. Miklós assured Anna that the Hungarian army had built tough defense lines in the mountains to stop the Russians.

The air raid alarms rang every second day after mid-August. Anna became frantic whenever she heard it. There was no bomb shelter close to their home, so they just ran down to the cellar below the store.

They heard a sharp, long whistle and then some blasts. Veronika cried out, so Anna tried to cover her ears to the earsplitting sound.

"God in heaven, this must have hit close!" Mother put her hands together and her mouth moved with no sound. Later, they found out that bombs had fallen on Radvánc, just half a kilometer from their home.

After a couple of days, Miklós arrived home with more creases on his brow than usual. He burst out before dinner.

"Romania has switched sides. They have joined the Soviets."

The silence around the table was thick. Mother's hand stopped midair with the ladle.

"Humph!" Stepfather said. "Hungary's finished."

Anna's eyes jumped between Miklós and Stepfather. "What do you mean?"

Stepfather went to the sideboard and took out a bottle. He put it on the table and poured two shots. Miklós nodded and grabbed one. The men looked at each other and knocked the shot back in unison. Stepfather filled the glasses once again. "The Soviets can now turn to the south and encircle Hungary. Or leave it to the Romanians so they can concentrate on breaking through the Carpathians."

The shrieking of the sirens became a daily event after that. Sometimes bombs fell on fields or buildings. Next Sunday, the sirens wailed nine times. Miklós forbade Anna to go to the city as the raids had become more focused on important targets, factories, and street crossings. Fighter planes were even shooting onto the streets with machine guns. Anna trembled with fear every day for Miklós as he continued to be on duty, mostly walking the streets, running errands, and helping ensure public safety in the aftermath of the bombings.

By the end of September, Miklós had made a decision.

"You must go to Zombor," he said one evening in a toneless voice after they had retired to their room. Anna was preparing to feed Veronika before putting her to sleep.

She looked at him and saw enough fear for both of them.

"The forces will evacuate the city soon. They will send me to the west, probably to Budapest, to help defend the capital and move valuables and documents. Who knows what else will happen? You must go as soon as you can."

She forced herself not to sob, but could not prevent tears from falling on her daughter's white swaddle. "How can I move with the baby? Where will we live?"

"I'd written to Imre requesting him to accommodate you. His answer has just arrived today confirming that you can stay in the same small room and kitchen we had slept in during our honeymoon. We'll send some packages by train and you'll travel only with the child." Miklós hugged them both close. "Take all the money we have saved and some other things, too, that you could sell. You always said linens make a good trade in Hungary. You can't remain here. The Russians might break through the mountains..."

His arms offered weak comfort that night, but she clutched his body with all her might.

Preparations to leave took Anna more than a week. She bought bedclothes and all the linen items she could find in the neighborhood. She filled three trunks with their belongings that they sent by a still-functioning post.

Stepfather did not make a fuss about her leaving—she could imagine it relieved him to have fewer mouths to feed. Mother shook her head in desperation and held her to her chest for several seconds too long.

"You could come with me," Anna whispered in Mother's ear.

"We are at home here, Ancika. Dad is Ukrainian; the Soviets will not harm us. You have a Hungarian husband."

Anna wiped the tears from her eyes and put up a bright smile as she turned to her little brother. He threw his arms around her neck, not meaning to release her.

"You choke me, you little tick!" She chortled. Somehow, it came out as a moan.

Miklós made sure he was not on duty that morning so that he could walk her to the station. Anna had a small bag and Veronika in a swaddle, wrapped in a large shawl. She tried to look elegant in her winter coat and beret. A squeezing sensation in her throat was building up during the walk to the station, and she could hardly breathe.

"When will I see you again?"

Miklós was speechless. She knew he did not have an answer, so she let him escape without it.

"You will come to us soon, won't you?" She saw his black eyes glisten with unshed tears and put her arms around his neck.

He nodded and held her tight until he heard Veronika's protest at being crushed between them. He breathed a light kiss on the child's pink cheeks and held on to Anna's trembling lips for several minutes. The conductor's whistle broke their embrace, and he helped her climb the high steps into the train car. Anna looked through the window, sticking her wet cheek to the cold, dirty glass until his waving arms got lost in the white clouds of smoke left behind by the train.

The horse-drawn carriage Imre had fetched carried Anna's three trunks from the station, depositing them at the front door. She had to unpack and organize her new life. Trying to find some excuse to delay the task, she changed Veronika's nappy and tried to feed her. Fortunately, she was hungry and sucked with relish. Anna sat on one of the two chairs in the kitchen. She looked around the small room and fortified herself. The double bed, now bare, with only a cumbrous straw mattress, awoke sweet-and-sour memories from their honeymoon. The bed would be half-empty. *For how long?*

Being sated, Veronika fell asleep. Anna opened the massive rustic wardrobe and noted that it would be more than enough for her meager collection of clothes and the little she had brought for the baby. There would be space for the extra linens. She could use the small commode under the window to change the baby. The bare whitish walls did not offer the warmth of home. The task was left to the stove, standing in the corner next to the door of the kitchen. She wondered if it could heat both the room and the kitchen. There was still a good part of the Indian summer weather left, but the nights would soon be cold, even freezing. She must talk to Imre about firewood. Or coal? She did not know.

The sideboard in the kitchen must have been there since the monarchy—its ivory paint missing in more places than not. A wooden bucket in the corner reminded her that there was no tap water. The wobbling table with the rickety chairs would have to do until she got Imre or somebody else to repair it. The faint smell of mildew hit her nose, and her inhaled breath ended in a deep sigh. Heating and ventilation would hopefully make it disappear.

The next morning, she asked Imre to look for a cow, a pig, and a couple of hens in the village for her. Her money was losing its value, and she needed milk. She would have to learn how to care for them. Her sister-in-law, Kati, had been keen to teach her about the garden the last time. She could give her a hand with the animals, too.

The animals arrived in a couple of days. She was amazed at how cheap they turned out to be—in Ungvár they would have cost triple the amount. She convinced Imre to accompany her to the market to Szerencs on Saturday, and they boarded a carriage together. Anna had a trunk full of bedclothes and linen with her. On the way back, the trunk was full of bacon, sacks of flour and corn, honey, and some vegetables. She had bartered her goods rather than sell them because she had a lot of cash, and how to spend it gave her a headache.

Imre promised to support her with food for a couple of weeks in exchange for her help with the grape harvest. She had never picked grapes before and was looking forward to it. Imre set the time for an early November day. It was freezing at dawn when they sat in a carriage along with all the neighbors. Another carriage with big tubs in it followed them to the vineyard. Everybody received a piece of bread and smoked lard, accompanied by a shot of pomace brandy. But the similarity to Miklós' tales about grape harvesting ended there.

Anna first put Veronika in a large basket between the rows on the ground, but she constantly cried, so Anna had to carry her on her back. The child was warmer there, close to her mother, and Anna's movements lulled her to sleep. The baby's weight, added to the weight of the grapes in Anna's wooden bucket, took its toll on her soon. By eleven o'clock, she was so worn out that she dropped to the ground as soon as Imre announced the lunch break. There was no warm stew or soup, but bread and lard again with some sweet peppers. The sun was up and the sky did not have a speck of cloud warming them soon. After her feed, Veronika fell asleep and Anna could put her in the linen basket. She worked uninterrupted for an hour before she had to put Veronika again on her back. It was a nightmare. She wanted to show that she could be just as useful as other women, but the amount she had picked was hardly half of the others. Imre did not comment until the end of the day.

"You're a hard worker, Noushi," he said and offered her his canteen as they swayed in the carriage on the way back from the vineyard. Anna could not straighten her back and looked at him from a stooping position, savoring the sweet wine from the bottle. It warmed her insides and brought back life into her.

The next day, Imre dropped her at the press house, at the lower end of the vineyard, where women were treading on grapes in big tubs and squeezing out the juice with big presses. Half of the team was still picking the grapes and supplying them to the pressing team. Anna learned how to pick out the aszú berries from the bunch of grapes. They looked like raisins but had a gray mold that sometimes covered them fully. They also had a characteristic smell that she remembered from the wine Imre had offered her the day before. Despite her initial aversion to the rotten grapes, she boldly tasted one and found it extremely delicious. *Good old raisins with a twist.*

The women poured the separated aszú berries into a sizable vat and trampled them into a paste. When Imre stopped by the vat, he smiled as he watched Anna trod in it with the other women. He explained that the men would pour old wine on the paste and leave it to leach out for a couple of days.

"This is the treasure of Tokaj, the aszú wine," he said with pride, and pointed to the waiting wooden barrels. "It will ferment and mature in those casks for at least two-three years. Then Miklós and I will make good money."

The harvest satisfied Imre, and he wanted to write to Miklós about it, but he did not know where to send the letter. He started some inquiries and came to Anna's door in the evening. "The Russians took Ungvár last week. I heard from a captain today," he said with gloom.

Anna stared at him and swayed with Veronika in her arms. Her first thought was of Miklós, who must be somewhere in Budapest by now. Then she thought of her parents. She somehow knew they would survive, being so insignificant in the entire scheme of things. This was what Mother had always been an expert at.

At dawn, Anna finished feeding the pig and the hens. Holding Veronika's basket in one hand and an empty bucket in the other, she stepped out of the barn. A strange man was standing in the yard with legs spread out and naked to the waist, washing himself in a washbasin. He was huffing and puffing as he splashed cold water on himself. The weather did not help: it had become freezing cold during the night. When he noticed her, he covered his hairy chest with a gray towel and rubbed himself.

"I beg your pardon, madam. Feldwebel Klaus at your service!" He spoke in slow German.

He was in his mid-thirties and had a bashful smile. His jacket with the insignias on the shoulder lay on the brim of the well. She nodded, wished him a good morning, and then went to the well to pull up some water to wash the bucket. The soldier grabbed his jacket to clear the space. Imre had told her that soldiers were lodging in different houses in the village, but she had not expected a German. Imre also had to offer a room to the soldiers, and his family squeezed into the other one.

"You speak German? What a relief! My Hungarian is not the best and has not improved during the last six months," he said. He looked into the child's basket and tossed his arms into the air. "You have a baby girl! I have three myself at home in Sachsen. They are older, though."

Anna told him her name when he asked, but was in no mood to fraternize. She went inside as soon as she had washed the bucket.

In the evening, he found her in the barn milking the cow.

"For your daughter." He put the small packet next to the

pail, saluted, and disappeared. She opened the chocolate bar only late in the evening because she had forgotten about it. The temptation to finish it was enormous, but she only took one cube and munched on it for half an hour. Veronika savored the rest of it for a week, one cube a day.

He brought her something every day. An apple, some biscuits, salt, sugar, and even a slice of smoked meat. He explained that he handled the food supplies in the army. Anna was embarrassed and did not want to accept his offerings, but he was adamant.

"Eat well so that your girl is healthy."

She noticed the holes in his shirt and uniform and offered to repair them. Herr Klaus refused, but Anna said she would not accept anything from him unless he agreed. He sat in her kitchen while she darned his clothes and entertained her with stories that were never about the war. It turned out that he had a butchery back home, and when he learned how close Anna was to his profession, there was no end to his tales about his experiences. He talked about how to prepare the best cuts and was willing to share other trade secrets. He had not seen his family for two years and did not mind the recent German retreat at all.

She found some used linen that she did not need and gave it to him for foot cloth. He thanked her by grabbing her hand and kissing it. Anna went purple. "It is late, you should go," she said, taking her hand back.

Herr Klaus apologized, saluted, and left. Anna found a bouquet of frozen asters in front of her door the next morning.

The German and Hungarian armies had emptied the village two days later. Herr Klaus did not come back to say goodbye. He was a shy man. Anna wondered if he ever got back to his village close to Dresden.

Chapter 20

The language was unfamiliar to her. Even when shouted, it had a lilt to it. The soldier's head popped up from behind the fence at the back of the yard. He aimed his rifle at Anna and accompanied his angry yelling with gestures of his gun, sending her back into the house. Anna released the handle of the draw well and let the pail fall back, clattering on its way. She ran inside without her water bucket and hid in the room with her child.

Two soldiers entered the kitchen a minute later. They had a strange helmet with a wide lower rim and wore a sandcolored uniform Anna had never seen before. They aimed their rifles at her, moving around the kitchen and looking into the room. Squeezing Veronika to her chest, Anna stood near the bed and held her head high, despite her terror. Veronika wailed. Anna rocked her left and right to quieten her.

"Soldiers? Germans?" One soldier yelled at her in broken

Hungarian.

Anna shook her head. "Gone. Two days ago."

The soldier nodded and stepped closer to her. Anna moved back and bumped into the bed. "Bread? Food? We hungry."

She nodded and plodded toward the kitchen with insecure steps. The soldiers did not stop aiming their guns at her. Anna pointed at one of the drawers on the sideboard and a white enameled jug. "I have bread and milk."

She stood in the corner, rocking her daughter, and watched how the soldiers sat on the rickety chairs, broke lumps of bread, and washed it with milk directly from the jug. They exchanged words in that melodic language that seemed chirpy and funny from the mouth of soldiers.

They shoved the remaining bread into their pockets, mumbled something, and left. Anna plopped into a chair, exhaled an unbelievable amount of air, and held Veronika close to her, kissing the top of her head.

Imre slipped into the door after some minutes. "Were the Romanians here? I hope they haven't hurt you."

"Romanians?" Anna asked, gaping at him. "They have just gobbled my bread and milk."

"Come into our rooms. The Russians might be here soon. It's better if we're all together."

They remained locked the whole day. It was after dusk when they heard the noise. Imre peeped through a hole in the blackout curtains and reported that tanks and several trucks were moving along the street. A van stopped in front of their house and soldiers dropped to the ground.

The door to the kitchen slowly opened. The soldier who entered had a wide face with accented cheekbones and almond-shaped, almost black eyes. His fur cap with the earflaps down had an unmistakable red star in the middle of the brow. He held his gun ready but was not aiming at them.

"Deutsch?"

Anna stood and answered in Ukrainian, explaining that the German and Hungarian soldiers had retreated a couple of days before. The soldier gaped at her as if she was an apparition, then he started to laugh. His Asian eyes almost disappeared into their slits.

"Where are you from, beautiful girl?" His Russian had an accent she could not place.

Anna took Veronika in her arms for protection.

"Uzhhorod, Subcarpathia."

"Zakarpattia! We were there a month ago. Your town has been liberated!"

Another soldier stepped in behind the first, who had moved into the room to make space for him. He seemed to be his superior and was wearing a coarse woolen trench coat with a stripe and a star on the shoulder. Instead of a machine gun, he had a bulging pistol holder attached to his belt. The first soldier explained to him something in rapid Russian and he looked at Anna with interest through piercing blue eyes. He inquired about her name and then nodded.

"Mrs. Móri, you are to report to the village mayor's office in the morning. We need interpreters."

The soldiers turned and left. Imre was quick to lock the door after them.

Anna arrived at the office of the village head at seven o'clock. Sándor Gajdos, the mustached, gray-headed corpulent "mayor", as he liked to title himself despite Zombor being just a big village instead of a town, was sitting behind his table. He was in deep discussion with another man who seemed quite his opposite: scrawny, small, and bald-headed but similarly in his fifties. Gajdos greeted her and proceeded to give introductions.

"Pali Balogh, our other interpreter. He was born in Zombor but fell into Russian captivity in the first war. We're lucky he made it back to Zombor by the early twenties. Anna Móri is our new citizen from Ungvár. You know Miklós, her husband, the policeman, don't you, Pali?"

Balogh nodded to Anna but did not make a move to stand or offer his hand. Anna stopped extending her arm in time and mirrored his nod.

"We need to be extremely careful with the Russians. They are already searching for local communists to put them in charge. I know there are some at the railway. I heard they also have somebody from Tokaj they trust..." Gajdos rubbed the back of his neck. A gleam of sweat covered his forehead despite the cold in the room.

They did not have more time to continue the discussion as two Soviet officers arrived, accompanied by two other soldiers. The younger officer was the one who had ordered Anna to report to the mayor's office, Junior Lieutenant Popov. He introduced the senior officer as Major Pachenko. The older man looked askance at Anna with narrowed, deep brown eyes below a frowning unibrow that lent him a foul image. He must have been in his early fifties, judging from the creases of hard battles and winters on his red face. A sweeping smile pushed away the wrinkles around his eyes as he heard her answering his questions in Ukrainian. He looked now like a loving father, at least as Anna imagined one would be.

"*Doroha divchinka*, how did you get here? Popov claims you're from Uzhhorod, *pravda*? But you speak Ukrainian like me, *bozhe moy*!" His Ukrainian surprised Anna. Anna had to bite her tongue not to ramble about her Hungarian heritage, so she told him about the Rusyn ancestors of her mother, about Stepfather from Galicia, and her Ukrainian teacher. Major Pachenko offered Anna *pálinka* she politely declined. She needed to concentrate on the language she did not use so frequently.

After an idle but mirthful chat about Ukraine and its people, Major Pachenko's attention turned to Mayor Gajdos. "We need a couple of things from you, Mr. Gajdos. For one, we want you to co-opt *tovarish* Kovács in the village council to represent the interests of the Red Army. He'll make sure there's good cooperation between the local authorities and our forces."

He bid Anna to translate and disregarded the scrawny Balogh. Gajdos nodded as Anna translated and scribbled notes onto a piece of paper in front of him.

"Second, we need you to compile a list of all men between the ages of 17 and 45 years and all women between 18 and 30 years. We need some help with restoration work due to war damages here and there. *Malenkaya robota.*" The major clicked his fingers as if saying how easy those works were supposed to be.

Gajdos raised his gray eyebrows but, again, only nodded.

"Third, we'll name a requisition committee with your participation. Don't be afraid, *tovarish* Kovács will help you collect grain and livestock from the village for the use of the Red Army. We highly appreciate your help in our ultimate victory over the fascists."

The little pearls of sweat that were appearing on the mayor's brow started to slip toward his eyes as Anna finished the translation. He stopped making notes, trying to stand up.

"Major Pachenko, the village is poor. People have hardly

enough for themselves," Gajdos said in a wailing voice, opening his arms.

The major did not wait for Anna to finish. He shrugged his arguments with a wave and stood. "*Tovarish* Kovács will be with you by noon. I expect your compiled list of the inhabitants by next Monday. We should set up the requisition committee today and start working immediately."

He waved Anna and Popov to join him and marched out of the room.

Anna worked with the Soviet officers till noon in a makeshift office. They addressed the complaints of the village people, created pamphlets about the regulations, and made lists of requisition requirements. She asked to leave at noon with the excuse that she had to tend to her daughter. They let her go but asked her to come every day in the morning for a couple of hours.

She went to take Veronika from Kati and saw Imre sitting at the table in the kitchen with his head in his hands, shuddering. She looked at Kati with questioning eyes.

"He was in the vineyard. A rocket hit the cellar. Soldiers took the remaining barrels, the neighbors said," Kati whispered with resignation. Anna's hand flew to her mouth to stifle a cry.

Imre raised his head and looked at Anna. The pain deformed his face and his eyes were swimming in tears. He opened his mouth, but just a croak escaped his lips. Anna dropped into a chair. *All that work with the grapes...*

"Nothing has remained," Imre answered Anna's unvoiced question and dropped his head on the table with a wail that broke out from the bottom of his throat.

"I could talk to the Soviet officers..." Anna said, looking at Kati.

"It could well have been the Romanians. It happened the

day before yesterday. The neighbors were not sure. They had just seen figures from a large distance carrying the barrels away." Kati held Imre's hand, standing above him with a tearless, frozen face. Anna noticed the children hiding behind her skirt only now—they were quiet, paralyzed by the shock of their strong father weeping.

The silence sat on Anna's chest and she had to collect all her strength to breathe. *Oh, God, have you not had enough yet? What else will you send on us? Must we be grateful that we live at all? If we have nothing to eat, how long will it last?*

Veronika's babbling and her gurgling laughter shook her out of her malediction. She floundered into the room and took her from the bed. She had a child. She had work to do.

Being with the Soviet officers several hours each morning proved to be invaluable. The Soviets were preparing a whole train to send the inhabitants for restoration work. Anna spotted a paper with the planned route and gasped. Names like Csap, Uzhhorod, Lvov, and Kiev were familiar, but there were at least another ten names that she had never heard of. This route would not be a couple of days long.

She looked for Gajdos and Balogh the following morning and told them about the train. Her predictions of a transport far east into the Soviet Union shocked them and they looked at her with wide eyes.

"I just can't believe this. What are we going to do?" The mayor's cluelessness repulsed her.

"If we want to save people, we must offer something in exchange," Anna said.

"They already want ten cows, twenty pigs, and ten hundredweight of wheat. We'll die of hunger if they take those."

"What about wine and *pálinka*? Everybody in the village has a vineyard and *pálinka* is more than enough in every household with a man."

Gajdos and Balogh looked at each other and then met Anna's look. They had sour faces.

"We could give a couple of barrels..."

"We need much more. We are paying ransom for our people. I suggest twenty barrels of wine and fifty liters of pomace brandy. The offer must overwhelm them to be successful. I'll talk to the major."

There was more whining from the two men, but eventually, they agreed and promised to talk to the most well-off farmers about the offer. Anna went to find Major Pachenko at his headquarters. She had to wait two hours for him to come back from an inspection.

In the past week, Anna became well accepted in the Red Army headquarters as word spread that she was doing interpreter work for Major Pachenko. She even received some smiles from the soldiers and officers who otherwise tried to be rigid and indifferent.

"Ahhh, our beautiful *divchinka*!" Major Pachenko doddered into the room and fell into a seat that creaked under his weight. The alcoholic smell around him was unmistakable. Lieutenant Popov peeped in at the door, but the major sent him away with a wave of the hand. His face was red and sweat beads were pooling into little streams on his temple. His dull smile changed to a somewhat livid one when he looked at her. "Did I tell you I have a daughter back in Moscow about your age? And a granddaughter, too, born just before the summer. She'll walk soon..."

Anna saw her chance. "She must be the same age as my daughter, Veronika. She was born at the end of April."

"Oh, that's fabulous! You must come and show her to me.

It would help me imagine my own grandchild..."

"I envy your daughter. My father is not curious about her granddaughter."

"How's that possible?"

Anna related her mother's story with tears in her eyes. "I would want a father like you. You'd have never behaved as he did," she said.

Major Pachenko mumbled something under his Stalin mustache and adjusted his belt. He looked at his table and searched among the papers. Eventually, he took a large sheet with a lot of names on it.

"Annychka, don't be afraid. Your name won't be on the list. You have a child to take care of. We want to pick up people with German names."

"Major Pachenko, this is a Hungarian and Rusyn village. Did you see the Greek Catholic Church on the east side? You must have come around it. All the Germans escaped with the retreating soldiers..."

"Hmm...we need people for restoration work..."

"If we don't have people, the fields won't be prepared and we'll starve next year..."

"But this is just *malenkaya robota,* just a couple of days..."

Anna looked at the major and held his eyes for some seconds. Eventually, he turned away. His face was redder than usual and he said in a low voice. "We need to fill the trains."

Anna nodded, then raised her head as if a thought had occurred to her. "I was wondering...this village could be useful to the Red Army in a different way..."

"What do you have in mind?"

"Wine and grape brandy... A bomb destroyed our cellar, and we lost everything, but other farmers...they would be willing to part with some barrels of wine and bottles of brandy in exchange for forgetting about the list..."

"Wine...and brandy?" Major Pachenko's eyes sparkled, and he looked at Anna with an amazed expression.

"I'm sure you'd keep your side of the deal, Major Pachenko. I'd expect nothing different. My father promised to support me when I went to high school. He never fulfilled his promise. You're not the type."

Major Pachenko stood up with a stagger, adjusted his jacket, and cleared his throat. "You can be sure of that, Annychka. A Ukrainian officer always keeps his promises."

"I'll come with my daughter tomorrow. You'll like her, she is an angel." Anna stood to go.

The major produced a lopsided smile, shook his head from side to side, and wagged his finger at Anna. "I didn't know we had witches in Zakarpattia, Annychka. Maybe it's good that you moved to Hungary."

Anna looked at him with her downcast eyes and nodded. "I'll talk to Mayor Gajdos. Thank you, *bat'ko* Pachenko."

"Annoushka, could you let me in?" The local schoolmaster stood in front of her door.

A whirl of snowflakes hit the kitchen floor as she opened the door to let the man enter. He hurried to close it and gave her an apologetic smile as he shook his coat and stamped his feet to get rid of the snow.

"Better to be inside in this weather," he said, "but I needed to talk to you."

"Have a seat, Mr. Csákány. I am afraid I have nothing to offer you," she said, ashamed.

"Don't worry, Annoushka, this is not a social visit."

Anna sat opposite the man, who did not even take off his coat.

"Now that the front has gone and will hopefully never come back, we are trying to organize life in the village. We want to open the school again." He took a checkered handkerchief out of his pocket and wiped his nose that had started to run in the kitchen's warmth. "Our teachers disappeared last year. Either to the army or in the transport of the Jews. The Arrow Cross men shot the last one in October, poor Pista Szabados, God rest his soul. I figured we have a couple of young women—Klára Márai and Ildikó Hárs—with high school diplomas in the village who want to help. Then I remembered you are here, too, and you are a teacher. So, I came to offer you a job. Would you like to join us at the school?"

This was what she had always wanted. She could finally teach! She could earn a living. There would be food on the table again.

She stood and searched in the boxes on the sideboard.

"What about a weak tea? I must have something somewhere. I got it from the Russian soldiers..."

The schoolmaster guffawed.

"Is that a yes?"

"With pleasure, Mr. Csákány. I am indebted to you that you thought of me at all."

"Apart from me, you seem to be the only skilled teacher around. It would be a pity to let you be idle. Would you have some brandy to line that tea?"

Anna sighed and took the bottle she had received from Imre when she had helped with the harvest in the vineyard. It was a good moment to celebrate, after all.

The school started right away in the first week of January.

Anna got the younger grades along with Klára, a smiling, blonde young woman of her age from a civic family. She had graduated from a grammar school in Miskolc, the regional big city, and then married a winemaker and ended up in Zombor. A neighbor was taking care of her two children, three and five years old, while she put herself into meaningful work that thrilled her.

Kati agreed to watch over Veronika along with her children during school hours, and Anna could devote herself to her first-ever job as a teacher. They split the small children among themselves. Klára got the first and second grades and Anna the third and fourth grades. Mr. Csákány and Ildikó Hárs took care of the higher grades.

Anna tried to catch the children's attention with games and stories. She used examples for teaching math from her commercial experience that they could relate to. There were only a couple of books to help with the curriculum, otherwise, the teachers were free to teach as they wanted. It was Anna's idea to introduce singing—she just had to learn several Hungarian songs from Klára. Fortunately, she found sheet music books in the little school library with well-known folk songs. The children loved her singing classes and she could then cajole them to enjoy her math lessons.

Mr. Csákány had agreed with the teachers that they would be paid with natural products the children's parents could provide: milk, curd, cheese, butter, eggs, dried fruit, and occasionally cured fat. It was a welcome possibility and hard currency. Anna could change some of it to get other items she needed. Veronika loved sweetened curd and thin slices of dried apple served as excellent chewing material to soothe her gums when she was suffering from teething pains. Anna had stopped feeding her, which gave her the freedom to pursue her teaching activities.

A lot of snow fell in February, almost a meter high. The village became a sleeping giant under a tender eiderdown. Traffic almost ceased, and it was an everyday battle to get out of the house to the school. But Anna did it with a smile on her face, turning the shovel with growing expertise to clean the path from her apartment to the street and beyond.

She was content like never before. They had little, but could have done with less. The small room and kitchen were warm thanks to the wood Imre was regularly giving her in exchange for the milk from her cow. Veronika was growing and was healthy. Anna was proud to provide for her little family, and although she thought of Miklós and sometimes longed for his embrace, she did not need him. It was an exhilarating feeling.

The late February sun warmed up the classroom, and it was cozier than other times. The sunlight played through the hair of the pupils as they looked at their papers, busy with their tasks. Anna wrote some sentences on the blackboard for the third-grade pupils to copy. The fourth-grade children read a tale loudly from a book she had copied for each of them for a reading exercise. She walked between the benches to check the work of the children and stopped next to little Marie. The child was frowning at the blackboard, chewing the end of her pencil. The graphite left black marks around her little lips. She then looked down at her paper.

"What is the matter, Marie?"

"I wrote the spelling of the word *faragott* differently. Mr. Szabados had taught us to write it with double *t*."

He was the teacher who had been shot in October, Anna recalled. She looked at the blackboard.

"I made a mistake deliberately to see if you could find it. You have eyes like a hawk, Marie!" The little girl beamed and Anna was able to hide her blush by turning to the blackboard and adding another *t* to the end of the word, as probably correct Hungarian grammar required. She was not sure. She checked the work of other pupils and found that half of them wrote the word with one *t*, whereas the other half put a double *t*.

Oh, my God! What other mistakes do I make every day that the children do not notice and learn the wrong spelling? If only I had more books here to check. Grammar books? Mr. Csákány could help. But how to approach him without embarrassing myself?

Her shortcomings rushed inside her in waves. *How can I teach in a language I have never learned myself at school? I will teach them poor grammar. They will realize it later and hate me. You learn it wrong and then you will always write it wrong. I am crippling a new generation.*

Tromping through the snowy streets and reaching her home was more difficult than on other days. She knocked on Kati's door, but nobody answered, and she noticed that the door was locked. *What's going on? Did she go to our rooms?* She went to her own apartment and heard wailing from behind the door. It was unlocked.

She tumbled into the kitchen. It was as cold as outside. She spotted Mother straightening up from the commode below the window where she was changing Veronika's clothes, putting the soiled, brownish garments into a bucket. The pungent smell made her stomach churn. Anna ran to her mother's side. "Mummy, how on earth..."

"I'll manage it now. I was wondering where you had toddled off and why this poor baby was alone in the cold, lying in her shit, wailing for who knows how long." Mother said with venom, and embraced her grudgingly, patting Anna's shuddering shoulders.

Chapter 21

Mother began to interrogate Anna as soon as Veronika had fallen asleep after being cleaned and fed. Anna rekindled the fire, and the small room and kitchen became cozy again. They whispered until the kitchen was warm and then closed the door.

"I teach. Finally, I teach! And I am capable of taking care of our little family!" Anna cried.

"I can see how capable you are. You leave my granddaughter to the mercy of irresponsible neighbors who let her freeze to death and cry in her soiled nappy!" Mother hissed and threw out a hand toward the closed door. "Teaching! Wake up from your dreams. The shop is running again and, with your contacts, we could make it flourish."

"Miklós may come home soon," Anna said. "My place is with my husband. I want to wait for him."

"He is not here, and God knows how long it will take them

to release the captured soldiers and policemen. He might even..." Mother coughed and took a sip of the tea Anna had prepared. "You could wait for him in Uzhhorod."

"I don't want to work for Dad again!" Anna jumped from her seat and started to pace the kitchen.

"Listen, Ancika. The Soviets are putting things back in order. Life is normal again. It's another order, stricter, but it allows us to prosper once more. Why do you need to teach children in a poor village for a pittance when you could do what you are really good at and make real money?"

Mother's eyes followed Anna as she squirmed on her rickety seat. "We can find a solution with Dad—you are a grown woman now and he has to respect that."

"Look at this house with its crumbling walls and thatched roof. Is this how you want to live?" Mother grimaced as she looked at the old sideboard with its chipping paint and the door that did not close properly, causing a nasty draft to reach their feet.

Anna fought back, but Mother could not understand her longing for independence and pride in feeding her little family on her own. Mother did not live for ideals. She was a pragmatic mother who wanted her daughter and grandchild to be safe. As soon as she had learned that the front had gone through Eastern Hungary, she had asked the authorities for permission to travel and find them. She had boarded a cattle wagon and traveled for a full day to reach them, a distance of 130 kilometers. Her train had to wait on idle rails several times to give priority to important army trains.

"It's possible to get permission to travel. With your contacts, you could find supplies. Industrial goods are missing in Uzhhorod. You could get it from Hungary." Mother grabbed Anna's hand, and she had to stop pacing. "Our customers would pay handsomely for candles, matches, shoes, and clothes. And the peasants from the Carpathians come with their food that would be worth gold in these poor regions now. This is a great opportunity!"

Anna thought of her city and her daily purchasing trips. She had been happy then. It was also a form of independence. Her heart jumped in her throat as she remembered how she had haggled with vendors and how she had served customers with a smile on her face. How they had left satisfied and how grateful they had been to have made a good deal.

Stepfather? *I am not a child anymore, but a married woman. I can prove my worth in business. He cannot terrorize me any longer.*

I can forget about my grammar faux pas problems at school. She felt her cheeks going pink as she recollected little Marie's frown in the classroom. Could she survive another humiliation? She loved children and wanted to educate them. But did not want to teach them wrong things.

Was teaching for her at all? After losing out on multiple opportunities, when the job fell into her lap unexpectedly, she realized that her Hungarian was not good enough. *I am a stranger among my people. I need to learn the written language somehow. If I had István with his vast knowledge of Hungarian literature and the language, he could have helped me. This is too much of a burden to shoulder alone.* Another thought occurred to her. Perhaps God does not want it. He was driving her back to trading. She had always believed in divine guidance.

I will not survive if another teacher or Mr. Csákány find out about my bad grammar. Mother is right, even if she does not know the real reason. I have to give up teaching for trading.

Anna felt empty. She had learned so much that she couldn't use. *I should fight! I should improve!* But now is not the time and place. Miklós is not here. Mother has come. Veronika needs safety and a warm home with her granny, not Kati, who could disappear anytime. She had apologized for being a bit late and for forgetting about the baby. But nothing had happened, right? It could have if Mother had not arrived on time.

In the morning, Anna went through the school day in a daze, and after classes, she knocked on the door of the headmaster. She steeled herself to not let her voice dither.

"Mr. Csákány, I will leave this weekend. My mother needs me. I'll go back to Ungvár until Miklós returns. I'm sure Klára can manage my class." The headmaster's mouth fell open, and she did not wait for him to close it. She turned and escaped from the school.

She put together a trunk and some food for the journey, and they boarded a cattle wagon on Saturday morning toward Uzhhorod. *I must be used to the old name again. The Soviets have changed it back to what it used to be in Czechoslovakia.*

"Your place is in Uzhhorod. You know those vendors of yours. I can't split myself between purchasing and serving customers in the shop. Mother can't handle the heavy items. You stay and *dostat'no!*" Stepfather's face was red like the ground paprika Anna had acquired from an adventurous Hungarian merchant from Szeged who had come to Uzhhorod on business. It had taken Anna two weeks to revive her contacts and build some new ones in place of the missing ones. The city had changed. Nobody spoke Hungarian on the streets anymore. Mostly Rusyn, Ukrainian, and even Russian were spoken—mainly by the Red Army soldiers.

"Dad, Jancsi is also here! He's a sturdy boy and can help Mum when you have to buy things. I want to go to Budapest. The capital needs food and they say it's possible to buy a lot of useful things on the black market."

Her brother was eager to help. Anna was counting on his support—the shop was much more fun than school.

"Jancsi must go to school, he must study." Stepfather was adamant.

"Dimitri, let the girl try her luck. There are not enough goods in Uzhhorod. I can manage the shop in the morning and Jancsi will help as soon as he comes back from school. Right, Jancsi?" Mother said and put a hand on Stepfather's shoulder.

He was boiling and could not sit anymore. He jumped up and darted to the yard, slamming the door shut with a deafening bang.

In the afternoon, Anna went to the station and met Zsófi, the young girl who was keen to accompany her on the trip. She was three years her junior, lived in a neighboring street, and had attended a Hungarian school. Anna remembered her from the group of children playing at the riverside. A couple of days ago, Zsófi had admitted to her that she had heard through the grapevine about Anna's plans to travel to Budapest to try her hand at the bartering business. The opportunity to make some money lured Zsófi. An adroit girl, she stood tall and was strong enough to carry a heavy bundle the entire day. She also had some relatives in Budapest, so Anna agreed. Anna was glad for the company, too. They easily found a train bound to Újhely, then a connection to Miskolc, then to Budapest. They would be traveling the entire night.

The cattle wagons had enough space to lie down, but the draft coming through every gap between the planks did not let them sleep. They shivered even in their woolen coats and, after some hours of misery, they huddled together for warmth.

Russian soldiers were supervising the travelers at every

station. The Red Army papers they had acquired in Uzhhorod, written in both Russian and Hungarian, proved to be useful in ensuring a swift check. Other travelers were not so lucky. The girls watched with dread as the soldiers dragged away an old man, beating him with their rifle butts.

They lost count of the many stops during the night. The rail line had been recently repaired to be used as single-railed, so their train was frequently halted on a sidetrack to let another train running in the opposite direction go past.

The train rattled into the Keleti Station of Budapest well after dawn on a bright morning. Their bundles, covered in dirty gray clothes, did not attract attention. But hidden under their clothes, they had real treasures: a large wheel of ewe cheese, beans, cured fat, lard, oil, and a dish with butter. With the bundles on their back, they looked like anybody around them—displaced residents after the war looking for a place to stay. The girls stepped through the destroyed doors of the station and stopped.

Anna had never seen anything like it. She had never been to a city bigger than Uzhhorod. Buildings with five to six stories lined the boulevard in front of them but were in total ruin. Entire walls had disappeared and debris covered the street. In some places, the debris had been piled into high clumps, and children were scavenging for anything that might be useful.

As they approached the city center, they noticed some shops open on the boulevard with empty, mostly broken windows with handwritten signs letting people know they were back in business. A cobbler, a cosmetician, a clothing store, a plumber, a solicitor...and a grocery shop. Anna hustled her companion to enter the shop.

The shelves were empty, as was the counter apart from a weighing machine sitting in the middle. An elderly, graying man stood behind the counter and leaned onto it with his palms as he followed them with suspicious eyes. "Morning. We have only yesterday's bread, canned sardines, and kerosene."

"Then we have more than you, sir," Anna said and let her bundle slip from her shoulders. "I wonder if you would be interested in some fresh cheese from the countryside, among other things."

The man's eyes almost popped out of their sockets. He stepped to the door and looked out onto the street, once to the left and then to the right. He then called out, "Hédi, come and replace me for a few minutes, will you?"

A woman of similar age as them appeared and took his place behind the counter. She gave Anna and Zsófi a once-over and nodded to the man. He invited them to the back of the shop with a nervous movement of his arms and hurried to close the door behind them. They found themselves in a storage area furnished with a desk on which some papers were kept. It must serve as an office.

As Anna and Zsófi opened their bundles and took out the ewe cheese wheels from the wax paper, the tangy smell hit the grocer's nose and his Adam's apple began to dance up and down. He rushed to take a penknife from his pocket. Anna nodded, and he cut a small piece of cheese and put it into his mouth. The young women giggled as he moaned.

He wanted to buy everything from them. Although the price he offered was double what they paid for the goods, Anna made him add a big stack of matches, which was a sought-after item in Uzhhorod.

They left the grocery store with empty bundles but a thick wad of cash and continued toward the Danube River. The cityscape became more ruinous but otherwise full of life. Groups of people were clearing the debris, a newsboy was hawking a paper, and people were hurrying through the streets on errands—always carrying some bags or packages. Red Army soldiers watched over the road crossings, occasionally asking for papers. They slipped through the checkpoints again without difficulty.

When they reached a square with high twin palaces on each side, they spotted a gigantic ornamented dirty ocher frame behind which the green of a hill shone through. The ocher frame was standing on the bank of the river. The chains of the bridge were underwater, and the pillar on the opposite bank disappeared in a mess of steel. As they looked to the left and the right, the ruins of all the other four bridges came into view, leaving the surface of the majestic Danube River almost undisturbed. To the north, at an island in the middle of the river, they saw a simple bridge structure being built by soldiers on stakes. It was too far, so they would not get to the other side.

They sat down on the stone steps of the bank, and Anna contemplated the destruction. It was like meeting a famous actor you knew only from the movies, in person, just to realize that he had a bald head and more wrinkles on his face than the plowed fields in the fall. She could not believe this destruction could be reversed. She thought it was final and the city would never recover.

They ate a simple lunch from the supply they had kept for themselves and set out for Zsófi's relatives' house to spend the night. It was late afternoon when they found the crowded tenement building at the edge of the inner city that had remained relatively untouched by bombs and gun shells.

The lady of the house offered them two cots in one of the dark rooms where two other members of the family also slept. An unendurable itching awakened Anna in the morning, and she found clusters of angry, red welts on her neck, wrists, and ankles. The ceiling was almost black, even though it was past dawn.

"Bedbugs, it's normal," Zsófi said, and asked for some soda bicarbonate. She made a paste with the white substance and applied it to the red marks. By the time they hit the road, the itching had become bearable.

The lady of the house suggested they go to the market in Teleki Square, close to the railway station. A throng of people crowded the aisles between the stalls. They had to jostle their way to the vendors and had a hard time haggling for candles, matches, cigarettes, yeast, sugar, ground paprika, shoes, and clothes. The vendors grimaced at the money they offered and asked if they had food to sell. Anna decided they would exchange their wares next time instead of using money. The market seemed the right place for it.

Their bundles were again full, and they were out of money by the time they returned to the railway station. It was only noon, but the train bound eastward was already standing on the platform. They went to find a place they could lie down. Anna decided that she preferred the draft to the bedbugs.

The handsome profit from the Budapest tour convinced Stepfather of the benefits. They had easily tripled the money they'd invested, and the acquired items from Budapest attracted more customers to the shop. Anna made the trip every week now, without the need to sleep over in the capital, saving her from the discomfort of the bedbugs. She knew where to go to sell her goods and buy the industrial gadgets for their shop. She would catch the train back the same day in the evening. Zsófi became her constant travel companion.

It was not without risk: the soldiers were sometimes violent and not all of them piped down when spoken to in Ukrainian. In those cases, they tried to save themselves by offering some brandy.

The train route went through Zombor so Anna would always place herself close to the car door and shout down to the platform, asking the locals about her husband. She always got the same answer: no, they hadn't seen Miklós. If a local boarded their car, she would interrogate the person. Who had returned to the village? How was Imre doing? Many of the soldiers had returned, but there was no news about Miklós. She consoled herself by imagining that, as a policeman, he must represent a more complicated case.

The thought that he might not return at all would work itself into her mind, squirming, wriggling in her neurons, and not letting her be at peace. She did not love him, but felt an attachment. It was not just the fact that they were married. They had lived together for a year and a half. He had become a part of her, and he was the father of their child. Some words stood out from Veronika's burble, but *Dad* was not one of them. She would learn to say *babusya* or granny first. Even before *mami,* mum. Although she tried to speak to her only in Hungarian, the Rusyn at Stepfather's household was overwhelming. Mother used it respectfully in his presence.

What would she do if Miklós... No, it was not possible. If he came back... no, when he came back, she could get away from Stepfather again. They would build their own home. Together, they could save enough money to buy a plot and build their own house in Zombor. She could then return to teaching slowly after taking some grammar classes. Or she could continue trading and Miklós could tend to the vineyard. Miklós must return home, she decided. He had done nothing wrong, hadn't killed people. Quite the opposite, he had helped the Jews. He had done his job as a policeman, ex-ecuting the orders of his superiors.

She felt weak alone. She knew she could stand up to Step-father and maybe she could even get Mother to support her. Having somebody to rely on was too comforting to decline.

Anna started to say her prayers again before falling asleep each night. Relying on God made her stronger in the same way as thinking about Miklós. And her prayers seemed to help. The days became warmer, and the debris disappeared from the streets and train tracks. Cars with wooden benches replaced the cattle carriages on the trains to Budapest, and the route took less time to complete. Trading was better than before, but there was no news from Zombor.

Chapter 22

The fresh morning breeze carried the fragrance of the blooming acacia along the railway line beyond the station. Anna crossed the last rails and joined the path leading to their house. She bade farewell to Zsófi, who turned onto the first street on the right. Anna had taken a liking to the girl. Their chatter shortened the journey, it was less dangerous when there were two of them, and she knew Budapest better because of her relatives. She could point out some special shops to find the items they needed. And, most importantly, Zsófi had become a confidante even though she could not replace Marika. Anna hadn't had the time to look for her after her friend had moved to Patak.

Close to her house, the sweet smell of linden trees in full bloom enveloped her nostrils. She opened the gate and the buzz of bees welcomed her. They swarmed around the flowering grapes of the arbor that now covered the bigger part of the concrete deck in the inner corner of the L-shaped house. The door was locked. Anna raised her eyebrows and searched for the keys in her purse. *They must have gone to the church, it's Sunday. Mother loves to push the pram around.*

The coolness of the kitchen refreshed her. The earthy smell of freshly cleaned vegetables and the pungent aroma of smoked bacon, prepared in the morning to be ready for lunch, took over the fragrance of the flowers outside. Her stomach made a protesting growl, and she stole a slice of bacon with a piece of bread. Lunch would be some time away yet, and she hadn't had breakfast. She dropped her bags in her room and went to wash her hands and face in the bathroom. The towel was missing near the washbasin. *Mother must have collected everything for a wash and forgotten to put out fresh ones.* She scurried into her parents' room to the robust chest of drawers.

The towels were usually in the lowest drawer, but it seemed like Mother had rearranged them. *Oh, here they are!* She picked up a beige cotton hand towel and a larger one for bathing when she noticed some papers below them. Curious, she reached for the envelopes. *Mother keeps all her documents in that scuffed suitcase under the bed... Does she hide something from Stepfather?* Anna grinned. She turned the envelope on top and read her own name on it, written by a hand she had once known so well.

She grabbed the entire stack, forgetting the towels on top of the chest, and darted into the kitchen. Four envelopes. Same hand. The lingering fragrance of cedarwood. Or was she just imagining it?

Dear Ancika,

They moved me immediately and permanently to Miskolc. No explanation was given, but there seems to be some political reason behind it that I cannot fathom. It must be a grave misunderstanding.

I have no time to reach you, I must leave today. Send me a letter to the Miskolc address below so that we can be in contact until all this is clarified. I hope you can still come for the agreed weekend and we could arrange for your stay here for longer... forever if you also want it. Looking forward to your answer soon.

With love, István

Anna could hardly read the last few sentences through her piling tears. The pressure in her lungs was unbearable. She saw his violet eyes again, the elegant suit, his delicate figure. She heard his voice and remembered his smart thoughts she did not always agree with, but that fascinated and stimulated her. And the cedarwood, his fragrance, was everywhere...

Her tears fell on the envelope and rolled onto the letter. By the time they stopped, the old ink was almost unreadable as it had dissolved into blotches of blue with a silver lining.

Three years. A husband. A child. A world turned upside down. No chance to rectify that.

Mother plotted this; I am sure. She never wanted me to be happy. She just wanted me not to walk the road she had. Find a prosperous husband, she said. And where did I end up?

A key rattled in the lock, hesitated, and then the door opened. Mother pushed the pram inside and entered the kitchen. Anna looked at her. Without a word, she took Veronika from the pram. Mother's eyes shifted to the kitchen table onto the envelopes. She opened her mouth to speak, but Anna put a hand up. Veronika blinked at her mother with heavy eyelashes and a faint smile. Anna took her into her room and put her into the crib. In minutes, she fell asleep.

Anna steeled herself, closed the door to her room, and turned to Mother.

"Now what? Fedor was a criminal, as I told you. I could

not have allowed him to bamboozle you any further, especially not allow you to escape to Miskolc like you're in some dime novel." Mother put a pot on the stove, threw in the slices of bacon, and let it sizzle.

"You manipulated me into marrying Miklós!" Anna hissed through her teeth.

"Now you have a respectable husband and a beautiful child."

"You spoiled my biggest love, Mother! You let me think he abandoned me."

"It was for your own sake, mind you."

"I could have been a teacher with a partner I love."

"And you could be dead now, following a political criminal, shot by the Germans or the Hungarian Nazis, what's their name—the Arrow Cross."

"I could be a widow now with Miklós being who knows where, if he is alive at all..." Anna said, and could not believe she had said it.

Mother turned to look at Anna but said nothing. She hesitated and then reached for the cutting board. The vegetables dropping into the sizzling fat sounded like marching soldiers in a battle.

Anna hated her. The pain squeezed her throat. Her vocal cords deflated like the strings of an abandoned guitar, incapable of producing any sound. She turned and staggered into her room with the last of her strength.

Anna went to the market early and returned home before noon with valuable food items that would ensure traffic to their shop and also leave her with some goods for her next tour to the capital. She thanked God that her bicycle was still working, not so much for riding—the chain fell down at every bump on the road so it made little sense to ride it—but at least it was useful for pushing the heavy bags and sacks to and from the market. That worked even when the chain was down.

It was a relief to be away from home. She had stayed in her room most of Sunday afternoon to avoid her parents. It was more than enough to hear Stepfather's grumbling about the wretched traffic in the shop. On Monday morning, Mother baked donuts so that they had something fresh to offer in the shop. Anna forced herself to steal some for breakfast, having eaten almost nothing the previous day. She did not want to exchange a word with Mother and slipped through the door.

Yesterday's idea had been circling in her mind the entire morning. *What would happen if Miklós did not return?* Her stomach churned, but the thought came back again and again, lurking in the background when she was bartering, and then jumping to her mind in full visibility when she finished a deal and was alone. It shocked her so much that she winced. *All the soldiers have returned by now, but there was no news about him. Could I manage with Veronika if he's gone?*

What kept her in Uzhhorod at all? Stepfather hated her, and she now knew how Mother manipulated her. *Can I ever forget it? Can I ever forgive her?* It is not home here anymore. Is there one in Zombor? Without Miklós? *I can't leave Veronika with Kati for a few days to go on my trips. Should I return to teaching?*

She looked at the Rusyn peasant in front of her as if she wanted an answer from him. He offered his wheel of fresh cheese, smiling and pressing her to taste a wee bit. It had a slightly tangy, sheep-like smell but tasted like heaven. She offered the peasant her last package of cigarettes and matches, and he seemed content.

"You want to vanish again? And who will help me keep the shop supplied?" Stepfather's grumbling turned to a bellow when Anna announced that she would travel to the capital the next day.

"I have left you half of my purchases, half of the bacon and the cheese, some meat, and curd. You can manage for a couple of days with the traffic we get."

"I wish your husband returns soon to curb you!" he said and slapped the table with his newspaper while going into his room. Mother did not comment. Since their quarrel about István's letters, she seemed to be unusually quiet when Anna was in the room.

Anna left for the station early in the morning with a cursory glimpse at Mother's broad shoulders while she stood over the stove watching the sizzling donuts. *I have Veronika to love me, at least.*

Zsófi was already waiting for her. She had her own sources and boasted of the sardines she had bought from the soldiers. Her biggest treasure was a large sack of dried beans that Anna envied. *Miklós would love it!* "Relatives of our neighbors came from the country and offered this from last year. It will be like gold at the capital market," she said with a giggle. "I am dreaming of bartering it for new shoes for myself."

They made a good pair, and it was safer to travel together, but they separated when they reached the market. They had their own methods of bartering. Zsófi flirted a lot; she could afford to do it being single. She could mesmerize potential customers beyond belief. Anna knew she did not need to flirt to get a good deal. It was enough to be amicable but bold at the same time. She was good with words and it helped her arguments, whether in Rusyn or Hungarian. Or in Russian, if she needed to handle the Red Army soldiers at the omnipresent checkpoints and, not rarely, when they simply started harassing people. She had polished her Russian in Uzhhorod with the Red Army at every corner.

"Zombor is the next stop," the conductor said. He strutted along the aisle, pushing away passengers' feet or the messy luggage in his way. His watery blue eyes stopped scanning the passengers for a second when he spotted Anna, and then he continued on his way.

Whistling, hissing, and puffing accompanied the slowing of the train at the station. Anna stumbled to the vestibule. She let some old people get off, then stepped on the stairs and shouted to a few waiting locals on the platform, asking about Miklós. Some were shaking their heads; others did not answer.

"I saw him arrive last night," said one woman on the platform.

Anna's heart stopped. She heard the conductor's whistle and dashed back to the car for her luggage.

"You will have to go alone. Miklós is back!" she shouted at Zsófi and ran to the vestibule.

The train was already moving when she jumped, but luckily, she fell on her bundle instead of the crushed stone on the platform. She ran toward Imre's home despite the weight of her bundle, bouncing left and right as she hopped over the rails.

Chapter 23

Finding the door to her room closed, Anna tumbled into Imre's apartment. Kati looked up from her cooking.

"Where's Miklós?" Anna asked, gasping for breath, and dropped the bundle to the floor.

"Noushika! He went to the vineyard with Imre."

Anna toppled into a chair.

Kati rushed to her and encased her shoulders, preventing her from letting her tears flow. "Why don't you make him dinner and wait till they return?" Anna nodded and sniffed and asked Kati for some fresh vegetables and beans. She had smoked bacon in her bundle that would not make it to Budapest today, but would be turned into a delicious bean goulash she knew Miklós loved.

The sun peeped into her kitchen through the open door the whole afternoon. She felt a shadow falling on her face as she leaned over the casserole to taste the rich soup after putting some hot paprika into it. A man stood at the door, a halo around his head, wearing an army cap. She could not see his face due to the glare of the sun, but she knew who it was.

"Miklós!" It was just three steps into his extended arms.

He did not say a word as his mouth was busy kissing her hard and long. He smelled of a mix of sweat, green leaves, and June wind—full of the fragrance of ripe wheat and grape flowers toned down by dust. Anna welcomed his embrace more than his kisses.

They stood there for a long time. Miklós seemed to understand that she needed him to hug her. It was only when he sniffed that she pushed him away playfully.

"You are hungry!"

"We worked in the vineyard the whole day and only ate some bread and cheese that Imre had brought. I smell bean goulash, is that right?" He smiled and peeped into the casserole on the stove eagerly. Anna moved it to the side and readied the plates.

Miklós talked about the vineyard during the meal. Anna asked questions about his captivity, but he brushed them off with curt, meaningless answers. She only learned that he had reached Austria where the Red Army had captured his contingent and, after several months, eventually let them return home. He refused to speak about those months, but his feverish eyes and pale, hollow cheeks spoke for themselves. *He must have suffered.*

Miklós understood that their stock of wine had been destroyed when the front went through the region, but he wanted to forget about it and look forward to the new harvest that fall. He told Anna about the end of the blooming of the grapes and the growth of the berries with an enthusiasm that was contagious. True, a lot of work would await them in the summer with shoot thinning, partial defoliation, cordoning, and, of course, spraying several times to protect against fungal diseases. Miklós did not want to go back to work in the police force during the summer. There would be enough work in the vineyard, and the return would be handsome in the fall.

He asked about Veronika and Anna told him how Mother had convinced her that it was better for them to stay in Uzhhorod until he returned. She told him about her work in the shop, how she had reorganized the supply chain, and her occasional trips to Budapest. He gave her a strange look.

"Now that I'm back, your place is here. We're a family and I can take care of you both. Go back to Uzhhorod and bring Veronika. I want to see her and have her with us."

She knew better than to argue. After all, he was a father who wanted to see his child. She caught the train the next morning back... home? She did not know where home was anymore. Some say home is where your loved ones are. Some say where your homeland is. Did she still have one? Miklós was right. They were a family and Veronika belonged with them.

Mother's face was sore after hearing the news. She dropped to her seat with a sigh. "You don't even have a decent place for yourselves. You live in a ruin. Miklós doesn't have a job. If you want to be with your husband, so be it. But why take the burden of the child now? You'll need to help him in the vineyard, not play nurse with the child."

"Mother, he wants to see her. I can't carry Veronika here and there. She'll be with us, with Kati and her children sometimes, but we'll be together as a family finally. I want them both."

Anna did not convince Mother, but got her way by force. She readied the child and returned to Zombor before the weekend.

She found their apartment empty. Seeing the light in Imre's flat and hearing some noise, she knocked on the door and entered. The two men sat around the kitchen table, holding their shot glasses high. They had just started to sing at the top of their lungs. Kati's face was dark, and as she pushed her children into the bedroom, she gave her a warning glance.

"My angels have arrived!" Miklós stopped singing, spread his arms, and tried to stand. It took him some seconds before he succeeded. Imre had a dull smile on his face. He put a hand on the bottle that Kati tried to seize and poured some transparent liquid into their shot glasses. The pungent smell of the pomace brandy hit Anna's nose.

Miklós beamed and hugged Anna along with the child. She turned Veronika away from him, but he took her from Anna's arms. He held the child high, shaking her a bit, smiling at her, and babbling something. Veronika looked at him somberly, and her lips curved down. Miklós lowered her to his face, planted a peck on her rosy cheek, and tossed her up in the air. The unknown experience frightened the child at first, but then she broke into a smile. Anna supported Miklós' shoulders as she noticed him teetering, but he straightened himself and tossed Veronika up once again. She emitted a gurgle and a clearly audible joyous shriek: *shche.*

"*Még*! You should say *még*, 'again'," Anna instructed, holding her hand out to secure her. But Miklós pulled the child close to him. He was swaying, so he had to lean against a chair.

"She doesn't speak Hungarian. It's high time we have her with us, for God's sake!"

Anna was silent. She didn't explain that she could not be with her every day. She had to make money for the whole family so that the shop could exist. In her head, she scolded Mother and cursed Stepfather for the language they spoke in the household. *It isn't enough that the Russians have occupied Ungvár and everything has changed—and not just on the streets, now they have to speak Ukrainian, even at home.*

Anna convinced Miklós to return home to put the child to bed and gave Imre a killer glance when he protested. Kati was able to snatch the bottle from the table and make it disappear. In their apartment, Miklós tried to play with the child as he was lying on the bed, but he dozed off soon. Anna put her in the cradle where she also fell asleep within seconds. Anna listened to Miklós's snores until late at night as she sat in the kitchen, alone, thinking.

It seems like he is searching for something. He is restless. His feverish eyes are jumping from one object to the other. Then he just sits, looking at nothing. I thought he would be happy to be with us again.

She missed the husband she had left in Ungvár. The man who had promised her so much... and who had eventually started to deliver. The eighteen months after their wedding were hard with her pregnancy, with Stepfather, with the Germans, with the horror of the transports, and the bombings, but she had been happy. Miklós had become the man she could rely on. Then he went away, and another man returned in his stead. It seemed the war had killed the Miklós she...she had started to love. Now she had to learn to love again.

Kati was more than happy to look after Veronika along with her children, and she swore that nothing like the incident would happen. She would be with the children all the time and not go gossiping with the neighbors. Anna had no choice; they had to go to the vineyard every morning—Imre, Miklós, and herself—and returned late in the afternoon.

Her dexterity, thoroughness, and quickness at learning made her the equal of the two men in the so-called "green work" with the grapes. She left the spraying to them, however, as the large wooden pail with the spraying liquid was too heavy for her and it was difficult to operate the pumping handle. She had become an expert in thinning the shoots, defoliation, cordoning, and hoeing as it required constant bending, and her body was more flexible than the men's. Sometimes, she would stop to straighten her sore back and look up the hill with a pride comparable to nothing. She was working in her own vineyard. She prayed it would bring just rewards.

Miklós had changed after returning from captivity. He became his former self when they worked in the vineyard but, as soon as they got home and she got busy with chores, he would just sit at the kitchen table and look at the scratched wood without a word. Anna tried to engage him in conversation or ask him to play with Veronika, but it worked only for a few minutes. He would turn within himself again, chewing on the inside of his mouth or his nails, only answering with grunts at her attempts to involve him in idle chatter.

On a Saturday in late July, she received a bottle of wine from Imre for her birthday. Miklós opened it in the evening. She had hardly drunk a glass and by the time she finished cleaning the dishes, he had poured the last few drops into his own simple tumbler. He drank it, stepped to the sideboard and took out another bottle, and raised it toward her.

"To your health, Noushika!" he said and drove in the corkscrew.

"We could have left it for another evening..." Anna said.

"I want to drink to the health of my wife on her birthday!" He snapped at her and poured his tumbler full. "Is there a problem with that?"

Anna stared at him as he drank the full glass, then poured another one. She left her own glass on the table and went to their bedroom. After checking on the sleeping child, she washed herself in the little enameled washbasin and slipped into bed. Miklós's words filtering through the thin door awakened her after a while.

"I told him to let them run! They just laughed at me and kept shooting and shooting...even when the bodies were quiet. Sanyi turned the bayonet against me, the swine!" There was silence for a while. "Nobody cared that I wasn't the same. I couldn't prove to the Soviets that I had helped the Jews. They called us Hitler's last henchmen. The beating was not the worst. It was the..." His voice thinned to a whisper.

Oh, dear. He must have been tortured. Why doesn't he open up to me about it?

Anna heard the hiccuping sobs, and her heart went out to him. Then there was silence again.

She found him sleeping at the table with his head in his arms in the morning.

Fruit trees edged the vineyard: apricot, plum, and apples. The plums and apples would take a long time to ripen, but by early July, the apricots had turned yellow. Some even had a slightly pink cindery skin that begged to be tasted. One afternoon, when they had finished work, Anna plucked some apricots.

"Careful, take only the ripe ones!" Imre said.

"We've had no fresh fruits this year. There are no strawberries or cherries, and the children would surely love some." Anna bit into a fruit. It was hard but sweet. "We will leave it for a couple of days in the kitchen to ripen to perfection. You don't want the insects or birds to eat it when they are ripe."

Anna did not have the patience to wait several days for the fruits to ripen. Veronika was teething. Her molars were not coming out easily, and she wanted to chew on something. The hard fruit seemed optimal. The child stopped crying and enjoyed the sensation of the pulp massaging her gums and emitting sweet juice at the same time.

The cries started the next morning, and Anna knew immediately that it was not due to teething. The men left for the vineyard, but Anna remained at home with the ailing baby. Veronika seemed to have stomach cramps because she curled up and was spitting up curdled milk. Kati was not so clueless and suggested she make tea with some salt and sugar. Anna used the last crumbs of sugar she had from her Budapest trips. Veronika did not improve and continued to suffer. Zombor had no doctor—not that Anna would have trusted a strange man. She left a note for Miklós, saying she was leaving for Uzhhorod.

Jancsi ran to fetch their family doctor, who used to treat them during their childhood. She was at home and came at once. She gave Veronika some pills and ordered a special herbal tea with salt, baking soda, and sugar. She assured Anna that the child would be better soon; she just had to be kept hydrated.

Anna did not leave Veronika alone for even a minute during the following week. The pills and the herbal tea helped. She became better and better, albeit still weak, and she presented them with her first smile and a few words after a couple of days.

"*Verka éhes,*" she said. Veronika is hungry.

"We'll go back after the weekend. She's much better now," Anna said while feeding the baby a proper meal for the first time in a week.

"Don't even think of it. Do you want to kill that child, for God's sake?" Mother turned to her from the stove where she was preparing lunch.

"It was an accident. We'll be careful. I can't leave Miklós alone when there's so much work to be done in the vineyard."

"That may be alright, but not with the child. You still don't have any lodgings of your own—living with those relatives of his. You said typhus is raging in Hungary, but we have none of it here. We have better food, and I can take care of Veronika now that Jancsi is big enough to help in the shop. Not that we have a lot of customers."

Anna was quiet. Miklós' interest in the child had languished in the past few weeks. Work sapped his strength, and he was just about able to indulge her for a few minutes in the evening. But he let go as soon as Anna prepared her bath. The child would be in much better care with Mother than with Kati. She could visit every weekend. She could even use the trips to do some trading—there was more food and cheaper clothes that would fetch a good price in Zombor or even Budapest if she could convince Miklós about the necessity and usefulness of such a trip.

"You must promise that you'll speak to her in Hungarian. Stepfather can speak to her in Rusyn but she must hear Hungarian from someone who speaks it well," Anna said.

"I used to talk to you in Hungarian. It is your mother tongue, after all. I can do the same with my granddaughter."

Anna went to see Stepfather in the shop. He was sitting on a stool behind the counter, but no customers arrived. The shelves were empty. He hid the only goods he had below the counter to serve the good customers.

"Dad, I will leave for Zombor on Monday. Mother has convinced me to leave Veronika behind until times get better. I thought I would ask you for payment as I will probably not be able to continue working in the shop. I have never got a pengő from the profits and God knows we could use it."

Stepfather looked at her through narrowed eyes. He turned the key in the cash drawer and pulled it from the keyhole. "You've lived here with the child for several months. The child will stay here, as I hear. We'll have to supply food and comfort. These are hard times. You must be happy that your mother will take care of her, despite my disapproval. I owe you nothing."

She took a sudden step back, as if she had been scalded. They had built this shop with Mother. She had given years of her life to it. If not for her ideas, contacts, efforts, and trips, they would have gone bust long ago. She had never seen a share of the profits.

She pivoted and almost fell as the dizziness took hold of her. Leaning on the doorpost, she floundered to the kitchen through the short corridor. Mother must have heard Stepfather's words. She took Anna's hand and closed it around two brand-new thousand pengő banknotes. The money could buy meters of linen, twenty kilos of flour, or ten kilos of salt. It was not much, but if Anna chose with care, she could double it. She hesitated only for a second, then she hugged Mother. Her anger over the hidden letters seemed to disappear.

Anna could not look at Stepfather again. She spent the Sunday asking around the neighborhood for usable stuff and went to the city early on Monday morning to look at what money could buy. She returned with a big bundle, mostly linen and fabric, that were cheap in Uzhhorod. The general currency, cigarettes, was also a good deal. Her mood changed. It was a heartache to leave Veronika behind, but she felt Mother was right. And she must help Miklós get back on his feet.

She slipped away from home in the afternoon while Veronika was sleeping, a large bundle on her back as she lumbered to the station. Her border-crossing permission slip bought her a smooth pass through the army inspection, and she found a quiet corner in the train to brood over her lot.

They would build their own place or find one that would be more comfortable than Imre's house. Their door did not close properly, the walls did not hold in warmth due to the falling plaster; the small stove wouldn't heat it next winter. Miklós should find a job. It would help him heal, get a purpose, and prove himself an honest man. Maybe she could find him something. The Germans were driven out of the country by early April, and the war had ended in Europe a month later. Hungary was in ruins—she had seen it for herself in Budapest—but now it was slowly gaining consciousness. Factories had started operations, shops had opened, and peasants had cleared the fields for fall sowing. Under the Soviet army's control, a new and temporary government had been created until the November elections. Things had started to work, there must be some possibilities. As soon as they had a secure place and some money, they could take Veronika back from Uzhhorod.

The thoughts promising a brighter future calmed her. The clatter of the train and the chatter of the travelers in the warm July evening worked like a lullaby. In her dream, she saw a white and yellow house with large windows, gladioli and roses in the front garden, and children chasing each other around a large walnut tree. She did not see Veronika among them, and the man coming out of the house had an unfamiliar face with watery blue eyes. She awakened with a shiver and a cold sweat as the conductor shouted, "Zombor!"

Anna shook her head, put her bundle on her back, and pushed through the narrow aisle. The conductor held her bundle while she jumped down to the platform and she thanked him, giving him a fleeting glimpse, looking into watery blue eyes that smiled.

She shivered again. Nausea held her stomach tight and her breathing was heavy during the entire walk to Imre's house.

Chapter 24

Miklós' mood did not get better. He took it hard when he heard that Anna had left Veronika in Uzhhorod, and his sorrow drove him into another drunken evening with Imre. Anna suspected that he was happy to find an excuse.

"Keep your hands off me, woman!" he mumbled, and shoved her away when she tried to get him to come home. "I have serious business with my brother...brother-in-law!" He smiled as he hiccuped and Imre's chuckle made him release a loud guffaw.

Kati's face was strained, and she took a deep breath. She placed some water on the table to dilute the *pálinka* and then collapsed into one of the chairs. She waved Anna to go home. Anna stood, took a hesitant pace toward the sideboard, and patted Kati's shoulder. Two newspapers on the shelf caught her attention.

"May I borrow them?" she asked. Kati nodded her assent.

Anna thanked Kati with a dip of her head that she remained with the men. It could be another hour until they finished the brandy they had opened.

Normally, she would not have had an interest in the paper because she had enough to worry about. The communist paper was enthusing about the Soviets and boasting about the agrarian reforms that had split the large estates and given a couple of acres each to half a million poor peasants. She thought the move was more to punish the rulers of the old regimes than to provide land to the needy. People talked about how the committees managing the reforms favored communists when deciding how much and which land the applicants would receive. She knew from their own example how hard it was to live on a couple of acres—they had eight and it was not enough to live on decently.

The smallholder's party paper was pushing for compensation for the land and calling for controlling the committees. They enjoyed a large base of followers in the agrarian country, but the communist influence under the Soviet occupation was dominant. The paper submitted to the Soviets' voice—the same as what she had seen in Uzhhorod. Just that the language used here was Hungarian. Both Subcarpathia and original Hungary were under the Soviet army's rule. She wondered if the November elections in Hungary would change that and in what direction.

It was a big advertisement in the communist paper that caught her eyes—an appeal to people to apply for the new democratic police force. Going through the places offered, she spotted Újhely. It was about halfway between Zombor and Uzhhorod. Commuting between Uzhhorod and Zombor every week was arduous. She had to catch the train early Saturday morning and arrive at her parents' house late in the afternoon. A change of trains was necessary at Újhely, with sometimes a long wait for a connecting train. Then she got back on Monday morning because there was no train service on Sunday. Moving with her bundle between trains and waiting at the station was neither easy nor safe. Sometimes she traveled with Zsófi, who continued her tours to Budapest alone and had more confidence now. How much easier would it be to have a direct train between Újhely and Uzhhorod! She could be there in a couple of hours! She folded the paper, put it on the shelf below the Hungarian cookbook she had received from Mother almost two years ago when she had moved to Zombor, and went to bed. She would not wait for her drunken husband to return.

"Look at this," she said to Miklós the following morning and placed the paper in front of him.

A hangover had made him even more morose. "What do the stupid communists say again?"

"Not that claptrap, just look at this ad."

Miklós bent his head and squinted while he bit into the thick slice of bread and dripping. He chewed slowly, mumbling something to himself while reading, and reached for an onion.

"The work in the vineyard will reduce in fall. I could handle it with Imre if there's no other way, and we could manage the grape harvest during a weekend or when you are off duty," Anna said. She smiled and put her hand on his shoulder. "I would love to see you in uniform again."

"I'll think about it," Miklós said, gulping down his tea. "Let's go, the vines are waiting."

He had to decide for himself—Anna knew that well. After almost four years of knowing him and with more than two years of marriage behind them, albeit separated by the war through one-third of it, she had learned how to bend him to her wishes. When he did not drink, that is. Anna desperately tried to remove any alcohol from the house, but Imre's secret stock overthrew her plans often.

"If I had a job, *and* the harvest succeeded, we could really save some money for the plot, couldn't we?" Miklós said on Friday.

"Of course we would," Anna said, placing some steaming potato stew on the table. She fondled his thick, black, wavy hair. "And you could make some new acquaintances in the Újhely police. I am sure with your experience..."

Miklós' neck showed signs of strain, and Anna realized she was treading on thin ice.

"Being a policeman is an important job and you can be sure of your pay. I agree, the current uniform is not as grand as it used to be, but it will suit you, my handsome husband." She planted a kiss on his stubbled cheek.

Miklós took her face in his palms and turned his mouth to meet hers.

"I will try it then," he babbled during the kiss, not taking his mouth away.

"Eat, or it will grow cold!" Anna laughed.

Anna suggested he accompany her to Újhely on Saturday and inquire at the recruitment office. She would know how he had fared on Monday once she was back with clothes from Uzhhorod that would be exchanged for food in Zombor.

He came through the door with a lopsided smile on Monday evening, returning from the vineyard.

"Woman, we're moving to Újhely on Friday!"

"What? Tell me more!"

"They have enrolled me. Provisionally, but still. I'll have to go through some training next year, but I'll be in the police from next Monday. They were rambling that my experience in the old force was not an advantage. They claimed they were not proud of the police of the old regime and its condemned practices like chasing and torturing communists, and such hogwash—it was more the gendarmes doing these dirty things but what do they know—but they are keen to have some people who know what to do." Miklós face darkened. "I made it clear I had never served the political police. I was mostly on the streets, keeping public order."

"They have no clue how you helped the Jews," Anna said, squeezing his hand. He blushed—a rare occurrence. He closed his eyes for a moment and then looked at her with glowing eyes. He cleared his throat.

"A lot of poor peasant boys who can hardly read and write and have only seen a weapon from a mile away apply for the job."

"I am sure they will need you like people need water. Wonderful news, dear." Anna hugged him and let him kiss and caress her. "You say we're to move?"

"I found a small apartment, but it's much better than this one. Good heating and even a small garden. We have to furnish and paint it. Half a kilo of sugar or butter per week for the rent. We can also agree to pay with oil. The widow landlady doesn't want money."

"We'll manage. I can get sugar from Uzhhorod or exchange clothes for butter in Zombor. As soon as we settle in, we could move Veronika." Anna was beaming.

She agreed to open the bottle of wine he presented. Probably got it from Imre, who always had a hidden stash to celebrate. She regretted it later. He was rough, and she did not enjoy the night at all.

✍

"No, you won't!"

"Miki, we need the money. I can't sit here and wait for you to come home."

"You wouldn't need to do this trafficking if your stepfather had given you part of the profits from the shop. I thought I had married a girl with means and this is how we ended up." Miklós started pacing up and down in the small kitchen.

His confession shocked Anna. The horror soon turned into scorn and disgust, but the words did not come out.

Miklós took an enameled mug from the sideboard and dipped it in the water can. He took several gulps and put the empty cup down. With both hands on the kitchen table, he looked into her eyes with a defiant frown. "You could also find a job at the tobacco factory. They have openings, especially for women."

Anna stared him down. "You want to hide me in that dusty, smelly factory and get my hands so brown that it won't be possible to clean them just for a couple of thousand a week? I know those women; they have no option. I have." She was adamant.

Miklós snorted.

"But not to Budapest. You can't be away for two days a week. I won't allow you to spend the night on trains with who knows what sort of travelers."

"Miskolc then. The capital is more lucrative, but Miskolc will also do. I can return in the evening if I start early."

They could not make ends meet without her trading trips, and he knew it. He was jealous of her going off on her own, running a successful business, and making more money than he could ever do in the police force. Since August, the prices had been doubling every month. Goods were missing, industries and agriculture were not operating well, and inflation was heating up with the government printing money in higher and higher denominations every month. Hungary was ordered to pay a huge war compensation to the Soviets. The army residing in its territory ate and consumed goods at the country's expense. It was not a good time for fixed wages. Miklós's weekly salary was spent straightaway in the evening on Friday, and it bought only bread, lard, and milk. To pay the rent and buy vegetables and other foods, they had to rely on what Anna could make. And she did. She exchanged clothes to get sugar, sugar to get salt, salt to get smoked meat, meat to get a bicycle, and the bicycle to triple the sugar she had started with. Sugar bought wine and *pálinka* with which she could buy cigarettes from the Soviets, and then exchange the tobacco for food. It was strenuous: she needed to move between cities and villages, sometimes with heavy bundles and bags, and she needed connections. She found some women to join her to make the trips safer, and everybody contributed with a new idea or opportunity. Her network grew.

Anna had to give some credit to Miklós, too, otherwise he became stubborn and bitter. "You know what? Now that we have food at home, we could buy some items with your salary that I could take to Uzhhorod and exchange for better things. It's great that they have doubled your salary from mid-September. We could further double your salary by next Monday."

She received some humming and murmurs in response, but at least there was no shouting. Anna started to warm to the idea. She began to plan what to buy with his salary. Oil and matches would fetch a good value in Uzhhorod.

It was the end of September. The forethoughtful prepared for the longer nights during fall and winter. She could still get an excellent price for kerosene and matches from the Újhely market on Friday evening. Food fetched the highest prices as everybody was spending their salary on it. Industrial products were cheap. She blessed herself for the idea.

The kerosene, matches, and cigars she had bought from women working at the tobacco factory were sold out in Uzhhorod in a matter of minutes on Saturday. She gained a new pair of army boots, several meters of woolen fabric, and fresh cheese from the Carpathians. A peasant threw in some sweat pears with the cheese because he was so happy with the kerosene. Veronika beamed as she bit into the yellowish skin of the soft pears; the juice coloring her tiny lips and, in a couple of minutes, her cheeks.

Anna could not kiss her enough during those weekends. The child was a lively little thing, toddling around the kitchen from one adult to the other. Her blabber was becoming more and more understandable and more and more Hungarian. Mother seemed to have kept her promise, and Anna was grateful whenever she heard Veronika uttering clear Hungarian words or even half-sentences. Anna told her daughter tales in the evening before she went to sleep and whispered little secrets in her ears that made little sense, but the child enjoyed them and rewarded her with gurgling chuckles. She inhaled her milky smell, and they fell asleep in each other's arms.

She delayed moving the child back with them until they could set up their rented apartment in Újhely so that it was suitable for her. They lived for several weeks with a table and two chairs, lay on old blankets, and saved up for more furniture. They repaired and painted the walls. She hoped that before the colder days in fall, she would be able to move Veronika into a comfortable and warm home. *Just a couple of weeks more.*

As always, Anna wanted to slip out on Monday morning to catch the early train, but Veronika was already up. She was sitting on the white jerry in the kitchen, and as she noticed Anna in the hall, opening the door with her coat on, she ran to the door shrieking. The jerry stuck to her small, chubby bum and was swinging from side to side as she ran.

"*Mama, ne menj el! Ne!*" Mummy, don't go away! Don't!

Anna's heart was in pieces. She went to the kitchen, grabbed Veronika, and swung her around several times. The jerry dropped to the floor with a big clunk. She kissed her with all her might, feeling the salty drops of tears that were slow to dry up. She reassured her that she would be back, but Veronika was inconsolable.

Anna missed her train that morning. She sat on the floor in the kitchen and played with the child, building houses with wooden blocks and looking at picture books. Mother took Veronika for an afternoon nap, so Anna could catch another train to Újhely in the afternoon. She was glad that they lived close enough for her to afford this delay.

The sky became dark in full daylight due to a flock of birds. They circled around several times in a whirling pattern and then landed on the vineyards. Imre and Miklós clacked long sticks against each other, running between the lines and shouting like madmen. The unwilling birds flew up in small batches but fell back immediately behind them. They stood no chance. The birds feasted on the bursting grapes clusters until noon.

Anna arrived late, and Miklós was waiting for her at the kitchen table. He was on the verge of tears as he described the scene in the vineyard. His voice broke as he talked about the mutilated clusters that remained on the vines, the precious juice dripping to the ground like the blood of a mortally wounded beast. They had started clipping the damaged clusters to give the remaining grapes a chance to recover, but it would take an entire week to complete. And what use would it be when they knew that what remained would hardly be enough for a single cask of wine? They should harvest as soon as they could. They would not need a lot of neighbors to help.

Anna tried to console him, standing behind him and hugging his trembling shoulders.

"We should let all the remaining grapes mature into *aszú*," she said, allowing a spark of an idea to come to light. She believed in it as she heard herself saying it.

"What are you speaking about?" Miklós raised his head to look at her with a confused expression. "If we leave the grapes, the starlings will eat them!"

"They'll go to other vineyards. There must be many untouched yet, much more attractive to them than our destroyed grapes. As you say, the grapes that remain would give us only a cask of wine. If we let them turn into *aszú* with the help of a good, long Indian summer, we can sell it for many times the price of a cask of wine."

"This is crazy. You'd take a risk that could destroy whatever remained."

"Or return half of what has been lost."

Miklós tossed and tumbled perhaps a thousand times that night. Anna knew why. It was his baby, the vineyard, and he always thought he was a competent winegrower. Accepting advice from anybody, especially an outsider, was testing his capabilities. Despite working with weather and nature, he hated taking risks. Anna did not talk about it again to let him reconsider. Days or weeks, if need be.

He was up before dawn the next morning, sitting at the kitchen table, when she emerged from the room. He was looking at the tea that he had made for himself, which was rare because he liked her to serve him. She made herself busy cutting slices of bread and preparing a hearty omelet by mixing some milk into the whipped eggs to start a better day.

"I'll tell you what," he said, using a piece of bread to wipe his plate clean of the melted butter that made the omelet especially delicious and to his liking. "We'll let the remaining grapes turn into *aszú* during October and make an early November harvest. Even later, should it not be freezing."

"Solid decision." She smiled at him, but he did not return it and stared at her. She quickly hid her smile, stacked the plates, and cleaned them. *I must let him take all the credit. It won't cost me anything. I had better focus on him letting me travel.*

Detecting her husband's improving mood, in the evening Anna presented her plan of going to Miskolc to exchange her wares before she went back to Uzhhorod during the weekend.

"I believe your plan with the *aszú* will work," she said, "but we still need food to sustain. The market will help us survive until the harvest from the vineyard."

Her logic was unimpeachable, and Miklós saw it. The way Anna had presented it also made it seem like his plan was genial. He rewarded her with a smile.

"You should buy yourself something nice. You work so hard; you deserve a present. There's nothing here that's worthy of you."

Anna kissed him. She was glad they had no more wine. Sweet sighs and contented hugs filled the night.

Anna was thinking of buying herself a pair of shoes. Her old beige pumps with the pyramid heel from before the war had become worn and uncomfortable with one heel run-down more than the other. She wore small-sized men's army boots in the vineyard and the garden. It had served well for heavy work and she had made it fit her tiny feet by stuffing two socks. She needed something that would show her to be a respectable woman and would be comfortable enough for the long walks to and from the station and market, or wherever the trips would take her.

She offered the new army boots she had got in Uzhhorod to a shoemaker in exchange for pumps and anything else he could give, but he was adamant about offering only one item. The black pumps were beautiful and felt like feathers on her feet. They fit perfectly. But she returned them with a grimace.

"They are tight on the sides."

"Madame, wear it for a week and it will take the form of your feet. Here, I will give you cream for it."

"No, they aren't comfortable."

She strolled along three more stalls, army boots in hand.

"Hey, madame, are those for sale?"

A middle-aged peasant stood behind a wooden table, graying hair peeping from below his black hat that matched his gray mustache, turned up at the end by wax. It was so funny that Anna could not suppress a smile.

"They are if you can give me a matching offer," she said and put the boots on the peasant's table.

The boots shone like they had just come out of a factory. She had put extreme effort into them in the morning at home and had packed them in a separate cloth in her bundle.

The peasant took the boots into his crusty hands and looked at them from all angles. Anna encouraged him to try it. It took him a few minutes to get rid of his old boots. He sat on a rickety stool and pushed his footcloth-covered feet into the new boots. They seemed to fit perfectly.

"I have some seed wheat to exchange it for."

Anna looked at him, shaking her head. "Do I look like someone who needs seed wheat?"

"I also have some fruit trees."

"Now that's better," she said, and produced a sour smile with a grunt. "We need to eat *now*, not in five years."

Wheat. Fruit trees. Miklós had an acre unused. They could not build a house on it as it was far away from the village, but could it be used for farming?

"If I do business with you, how will you deliver your wares?"

"I'm returning this afternoon to Szada. I can deliver it somewhere close."

They agreed on a hundredweight of wheat and fifty fruit trees—plums, apples, and apricots—for the army boots. He would deliver it the next day to Zombor, to Imre's address.

Anna did not lose time. She exchanged her fabrics for canned food, some kerosene, and sugar, and again she had a heavy bundle to carry to the railway station. She caught the afternoon train and was back in Újhely by six just before Miklós was off duty.

She was impatient to tell him the news. He was shocked at first, but then hugged her and planted a kiss on her cheek. It felt good again. They were a good team.

"A hundred kilos of wheat would cover a whole acre, just the idle one. We could plant the fruit trees around the edge of the field. It would be wonderful!"

Anna traveled to Zombor on Friday to meet the peasant at Imre's house. He was already there and in the middle of an animated discussion with Imre when she arrived. The men unloaded the wheat into wooden casks and put the fruit trees into the shed. Their naked roots were asking to be planted as soon as possible. A sudden icy shiver ran through her back when Anna realized all the work she would have to do, Miklós being on duty most of the time. She knew close to nothing about sowing wheat or planting trees.

"I'll help you with it, don't worry," Imre said, looking at the deepening wrinkles on her forehead. "By next summer, you'll be a proper countrywoman."

Chapter 25

The journey from Újhely to Uzhhorod would have taken only an hour, but for the stops at every village. Looking out of the window, Anna remembered her first honeymoon trip with Miklós a mere two and half years ago. The green plains in the May of '43 had turned into trampled prairie after soldiers with tanks fought there a year ago. The reeds grew fast to mask the destruction, popping up around the brooks and lakes of the floodplain of the Bodrog River, but could not make the omnipresent bomb craters disappear. In some places, skeletons of the destroyed German army vehicles lay scattered that nobody had taken the care to clear away. Temporary reinforcements made the damaged long bridge usable, but the train had to slow to walking speed to avoid destroying the fragile construction. Anna turned away from the gray and brown nature that did not match her memories.

We have a child, the sweetest creature on the globe. We survived the war despite everything. Miklós returned from captivity. We are together again in a cozy little apartment that allows us to have Veronika with us. She agreed with Miklós that they would move the child back to Hungary the following week, even if Mother protested.

"It's better to move everything now. You never know what the *Ruskis* are up to," she heard the man next to her saying to his comrade, who sat between two burly peasant women in black vests, skirts, and gray headscarves. The men also wore black and smelled of sweat, earth, and animals. At least the one sitting next to Anna. She moved closer to the window, but this encouraged the man to take up more space, so she gave up on it. The wooden planks of the third-class seats cut into her bottom and thigh with every jerk. She was happy the journey was only two hours.

"You're right," the comrade said. "We'll pack and move latest in November. The *Ruskis* inquired about the Hungarians in the village. Like when the Germans had asked about the Jews. God forbid we end up there."

What are these men gabbing about? Are the Russians interning Hungarians in Subcarpathia? What's happening there? Sarah Rosenberg's pallid smile occupied Anna's imagination as vivid as on that May morning a mere eighteen months ago. She had thrust the package into the Jewish woman's hand in the railway station before they loaded her into a cattle wagon with her husband and three children. She wanted to believe that it had helped her. Everybody knew by now where they had ended up. Anna had heard that less than a hundred survivors out of the nearly twenty thousand that had been captured returned from the transports from Ungvár.

"There are whispers that the Czechoslovaks have come to an agreement with the *Ruskis*. They will give Subcarpathia to them," the man next to Anna said.

"They are everywhere, aren't they?" The man opposite spat.

"Like cockroaches. Just more dangerous."

Anna's heart was in her throat. *Was the war not enough that now they will cut us into pieces?*

She looked out the window again. Even this gray and brown destroyed nature was better than the fretting rumors of these sods. The train stopped again, and she watched as people boarded it. She sighed. *We'll never be in Uzhhorod at this pace.*

After an hour, the train clattered into the station of Csap. The platform was full of Russian soldiers, with the red collar ranking on their khaki uniforms and the unmistakable red star on their caps, standing at every meter with a hand on their machine guns. The train slowed to a stop with a screech, the locomotive emitting sniffing noises as if it did not enjoy stopping at this place. Then there was silence. Nobody moved. The soldiers kept their eyes on the dirty windows and doors while the travelers tried to look around and behind the soldiers, searching for the authorities or anything that could explain the picket line.

After several minutes of total silence, the travelers started to whisper to each other. The soldiers did not move at all. The man next to Anna stood and stretched his limbs, so she tried to recover some of her lost space.

People moved around the car—talking, smoking, and eating—resigned to the unwanted stop and waiting for it to end. Nobody was leaving the train, and the platform was empty of travelers. Anna remained in her seat and looked outside the window, but there was no change. After half an hour, she noticed some commotion at the side of the railway station building. An army jeep came to a halt and two officers jumped out of the car and hastened into the building. Nothing happened for another five minutes.

Anna heard sharp shouts, and more officers came out of the building and spread across the length of the platform. Some soldiers started boarding the train at a brisk pace and, within a minute, they flooded their cars. Russian commands sounded, and the soldiers pushed everybody off the train. Some travelers were indignant at the soldiers' behavior, others simply followed instructions, but one by one they had to hop off the train. The officers directed the soldiers to herd the passengers into a long line.

Anna stood behind the man who had been sitting next to her in the car. She was trying to make sense of the whole commotion, but her knowledge of Russian did not help. The commands were just about getting everybody in a queue and thoroughly checking their papers and belongings. Passengers soothed each other by saying that the soldiers were surely looking for some criminals, so normal people had no reason to worry. Anna wanted to believe it.

The soldiers at the front of the line began to split the crowd: they sent some passengers ahead to the eastern part of the station building where other soldiers kept watch on them. They directed others to the back of the train under the supervision of another group of soldiers. The latter group of passengers protested. They kept shouting until an officer pulled out his pistol and fired a shot in the air, and another soldier hit a man on the head with the butt of his gun. The injured man collapsed, held his head in his hands, and slowly crawled to where he was directed.

The man in front of Anna was just showing his papers to the soldiers. He spoke Rusyn and explained that he had visited the market in Újhely. The soldiers opened his bundle and took out everything: several packages, sacks, and a loaf of bread. They gave only the loaf back to him and sent him to stand with the people at the eastern wall of the station.

"My permission! I need my permission!" The man raised his voice.

"No permission. It's invalid," one soldier said and tore the paper in half and put it in his pocket.

"But…"

The soldier raised his gun, and the man doddered toward the far group.

The soldier shouted at Anna even though she was less than a meter away from him, "Papers!"

She handed over her border-crossing pass.

"Residence in Újhely?"

Anna nodded.

"You go back to the train!"

Anna looked at the young soldier with cold blue eyes and saw emptiness there. She stretched out her hand to take her permission, but the soldier snatched it from her.

"Invalid!" He tore it in two and pocketed the pieces.

"You don't understand! I am from Uzhhorod. My mother is there, my daughter is waiting for me…" she said in good Russian, her voice rising to a shriek.

The soldier, confused by her language, took the paper from his pocket and looked at it again. Now suspicion sneaked into his cold eyes.

"You live in Újhely. Get back to the train!" He pushed her with his left arm. Anna almost fell.

She screamed. Dropping to her knees, she hugged the soldier's legs. "I must go to my daughter! Let me go to my daughter, please, let me…"

The young soldier tried to get rid of her by putting a foot on her shoulder and pushing with all his might. An officer shouted something and the other soldier moved in with his gun.

The sharp pain stopped Anna in mid-sentence and the world went black.

"Madam, take this! Madam! What's your name?"

She opened her eyes. As she focused on the voice, she saw a strange man with a mustache fanning her with his hat.

"What's your name, madam?"

"An...na," she said and tried to sit up, but fell back at once. Her head seemed to weigh a ton.

"Anna, stay put. You're on the train back to Újhely."

It dawned on her suddenly. "I must go to Uzhhorod, to Ungvár..." This time she succeeded in sitting and leaned against the bench. The pain jolted into her head, and she squeezed her eyes shut for a moment. "... to my daughter..."

"The Russians have closed the border. Nobody can cross. They sent all the Hungarian residents back to Újhely. Where's your daughter?"

"With my mother, in Ungvár... I was born there..."

"You've somebody in Hungary?"

Anna looked blank, then she remembered. "My husband."

The man nodded and put his water flask to her mouth. Anna gulped down some water. She felt the train moving.

"Where are we going?" Her voice broke as she suddenly inhaled.

"Back to Újhely."

"I can't go back to Újhely. I must go to my daughter!"

"Anna, it's not possible now. Calm down. Go to the Soviet headquarters in Újhely and try to explain. Here you can't do anything."

Anna looked at the man. He had helped her sit on the

bench and was now coaxing her to lie down. The train was half-empty now that all the Subcarpathian residents had been held back in Csap. They were let into Soviet territory to go to their destinations, the man told her. The passengers on the train did not speak. They all had their fears and losses, cut off from their loved ones, their birthplaces, their friends, and their pasts. The monotone clattering of the train and the silence in the car made her head heavy again, and she escaped into a fitful sleep.

Veronika was running toward her with her potty seat stuck to her chubby buttocks and her arms wide open, asking her not to leave. Anna awoke with a start. The train's wheels screeched as it slowed down and rattled through the turnout tracks in front of the station.

An uncontrollable shiver seized her as she recognized the two-storied Újhely station building.

Chapter 26

Miklós was shocked at first, but he soon found some consoling words. He paced the kitchen and tried to reason that they must allow her to move their daughter. She just needed to go to the army headquarters to explain. Anna sat at the table in the kitchen, immune to his caresses, hugs, and kisses. When he wanted to move her to the bedroom, she protested and insisted on staying in the kitchen. Miklós sat with her for a while, then went to sleep.

Anna switched off the light bulb to save the expensive electricity, lit the kerosene lamp, and placed it in front of her. The yellowish curved glass of the lamp was greasy from the many touches that had left a collection of fingerprints on it. She looked into the small flame—the shape of a birch leaf—which was enough to light the kitchen table but left the rest of the room in furtive grayness. The table was almost identical to their old wooden one in Ungvár. She shuddered, the tears flowing freely. Mother would worry about where she was and what had happened. She would inquire the following day at the neighbors or with the customers, but she would need to explain it to Veronika, who would have been waiting for her since morning, and for sure would still be waiting tonight.

I must visit the Red Army Headquarters. Maybe I can find Major Pachenko. He will surely help. I must get the permission slip and bring Veronika back to us. I can't live without my daughter!

She took out the only photo she had of Veronika from her purse. They had it taken when Miklós had returned early in July before she got sick from the apricots. Veronika was looking directly at the camera with those vivid eyes of hers that were an exact copy of her mother and grandmother. *Like she would look at me, exactly like she was looking at me yesterday. Don't go, Mummy, she had cried.*

More tears were coming, dropping to the checkered oil-cloth on the table and making little pools. Her shoulders quivered silently. The tears dried and apathy took over. She clenched her hands into fists. Her eyes burned, but the kitchen's shadows became sharp again. She would fight for her, fight for her daughter. Veronika was the only thing she had.

The corridor of the Red Army Headquarters smelled of wet woolen uniforms, sweat, pungent cigarette smoke, and kerosene. Anna had been sitting for two hours with several other people on the wooden benches in front of the office of the deputy city commander, Major Sidorov. The two Russian soldiers sitting in front of the officer's door were playing a game of dice and laughing. Another soldier was standing guard and watching the civilians with cold suspicion.

Her turn came in the afternoon after six hours of waiting when Sidorov returned from a long lunch. He was a tall, dirty-blond man with a brown Stalin mustache and a nascent potbelly, which was surely the result of his new comfortable office and the Hungarian kitchen. He strode in with his secretary, a strict woman in a sergeant's uniform, and asked for the next person.

"Móri!" The secretary stood at the doorstep and shouted as if she was on a battlefield.

Anna jumped and edged closer to the door, then straightened and scuttled in.

"I suppose we can speak Russian, is that right?" The Major asked instead of greeting her. He bade her sit in front of his massive desk. He fished out a pipe from his pocket and filled it with tobacco from the local factory's sack.

Anna explained her situation in passable Russian, with some Ukrainian words mixed in, first stuttering, then getting more confident. Major Sidorov grimaced as he heard her speak while studying her written appeal that she had submitted to the secretary early in the morning.

"I'm surprised you left Uzhhorod, Gospozha Móri." The Major lit his pipe and drew on it, letting the smoke escape through his mouth. He looked at her with narrowed eyes after the smoke thinned.

"My husband is from Hungary, he has..."

"Ah, policeman Móri. The previous regime's obedient servant. We wouldn't want him in the Soviet Union, for sure."

"Miklós was just hired back into the force, tovarish Krupnyy Sidorov."

"We know it. We'll see how he fares."

"I would need my permission slip back to visit my daughter and...and ask for family unification."

"Subcarpathia has returned to the Ukrainian Soviet Socialist Republic that is part of the Soviet Union as per its population's longstanding wish. The borders are closed. We don't allow suspicious individuals to enter our society."

"Suspicious...?"

"You married a Hungarian policeman and left Uzhhorod. We don't trust you."

"But my daughter..."

"We'll bring up your daughter as a socialist citizen with your mother hopefully supporting our endeavors. If not, we'll take care of that, too. You can go." Major Sidorov waved with his hand in the air and looked down at his papers, sucking on his pipe.

The blood froze in Anna's veins. She could not even protest when the austere secretary led her out of the office, holding her arm in an iron grip and releasing her only after she had crossed the door.

Major Pachenko. He is my only hope.

Fortunately, Miklós had a night shift and had already left by the time she stumbled home. She wanted to go to bed early, exhausted from almost no sleep the night before. She had to get up early for the train to Zombor. She must find the Major. Her mind was chasing ideas about what else she could do. Sleep avoided her again, and she sat in the kitchen looking at the flame of the kerosene lamp and thinking about her daughter.

She left before Miklós arrived, leaving a note that she had received no help in Újhely and would try in Zombor. It was still dark when she caught the train.

The new army station was housed in Mayor Gajdos' office

building. Only a simple soldier stood guard, who decided not to give her any information. He told her to come back in the afternoon. She pulled together all her courage, sat down on one of the chairs in the small anteroom, and said that she would wait. The soldier shrugged and lit a cigarette.

Anna was sure that Major Pachenko would help her. He liked her and he had played with Veronika. He would surely have some power to convince Sidorov to get her a border pass. Maybe he could even arrange for the straight moving of the child. He would know what worked in the Soviet army.

She must have dozed off because a sudden whirl of ice-cold air awakened her. A scrawny man in civilian clothes entered the anteroom and, without giving her a glance, stalked into the office. The sun was high in the sky, but the chilly air coming through the open door made her shudder. The soldier did not bother to close it but went into the office. When he came out, he beckoned her to go in.

"I am József Kovács, working for the Red Army as the local deputy," the scrawny man introduced himself with an affable smile on his bony face, but did not offer a seat. Anna stood in front of his desk with interlocked hands that were slightly trembling. "We had to change the previous village management for political reasons." He sat back in his chair with a smirk.

So, Mayor Gajdos is gone. She recollected the name—*tovarish* Kovács, the communist who Major Pachenko had pushed on the Zombor people. She had never met him.

"I'm looking for Major Pachenko," she said after explaining that she had lived in Zombor during the liberation and had even taught for some months at the school.

He looked at her, and the smile disappeared from his face. "Major Pachenko is not here."

"When will he return?" Cold sweat flooded onto her forehead.

"They arrested him in the summer and transferred him back to the Soviet Union," Kovács said. Anna swayed and bumped into the wall. She would have fallen lest Kovács hadn't swiftly caught her. He led her to a seat. "Do you want a glass of water?"

Anna could not answer. She just looked at the man with hazy eyes. Kovács held a glass of water to her lips.

"He must have done some black business with the requisitions they had entrusted him," Kovács said as she gained some strength and could sit up without slipping from the chair. "What did you want with him?"

"I... I am here to work on our field, and I wanted to show a picture of our daughter...he told me he had a granddaughter of the same age..."

Kovács contemplated her for some seconds. "If I were you, I would stop looking for him."

Anna nodded. She gazed at him for a minute without moving, but Kovács did not offer further information. She tried to rise. Her knees were still weak, but she forced herself to stand straight. "I need to go. Thank you." She got only a curt nod in response.

She floundered out of the building and turned toward the station. She didn't bother to visit Imre and Kati. A sharp northwestern wind found its way into her coat and she quivered. Exhaustion fell upon her, and her head felt like it weighed a ton. A child propelling a flock of geese along the muddy street greeted her, but she just nodded. Two days without sleep and food, and the burden on her heart took its toll. She fell on the bench in a nook of the station building, relieved at the shelter it provided from the cutting wind. It was quiet there, and her head lulled to the side. The screech of a train's wheels and a splitting headache awakened her.

There was no heating on the train, and not enough people to warm it up. She shivered in a corner, looking outside at the blue hills, green vineyards, and poor villages. She had never been so forlorn. There was no help. Her daughter was just a hundred kilometers away, but she might as well be as far as the moon. The Russians wouldn't allow Anna into their country. Major Sidorov was a cruel bastard. Major Pachenko had disappeared. Who knows if he was still alive?

I should not have left her in Ungvár. I wanted her to be safe and now I have left her in the hands of the bloody Russian communists. My only daughter! My only love!

Miklós? He was not even bothered. His vineyard is more important to him than his daughter. He is happy that we do not need to take care of her. How could I have been this feckless?

She looked around in the darkening car, seeing only a few passengers returning home from work or market trips. She could not see their faces in the darkness of the car. No heating, no electricity.

Mother is there to watch her. The Lord is there to watch her. I am banned from watching her. I am damned. Her head was pulsating, and she felt nausea building up in her stomach. Fresh air would help. She tried to open the window, but it did not relent. Stumbling through the gangway, she caused a sleeping passenger to protest as she bumped into him. She opened the door to the vestibule and found the right door ajar. The swishing of the wind cut into her face. She gripped the handrails. The running bushes along the tracks were gray but seemed like tender pillows. Breathing hard, she gazed into the gaping abyss. It filled her lungs and promised redemption.

She released the handrail and hugged the dusk with both arms.

A brawny arm gripped her waist, saving her from falling into the inviting abyss. She felt delusional. The arm held her for a second and time stopped. She heard the cold air whistling around her body and felt it cutting into her eyes and forcing tears. Her arms were freely hovering, with just the tips of her toes touching the steps. The clattering of the wheels, nothing else. *Tackatta-too, tackatta-too, tackatta...*

Then the arm dragged her with unstoppable force back into the vestibule. The door slammed with a metallic bang.

She was lying on somebody, the arm still holding her tight. Then it released her.

"Madame..." A man below her wheezed.

She turned her head, and through the tears, she spotted those watery blue eyes. *Where have I seen those before?*

Anna sat up and let her back fall to the wall. "I needed some air."

The blue eyes gazed at her. "You better come and sit down inside," the conductor said and pulled her up, still gripping her arm as he led her to her seat where her small handbag waited patiently. He sat with her, not letting his eyes leave her for a second.

Anna closed her eyes. *You should have let me fly. I would have found forgiveness. I have failed her.*

She heard him babble. Something about traveling, people moving all the time, looking for something, about hunger and how to help it. Sugar and wine and smoked meat, money having no value, and that it would become even worse. Who cares? It was so petty. None of it mattered anymore.

She wanted him to let her be, but the conductor had abandoned his job of checking new passengers after every stop in favor of sitting with her and blabbering. He stayed with her till Újhely and helped her get off the train. He asked her something, but her mind could not decipher the words and she left without an answer.

As she trudged home on the black streets, led only by the rising moon, she thought that it was good to feel that she mattered. At least to somebody.

Chapter 27

Daily trips to the field in Zombor. Carrying hundreds of pails of water to the fruit trees. Asking Imre to plow the field for sowing. Sowing the wheat. Anna worked every day from dawn to dusk on the field. Miklós joined her on his days off, that sometimes included weekends, more frequently not. It was back-breaking work, but not mind-numbing enough. Her thoughts buzzed around her daughter. Every day, new ways came to her mind about how to get to her. She wanted to go to Budapest to hire a lawyer. To contact higher-level authorities of the Red Army. To contact the government, the Greek Catholic Church.

"They won't even talk to you. We don't have money for lawyers. You'll just make a fool of yourself in front of the authorities," Miklós said. He tried to make inquiries with the police, but his superior stopped it at once. The Soviets were untouchable.

"I have to do something. Should I just twirl my fingers, waiting for something to happen? I have to save my daughter!" And the tears started.

Anna traveled to Miskolc, where the Red Cross had a regional center. She waited in a long queue for three hours to come to a small window that accepted new inquiries. She heard how the others were looking for their loved ones who were lost or had been carried away during the war or even afterward. The form had a template for specific questions in specific situations. It did not fit her problem.

"No, she was not lost. She was in Ungvár with her granny while I was in Hungary, and the Soviets closed the borders."

The woman behind the window blinked and cast down her eyes. "We have little help from the Soviet authorities." She seemed to change her mind. "None. But leave the form here with the data about your daughter, address and all, and we'll try to get in contact with her. You must be patient; it can take time."

One day, when returning home one stormy afternoon from Zombor because she could do no reasonable work in the soaking downpour, she spotted a familiar face at the Újhely station among the waiting crowd. The woman had a beige trench coat on, a simple brown shawl to protect against the windy weather, and a fashionable matching beret.

"Marika! Is that you?" she said and made a tentative step toward the elegant woman.

"Ancika? You're alive!"

The embrace of the two friends did not want to end. Marika was on her way back to Patak, just one stop away, having run some errands in the district capital town. She decided to skip her train and wait for the next, the last one that day.

They hid from the rain in the waiting room. They reminisced about their afternoon coffees in their city and sent wishful glimpses at the locked buffet window with a grid. Nobody had the money for coffee anymore, not that any coffee existed. It was a temporary escape for Anna from her desolation.

Anna looked at her with slight envy. It surprised her that Marika had recognized her in soaked working garments.

"As an engineer, Karcsi has a lot of work, fortunately, with all the restoration going on. I am busy with our little son, Ádám—you should see him. He takes after Karcsi even though he's only two! You can't let him alone for a minute, the little rascal!" Marika said, and squeezed Anna's hands. "Veronika must be one and a half already. Does she speak?"

Anna could not hold it anymore and broke down.

Marika's face was full of horror. "Ancika, what happened?"

"She is in Ungvár," Anna said between sobs. "The border...they closed it when I was here..."

"They did not let you back, right?" Marika's arms were immediately around her, just like in the old times. Anna realized how she had missed them.

Anna shook her head. "I have been everywhere: the Red Army, the Red Cross. I wanted to go to the capital to ask for help..."

"Nobody can go to Subcarpathia, I know. Karcsi also tried. We're happy we found a way to send and receive letters from our parents."

"I sent two letters but got no answer."

"Ancika, you can't send them letters directly," Marika said. She *tsked* with her tongue and shook her head, letting a curl free from the beret. "The Soviets are monitoring the post. We have a friend who works in Budapest at the Soviet Headquarters. They allow him to correspond with his relatives in

Ungvár." She took Anna's hand in hers. "If you give me your letter, I can include it in ours with instructions to pass it to your mother. She could use the same route back to let you know about them, too."

Anna looked at Marika with rising hope in her eyes. "I have missed you!"

"Silly, come on!" She embraced her again and Anna let herself indulge in her sweet, comfortable fragrance.

They exchanged addresses and promised to meet soon. It was difficult to let her go, but her train had arrived.

The Indian summer ended and there was constant rain every day. To prevent the *aszú* grapes from rotting in the weather, they harvested everything the next weekend with Imre's help. They had to put oilcloth on the floor of the shed and in their old apartment to let the berries dry. The room smelled of the zesty scent of the *aszú* that promised a rich reward when they sold it to the large wine-growers.

They sold the berries in early November, and they had to accept cash. They spent some money on smoked bacon and butter, which was cheaper in the village, and hurried home to buy firewood. Anna suggested buying more than they needed, as much as they could store in the shed behind their apartment. It turned out to be an excellent investment. Prices doubled every month. They still had some money left that Anna had saved for worse times.

"I'll go with Mrs. Szabó, our neighbor, to Miskolc next Monday to buy some things we could exchange here. Your weekly salary's enough only for two days and then we're eating bread again," Anna said at their meager dinner. The paprika potatoes were thin without vegetables and smoked sausage.

Miklós broke the end of the brown bread loaf and dipped in the dish that looked like red soup with potato wedges swimming in it, which was not enough to make it thick. Without the bread, it would not have been enough for him. He looked at Anna while chewing. "At least we have one salary. You could also find a decent job in Újhely. I told you about the tobacco..."

"We've been there. I won't have anything to do with that place till I can make some pengő trading."

"Why are you so keen to travel, can you tell me?"

"How else to trade and make money?"

"Who's the man you're traveling for?" His black eyes pierced into hers with suspicion.

"Have you gone crazy? I'm going with Mrs. Szabó and..."

"I don't like those trips. A wife's place is at home, not dawdling about the countryside and trafficking with who knows what people..."

"What are you saying?" Anna's eyes widened, and she sat up erect. She could not help raising her voice. "I'm dragging along heavy bundles through trains and towns and markets, haggling with sly customers and dirty soldiers to double our money and to be able to prosper. To be able to buy more than bread and lard. Do you think I'm doing this for fun?"

"Watch out. I'll kill you if you cheat on me!" Miklós banged his spoon into the empty plate and dashed out of the kitchen, grabbing his coat from the peg at the door.

What is wrong with him? He distrusts me? He is the one who cheated on me just because he could not wait for our wedding for a couple of months!

He came home drunk. Anna was already in bed, thankful when he passed out and began to snore and did not touch her. The smell of vapid wine nauseated her.

Everybody feared the communists would win the November general elections, but it did not turn out that way. The smallholder's party was an absolute winner with a high margin, the rest was shared by the communists, social democrats, and the peasant party. Miklós was elated as he was a firm supporter of the smallholders, himself being one. He believed the win would ensure the support that simple people needed and would limit the communists despite their Soviet backing.

One evening, he came home in a bad mood. He threw the newspaper on the kitchen table and fumed. "Coalition government! Bullshit!"

Anna looked at him and stretched her hand for the paper, but then changed her mind. She served the soup containing everything Miklós liked. She hoped it would change his mood for the better, and she was right.

"Bean goulash? At least some good news today!" Miklós said with a deep sigh, and Anna suppressed a smile as she turned to cut some bread. She knew better than to comment. He needed his time to come to terms with everything.

Miklós devoured the reddish soup with the big white beans, carrots, and turnips. The smoked pork flank she had secured in Miskolc elevated the meal into a feast. *I was right not to change it for the sugar the woman offered today, although that would have been a great deal.*

Halfway through the meal, when he had silenced his urgent hunger and dulled his taste buds, Miklós explained that the Soviets must have forced the smallholders to make a wide coalition. Although the smallholders had nominated the Prime Minister and kept finance, foreign affairs, and agriculture, the communists had grabbed interior, welfare, and transport that were key to managing the country. He was most angry about the police remaining under communist rule.

Anna was half-listening. She never liked politics and thought it a waste of time. She could not deny that those big decisions had a major effect on life in general, but she believed one should still be responsible for one's own fate through action. *I will not leave Veronika in fate's hands.* She wanted to cry again but forced her thoughts instead on the letter she had written and sent to Marika to be posted to Uzhhorod among theirs through the clandestine route. *May Mother get it soon.* The Red Cross had no news so far.

Anna tried to save some of the money they had got for the *aszú;* she could not add to it during the last month and a half. They lived from one day to the other. Miklós' salary disappeared in a couple of days, and what she could make by trading was hardly enough for the rest. Fortunately, they stopped traveling to Zombor in the winter, thus saving on travel fares, after having sown the wheat and sold the *aszú.* The fruit trees just needed to take root and get stronger to survive the cold.

Trading was more difficult in winter. Miklós allowed her to go only once a week and only to Miskolc, and this did not create enough opportunity. She boiled over with rage about his jealousy and stubbornness, but he was adamant and she was afraid to overstrain their arguments. She could have started down a slippery slope.

Christmas was nigh. It would again be a quiet matter

without presents. Food on the table would have to do.

She was finishing a dinner of noodles, turning them in sizzling fat from a bit of smoked bacon that created heavenly-smelling cracklings. The curd waited on the table to be put on top, but she missed the sour cream that made the pasta slippery and delicious at the same time. She could have gone with noodles and curd only, but they needed fat. They both had lost weight in the past months. Her own leanness reminded her of the times when Mother, Jancsi and she were surviving on mushrooms.

Miklós opened the door, and she spotted his drawn face. Her brows up, she opened her mouth to ask what had happened when he blurted it out. "They will devalue the money to the fourth."

"What?" Anna got panicked. She had still some cash in the cupboard.

"From tomorrow, banknotes will have a quarter of the original value. You need stamps to have them marked to the full value but those will cost you the difference."

Anna forced herself to shrug while her heart jumped into her throat. She thought her voice came out like a whistle.

"We're alright, we have no money." She thought of the hundred thousand pengő in her drawer below her briefs. A month's salary had changed to a week's. "Will they compensate you?"

"The captain made some dirty jokes that I don't need it, having the fields and the vineyard. He even called me *kulak*—must've heard it from his Russian and communist friends. I don't even know what it is."

"Nonsense," Anna waved in dismissal. "Those were rich peasants in Russia. Stalin sent them to camps and confiscated their fields."

Miklós looked alarmed, then dismissed the thought. "We

live in a democracy. It can't happen here. They talk about a salary raise but only from January. You were right about investing in the firewood. If we are frugal, we could sell some..."

Putting the meal in front of him, she said. "I could bring more money if you let me go with Ella, Mrs. Szabó, more often."

Miklós chewed on some bacon cracklings for an entire minute, dragging it out. "I don't like that woman. Where do you want to go?"

"Wherever the opportunity comes up. She said she had other contacts. People always want something. But we will surely do just day trips. I will be home by evening."

He kept quiet until the last scraps disappeared from his plate. "The police are monitoring trafficking activity. I'm risking my job with this game of yours."

Anna guffawed. "Game? If I don't trade, we go hungry to bed every second evening! Do you remember we wanted to buy a plot? Do you want to live in a rented room all your life? We have to help ourselves."

"I don't know about this trading, I tell you. But if you cheat on me..."

"Miki, *I* am not the type." She could not help saying it. She received a stare. He stood and took the newspapers.

Half the battle is won. Now I need to make money. I hope Ella really has connections.

She could not fall asleep for a long time that night. *He is too comfortable and gives up fast. Why can't he be more enterprising?* His snoring irritated her.

Chapter 28

Ella Szabó was sipping on thin, bitter tea with a moody grimace. She waved at Anna's apologies. "It's not about the tea, Noushi. At least you have something to offer. I've only water at home. It grieves me that we couldn't get any proper business last month."

They were sitting at the kitchen table in the darkening late February afternoon. Miklós was on duty and they had had no opportunity for any good trading in the past week. Their pantries showed aching emptiness.

Anna tried to cheer her up. "That fat clerk you found with that woolen coat was not bad at all. It was great value for the bacon we had."

"Maybe, but then we had to exchange that coat for such little sugar and cigarettes that we got just one bite bigger bacon than we had started with. Two days' work for a day's dinner—this won't last long!"

"True...the prices are..."

"Don't even mention them!" Ella said, throwing her arms in the air. "The rent has doubled again this month. Bread is fifteen thousand pengő, potatoes are six thousand for a kilo, and an egg costs ten thousand. Can you imagine that? We haven't had an egg for months! I forbid Józsi to buy newspapers. This month, it went up from two to ten thousand! He can choose: paper or bread..."

"We'll be millionaires soon! Miklós's salary is a hundred and fifty thousand a week." Anna tried to laugh, but Ella did not react.

Silence reigned over the table. Anna looked at her neighbor's hollow face and wondered how strained she must look herself. She remembered Ella's promises a couple of months ago. "You said you knew more people on the railway line to Miskolc..."

"True, but the resourceful ones travel to the capital. The real market is there. Whoever remains here has little and they don't have the right connections...unless..."

"Miklós won't let me go to Budapest."

"Well... I know this Bodnár on the railway. Tibor is his first name. He is on the move all the time. He seems to be an enterprising chap, although a bit silly."

"I don't like silly men."

"No, he is just unfortunate with women," Ella said and dismissed the thought with her shake of the head. "But he can be an excellent source for business. I'll try to catch him tomorrow at the railway station."

Anna was washing in the tin washtub using her last piece of soap when she heard a knock on the door. It was cheap smelly soap that she despised, and she craved for her lavender soaps from Ungvár. Such luxuries were a matter of the past—as if they had never existed. She promised herself that she would buy lavender soap as soon as she made a good deal. If...

The knock sounded again. She dried her hands on her apron and rushed to open the door when she noticed Ella's slim figure through the windowpane. During the day, she always left the heavy curtains away from the door to allow light into the otherwise dark kitchen.

"I found Bodnár, and he promised some trade," Ella said and darted in, hurrying to close the door behind her. It was freezing outside.

"I'll put on some tea, what do you say?" Anna said and filled the kettle.

"That will revive me. What nasty weather. But listen, you told me you had a bicycle. Do you still have it?"

"No, I wanted to move it from Uzhhorod piece by piece and I brought only the wheels...before they closed the border..."

Ella realized what she had touched upon. "Now, don't cry. Listen to me. He's looking for a bicycle—or at least parts. I'll meet him at the station in the afternoon when he returns from Miskolc. I could offer him the wheels, let him come up with some equivalent."

Anna blew her nose into a kerchief she fished out of her apron pocket and poured water on the tea leaves. They made a reddish yellow brew as she put in some more leaves to make a decent drink. It was her way of celebrating a good deal in advance. *I hope it is not premature...*

Anna spread some rendered fat on bread for lunch, which went well with the tea. They were planning what else they could free up for trading. Ella came up with some linen she would not need and Anna remembered that she could offer her wristwatch. She had received it from Mother on her twentieth birthday. It would fetch good value.

Ella slipped out of Anna's apartment later in the afternoon and Anna looked around to see what she could prepare for dinner. Three potatoes, some carrots, and turnips did not offer a great variety of meals. She thanked herself for not throwing out the pork rind from the side of the smoked lard they had finished last month. It would grease up the potato stew and give it a better taste. If cooked, it could even be palatable.

Miklós was again in a bad mood—lately, he was always upset. The communists pestered him at the police force. His fields and vineyard were a constant reason for jibe and mockery. Anna assuaged him by saying that envy made his colleagues tease him so, but Miklós claimed it was not teasing. He felt ashamed to have property.

"Don't be silly! If we did not have the fields, we would have no hope of standing on our feet again after the wheat comes in and the grapes ripen later in the summer," Anna said and put in front of him the steaming potato stew that at least had the smell of smoked meat. Seeing the question in his eyes, she remarked. "Rest of the bacon...rind. Try it if it's soft."

She was content with the thin soup from the stew and soaked some bread into it, leaving most of the potato, vegetables, and the rind for Miklós.

Ella informed Anna early in the morning that Tibor Bodnár had offered ten kilos of sugar for the bicycle wheels. Ella knew that Miklós did not like her, so she waited until he had left for work, and then knocked on Anna's door.

Sugar was the hard currency that could be exchanged for anything, especially for food they needed. Anna thought this was great value. She put on some warm clothes and grabbed the wheels to go to the station with Ella to meet Bodnár. He had promised to be on the mid-morning train that day, her neighbor said.

When they got to the station, Anna spotted the blue-eyed conductor in his uniform as he came out of the stationmaster's office. She wanted to turn away, but Ella pulled her toward him.

"Tibor, this is the Anna Móri I talked to you about. She has those bicycle wheels," Ella said and pointed to the wares. She kept pulling on Anna's sleeve and exchanged glances between her neighbor and the man.

The conductor's thin lips curved into a handsome smile. "We've met before, haven't we? Mrs. Móri? Tibor Bodnár, at your service." The conductor looked for her hand.

Anna gazed into the watery blue eyes, struggling to suppress the hot wave that overcame her face and chest. She thought it was shame, but she was not sure. She remembered to offer her hand only after Ella nudged her. The conductor took it and bent over it without actually kissing it. His hand was warm despite the freezing cold.

Bodnár promised to get the sugar by the afternoon when he finished his shift. He offered to deliver it to her place, but Anna objected. They agreed that she would be at the station at four in the afternoon.

"I couldn't let the man come to our apartment. Miklós is jealous enough. I'd rather come to the station with you," Anna said to Ella on their way home, already thinking about what she could exchange the sugar for.

"Well, my dear, you'll have to go alone. We're off with

Józsi tonight to visit his ailing parents," Ella said.

"No, you can't do this to me! He's a stranger!"

"A stranger who owes you ten kilos of sugar. The trip is worth it."

Ella lent her a small handcart to carry the sugar. Anna left a note to Miklós on the kitchen table saying she was going to arrange for some bartering. She would be back earlier than Miklós, but it was safer to let him know. He could look for her and become nervous. He was jealous even of Ella, but a man, a stranger... Anna's brow furrowed. *What does he think of me? I know he is not happy in the police force. Now that there is no vineyard work, he is restless again.* She remembered catching his covert glimpses, the way he looked at her when she came home from their bartering trip with Ella, with a bag full of food. It was long ago, but she still remembered this look. It dawned on her now. *He was envious. He just can't stand it that I am more capable than him.*

The thought hit her so hard in the chest that she stumbled and almost dropped to the chair. It took her a minute to pull herself together. She grabbed her coat and beret and slipped through the door. She felt colder inside than the freezing February wind as she plodded toward the railway station.

She was waiting in the station building when she heard the clattering and puffing of the afternoon train from Miskolc. She went out to the platform and scanned it. Bodnár jumped from the first car, helped a woman with a child get down to the platform, then turned and waved to her. She nodded but did not come closer, waiting.

Bodnár also waited until all the passengers got off the train and dispersed. It was the terminal for the train and it had finished its journey for the day, so no other passengers were waiting to get on. After the platform had emptied, he climbed into the car and reappeared with two gray linen sacks.

Anna ventured closer, pulling her cart behind her. Bodnár jumped down again, now a bit more heavily with the two bundles. He placed them in her cart. "Five kilos each. Let's go to the waiting room."

Anna nodded, and they cleared the platform. Only a railway man remained there, knocking on the wheels with his long-handled hammer as he walked along the train.

They sat on the same bench where Anna had met with Marika a couple of months ago. *I must visit her soon. Maybe she has received some news from Ungvár by now.*

She could not resist reaching into the bundles, taking a pinch of the crystals, and tasting them. Bodnár smiled and said, "We could do more business, Mrs. Móri."

"I don't have more bicycle parts." Anna's voice was hesitant.

"I am looking for wine this time. Could you find me at least ten liters—Tokaj wine, of course?"

Anna's thoughts moved around in a flash. She could not contact Imre or any of Miklós's relatives. *Let's hope Ella knows some wine-growers.* "Give me a couple of days. What will you give for it?"

"Ten kilos of sugar and two kilos of salt."

"Ten plus three."

"Deal," he said swiftly, and produced the handsome smile again. His confidence impressed Anna. She wondered why.

"I'll let you know through Ella soon." Anna stood and nodded. She turned to go, but after some steps, she looked back. "Thank you for...you know..."

Bodnár's eyes brightened up. "I need business partners, madame. I can't let them fall off trains."

Anna shook her head and tittered.

She went through the market to see if she could buy some food for part of the sugar. She arrived home with two pairs of sausages, rendered fat, apples, eggs, flour, and bread, and still had half of the sugar left. *Miklós will be content.*

"Now that you mention," Ella said, cutting a piece of the apple pie Anna put in front of her to accompany the afternoon tea, "I might have a contact in Tolcsva. He's Józsi's old schoolmate, and he has a vineyard. We were there to help with the harvest last year and it was a rich one. He must have some wine for sale."

Anna expected she could pay for the wine with the rest of the sugar. Five kilos must be enough, she figured. She offered one-third of the proceeds of the deal to Ella if they went there together. After all, it was Ella's contact, and Anna could not have brought the wine home alone. As her neighbor described, the vineyard was a one and a half-hour walk from the train stop.

Anna calculated that if they left early in the morning, they could be back well before Miklós arrived home. She decided not to tell him in advance about their trip. Ella informed Bodnár that they would come back the next evening with the wine.

Daybreak found them on the train. It was just three stops from Újhely, half an hour's journey. It was a week into March but still freezing in the morning, and the languid sun promised little warmth that day. Ella found the way soon, and leaving the village, they started toward the hills. The road got steeper and meandered into small valleys. Looking back, they saw the frozen plains along the yellow Bodrog River. The five kilos of sugar and the two large, empty demijohns made the journey seem twice as long. Anna thought her arms would split from her shoulders. Their limbs had frozen and she could not feel her toes. Eventually, a small cemetery appeared on their left, behind which old houses popped up like mushrooms in the forest, mostly cellars, some with little fields around them. Ella hesitated for a minute, then started off to a house with red roof tiles. A dog barked when she stopped at the gate and she called out. "Feri!" A middle-aged man in a rough sheepskin jacket and a fur cap appeared as she was about to call out again. He looked at them with suspicion.

"Feri, I'm Ella, Józsi Szabó's wife. We were here during the harvest in October."

"How did you get here, Ella? Come in, come in." He invited them into the warm kitchen and offered them seats. A bottle of *pálinka* materialized on the table in seconds. "You must be frozen; this will cure you."

The strong brandy forced tears into Anna's eyes, but it spread through her veins and revived her after the strenuous journey. Feri accompanied them to the next building, his cellar, and offered them his wine to taste. Ella did not hesitate to accept. Anna was still dizzy from the *pálinka,* so she declined. Ella's almost imperceptible nod approved of the wine and Anna offered Feri the five kilos of sugar they had in their bundle. Feri grimaced and asked if they could find him some salt. Ella promised that if he visited them the following week, he would get some salt for more wine. That sealed the deal.

Their journey downward was easier, but the heavy demijohns weighed them down. They stopped for a brief break to eat their bread and dripping for lunch.

"We should have been back in the village already, shouldn't we?" Anna asked and looked around the valley. The sun had already left its highest point in the sky. They had left several crossings behind them. Ella claimed they were on the right path. In another half an hour, they got out of the valley and glimpsed the river below, but they could not see the village.

"Damn, we are lost!" Ella said.

They kept moving in a downward direction and reached another village. It was one stop further than their original destination and, by the time they got to the railway station, they could only follow the white clouds of their train pulling away. The stationmaster told them that there were no more trains to Újhely that day. They had to go back to the main road and wait for a carriage or car that would take them to their town.

It took the horse-drawn carriage three hours to reach Újhely, and it was dusk when they reached the outskirts of the town. They still had half an hour to go on foot. Anna asked Ella to take the wine and hide it in their apartment. Józsi worked as a blacksmith at a small factory and never drank, bless God. The wine was safe at their place.

Miklós was sitting at the kitchen table with his back to her when she opened the door. She greeted him, but he did not answer. Then she noticed the two empty bottles in front of him. Anna's stomach jumped to her throat.

"Where the hell have you been?" he asked in a strangled, faltering voice. Shouting would have been better.

"We were bartering with Ella."

"I've been home for over two hours. No dinner, no wife. She's out bartering with her friend, that tramp, instead of cooking dinner. And what did you trade, if I may ask?"

"We were in Tolcsva to change sugar for wine at a wine-grower, Ella knows. Somebody wanted wine from us in Újhely, promising double the reward in sugar and salt."

Miklós stood, his bloodshot eyes moving around Anna and the kitchen, viewing it like a spectacle. "And where's the wine, if I may ask? I don't see any and my bottles are empty. I could well use that wine..."

"I left it with Ella... I thought..."

"You thought...you think you're so clever, don't you? You wanted to hide the wine from your husband, you...come here!" he shouted. Anna tried to leave, but he stood in the way and groped her. Anna flinched at his touch. *God, let me escape from him. He will kill me!*

"Come here, I say!" Miklós made a wavering step toward her, his voice rising to a shout. He had to support himself by leaning on the table, but still stood between Anna and the door.

"Let me go to the outhouse, please. I must..." Suddenly, she felt her bladder would burst. She realized she had not relieved herself since morning.

"Somebody is waiting for you outside, huh? Who's he? Who ordered the wine?"

"Nobody...it's a railwayman, Bodnár..."

"You're fooling around with a railwayman, then...another uniform. These are your trading trips, you! Come here, I said! I'll teach you how to behave with your husband, you Rusyn slut..."

Anna stopped dead. She looked at her husband like she had never seen him before. His black eyes swam in a cobweb of bloody veins on the whites, jumping from the table to her and back, trying to figure her next move. He was seething with fury. *I don't know this man.*

She gathered her courage and stepped closer.

"I must go to the privy. Please." *He must let me out.*

He panted and straightened in front of the door. She stepped closer and reached for the door handle. Miklós grabbed her hand.

"Let me go," she said and pushed his hand back, trying to get to the door as he stumbled.

He got back his balance and shouted.

"Don't you push me!"

The tremendous blow hit her stomach and sucked the air from her lungs. She doubled over, opening her mouth, but couldn't breathe. She heard a clap of thunder in her left ear and fell. Then it was black.

Ella heard the shouting from the Móris' apartment when she put the warmed-up dinner in front of her husband. Yesterday's kale stew without meatloaf. But tomorrow it would be better. She thought she should look up the Móris, but Józsi had just started eating and she did not want to interrupt him. She had been telling him about their adventure during the day, cursing herself for missing the right path and getting lost.

Józsi asked about Feri, and Ella fed him with scraps of gossip his old schoolmate had told them in the brief time they had spent at his house. He had a lot of wine but it was difficult to sell it. You had to have a better clientele than the ordinary folks who could afford to spend on alcohol. They were lucky Bodnár knew such people.

During their dinner, the shouts from the neighboring apartment died off, and she forgot about the Móris'. They began to discuss what they could buy with the sugar and salt they would get from Anna after she had exchanged the wine with Bodnár. Ella was also wondering how they could find more customers for Feri's wine. It could become a continuous stream of income for them for the next few months. Józsi promised to ask his master in the workshop who knew the elite of the town.

Józsi went for a smoke outside before turning in for the night—the only vice he had and which Ella tolerated. When he returned, he said, "They are not saving electricity, the Móris. It's almost ten and all the lights are on in the kitchen."

Ella stopped short. *Noushi doesn't waste electricity. Strange.*

"Go to bed. I'll peep on them through the window to see if everything's alright," she said and pecked him on the cheek.

She put on a scarf and sneaked below the Móris' window. It was dark in the room, the only light seeping from the kitchen, throwing some shadows. The room seemed empty. She tiptoed to the door. *It's unlike Noushi to let the whole yard look into their kitchen with the lights on. She would have pulled the blackout curtain across the window.* The kitchen was empty. She saw it clearly through the crocheted curtain on the door window. The yellow light from the single bulb above the table fell onto two empty wine bottles. She noticed one chair overturned.

What happened here?

She ventured a timid knock but got no answer. She tried the handle, and the door opened. Ella yelped but immediately muffled her voice with a hand to her mouth. Her eyes widened, and she froze.

Anna was lying on the floor next to the overthrown chair, her legs crossed in a weird, unnatural position.

Ella bent to her, her hand still at her mouth, putting her ear on Anna's chest. She breathed deeply and dashed to the door.

"Józsi, get up, help me! Noushi is unconscious!" She shook her husband's shoulders. In a fuddled state, Józsi rubbed his eyes open and doddered after his wife in his pajamas, taking his coat on his shoulders. Ella began to look for something in the sideboard. He darted to the Móris' apartment.

He was trying to shake Anna to consciousness when Ella appeared with a small bottle in her hands. She noticed his grimace when she unplugged the stopper.

Ella busily rubbed the smelling salts onto Anna's chest, while Józsi put the vial closer to her nose. Anna jerked her head away from the glass but did not open her eyes.

"Run to the police station and call the hospital for an ambulance!" Ella instructed her husband. Luckily, the large city hospital had some ambulance cars, else there was no such service in the town. He jumped at the opportunity to do something useful.

Anna opened her unfocused eyes and started to cough. She screamed and panted with quick breaths. Tears ran down her face. Saliva was drooping from her twisted mouth. She moaned.

"Thank goodness! Don't move. It'll be alright, Noushi, Ella's here," Ella said and held Anna's hand. *Where is that ambulance, for God's sake?*

Anna looked around the white ceiling, the bed railings, and the bedsheets, and spotted a row of people lying in beds next to her and at the opposite wall. To her right, there was a window. The last rays of a tired afternoon sun fell on the windowsill. She moved her head to better see the sycamore trees outside and almost screamed with pain as she inadvertently moved her torso. A stitch in her side stopped her breath, and she tried to catch it again. She had to breathe several times, always just a little, panting, trying to get enough air. The tight clothes wrapping her torso all but immobilized her...

"Mrs. Móri, happy to see you back!" She heard a faint voice from the foot of the bed as if it was coming from a tunnel. She forced her eyes to turn without moving her head.

The woman was in white with a cap covering her brown hair. A nurse, she realized. She tried to wet her mouth, but swallowing was impossible. Her jaw could not move without a dull pain in her entire face. Anna tried to speak in spite of the ache. "What...happened?"

"*You* tell me...you were hospitalized yesterday with at least two broken ribs, severe bruises on the left side of your face, and a displaced jaw. Also, your shoulders are bruised. Did you have a fight?"

A fight. Miklós. The blow to her stomach. She had heard a thunderclap and then nothing.

"He beat me..." She saw the nurse nodding.

"I'll ask the doctor to see you. You slept through the ward rounds today. We gave you tranquilizers. If you need something, just shout, but we'll look over you every hour."

The nurse helped her use the bedpan, but it wasn't without pain.

Anna closed her eyes but could not sleep. *Why did he do this to me? I can't believe he could do this... He hit me...in his drunken stupor, or was he always this person?*

"Mrs. Móri?"

She opened her eyes and saw a young man in white bending over her. His voice was muffled and very weak.

"I am Dr. Nagy. I treated you last night after the ambulance brought you here. Two broken ribs..."

"Can you speak up, doctor?"

The young man seemed confused. "Do you not hear me well, madame?"

"You speak in a low voice..."

The doctor went to the window, to Anna's right side, and bent over her head. "Do you hear me better now?"

"Yes, you don't need to shout." She tried to force a smile, but abandoned it as the pain became more pronounced.

Dr. Nagy nodded and asked, "Did you receive a slap on the left side of your face?"

Anna squinted her eyes. It was black. But the thunder... "I don't remember. I heard a sharp blast..."

"I am afraid the hearing in your left ear is impaired. We'll examine you tomorrow. Now rest, please." He disappeared, leaving Anna alone with her doubts.

It was dark outside when Ella came to the room and scurried to her bed, smiling from ear to ear.

"Hey, you made me sick with worry yesterday!" She pecked her forehead. Anna thought she had never done that before. *I must look horrible.*

"Come to my right side, I hear better there," Anna said.

Ella's eyebrows rose, but she went around the bed and sat on the edge, making sure she did not bump into Anna.

"Bodnár took the wine in the morning and brought the sugar and salt this afternoon, as we had agreed," Ella said, excited. "He needs more wine next week, and I asked him to exchange it for salt and a large sack of potatoes. We can give the salt to Feri and keep the potatoes. It will feed both of us for a week or longer."

Anna looked at her flushed cheek and shook her head with a wince. "Will I be alright by next week?"

"Come on, they'll release you on Monday. I talked to the doctor. We will..."

She was rambling, and Anna lost the thread of the conversation soon. Miklós was on her mind. "Where's he?"

Ella looked at her and hesitated, eyes jumping from

Anna's face to the window, then back. "He disappeared. I went to the police station, and they said he had asked to be moved to Szerencs. And..."

"And what?"

"I've found a key to your apartment in our postbox this afternoon."

The silence became unbearable. Anna wished Ella would continue her babbling, but she seemed to have lost the mood to talk. She put an apple on the bedside table and promised to be back the next day. Anna squeezed her hand and let her go.

He beat me and left.

Chapter 29

Ella was almost right. They released Anna from the hospital the following Wednesday, a week after her "accident". She walked home with the doctor's papers under her arm, flinching when she had to turn her head to look around at the crossing. The stabs in her side had become bearable, but did not fully disappear. She could chew, but not without pain. She learned how to breathe: small, frequent panting, like when she was bearing the child. *The child...*

She noticed the passersby looking at her, amazed and confused. Only then did she realize the tears coming down her cheeks. She wiped them onto the sleeve of her threadbare woolen coat like an urchin and sniffled. She could not care less.

The coat Ella had brought her on Sunday to have something to wear was too warm in the sunny, late March weather, so she unbuttoned it. The crisp breeze worked like the tranquilizers she had had to swallow in the hospital.

Veronika filled her thoughts. *Maybe there is a letter waiting at home. I have to call on Marika to check with her. It has been so long and there is no answer. I hope Miklós lets me go...what am I babbling about? He left, after all...*

The apartment was empty. Ella must have cleaned it. She went to the wardrobe in the room. *He took his clothes.*

She dropped to one of the kitchen chairs. Sobbing was not good. It induced constant stitching as her body trembled, and the air she could breathe was not enough. She forced herself to stop.

How would she be able to trade with such pain? She couldn't carry goods. There was no money. Ella had to go for the wine alone. They had agreed with Bodnár to do it on Tuesday. How would she manage?

She looked into the small pantry. The racks were empty but for a jar of fat. There was a large half-full sack on the floor. She caught herself as she was about to bend and opened it with her foot. Potatoes. Ella must have done the trip.

Anna put some water on the stove and prepared the fire. She felt that she could move better and risked some bending to pick up some potatoes. If she did it slowly, the pain was bearable.

Boiled potatoes turned in heated fat tasted strange, but it was better than nothing. She had taken the last bite when she spotted Ella's head peeping through the door pane and heard a knock afterward.

"Come in, it's open," Anna said.

"You are home finally, Noushi! Did you find the potatoes? I could save nothing more yesterday but look at this." Ella put a loaf, a greasy package, and an enameled can on the table. Bread, butter, and milk.

"You can't do this, Ella," Anna said and looked at her friend with tired eyes.

"I can and I will. I exchanged some of the salt, now it has a good price. You must recover fast. I can't wait to travel with you again."

Anna took inventory in the evening. She still had her golden wristwatch and the gold chain with the medallion she had received from Mother as a wedding present. They would have to go. She would pay Ella back for her help and would have some food until she could make money herself. Not money, as it was still worth nothing. And only reducing in value. In the week she was in the hospital, prices had tripled. It was unbelievable. Nobody in their right mind would accept money or keep it for longer than a day. Ella told her they had introduced a one-million pengő banknote last month. By now, it would not feed a family for a week.

She bought sugar, salt, rice, and cigarettes. The black market considered a kilo of rice or a hundred cigarettes as the equivalent of an American dollar. It was theoretical as only the richest speculators had access to dollar banknotes, but it served well as a standard in the raging hyperinflation. As Ella put it, rice as a currency was the best: if you can't exchange it for something, you can at least eat it.

Anna joined Ella for a trading trip the following week. Her pains became sporadic, and she learned to move gingerly. Her hearing also improved, but she still heard better through her right ear. However, carrying a bundle on her back was out of the question. It would not have worked without Ella's handcart. Tibor Bodnár offered them a new opportunity every week. Sometimes they could turn around twice. By the second week, she had already built some reserves and did not need to spend everything on food, but could further exchange goods that increased her profits.

"Noushi, listen to me," Bodnár said, taking over the name he had heard from Ella. Anna winced at hearing another man calling her by the name Miklós had christened her with. "I feel responsible for what happened to you. Let me offer some help. I could arrange a permanent train ticket for you so that you don't need to pay these ever-increasing rates."

"I don't want your help. I'm grateful for your trading tips, but I'm not accepting charity." She had to look away from the watery blue eyes so as not to change her mind.

The evenings were lonesome. Anna left the electric light on all the time so as not to feel so alone. One night, she was looking for some documents in the drawer of her commode when the doctor's papers caught her eye. She had forgotten about them in the commotion of barely surviving. She had not even read them when she had left the infirmary.

She sat down and studied the sheets under the kitchen light. The papers detailed all her injuries. The doctor not only described them, but also commented on their origin.

These injuries clearly show that Anna Móri suffered a brutal attack that would leave permanent damage to her left eardrum, causing hearing impairment. We cannot exclude that her broken ribs will not heal properly, given the fact that the hospital does not have the proper equipment to examine the damage and, under the current circumstances, cannot perform anything other than critical medical surgeries. Her displaced jaw was fixed and it will not result in permanent damage. Given that the attack happened in Mrs. Móri's apartment, where she lived with her husband, suspicion of domestic violence arises as the root cause of the injuries.

Anna stared at the paper and could not help the trembling that took over her body. His voice full of venom. His bloody eyes. *He called me a Rusyn slut. I, who can speak better Hungarian than him. I have never even looked at another man from the time we have been together. I thought he loved me. If I can't love him, at least this marriage could have given me a haven. Michal was right. Marriage was too pricey a way to escape Stepfather.*

Anna could not sit idle anymore. She had to do something. Tibor Bodnár had given her some wool the other day and asked if she could knit sweaters for children. She never thought Mother's lessons would come in handy. Ella got two knitting needles from somewhere and gave them to her. They were thick and crooked, but it was no time to be picky. Anna took the yarn and started rolling it into a ball.

The doctor had written those papers with an intention. He wanted to help. Did he? What other reason could he have to include his suspicions?

I had no choice, Mother forced me. Yes, he was handsome in his uniform. I saw women turning when we paraded on the embankment...a thousand years ago. He cheated on me when we were engaged. Then he promised the stars. He promised a home. It would have been enough to love. Not only at night, but in daylight. And to trust me.

The yarn stopped in her hand. She turned her pale, thin wedding band on her finger.

He was not even upset about Veronika. Not even asking about her. Who did I marry, sweet Lord?

She stacked the papers and put them back into their envelope, leaving it on the kitchen table. She used the ring as a paperweight. *Futile.*

Anna jutted her chin and looked defiantly into the skeptical, sleepy eyes of the clerk. "Yes, this is what I want."

"As you wish, madame. Here is the form to fill in. Can you write?"

He is trying my patience. Don't fret. Instead of answering, she started filling in the lines on the form with her personal data.

"Could you move to the table there? I've other clients waiting. It'll take you some time," the clerk said. His malignant voice made her blood boil, but she knew better than to fight with an irksome scrivener.

The form required a lot of details that hurt to disclose. Anna felt pressed to breathe in deeply, then caught herself. Instead, she grabbed the desk with her left hand and forced herself to cool down. She felt her cheeks turn hot at some questions, delving into their privacy. *Just get through this, once and for all.*

She thought about the ponderous decisions she had made in her life. Giving up her teacher's job far away from Ungvár for the sake of Mother and the shop. Accepting Miklós when she still loved István, although he had disappeared. Agreeing to marry Miklós even after he had cheated on her. Yes, Mother's "arguments" were intimidating. She had even accepted that there was no house, no own home in Zombor as he had promised. Letting Mother take care of Veronika for her safety.

She had never looked out for her own benefit. She had always let fate or somebody else decide, except once, when she refused to take the Jews' apartment. She felt her stomach churn even now, thinking about it.

She could do it. Her body was healing. It would take longer with her soul, but it would come. She had a purpose in fighting for her baby. Now that she was back to bartering, she could prosper. *I was always good at trading, whatever Stepfather said.*

The air in the crowded room of the city council department began to suffocate her. She scratched her name at the bottom of the form and it took special care to force her hand to write "Móri".

Perhaps it is for the last time.

She stacked the papers behind the form and looked at the heading. *Petition for dissolution of marriage.* The clerk took it from her, stamped it, and wrote out an acknowledgment.

The divorce came through in a mere two weeks, despite Miklós's protests. The doctor's papers had worked.

Chapter 30

The night train was safer than it had been a year ago and was much less crowded. Ella was snoring next to Anna. They sat with their feet on top of the unoccupied bench, a primitive comfort. Wooden benches still felt hard, especially with their thin skirts in the sweltering summer. But a better class would have been a waste of money. Anna remembered her first trip to Budapest in the cattle wagon, and her bottom felt much better. *What a luxury now!*

They took turns to sleep at night, and now it was Anna's turn to watch their bags in the luggage rack and the handcart below their feet. The July heat had reduced as the night came, but passengers left most windows open to lessen the warmth radiating from the car walls and benches. It was quiet in the car with the occasional passengers getting on and off in the dimmed emergency light. The letter was in her purse and she pulled it out. The window lights just above her head proved enough for reading with her sharp eyes.

She could not believe the letter had reached her after such an adventurous journey. First, it must have traveled from Ungvár to the Budapest headquarters of the Red Army, hidden in the private correspondence of Marika's husband's friend. The friend must have waited for several weeks not to raise suspicion before sending it to Patak, together with Marika's own clandestine correspondence with her parents. It had been nine months ago when she had sent her first note to Mother on Marika's encouragement through this hidden route. Mother had waited a long time to include a fresh picture of Veronika. She was standing in front of the camera, clutching a teddy bear to her chest, looking directly into the lens, afraid but curious. The dress she wore was like a feather. Surely it was Mother's work. The light gray color on the black-and-white photo could mean pink. Veronika's unruly, wavy, light brown hair was braided into two pigtails, fixed by cheerful polka dot ribbons. Mother wrote she had just turned two years old when they had the photo taken, so it had to be early May at the latest. Over two months ago.

Anna pressed the photo to her chest and wiped her tears to clear her vision so that she could go through the letter once again. It was frightening, but soothing at the same time. Soon after the October border closure, rumors had spread about executions, houses on fire, and the interning and dragging away of Hungarian inhabitants from Ungvár to Siberian work camps as they had done with those from the Hungarian villages after liberation. *Malenkaya robota.* Anna entertained no illusions about the truth of those rumors. It had to be a grave risk writing about such things, and she understood if Mother mentioned nothing of that.

Mother wrote about their deprivatized shop. Anna had heard about the socialization of large factories and fields above 500 acres in Hungary—but a small shop? Luckily, they had allowed Stepfather to work there as a state employee with a low salary that was hardly enough for the family. They had strongly advised Mother to work in a factory and put Veronika in kindergarten. Instead, she had tended the garden during spring, she wrote, and taken the odd sewing and mending jobs in the neighborhood that she was famous for, resisting the authorities for now.

When Anna reached the section where Mother mentioned Veronika asking a lot about her mother, her face crumpled again. She knew the words by heart now and did not resist the tears blurring her vision. The assurance from Mother that the child spoke Hungarian, besides Rusyn, strengthened her resolution. *I will move my child to Hungary. The Red Cross has yielded no results so far, but all is not lost.* Anna had submitted her petition for a passport to the police in Újhely without results. Did Miklós have a hand in it? She would go higher if she must.

She had achieved so much during the spring and summer. She had no doubt she could get anywhere. Miklós was history, and would not pull her back anymore. Her bartering business flourished at the height of hyperinflation. Anna was able to buy back her chain with the medallion although her watch was gone, but she thought it a luxury, anyway. She had all the time in the world, so measuring it was not a priority. Instead, she bought other gold objects to preserve the value of her profits.

She had not forgotten her dream of owning a home. The new stable currency would arrive in August, the papers promised. Just a couple of weeks to go. She had enough gold to open her own shop. She had made a deal with a house owner for suitable premises in the city center and had even paid a deposit. It would be cleaned and modestly furnished, ready by early September, and she could end the bartering business. Or maybe she could do it on the side but in the safety of her own shop. Now it was about food, but soon it would be about clothes and other items that customers needed. She would build it for her daughter. Beautiful fabrics would be arranged on the shoulders of Paris dolls, encircling their slim waists. Her hat collection would be in a corner, wide-rimmed cartwheel hats she had always loved but could never afford, or the berets she wore herself, the tam hats, pillboxes, and turbans in a million bright colors. The fragrance of lavender would invite people from the street and create a cozy atmosphere that customers would not want to part with. The mannequins in the shop window would be covered in chic robes from Budapest, or even better, models copied and sewed locally, with increased profit. A real fashion house at the edge of the country. The Slovaks would come over the border to buy her goods. Her insides trembled in anticipation and she choked on her breath. She felt like waking up Ella and telling her. Until now, nobody knew of her plans. It was her secret.

Ella opened her eyes as the conductor announced another stop. She looked at Anna with blurry eyes, but sleep hugged her back in seconds. Her snoring soon counterpointed the train's clattering. Anna smiled. *A little night music.*

No more pushing the bicycles on Ungvár's cobblestoned streets. Forget the drudgery for Stepfather's profits. No more cattle wagons or night trains to struggle to exchange cheese for sugar and salt for wine. She would own a shop that would be her and her daughter's pride. *Noushi's. Or Veronika's?* She grinned and felt a lightness in her body. The July night breeze from the open window hit her hot cheeks, and she was grateful for the refreshment.

Tibor Bodnár had tried to get close to her. They had

worked together for half a year now. He had proved to be the right business partner, and Anna had made it clear that she did not wish for more even though she felt an attraction to those watery blue eyes, his manly posture, his ambition, and the railwayman's uniform. *I don't need a man.*

All that was lost did not matter if there was a future to gain it back. She would get her daughter back. She would create her own home and live in this country that worked against her as a foe for now. The country whose language she spoke but where she had nobody. She must have her daughter here. She needed no one else.

Her heart ached for Ungvár, but she really needed only her daughter. Her city had been lost to the new rulers who would do their utmost to change it beyond recognition. Her city, her home, her friends—all gone or dispersed in the surrounding countries. Her homeland had disappeared. There was nothing to return to. Mother would survive with Stepfather under the new rulers. *I need only to save my daughter.*

Anna believed that with Veronika at her side, she could even find a homeland again.

Maps

Fig. 1: The region before 1918

Fig. 2: The region between 1918 and 1938

Fig. 3: The region in 1940

100 km

1: 8 500 000

Author's Note

Subcarpathia (or Transcarpathia—from a Ukrainian or Russian perspective, the land beyond the Carpathians) has always been one of the poorest regions of all states it has been part of: Hungary or from time to time Transylvania (1000-1918), Austria-Hungary (1867-1920), Czechoslovakia (1920-1939), Hungary (1939-1945), the Soviet Union (1945-1991). It maintains the status even in today's Ukraine (1991-present). Situated in a godforsaken corner of all these countries, it has never received the proper attention it deserved.

The above historical reality contributed to the already existing multinational color of the region. Until WWI, Rusyn, Ukrainian, and Russian populations dominated the villages, while the towns and cities had a Hungarian majority. A significant Jewish population was also characteristic of the region (about 13%) that held most of commercial activity in their hands, but the majority, however, identified as Hungarian.

After the region became part of Czechoslovakia as a result of the peace treaty after WWI, its Slovak and Czech population significantly increased. For the first time, the Jewish population was considered as a separate nation in the census of 1921.

The Hungarian rule after the first Vienna Awards (1938)

and the occupation of the whole Subcarpathia by the Hungarian army in March 1939 again increased the Hungarian population, both by migration and convenience (it became more useful to declare a belonging to the Hungarian nationality than to Rusyn or Slovak). The transport of Jews to the death camps and their annihilation totally destroyed the Jewish population of Subcarpathia: 85 thousand people were deported and only some hundreds returned after the war.

The Soviet rule after WWII contributed to the shift in the population of the region in multiple ways. About thirty thousand men of Hungarian nationality were deported to Gulags, mostly to Siberia, in the fall of 1944. Similar number of Hungarians left Subcarpathia from the fear of the Soviets, mostly to Hungary. Thousands belonging to the German minority have also escaped to Hungary. They were soon replaced with ten, maybe even hundreds of thousands, Ukrainians and Russians that moved to Subcarpathia after WWII.

Anna, the heroine of the novel, considered herself Hungarian, while her mother was Rusyn and her stepfather, Ukrainian. Close relatives of the real Anna, living in today's Subcarpathia, mostly declare themselves Rusyn, while they speak Hungarian, Rusyn, Russian and Ukrainian, sometimes even Slovak. In this environment, national identity becomes an emotional matter and a personal choice.

Moving the borders and forcing minorities to accept the ruling nation's language, customs and culture was commonplace during the past century, not only in Subcarpathia. Hundreds of thousands had to leave their homeland. They either perished or tried to find a new one. Most, however, had to come to terms with the changes and make the best of it. Little is told about the struggle of their self-identity.

Anna's story is here to remind us of those who have lost their identity, homeland, language or more due to the war eighty years ago, and the war happening in front of our own eyes even today.

July, 2022

Acknowledgment

This book could not have come into being without the rich memoirs the real Anna wrote some twenty years ago that served as inspiration for the novel. I am indebted to her for entrusting me with her writings, and my thanks will find her in heaven for all the stories she told me about her life. Some of them found their place in the book and others contributed to the world around it.

During my research of the historical background, I have come across numerous studies and publications from Czech, Hungarian, Slovak and Ukrainian authors that helped create a vivid picture of the one-time Subcarpathia. I wish to highlight the name of Hungarian historian, Dr. Csilla Fedinec, whose publications were invaluable to better understand the historical reality of the region and age.

The encouragement and gentle critique of my alpha and beta readers kept me motivated when I was writing, and convinced me to finish the book and publish it. Thank you to Imani Cofield, Marc DeGeorge, Dominika Mars, Marva Boehm Mason, Márcio Sampaio, Brysen Taylor and Katerina Vavoulidou.

I was lucky to find my editor, Aanchal Jain of Read.Write.Relate, who helped me immensely to make the story flow naturally, more enjoyable, and the novel—hopefully—error-free. She has been a great professional to work with.

I am indebted to Dominika Mars for the cover design, Viviana Bordas for modeling, and Todd Trapani for the background photo.

Last but not least, I owe truthful thanks to my family, my wife Iva, and our daughters, Dominika and Viviana, who graciously endured my year-long obsession with the novel and helped finish it with their love and valuable advice.

About the Author

Dear Reader,

An early retirement from a satisfying business career has recently allowed Robert Bordas to devote himself only to writing, his dream of his younger years. He is interested in history, languages, self-identity, genealogy, and more. If not writing, he is reading on his Kindle, learning another language, traveling, enjoying outdoors or giving invaluable advice to his family. 'The Hand We Are Dealt' is Robert's debut novel, based on his own mother's memoirs.

If you want to learn more about the author, how this book was born, and what he currently works on, please visit **www.robertbordas.com**.

Robert loves to hear from his readers. Should you have any comment, questions or suggestions, don't hesitate to contact him either through the above webpage or directly by e-mail: **robert.bordas.author@gmail.com**.

If you liked the book, please, don't forget to leave a review on Amazon or Goodreads. It's enough to say: 'I liked it.' Authors live on and for their readers' praise.

www.ingramcontent.com/pod-product-compliance
Lightning Source LLC
LaVergne TN
LVHW042346190726
843493LV00005B/936